Cockatoo

The Navy Cadets

C.R. Cummings

Cockatoo

The Navy Cadets

C.R. Cummings

DoctorZed
Publishing
www.doctorzed.com

First Print Edition Published 2020 by DoctorZed Publishing

DoctorZed Publishing books may be ordered through booksellers or by contacting:

DoctorZed Publishing
10 Vista Ave
Skye, South Australia 5072
www.doctorzed.com

ISBN: 978-0-6488271-8-4 (hc)
ISBN: 978-0-6488271-7-7 (sc)
ISBN: 978-0-6488271-6-0 (ebk, 2nd ed)

National Library of Australia Cataloguing-in-Publication entry

Author: Cummings, C. R., author.
Title: Cockatoo/ Christopher Cummings.
ISBN: 978-0-6488271-8-4 (hardcover)
Series: Cummings, C. R. The navy cadets.
Target Audience: For young adults.
Subjects: Adventure stories, Australian.
Military cadets--Queensland--Fiction.

Cover image © Christoph Lischetzki| Dreamstime.com
Cover design © Scott Zarcinas

Printed in Australia, UK & USA

DoctorZed Publishing rev. date: 18/09/2020

**Special Thanks
to Tina**

May she prosper and have a very good life.

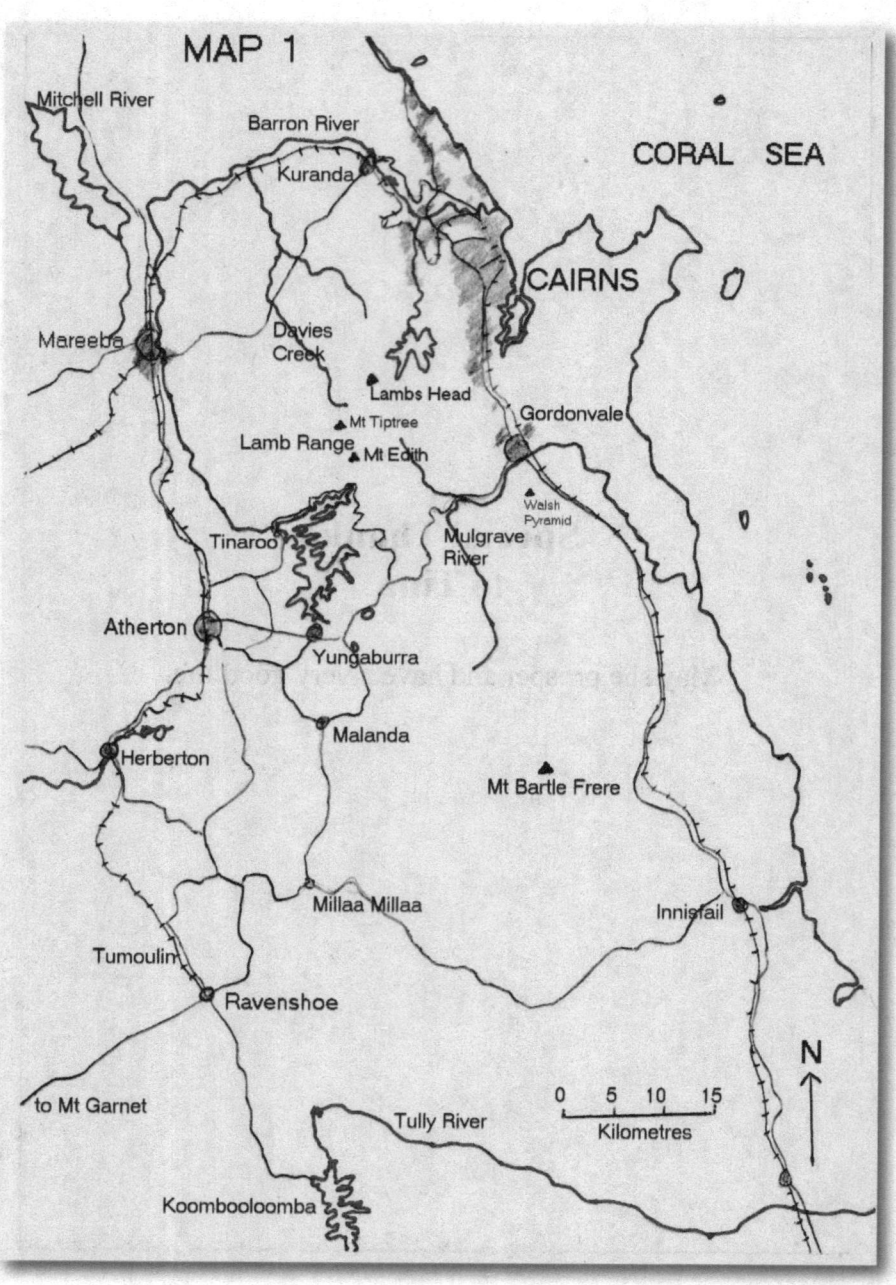

MAP 1

Mitchell River

Barron River

Kuranda

CORAL SEA

CAIRNS

Davies
Creek

Mareeba

Lambs Head

▲ Mt Tiptree

Gordonvale

Lamb Range   ▲ Mt Edith

Walsh
Pyramid

Tinaroo

Mulgrave
River

Atherton

Yungaburra

Malanda

Mt Bartle Frere

Herberton

Millaa Millaa

Innisfail

Tumoulin

to Mt Garnet

Ravenshoe

Tully River

Koombooloomba

N

0   5   10   15
Kilometres

Chapter 1

KOOMBOOLOOMBA

Dawn on the lake 5 kilometres south of the Koombooloomba Dam in Far North Queensland.

The first golden kiss of sunrise was just tinting the treetops across the still waters of the lake. Being April there was a hint of chill, but the clear sky and high humidity bore the promise of a hot day to come. Tina Babcock, 14 and a navy cadet, shifted to a more comfortable position in the Canadian canoe she was in and felt that her plan was at last working.

The object of that plan was to get the boy seated behind her to notice that she existed. The boy, fair-haired, blue-eyed and in the same class at her school, was Andrew Collins. Andrew was the same rank in the Navy Cadets as Tina, an Able Seaman, and both were in their third year in the cadets and in Year 10 at school.

Sitting in the front of the canoe was Tina's red-headed friend Sarah, another class-mate and also an Able Seaman. It had taken quite a bit of behind-the-scenes manoeuvring to arrange it so that Andrew had ended up in the same canoe but Tina had managed it. Andrew had been a bit grumpy but as there were only four canoes allocated to the Port Watch it had not been all that difficult. It also seemed, from Andrew's attitude and comments, that he was quite unaware of what had been arranged.

Oh! If only he would notice me! Tina thought.

She had been in love with Andrew ever since she had first laid eyes on him, but he did not seem to be aware that she was anyone special. An almost crippling shyness prevented Tina from making her feelings known and she was just hoping that being together might change things for the better.

But so far it did not seem to have. All the previous day Andrew had spoken more to his male friends in other canoes than to the two girls in his. It wasn't that Andrew didn't like girls. To Tina's jealous chagrin there were quite a number of serious rivals for his affections, and comments and stories had fuelled her annoyance and made her a little desperate.

One of those rivals was in one of the canoes following along behind-the golden-haired English girl Jennifer Jervis. Andrew had been smitten by her for a year but so far she had not reciprocated his interest. In fact it gave Tina malicious pleasure to note that Jennifer was happily helping to crew the canoe of the unit Coxswain, Cadet Petty Officer Michael O'Leary. That Andrew was not pleased by this had been very obvious the previous day when the expedition had set out.

The canoe expedition was a weekend camp being run by their part time, volunteer Navy Cadet unit. The group comprised four adult staff and 22 cadets. They had driven up from Cairns the previous morning, lunching in the small town of Ravenshoe before driving south for 40 kilometres along the winding bitumen road through dense tropical rainforest. On the way they had detoured to visit the Tully Falls Lookout and to view the actual Koombooloomba Dam, a large concrete structure.

The group had then taken to the water in 8 Canadians, plus two power boats for safety and admin. For nearly five hours they had paddled south to the far end of the lake. This was about 10 kilometres and by the time the group had arrived at their planned campsite it had been almost dusk, and Tina had been feeling quite exhausted. She was no athlete and the unaccustomed exercise had tested muscles and raised blisters.

The trip had been interesting enough, the lake being a flooded valley in the mountains, with numerous islands and winding inlets snaking off into the overhanging jungle. What had really interested Tina were the birds. She was thrilled to watch the hundreds of wild birds. In particular she loved watching the cockatoos. To her delight she had seen dozens of white, sulphur-crested cockatoos as well as large numbers of black cockatoos. She actually thought that the black cockatoos with their red beaks and flashes of red under the wings were the most impressive but loyalty to her own pet cockatoo 'Beaky' made her admire the white ones.

The ducks, pelicans, cormorants, and water-waders all gave her pleasure just to watch and it had been a rewarding experience to see so many in the wild. She was now experiencing this again as the canoes glided along almost silently on the mirror-calm water. Whole flocks of water birds were bobbing quietly on the lake, or were pecking along among the mud and reeds on the lake's margins.

With a requirement to be back at the vehicles at the Dam by 1100hrs so as to be back in Cairns by 1400hrs the group had risen before daybreak and packed up in the first grey light of dawn. The bulk of the camping gear had been loaded into the flat-nosed 'tinnie' crewed by Lieutenant Mullion, the lady officer who was QM and a cadet. The tinnie had set off immediately to set up for breakfast at an island halfway along the lake.

The canoes full of cadets and Lt Ryan, the Executive Officer (or XO) of the unit had then set off happily enough, only a few grumbling about not eating and about the cold. As it was not even cool enough to need a pullover this last was pooh-poohed by the majority.

As soon as it was light enough for safety, the canoes had been launched and now they were skimming quickly along, their bow waves rippling the otherwise glass-like surface of the water. To begin with it had been a bit of a race but the novelty of that had quickly declined as most were too unfit. Even so Tina's canoe was now well ahead of the others, the nearest being at least 200 metres behind. Of the safety boat which had still been beached at the campsite there was, as yet, no sign.

Andrew had taken the role of captain and Tina was content to let him but she did wish it was just them alone in the canoe, and with no other canoes on the lake. She pondered this little fantasy for a few minutes and found she was at a loss to know what to do if that was in fact the case.

I still wouldn't be game to tell him how I feel, she thought.

Again she shifted her position, uncomfortably aware that the sore muscles were returning with depressing speed. Chafed and constricted by her buoyancy vest she fidgeted to make it more comfortable. She did not like wearing buoyancy vests or lifejackets. Part of the reason was that her breasts were quite large for her age and she had trouble doing the vest up over them. This was not only uncomfortable, but she felt it made her look bulkier and fatter than she wanted to. She was well aware that her waist was not as slim as she desired, and she feared that in the buoyancy vest she would look even worse. With a huff of annoyance she wriggled to try to make the vest more comfortable, then resumed paddling.

By then they were skimming close to the end of one of the many jungle-covered peninsulas. This was just to port and Andrew steered them to cut through a stand of dead trees which were sticking out of the lake. These were a relic of the drowning of the valley when the dam had been constructed way back in the 1950s and Tina studied the bare grey trunks with annoyance. Such environmental destruction would never be tolerated now, and she was glad of that.

The canoe suddenly rocked as it slid against a submerged log. Sarah cried out in fright and Tina held her paddle ready to keep the balance. She frowned and called over her shoulder, "Careful Andrew, you nearly had us over then."

Andrew laughed and replied, "She'll be right. It was only a stump I didn't see."

"Here's another one coming up," Tina warned, her anxious eyes detecting the darker shape in the black water.

In truth she didn't much like the lake. The water was quite cold and dark and the shores were black muddy soil surrounded by the gloomy wall of dark rainforest. The thought of having to swim in the black looking water did not appeal at all. She pointed ahead and said, "Do we have to go through these dead trees. Can't we detour around them?"

"We could," Andrew conceded. "But then the others would catch up more quickly."

Tina stopped her protest and between paddle strokes concentrated on watching for snags. Andrew steered the canoe to shave the tip of the point, then swung them to port around it, the canoe almost grounding as it did.

"Look out!" Sarah suddenly cried.

"What?" Tina called, her eyes searching ahead.

Then Sarah cried out again and the canoe began slowing suddenly. Tina felt a surge of panic as she tried to back-paddle. Then she felt something drape over her and catch at her.

A net! she noted with astonishment. The thought of being tangled in a net and drowning sent a spasm of near panic through her.

The canoe came to a standstill and then rode back a metre or so. Sarah struggled to extract her paddle from the net which was now tangled around it. Tina stopped moving and studied the net. At first she had thought it must be a fishing net, but now she saw that it was not in the water but was strung up in the air between two dead trees. It was made of such thin, fine nylon that it was all but invisible. The net was so finely made that Sarah's struggles had torn part of it.

"It's a mist net!" Tina cried in surprise.

"A what?" Andrew asked as he put his paddle down and reached for his clasp knife.

"A mist net, a net made of such fine threads that it looks like mist from a distance," Tina replied. "People use them to catch insects and birds."

Now that she looked at it more carefully Tina noted that the net was all but invisible against the sky but showed up clearly against the black water. She grabbed at it and was able to lift it away from Sarah's head. Sarah still had her paddle entangled and her efforts to free it tore more of the net. Tina noted that the net was strung up between two dead trees and must have been at least 5 metres high and 10 metres wide.

"I wonder who put it here?" Andrew said.

Sarah heaved herself free of the net and then again tried to free her paddle. "University researchers perhaps?" she suggested.

Tina studied the net and considered this, but another idea moved her to speak. "Bird poachers use them too," she said.

"Bird poachers?" Andrew asked. He hauled on part of the net and pulled the canoe up against one side of the net, then began to cut at it to free Sarah's paddle. The thin mesh proved surprisingly strong when twisted in a bundle.

"People who catch native birds and sell them on the black market," Tina replied. "I was reading about them the other day."

"Why would anyone bother?" Andrew asked as he cut at the end of the net.

"Australian native birds are worth a lot of money in places like England and America," Tina replied.

"Huh! Can't imagine that," Andrew replied. He had now freed Sarah's paddle and proceeded to pull at the net so that it tore free from the top of the dead tree next to them.

"They are," Tina insisted. "It's against the law to own or sell most Australian birds and they can't be taken out of the country."

"Why not?" Andrew asked.

"Because they are rare or endangered," Tina replied.

"Rare! There are millions of the buggers!" Andrew replied incredulously. He dug his paddle in and started the canoe moving, sliding it forward over the net, which now hung in the water.

Tina resumed paddling as well. She was feeling troubled about the damaged net, which was now only attached at the bottom between the two trees. "Shouldn't we try to fix the net?" she asked. "It might be part of a research project."

Andrew muttered a reply which was interrupted by Sarah calling out, "Lookout! There's another net just ahead."

Tina saw this one and they back paddled and changed direction to avoid it. They slid past the left side of the second net so that they almost grounded on the shallows. As they did Sarah pointed over the side.

"There's a dead bird caught in this one."

Tina looked and saw the white feathers and shook her head with regret. She loved birds and hated to see them hurt. "Oh dear! It's a white cockatoo," she said.

She was about to say more when a sharp, flat sound made them all look suddenly to their left.

"That was a shot!" Andrew said.

Sarah pointed to their left along the shore of the next bay on their port side. "There. Oh look! What's going on?" she cried.

Tina looked and tried to work out what it was she was seeing. The first thing she noticed was a power boat over against the beach. Then she heard a second shot and saw people. Her first thought had been that the people must be shooting at birds and that started her anger rising. Then she realised it was altogether more serious.

Running along the beach towards them, perhaps 200 metres away, was a man dressed in a short sleeved khaki shirt and khaki shorts. He was being pursued by three other men in non-descript grey, dark green or black clothing. That the man in khaki was trying to escape was at once obvious. Tina opened her mouth to say this, but her voice was choked off by a gasp of alarm as another shot was fired. The man in khaki stumbled and pitched forward on his face.

Sarah cried in dismay and Tina gasped, then cried, "They shot him!"

All the while the canoe had been gliding towards the men and they were now only about 100 metres away. Temporarily stunned by what she had just seen Tina could only gape and wonder. She noted a boat trailer and the rear end of a brown 4 Wheel Drive vehicle protruding from the edge of the jungle near the motorboat. She also studied the three men.

At that moment the three men became aware of them. Tina saw one of them grab at the sleeve of the second one and point towards them. Only then did it begin to dawn on Tina that they might not just be observers of the drama. A stab of fear caused her heart to begin to hammer.

Andrew had obviously made the same deduction as he was already back paddling and now hissed, "They just shot that man and we are witnesses. Let's get out of here!"

"Oh surely they didn't!" Sarah gasped.

"They did!" Andrew snapped. "They just shot him and we saw them do it. Now start paddling, port side, fast!"

Tina obeyed, digging her paddle in and hauling back with all her strength. Even now she was still bemused by the unreality and suddenness of the event. She saw the first of the three men reach the figure sprawled on the black sand and noted that he was carrying a gun of some sort. To her growing alarm she saw him glance at the body, then continue running towards them.

The man, dressed in jeans and a dark green shirt, yelled as he ran, "Hey! You kids, we are the police! Come here!"

That caused another stab of concern to Tina and she half turned to gasp at Andrew, "What should we do?"

"Paddle like hell!" Andrew replied. By this time they were moving fast and were starting a wide, sweeping turn out away from the beach.

"But he said they are the police," Sarah cried, her voice trembling with anxiety.

"I know he did," Andrew replied, "But that doesn't mean they are."

"But we could get into trouble!" Sarah wailed.

"We already are!" Andrew replied grimly, paddling for all he was worth.

"But if they are the police and we don't go back won't they arrest us or something?" Sarah cried.

"And if they aren't we could end up very dead!" Andrew snapped, "Now shut up and paddle."

"Oh they wouldn't hurt us!" Sarah gasped.

Tina had been saving her breath to paddle but now she snapped in exasperation, "Oh shut up Sarah! If they just shot one man then they will shoot us too because we saw it. Now row!"

"Paddle you mean," gasped Andrew.

"What?"

"Paddle," Andrew replied, between gasps. "These aren't oars so we can't row."

Tina thought that a silly comment to make at a time like that but just shook her head and kept paddling. By then they were more than halfway round the turn. She glanced over her shoulder at the men, noting that the second one was a big, solid brute with curly black hair and a moustache. The third man was tall and thin and had a beard and longish brown hair.

The first man was now only about 75 metres away. He again shouted at them, "Stop where you are! Stop or I shoot!"

"He's bluffing surely?" Sarah cried, pausing in her paddling to look.

"He's not! Keep paddling!" Andrew ordered.

Tina was really scared now and she snatched another glance over her shoulder, just in time to see that the first man had stopped and had raised the gun. "He's going to shoot!" she gasped incredulously. It all seemed too unreal to be true.

Boom!

The sound of the shot echoed across the lake. Tina felt a stinging blow to her left shoulder and was astonished to see the water beside her suddenly whipped into a flurry by dozens of small splashes.

"Argh! Shotgun," Andrew gasped. "Keep rowing."

"Paddling," Tina replied, as much to try to stop herself from becoming hysterical. Her mind was now screaming with mounting terror and she felt the edge of panic.

Sarah began to scream and stopped paddling. Tina tried to ignore her and concentrated on her paddling, dimly noting that they were now heading back the way they had come. "They tried to kill us," she croaked incredulously.

Andrew grunted a reply, then shouted, "Sarah, shut up and paddle!"

Sarah kept wailing in fright and Tina noted that her paddle was now trailing in the water. She used her own to scoop it upwards. "Sarah, are you alright? Did they hit you?" she yelled.

Sarah shook her head but kept on sobbing and calling out. Driven by the instinct for self-preservation Tina reached forward and hit her hard on the shoulder. "Be quiet and paddle!" she yelled.

To her relief Sarah stopped calling out and began to paddle. All this time Tina had been mentally cringing and tensing in anticipation of another shot and she now glanced back. To her relief she saw that the man had stopped running after them.

"They've given up," she gasped.

Even as she said this, she heard the second man shouting, "Danny! Back to the boat! We won't catch them that way."

The motorboat! Tina felt her blood freeze with fear. *We won't be able to outrun that!* she thought.

"They are getting their boat," she gasped.

"I heard," Andrew replied.

"We won't be able to get away from that," Tina said.

"We have to get back to the others," Andrew replied, "It is our only chance. Now stop talking and paddle!" As he did, he raised the small radio that was looped around his neck and called. Tina turned to look, anxious that they get radio communication with the adult officers at once. But there was no answer. Andrew tried again but then shook his head.

"Not answering. I'm not sure if it is transmitting. Keep paddling while I try again."

Tina nodded and dug her paddle in. As she did, Andrew called again. Still no response. Tina glanced back and said, "Maybe it's got water in it?"

But the radio was in a plastic bag and Andrew held it up to show her it was dry. "No, and the battery symbol shows it has plenty of power." He tried again but with each unanswered call Tina's dread intensified. Sarah began to blubber and was obviously on the edge of hysteria.

Andrew muttered an oath and then said, "Might be all this jungle screening the transmission. We should be right once we get around the point." With that he let the radio go and resumed paddling with deep, powerful strokes.

Sobbing with exertion and tensed by mounting desperation Tina paddled as hard as she could. As she did, she glanced back, noting the three men run back past the body on the beach and on towards their motorboat. Even before the canoe had reached the tip of the peninsula, she saw with dismay that the men had reached the motorboat. Two scrambled aboard, including the man Danny. The tall, thin bearded one stayed on the beach and shoved the motorboat out into deeper water. A second later Tina saw foam boil at the stern of the motorboat and it began to move.

"Oh no! Here they come!" she gasped.

Chapter 2

ESCAPE

By then Tina noted they were skimming through the stand of dead trees off the point.

"Andrew! Be careful we don't hit a snag," she gasped.

She was becoming increasingly desperate as awareness of approaching physical exhaustion made itself obvious. Already she was panting, sweat was trickling down her face, and her arm muscles felt heavy and strained.

I don't think I can keep this up much longer, she thought.

Then another worrying thought came to her as she glanced back at the motorboat, which was now accelerating at dismaying speed. "Andrew, watch out for those nets."

"I will," Andrew replied, his voice tense with anxiety.

Tina noted that they were almost scraping the beach and she glimpsed the mist net with the drowned cockatoo in it go slipping past close on her left. Then she saw that Andrew was aiming them at where she thought the first net was.

"Andrew, watch out for that net!" she cried.

"Just make sure your paddle doesn't snag in it," he replied. "If it does just let it go and dig out the spare."

Tina was now looking anxiously ahead, hoping at any moment to see the other canoes. She thought she knew what Andrew had in mind but was doubtful if it would help. She also noted that he was still turning them to starboard, hugging the beach.

"If they look like catching up," Andrew said between laboured gasps, "I am going to beach us and you are to run into the jungle."

Tina glanced at the wall of greenery slipping by only 10 metres away and was simultaneously cheered and depressed by its proximity. The jungle certainly offered some sort of safety but was also, in her limited experience, an unpleasant environment. Concern about becoming lost in the jungle flitted across her mind but she then smiled grimly, realising that it was the least of their worries.

That will mean we are still alive! she reasoned.

Sarah glanced back and sobbed. "Oh where are the others!" she wailed. She was panting hard and now stopped paddling.

Tina gritted her teeth and forced herself to dig her paddle in and haul back. She found temporary relief in the fact that they had slid out of sight of the motorboat as they rounded the point but she could hear the sound of its motor growing rapidly louder.

Andrew called on them to paddle port side and began turning them to starboard, towards the beach. "Get ready to run for it!" he gasped.

As Tina glanced back the motorboat roared into view. She saw Danny kneeling in the bows and even as she watched she saw him point in their direction. The bow of the boat turned towards them.

By then the canoe was only metres from the beach. *We've left it too late!* Tina thought, her heart pounding frantically.

She saw the motorboat suddenly swerve and knew it was avoiding the mist net. Then it aimed straight for them and its motor roared. The bow rose and the spray flew higher and she knew it would be on them in seconds. Through eyes that seemed to be blurred around the edges she saw Danny lifting his gun up to his shoulder.

At that moment, the canoe ran up onto the beach. "Out!" shouted Andrew. At the same time he dug his paddle in to keep the canoe steady.

Sarah rose unsteadily and dropped her paddle. Tina used hers to keep her balance as she untangled her legs and stood up. Then she leapt into the shallows. The water shelved faster than she had expected and she went in thigh deep. This caused her to stumble, but fear kept her moving and she floundered up onto the beach in a flurry of splashes. By then Sarah had also climbed out. Tina paused and looked back, anxious that Andrew also escape.

She saw that he was scrambling to get out of the canoe but it was slipping back off the beach. Without thinking she pounced and held it steady.

"Run!" Andrew shouted. "Never mind me, run!"

Tina ignored him and he sprang into the shallows next to her. She grabbed at his sleeve as he stumbled and then looked up with resignation as the motorboat came racing towards them. By then it was only 50 metres away and she could clearly see Danny aiming his gun. Sobbing with fear she turned and began running up the narrow beach.

As she did, she heard Danny shouting at them to stop. A peculiar change in his tone of voice made her glance over as she reached the edge of the rainforest. To her astonishment she saw Danny bending forward over the foredeck of the motorboat. He was scrabbling to hold on and his gun was hanging over the side. With some astonishment she saw the barrel of the gun go into the water and be dragged out of sight.

The boat came to a shuddering stop and its motor began making loud rattling and spluttering sounds. Danny went on sliding and went slowly over the side. He managed to hang on but still went in over his head. The gun went out of sight.

"Stop! Stop!" Andrew called, snatching at Tina's vest. "They've hit the other net. Quick! Back to the canoe."

Sarah was already struggling to get through a tangle of vines beside Tina. The expression on her face was one of sheer terror and she only goggled and gibbered as Tina called to her. She had to grab Sarah and shout in her ear.

"Back into the canoe, quick!"

Shaking her head in fear and gasping great gulps of air Sarah turned and followed. Tina ran down the beach behind Andrew. The canoe had slid back out into deeper water but Andrew just dived in and swam out to it with a few strong strokes. By the time Sarah reached the edge of the water he had pushed it back into the shallows.

Paddles were then the problem. Tina and Andrew had both dropped theirs on the beach but Sarah's was floating 10 metres away.

"Get in!" Tina cried, shoving Sarah towards the canoe. She snatched up her own paddle and tossed it in, then grabbed Andrew's and handed it to him as he came splashing up out of the water.

"Thanks!" he gasped, adding, "Bloody hell, that's cold!"

Sarah had got tangled up with their camping gear, but Tina simply pushed her and said, "Lie still!" She then scrambled in while Andrew held the canoe steady. Next, she used her paddle to hold the canoe while Andrew shoved off and sprang aboard. It was now that the training and experience of the cadets paid off. The canoe rocked alarmingly as Andrew scrambled into position but it did not roll over. Paddles were brought into use and they began turning the canoe around.

All the while Tina had been flicking glances towards the motorboat, fearing that the other man might also have a gun. He did not seem to have and was busy swearing and looking over the back. Danny was still struggling in the water and to Tina's dismay he reached up and slid the dripping gun into the boat, then moved to heave himself back aboard. As he did, he yelled, "Help me Marco, you dumb shit!"

Maybe we should have run into the jungle? Tina wondered as, heart in mouth, she began paddling.

The motor suddenly cut out and in the silence she clearly heard a flow of obscenities issuing from the second man, Marco. Andrew back paddled and turned the canoe and got them moving again. Tina was now almost completely winded. She sobbed with the effort but grimly dug her paddle in and dragged it back. She had to wipe perspiration away from her eyes and was painfully aware of how unfit she was.

As the canoe began moving away from the motorboat she glanced back, still fearing to be shot. She saw Danny drag himself aboard and that got her anxiety up again. Then he began angrily gesticulating. Next, he reached down and Tina's blood ran cold as she saw him pick up the gun.

"He's going to shoot again!" she sobbed.

"He's a fool if he doesn't check the gun first," Andrew croaked, but he redoubled his efforts to paddle, glancing back every second.

Tina did likewise and saw Danny hold the gun downwards. The sight of muddy water dribbling out of the barrel gave her a great surge of hope. Then Danny broke the gun open and looked in before snapping it shut.

"Get ready to lie flat," Andrew cautioned.

"Won't the bullet just go straight through the canoe?" Tina asked, uncomfortably aware that the hull of the canoe was only a few millimetres thickness of fibreglass.

"It's a shotgun," Andrew replied, "And I think he's only got bird shot. If we can keep paddling we will be out of range in a minute or so."

Tina knew very little about shotguns but enough to understand that a rifle was much more deadly at long range. Having fired rifles at the range she was aware of their capabilities. She glanced back again and saw that Danny was now raising the gun to point it in their direction.

Andrew saw the movement as well and snapped, "Get down! Lie as flat as you can."

He ignored his own order and dug his paddle in again. Tina cried at him to duck, her eye's flicking to Danny. Thus she saw Danny shake his head angrily, then lower the gun and point off to their port beam.

A single look told the story. Sweeping into view around the next point were the other seven canoes!

"Saved!" she gasped.

"What if they try to shoot them as well?" Sarah wailed anxiously.

Tina thought this very unlikely and Andrew just snorted and said, "They are bird poachers, not mass murderers!"

Tina sat up and resumed paddling. At every stroke they slid another 5 metres away from the stationary motorboat. Each glance showed the distance widening and Andrew slowed down and said, "OK, take it easy. We are safe now."

"What will we do?" Sarah asked.

"Warn the others then try to contact the police I suppose," Andrew replied.

He looked back repeatedly and then began calling out to the approaching canoes to stop. They ignored this until they were only about 50 metres off. Then they came to a bobbing standstill.

"Lieutenant Ryan sir! Stop there! Danger!" Andrew hailed.

Tina saw the black-bearded figure of Lt Ryan nod and then order the others to stop.

"What's going on? What were those shots?" the officer called back.

"Those men shot someone on the beach and then chased us and tried to shoot us sir," Andrew replied. By then they were only 50 metres away and he could lower his voice.

"You're joking!" Lt Ryan called back, but Tina could tell from the look on his face that he believed them.

"Call the police sir, quick!" Tina called.

Lt Ryan nodded but first he turned to those around him. "All you people turn back and paddle. We will put some more distance between those fellows and us," he ordered.

Then he reached into his shirt pocket and extracted, not without difficulty because of the buoyancy vest, a mobile phone in a plastic bag. He turned this on and looked at it, then shook his head.

"No service," he said.

"What about that emergency number you are supposed to be able to get sir?" called Cadet Midshipman Ken George, the stocky lad sitting in front of the officer.

Lt Ryan shook his head. "No use. If there is no signal we can't get it. We don't have the transmission power. Get on the radio and ask Petty Officer Evans to get that safety boat here ASAP."

Ken, who was Tina and Andrew's divisional Cadet Officer, picked up a radio handset and began calling. By the time he made contact all the other canoes had turned around and Tina's canoe had caught up with them. That put them at least 300 metres away from the motorboat and she now felt much safer.

So did Sarah who began to sob uncontrollably. That annoyed Tina, although she had also begun to shake as the reaction set in. She lowered her head and said a quiet prayer, then tried to relax. That was hard as she ached all over and her left shoulder throbbed. She was further dismayed to hear Ken tell Lt Ryan that the safety boat, which was a fast motorboat, was still at the campsite with an engine problem.

Lt Ryan frowned and swore under his breath. "Try the tinnie then," he ordered."

CDTMID George called again and after two attempts made contact. A short conversation followed. He then said, "Sub Lt Mullion said they are on the beach cooking breakfast, but she and Seaman Ferguson will come as quickly as they can."

Lt Ryan frowned again and again swore under his breath. He then turned back to Tina and Andrew. "OK, finish your report. What the hell's going on?"

He directed this to Andrew, which peeved Tina a bit. Andrew repeated the outline and then added more detail to the story and as eh spoke Tina saw Lt Ryan's expression change to looking very worried and grim. He tugged at his thick, black beard and nodded, his eyes continually watching the now distant motorboat with the crooks in it.

Taking the radio handset he said, "Petty Officer Evans, we need the safety boat now. This is urgent! Never mind tuning the motor. Get it going and catch up with us, fast! Over!"

"Roger, as quickly as we can; 10 minutes, over," came the reply in a female voice.

Petty Officer Ferguson, Tina thought, identifying the voice of their female Instructor of Cadets (and mother of Cadet Seaman Ferguson).

"And get on that satellite phone and call the police," Lt Ryan added.

"Roger that," PO Ferguson replied.

"What do we do now sir?" Andrew asked.

"We get a bit further away. We will cross over to the far side of the lake and slip past," Lt Ryan replied.

Andrew pointed across the lake. "We should hug the shore sir, so we can run into the jungle to hide if they come after us," he added.

Lt Ryan nodded. "That's good tactics," he agreed. He loudly instructed the others to do this, then set them slowly paddling.

With an effort Tina dug in her paddle and set to work. She was amazed at how tired she felt and at how her shoulder ached. *I must have pulled a muscle,* she decided. She was also a bit peeved that Sarah just sat crying and shivering in the front. She was shaking herself but was determined not to give up, particularly in front of Andrew.

She glanced back at him and saw him looking across towards the motorboat, his handsome face a mask of seriousness. *Oh he is wonderful!* she thought. *My hero!*

That cheered her and she was boosted even more when his bright blue eyes met hers and he gave her an encouraging smile. "Good work, well done!" he said.

That rendered Tina speechless and she could only nod and resume paddling. A warm glow spread through her as his praise sank in. Her gaze then swept across to the other side of the lake and she was concerned to see that it was only another hundred metres away. In fact the lake constricted beyond that so that it was only about 300 metres wide at the place opposite the motorboat.

All this time the men in the motorboat had been working over the stern and Tina noted that Danny had slid into the water again. *Clearing the mist net from their propeller,* she deduced.

As the small flotilla of canoes began snaking along beside the eastern shore Tina saw Danny climb back into the motorboat. Then Marco started working on the motor. Across the water came the splutter of engine noises as it started up. That got Sarah staring anxiously at it. She cried out, "Oh no! They are moving. Now they can catch us and shoot us!"

The tone of near hysteria in Sarah's voice sent chills through Tina, but it also annoyed her. "They won't!" she snapped back.

"They will!" Sarah shrilled.

"Oh shut up!" Andrew cried angrily. "They can't shoot us all!"

Ken George nodded. "They probably haven't got enough ammo," he added.

"That's enough!" Lt Ryan ordered. "Turn towards the beach and get ready to hide."

That at least got them doing things. But it didn't stop Tina glancing back at every left-handed stroke though. To her relief she saw that the motorboat was only moving slowly. From the irregular chugging and spluttering it had a damaged motor or propeller. She was even more relieved to see it turn and head back around the point.

Arthur Blake, another classmate pointed towards the boat. "They are running away!" he called.

Andrew nodded. "Or going back to their vehicle," he replied.

"Vehicle?" Lt Ryan queried.

Andrew pointed. "Yes sir. They have a Four-Wheel Drive with a boat trailer down on the edge of the lake," he replied.

Peter Parsons, a cadet who sat in the front of Lt Ryan's canoe, asked, "How did it get there?"

"There are sure to be old logging tracks leading in off the main road," Lt Ryan replied.

"They will get away!" Tina said. Now that they were safe she was angry at having been frightened so much.

Andrew shook his head. "Not if our safety boat can get back to the dam quickly," he replied.

"What do you mean?" Tina asked.

Andrew picked up a map in a plastic bag. "According to this map there is only one road along the other side of the lake. It winds through the jungle and passes close to the dam. If the safety boat gets there first they might get a look at the vehicle."

Lt Ryan had also picked up his map, the army topographic 1:50 000 scale. He studied it and shook his head. "No. It is about 3 kilometres from where we left our vehicles to that road junction. Besides, the road over there also goes on southwards. I think it links up with several other roads down that way."

"Worth a try sir," Andrew persisted.

Lt Ryan shook his head. "No. Too dangerous. We will hand this over to the police. Everyone start paddling and we will try to keep these fellows in sight and at the same time get closer to the dam."

Tina heartily agreed with that. The glance at Andrew's map had made her very aware of just how isolated they were. She knew that it was roughly 3 kilometres to the dam where they just might find a workman of some sort, but then it was at least 40 kilometres of winding jungle road back to the nearest town, with only a few farms near it. There were buildings at the Tully Falls Weir about 10 kilometres back but there had been no-one there when they had visited the previous day.

By this time, the crooks' motorboat had vanished around the point on the other side. Tina found she was fuelled by a strong desire to see the men brought to justice and that gave her the energy to keep paddling. To her satisfaction only a short paddle allowed them to see around the point and along the long arm of the lake where the men had their vehicle.

"There they are!" cried Dimity Bates, a First Year Ordinary Seaman in Cadet Petty Officer Hayley Booker's canoe.

Tina had to strain her eyes to see clearly as the motorboat was now over half a kilometre away and was just a tiny greyish shape. The men looked like tiny ants as they climbed out onto the beach.

"They are going to pull the boat onto its trailer," Andrew observed. "Oh damn it! Now they will get away!"

"There are three of them," commented Ken George.

"No, I can see four," corrected Lt Ryan, who was now using a pair of small binoculars.

"One of them might be the man they shot?" suggested Tina, puzzled.

Lt Ryan shook his head. "No, I can see the body on the beach," he replied. "There is a man wearing dark shorts and a white, short-sleeved shirt. He has dark glasses on."

"We didn't see him," Andrew commented.

Lt Ryan frowned. "Hello! They are not putting the boat on the trailer at all," he said. "They are loading boxes in."

The group had now come to a bobbing standstill. All stared across the lake and watched as the man in the white shirt climbed into the boat with a man in grey clothes Tina recognised as Marco. The boat was started up and turned to go slowly away from them. Tina was surprised to see it head directly for what she took to be a small cape or point jutting into the lake. She was even more astonished by what happened next.

The motorboat stopped at the edge of a green mass which suddenly seemed to lift up. For a few minutes she could not make out at all what it was she was seeing.

It was Lt Ryan with his binoculars who enlightened them. "By thunder! That is a camouflage net they are moving. There's a plane under it, a floatplane!"

Now it made sense. Tina was able to make out the straight line of the aircraft's wing. The floatplane was painted a dull grey colour and was very hard to make out. She shook her head in disbelief, then nodded when Andrew said, "They probably use the floatplane to fly out to meet ships at sea and transfer the wildlife."

"That makes sense," Lt Ryan agreed. "They are loading those boxes into it now."

"Oh where's that safety boat?" muttered Tina in annoyance. She was troubled by the fits of shivering which were now sweeping over her and she let out a groan when she tried to ease her sore shoulder.

Several minutes went by before the watching cadets saw the net hauled down and rolled into the motorboat. The man in the white shirt climbed into the floatplane. A few moments later the sharp vibrations of its engine starting up carried across the water to them.

Cadet Midshipman Pike, the second cadet officer with the group, shook his head. "It's going to take off, he commented

Andrew scowled. "Oh bummer! They will get away," he cried angrily.

"Not much we can do to stop them," Lt Ryan replied.

There wasn't. Tine and the others could only sit in their canoes and watch as the motorboat turned and made its way back towards the place where the other two men and the 4WD waited. There was a surge of revving sounds as the pilot warmed up and tested his engine and then the floatplane began moving forward. Tina found it very frustrating and not a little scary to be able to do nothing but sit and watch.

The floatplane moved faster and faster until great creamy waves of white spray were being hurled out by its two floats. It was running on a course diagonally across their front but to her surprise it did not seem to accelerate to the sort of speed she expected for a take-off. Then, when the plane was about a kilometre to the north of them, it suddenly slowed down.

To Tina's puzzlement it began slowly turning in a wide circle. "What's it doing?" she asked.

It was Ken George who answered. "I think he was just warming up the engine and churning up the surface of the lake at the same time."

Lt Ryan nodded. "I agree. There's no wind so his take-off direction is irrelevant."

"But why roar up and down sir?" Tina asked.

Andrew answered her. "I read somewhere that floatplanes have trouble unsticking from perfectly calm water. They need a few waves to get a bit of a kick."

That made sense to Tina and she nodded and studied the widening ripples now spreading across the lake. The first of these arrived to set the canoes rocking gently as the floatplane completed its turn. Its engine now roared and it began its take-off run.

"No markings," CDTMID Pike observed.

"No, just that dull grey and black underneath," Andrew agreed. "They are up to no good alright."

"What type is it?" Lt Ryan asked.

"No idea," Ken George replied.

"Willy would know," Andrew added. Tina nodded. Willy Williams was an air cadet at their school and an authority on all things that flew.

Nobody else knew. All they could do was sit and watch the machine race across the water. It began bumping over the small waves of its own earlier progress. Small clouds of spray were flung up and then suddenly the aircraft 'unstuck' and began climbing. By then it had travelled more than halfway back across the lake.

The floatplane made no attempt to gain altitude, other than to clear the treetops on the far side of the lake. Within seconds it was lost to sight, heading west.

"I wonder where his base is?" Andrew said.

"I.... hello, here's our safety boat," Lt Ryan said.

Tina looked towards the sound of buzzing off to her left and saw the unit's white coloured power boat racing towards them. *At last!* she thought. Then she looked across the lake and saw that the men there were just hauling their motorboat onto the boat trailer.

"Sir, if the safety boat is quick it might be able to get across there and see something, the vehicle's number plate maybe."

Lt Ryan shook his head. "Too dangerous. I will send it to the dam."

"What about that man they shot sir? Shouldn't we check if he is really dead?" said Tina, stubbornly wishing to catch the men.

That got Lt Ryan tugging at his beard and he had to nod. As the safety boat came skimming up to join them, he nodded. "Yes, you might be right. But it will be adults only. As soon as I leave, you kids start paddling north as fast as you can."

That answer both pleased and relieved Tina. She did not really want to see a dead man but was gripped by a dreadful anxiety now that it had occurred to her that the man might still be alive.

"Oh hurry sir!" she cried.

Chapter 3

CLOSE!

Lt Ryan at once clambered from his canoe into the safety boat. He then ordered the two cadets already in the safety boat: CDTCPO Josh Neville and CDTAB Tracey Atwell, to transfer to his canoe and to another canoe which had only two cadets in it.

As soon as the two cadets had done so, he called out, "Cadet Midshipman George, you are in charge of the canoe group. Start paddling for the dam. Get there as quickly as you can and load the canoes on the trailers. We will follow you. Now get going!"

CDTMID George at once replied, "Aye, aye sir!" then called to the cadets to start paddling. Tina did so but found her shoulder so sore she groaned as she forced her muscles to move. The safety boat then roared away, curving to port and heading directly across the lake towards the 4WD and motorboat.

"Those men are looking," Andrew commented. He was grunting and panting, and Tina suspected he might also be feeling the strain. As her body twisted with every second stroke, she looked across the lake to watch.

To her consternation she saw one of the men was walking towards the body. 'Going to make sure he is dead, or to take the body to hide it,' she thought. Then she saw the man stop and look towards the approaching safety boat. It was too far for her to be sure but she thought that one of the other men called him back. At any rate the man suddenly turned on his heel and walked quickly back towards the vehicle.

By the time the safety boat was a couple of hundred metres away the three men had all climbed into the vehicle and it had vanished from sight into the jungle, towing the boat and trailer behind it. 'Oh drat! They are getting away,' she thought.

The safety boat slowed down and very cautiously went past the place where the vehicle had been, keeping a couple of hundred metres out. It then turned and slowly nosed in to where the body lay on the beach. Tina saw Lt Ryan and Petty Officer Evans, both easily recognizable even at that distance by their beards, get out and go up the beach to the body. They knelt and began examining it. Tina's stomach turned over at the thought of what they might be seeing.

By then the canoes had paddled several hundred metres and they were approaching another narrow stretch of the lake. A small jungle covered island stood in the narrowest point but even that was 200 metres wide, so they slipped past with no concern. As they did the safety boat was lost to sight, but Tina was so interested in the drama behind her that she was attuned to every clue. Thus she distinctly overheard CDTMID George say, "Alive!"

At that Tina stopped paddling and looked over towards the officer's canoe. He was talking on one of the CB Radios one person in each canoe carried for safety. As he put down the handset Tina could restrain her curiosity no longer.

"Sir, what did they say please?" she called.

"The man is still alive but very seriously wounded. They are loading him aboard and are going to rush him to the dam," CDTMID called back.

"Oh, thank God!" Tina cried. She felt tears prickle and she sighed with relief and pent up emotion. She went to resume paddling but found she could hardly make her left shoulder work. Shaking her head she gritted her teeth and made a determined effort. A wave of dizziness then swept over her and she found her eyes going out of focus.

'I'm going to faint!' she thought in dismay.

Andrew cried out in annoyance as her paddle began to drag in the water. Then he reached forward and tapped her back. "Hey Tina, are you alright?" he asked.

Tina gripped the paddle and fought off another wave of dizziness. A throbbing pain burned hotly in her left shoulder and suddenly she felt Andrew's hand on her arm.

"Hey! That's blood! You've been hit!" he cried.

Tina struggled to stay conscious. Glancing at her left arm she noted that the white Able Seaman's badge on the long sleeve of her dark blue uniform shirt was stained red. She reached across with her right hand and touched her shoulder, then looked in dismay at her fingers. They were red with blood.

She could smell it now and that did make her faint. She just blacked out and slumped into the canoe. Even in that state she was dimly aware she had dropped her paddle as Andrew cried out and she got splashed with cold drops as he retrieved it. That helped her open her eyes and regain consciousness.

Andrew placed the dripping paddle beside her in the canoe, then yelled out, "Hey sir! Tina is wounded! She has been shot!"

That stopped all the paddling except for CDTMID George's canoe which came sweeping alongside a minute later.

"Where? Show me!" he snapped.

Tina struggled to sit up and managed to lean over and point. "Here sir. I don't think it's very bad," she said.

As CDTMID George leaned over to look at Tina's back Hayley Booker called from another canoe, "Sir, you'd better look at Andrew as well. He's got blood on his neck and back."

That got Tina sitting up. She twisted around, in her anxiety ignoring her own pain. "Oh Andrew! Are you alright?" she cried.

"Aw! I reckon," Andrew replied.

"Have you been hit?" Tina asked, concern becoming her dominant emotion.

Andrew met her eyes and gave a lop-sided grin as he nodded. "Yes."

"Why didn't you say?" Tina snapped angrily.

"Because I didn't want to frighten you or Sarah," Andrew replied. "Besides I didn't think it was much."

CDTMID George had now transferred his attention to Andrew. "Where exactly are you hit?" he asked.

"A few pellets in the arm and a couple in the back and neck and one or two in the back of my head," Andrew replied.

Tina twisted round to look at him in horror. He gave her another wry grin, but she could tell he was in pain. "Does it hurt?" she asked.

Andrew nodded. "The ones in the arm are starting to really throb and I've got a splitting headache," he replied.

CDTMID George reached up and got Andrew to turn his head. Tina was dismayed to see that the back of his head was a sticky matt of bloody hair. The cadet officer sucked his teeth and shook his head.

"Bloody hell! This could be serious. You just sit still," he ordered Andrew. Then he snatched up the radio handset. "Safety boat, this is Cadet Midshipman George, over."

"Go ahead, over," crackled the reply.

"We've got a couple of cadets here with gunshot wounds. Get here fast, over."

"On our way! Over," replied Lt Ryan's voice.

CDTMID George next asked Sarah if she was alright. She said yes but then burst into tears and sat sobbing uncontrollably. Tina again felt dizzy and slumped down, the shock making her shiver violently. Thankfully she heard the sound of the safety boat's engine growing rapidly louder and a minute later it roared into view, bow wave creaming. Another minute later it was bobbing alongside and CDTMID George was explaining the situation.

Lt Ryan nodded grimly and snapped, "Andrew! Tina! Get into the safety boat. We will get to you to hospital. Hold the canoe steady you others."

Tina felt so groggy she had difficulty getting her balance. Lt Ryan gripped her arm and helped her to half-slide, half-step into the launch. As she stumbled over the gunwale, she saw the wounded man lying at her feet. His back was towards her and it was just a soggy red mass of tattered shirt and blood-soaked bandages. That made her blanch and go nauseous but Petty Officer Ferguson steadied her and sat her down at the stern.

As Andrew was helped aboard Tina found her eyes drawn back to the wounded man. Despite her own shock she was able to note that the officers had done the right thing and had laid the man on his injured side. *So he doesn't drown in his own blood,* she remembered from her First Aid training. It was obvious he had taken most of the shotgun blast in his left side and that the lung must have been damaged.

She also noted the round, coloured cloth badges on the sleeve of the man's khaki shirt. *A Parks and Wildlife Ranger,* she told herself.

By then Lt Ryan had moved CDTCPO Neville and CDTAB Arthur Blake to her canoe. He gave instructions to keep paddling for the dam. "Stay in radio contact every 2 minutes," he said, "and don't stop for breakfast."

"Aw sir!" Blake grumbled.

Then the engine of the safety boat roared and Tina was pressed back into the seat as it accelerated. She felt a great surge of relief now that the adults had things under control and her safe. Despite that, her anxiety stayed high as she worried about Andrew and the wounded Ranger.

As the safety boat raced across the glassy surface of the lake Petty Officer Ferguson began examining Andrew's head. Lt Ryan began calling the emergency services on the satellite phone the unit had hired for safety. There seemed to be some difficulty in getting this to work and Andrew pointed to the boat's marine radio.

"Try the radio sir," he suggested.

"I have," Lt Ryan replied. "No luck. The system is designed for the open sea," he explained. "Here we are surrounded by mountains which would screen the transmissions." He then concentrated on using the satellite phone and to Tina's intense relief he made contact. After explaining the situation he kept the phone to his ear.

Petty Officer Evans who was steering the boat looked around. "We could activate the EPIRB (Emergency Position Indicator Beacon, a radio transmitter which worked via satellite) sir," he suggested. He turned back to steering the boat and divided his time between looking ahead and glancing at the map on the chart table next to him.

Lt Ryan shook his head. "Not worth it. We will be at the dam in 15 minute at the most. How is he Mary?" This to Petty Officer Ferguson about Andrew.

"He's got at least two bullets in embedded in the back of his skull," she replied.

Andrew shook his head. "Pellets Miss, not bullets," he corrected.

"I don't care! You are a very lucky boy!" she snapped angrily.

"Yes Ma'am."

Lt Ryan grunted. "Huh! Thick skull and no brain probably," he commented. "How is Tina?"

"I will look at her now. Andrew, you get that buoyancy vest and shirt off. You too Tina," she ordered.

When Tina realised the implication of what the instructor had said she blushed and opened her mouth in dismay. "Oh Miss! I can't take my shirt off! There are men here!"

"Oh don't be silly girl! They won't look! Now get it off so I can do some First Aid!" Petty Officer Ferguson ordered.

With trembling, fumbling fingers Tina undid the buoyancy vest. Petty Officer Ferguson helped her and Lt Ryan helped Andrew. Then Petty Officer Ferguson said, "And the shirt! This is no time to be coy."

"Miss!" Tina muttered, blushing again. She looked at the men, but they all stood in front of her facing the front of the boat. Hesitantly she began undoing the buttons. Her reluctance came not only from a natural modesty but from the fact that she was wearing a sheer nylon bra and it was almost transparent. As it was she was highly embarrassed to have the female instructor seeing her. Very slowly she undid the buttons and then slipped the shirt half off, hoping that would do.

"Oh, all the way for heaven's sake!" Petty Officer Ferguson cried. "I've got two daughters dearie. It's hardly a novelty to me."

"It is for me!" Andrew quipped.

Tina saw his head half turn as he slipped off his own shirt. "Don't you dare look!" she cried, although she had often fantasised about Andrew seeing her that way. Now she found her heart hammering very fast and the blush warmed her neck and cheeks. Anxiously she held the bunched-up shirt over her front.

Then she forgot about herself when she saw Andrew's back. It was peppered with a dozen tiny bluish marks. Blood was still trickling from a couple. She also noted that the back of his buoyancy vest was riddled with a dozen holes.

He must have been in great pain while we were trying to escape, she thought, her admiration increasing.

Petty Officer Ferguson had Tina turn around and began washing and then wiping her wounds with antiseptic. That stung and Tina gasped a few times.

"Sorry, but it has to be done," Petty Officer Ferguson replied.

"How is she?" Lt Ryan asked.

"I can see three wounds in her left arm and shoulder," Petty Officer Ferguson replied. "I don't think any are life-threatening. The bleeding has almost stopped."

"What about Andrew?" Lt Ryan asked.

"At least a dozen. Let's see. He's got seven, no eight, in his left arm and shoulder and three more in his back, and the two in his head." Petty Officer Ferguson reported. She then turned back to Tina and placed anti-septic pads on each wound and began bandaging.

All the while the boat had been roaring across the water, occasionally slapping into a small wave as the first of the morning breezes began to ruffle the surface. They raced close past three jungle-covered islands and skirted several stands of dead timber, then straightened out.

"5 kilometres," Petty Officer Evans said. "10 minutes at most."

Here they me the tinnie with Sub Lt Mullion and CDT Ferguson. After a quick explanation they were sent back to be a safety boat with the canoes. "They will just have to miss breakfast," Lt Ryan added.

Petty Officer Ferguson finished bandaging and patted Tina on the shoulder. "Ok Tina, put your shirt back on," she instructed.

Tina tried. She easily slid her right arm through that sleeve, but when she tried to pull on the left sleeve she found her arm and shoulder really hurt to move. "Ouch Miss!" she cried. "Help me please," she asked, hotly aware of her cleavage and of the cool wind on her bare skin.

Petty Officer Ferguson turned to help her. Tina knelt on the back seat and moved across to allow her more room. The officer said, "You could just leave it draped over your shoulders."

"Miss!" Tina cried in embarrassment. "I couldn't do that!"

"The ambulance people will probably just take it off again," Petty Officer Ferguson said, but she helped Tina slide the left sleeve on while saying, "I don't know what you are fussing about. You probably wear less at the beach!"

Tina didn't but did not say so. She pulled her shirt around her and began to fumble with the buttons. As she did, she glanced down and got a shock. The wounded Ranger had opened his eyes and was looking up at her.

"Miss! He's awake!" Tina cried.

Then she realised she should have made sure of her shirt first because all of the males spun round to look. She gripped her shirt across her front, hotly aware that it had gaped open. However the others had eyes only for the wounded man. Lt Ryan and Petty Officer Ferguson knelt and blocked Tina's view. She briefly met Andrew's eyes and she saw his flick down to her bulging front for a fraction of a second before he looked away.

"He's passed out again," Lt Ryan said, straightening up.

"He's lost a lot of blood. His pulse is very weak and his skin is ice cold," Petty Officer Ferguson commented.

That caused Tina's heart to flutter with dread and she experienced a wave of nausea. To keep steady she sat down again and looked away. There was nothing she could do to help except pray and she did that. She also found her gaze wandering to Andrew, who had sat side on to her near the chart table.

Oh, he's handsome! she thought, taking in his tanned skin, fair hair ruffling in the breeze, and the strong muscles. *I do hope he notices me now!*

That gave her the impish thought that if she let her shirt fall open he would be more likely to notice, but the very idea made her blush and she quickly buttoned it up. It also made her anxiously jealous about the stories she had heard about the busty blonde named Letitia that had apparently let Andrew see plenty during holiday trips to Townsville.

And probably more than just a few looks! she thought, half-angrily, half-wistfully.

Tina had never allowed a boy to touch her breasts and now she bit her lip and wondered what she would do if Andrew did notice her and wanted to. That got her all anxious again and she then became dizzy and shivered. She shook her head and put that down to the wounds and shock.

"There's the dam wall," Petty Officer Evans called as the boat began turning to port around yet another jungle-covered headland.

"Oh thank God!" Tina muttered. She strained to see and when her eyes detected the cluster of tiny buildings a few kilometres ahead she sat back and closed her eyes with relief.

Chapter 4

SUSPICIONS

Because it was isolated Koombooloomba Dam had no resident staff and very few facilities. There was no proper boat ramp, only a rough gravel vehicle track which led down through a belt of trees. To Tina it all looked somewhat hostile and forbidding. As the launch approached the 'boat ramp' at the end of the western arm of the lake she studied the dark wall of trees and shivered. The anxious thought that the men might be there waiting for them crossed her mind.

To add to her depression it began to drizzle. Glancing up she noted with surprise that low cloud now covered much of the sky. *I hope that doesn't prevent the rescue helicopter from reaching us,* she thought. She was now feeling very stressed and sick.

As soon as the safety boat reached the boat ramp Lt Ryan jumped out and raced up through the belt of trees. As he did, he took the satellite phone with him and Tina saw that he was also casting anxious glances at the overcast. She and Andrew were helped out and then used their good arms to assist in lifting out the gravely wounded Ranger. Feeling the man's clammy flesh made Tina nauseous again and she quickly sat down.

It was obvious the man was in urgent need of medical aid as blood was trickling out of his mouth and his pulse was all but gone. *What a dreadful shame!* Tina thought. The man looked to be only in his twenties, and she judged him to be quite handsome.

Petty Officer Evans then backed the safety boat out and headed back along the lake to re-join the canoes. "In case they need another safety boat," he explained.

Being left lying on the wet gravel beside the boat ramp with just Andrew, the wounded Ranger and Petty Officer Ferguson got Tina all anxious again. *What if those men come here?* she wondered. All the while she became sicker and sicker, her own wounds throbbing and a headache growing by the minute.

To her great relief Lt Ryan returned 5 minutes later with his station wagon. He reversed this down to where they waited and then quickly climbed out and opened up the back. Tina saw this was now empty of its usual clutter of camping and sailing equipment. He gestured to the back.

"Let's lift this fellow in out of the weather," he said.

Despite feeling nauseous Tina stood up and helped, being told to hold the man's ankles. As they lifted the wounded Ranger gently into the vehicle Andrew asked, "Are the ambulance on their way sir?"

"I've been on to the police and the emergency services. They are sending a helicopter from Cairns and said a policeman was on his way from Ravenshoe."

"But that will take half an hour at least!" Sub Lt Mullion cried

Lt Ryan nodded. "A bit less I hope," he replied. He checked his watch. "It is now about 20 minutes since I first contacted them." He then turned his attention to making the wounded ranger comfortable. That done he climbed into the driver's seat. "Walk up to the car park. That is where the helicopter will land," he said.

Andrew glanced upwards. "If it can," he added gloomily. He then held out is arm to Tina. "Lean on me if you need to," he said.

Despite her dizziness and dread Tina felt a thrill of happiness. *He is so thoughtful!* she told herself.

Helped by Petty Officer Ferguson, she and Andrew made their way up the track the 100 paces to the large flat clearing which was a combined camping ground and car park. This was just a clearing in the forest with no facilities. Apart from the cars belonging to the cadet staff and their mini-bus the place was deserted.

Then all they could do was wait, anxiously monitoring the wounded Ranger's steadily failing vital signs and watching the cloud thicken overhead.

First to arrive, after about half an hour, was a uniformed police sergeant who had driven from Ravenshoe. Seeing the car with its red and blue lights was an enormous relief to Tina and she sobbed with emotion. Next was an ambulance a few minutes later. That made her even more relieved. Two paramedics set to work on the wounded Ranger with obvious professional competence.

To Tina's surprise they did not put the wounded Ranger straight into the ambulance and set off. That got her all worried till she heard that they were waiting for a rescue helicopter to come from Cairns. While they waited a female paramedic inspected her wounds and then Andrew's. As

Petty Officer Ferguson suggested she had to slip her shirt off, but she was able to turn her back on the males and only slid it down enough to expose her shoulder blades.

The ambulance officer studied what had been done and decided it was satisfactory. "That looks fine," she said. "I'll leave it as it is."

She then moved to talk on the radio in the ambulance. To Tina's relief she heard him talking to the rescue helicopter, but it was another five nail-biting minutes before it arrived overhead. There was then a few anxious moments while the helicopter descended slowly through the layer of cloud. Tina saw that this was not as thick as she had thought. But it was still enough to wet her with another sprinkle of drizzle and that set her shivering again.

As soon as the helicopter was on the ground there were a few minutes of rapid work by the adults to transfer the wounded Ranger to it before it lifted off and headed for Cairns. Only then did Tina really begin to relax.

As she was led towards the waiting ambulance, she asked the policeman if he had seen a brown 4WD towing a boat. He shook his head but took note of the details. She was then ushered in to sit beside Andrew in the back of the ambulance. She liked that and gave him a shy smile, dearly wishing she could hug him and have him hold her. Instead he chattered away to the paramedics about the adventure.

Petty Officer Ferguson got in as well and the ambulance set off. Tina did not enjoy the drive. Because there were no windows and as the road had so many curves, she quickly became car-sick. Only by lying down did she manage to control her now empty stomach, but it was an unpleasant trip. It took nearly an hour and a half as the nearest properly equipped hospital was in Atherton.

On arrival at the hospital she and Andrew were helped inside and taken straight in to be seen by a doctor. Andrew was judged to be the more seriously hurt so went in first. Tina was seated in a waiting room and a no-nonsense Nursing Sister took her details. By then Tina knew her parents had been notified and Petty Officer Ferguson informed her they were on their way.

They had not arrived by the time Tina was taken in to the doctor. By then she was feeling feverish and exhausted. The doctor was a nice young man and that got her all anxious about her modesty again. He insisted she take off her shirt but as the Sister was there to help and gave her a slip-on gown to wear on her front. Tina was quickly set at ease. The doctor then gave her a needle. This was local anaesthetic and caused her left shoulder to go numb.

Half an hour later the doctor had extracted the four shotgun pellets and placed them in a small plastic container. "Birdshot," he said, "If it had been larger pellets you could have been seriously injured, or killed."

After being helped on with her shirt by the Sister Tina was taken out to the waiting room. Waiting for her were her parents and her little brother Garth. There were tears and hugs from her mother and anxious smiles from her father, who then embarrassed her by handing her teddy bear to her. Tina blushed as she tucked the big brown bear under her arm but no-one else seemed to be concerned.

"Is Andrew alright?" she asked Petty Officer Ferguson as soon as the introductions were over.

"Yes, but they are keeping him in overnight for observation because of the head wound," Petty Officer Ferguson replied.

"Who is Andrew?" Tina's mum asked.

Tina blushed and mumbled. Petty Officer Ferguson answered for her, "The boy who was with Tina in the canoe. She thinks he is just wonderful."

Now Tina flamed with embarrassment and she hotly denied this, all the while conscious of her little brother's teasing smirk and her mother's knowing smile. "It's not like that!" she insisted. "Now, can we go home please?"

"The police want to interview you first," Petty Officer Ferguson said. "That is if you feel up to it."

Tina nodded. *Better to get it over with*, she thought, even though she really felt drained and just wanted to sleep.

So the next hour was spent at the Atherton police station answering questions and making a statement. Before she left, she asked if the wounded ranger was safe and was immensely relieved to learn that he had reached Cairns alive and was being operated on.

"His condition is very serious, but the hospital is hopeful," the policeman said.

Then it was home to Cairns. Using her bear as a pillow Tina slept most of the way. The drive took a bit over an hour and she was sick and feverish when woken on arrival at her home. Despite this she did not go immediately to bed. First, she ruffled the ears of 'Puddles', the family dog, a yappy little Wire-haired Terrier. Then she made her way through to the back yard to where her pet cockatoo was kept in a large aviary.

As soon as the cockatoo saw her it fluffed up its crest and began to squawk. That made Tina feel instantly better. She went up to the wire mesh and poked a finger through.

"Hello 'Beaky'. Are you glad to see me? I'm very glad to see you," she said.

The cockatoo bobbed up and down and squawked loudly, then gently nibbled at her finger. Pleased at the bird's display of affection Tina leaned closer and put the fingers of her other hand through to lightly stroke the feathers of his neck. "Good bird!" she cooed. Then she tugged backwards. "Oh, naughty bird!"

That was because Beaky had leaned across and seized the fluffy left ear of her brown teddy bear. The bird latched on and began to worry the ear. Tina pulled the bear free and waggled her finger at the cockatoo, who screeched his displeasure.

"Oh, naughty Beaky! Are you jealous?" Tina said. Then she had to laugh at the cockatoo's reaction. To settle him down she offered him a cracker from the packet on the nearby table. Mollified, the cockatoo began crunching the biscuit into pieces. As he nibbled and gulped at the crumbs Tina again stroked his neck feathers, this time making sure to keep Brown Bear safely out of sight behind her back.

Satisfied her pet was safe Tina went back inside and was immediately ordered to bed by her mother. This time she did not resist. Within 10 minutes she was securely tucked between the sheets, her bear snuggled against her left side. Her mother sat with her and gently stroked her hair while she relaxed. Then reaction set in and with it bouts of tears and shivering.

"It was awful Mum. I was terrified," Tina confessed.

"You were very lucky. Maybe you should not go on those expeditions," her mother replied.

That thought appalled Tina. "Oh Mum! Fair go! It was just a coincidence."

"Well, we will see," her mother replied doubtfully.

"But Mum, Navy Cadets is the main thing in my life," Tina argued.

Her mother sighed and nodded. "Yes, we know. We wish it wasn't," she replied. "We wish you would spend more effort on your schoolwork."

That was another worrying thought to Tina. She tried to argue that her marks were good, but she knew she could do better. *I'm capable of getting 'Very Highs', not just 'Highs',* she told herself.

She also sensed that the real problem was motivation: she just did not know what career she wanted. To end the discussion she pretended she was tired and closed her eyes. That worked and very soon she actually was asleep.

* * * * *

Monday was a school day, but Tina felt so feverish that her mother kept her home. She spent a day in bed, mostly sleeping but occasionally walking around the house. Her home was a one-story 'brick-veneer' in a suburb of similar houses. It was built off a court so was in a very quiet neighbourhood. The house itself was constructed around a courtyard that her father and mother frequently talked about roofing over to make more covered space. At the front of the house were a car port, lounge room and dining room. Along the east side were the kitchen, bathroom, toilet and two bedrooms. Across the back were two more bedrooms, including Tina's and her parent's master bedroom. On the west side, separated from the main bed room by a breezeway leading to a back door, were a store room, laundry and a large open area that was filled with a catamaran on a trailer, a Canadian canoe, and a mass of assorted paddles, life jackets, ropes, sails and other similar items.

The yard was very small, something Tina's father thought was a good idea as it meant less mowing. The back yard was only 5 metres wide and part of it, in the corner near the clothesline, was Beaky's cage. She could see him through her back window when she was sitting at her desk. Directly behind the clothesline and Beaky's cage, from the corner of the neighbour's yard at the back, was a shed and then a large aviary that extend right across the back of that property.

Tina liked that cage because the back neighbours also had pet birds and there were usually half a dozen fluttering around or chirping. Six were sulphur-crested cockatoos and they often squawked with Beaky. Knowing that Beaky wasn't alone did something to ease the niggling concern that Tina had about keeping a bird a prisoner in a cage. The other birds at the back, in separate sections of the big aviary, were parrots and budgerigars.

They are lovely birds, Tina mused as she sat and did her homework.

As darkness set in, she pulled her thick curtains across and turned on her air-conditioner. It made her very uneasy to have her curtains open at night. Her sliding windows had security screens on them, but she was still a little paranoid about prowlers. The thought of a stranger peering in at her from the darkness while she was asleep in her bed was not something she liked to think about. Even the thought that the back neighbours might glimpse her changing or doing something private like looking at herself in the mirror made her feel anxious.

Not that I ever see the neighbours much, she mused. They were a man and a woman in their thirties. There were two children, girls of about seven or eight, but they rarely came into the back yard and were very stand-offish, so she had never invited them over to play.

That night the TV News was full of the drama at Koombooloomba Dam and there was a short clip of the helicopter landing at Cairns Base Hospital and then of the CO of TS *Endeavour*, Lt Cdr Hazard, being interviewed. A few shots of the dam area followed but it was obvious to Tina that the TV crew had not been there. *It is a very remote location,* she told herself, to excuse this.

Seeing the pictures and hearing more detail caused her some unpleasant flashbacks and she found she was trembling and breathing fast. It also made her aware that her wounds were itching and sore. But the best part of the news was hearing that the wounded Ranger was still alive.

No sooner had the news finished than the doorbell rang. Tina's heart skipped, hoping it might be Andrew, but even as she thought it she knew it was a foolish idea.

He is probably still in hospital, she thought.

The visitors were four girls from the Navy Cadets: Hayley Page, Stella, Carmen Collins and Jennifer Jervis. Seeing Jennifer caused Tina very mixed feelings. Part of her wished her to the devil because Andrew liked her, but the other part had to concede that Jennifer was very nice. Tina conceded that she was friendly and helpful and not deliberately trying to attract Andrew.

But it would be better if she went back to England.

The girls discussed the weekend in detail and the others fussed over Tina, making her feel very special. The visit certainly helped calm her down so that she slept better, with only one bad dream where her canoe was being dragged by a strong current towards some unnamed but dreaded danger.

When Tina woke in the morning, she felt much better. There were still a few minor aches and pains, but she felt well enough to go to school, and wanted to, in the hope of seeing Andrew and also to discuss the adventure with her friends. Whistling happily she got out of bed and went to the window. As she drew the curtains she stretched and noted it was a bright sunny day.

To herself she said what she often did on such mornings: "The sun is shining; the birds are singing!" As she said it, she picked up her hair brush and looked out at Beaky and the other birds. Some of these were indeed singing. Smiling and chirping along with the birds Tina began to brush her hair.

Then she stopped and frowned. Something was different but it took her a few minutes to work out what it was. Then she shook her head in puzzlement.

All the cockatoos from next door are gone, she thought. *But when were they taken?*

Chapter 5

ANNOYED

Tina turned away from the window feeling both suspicious and a little puzzled.

Why did the neighbours take all cockatoos away? And when? she thought. She was sure that the birds had been there when she went to bed. *I wonder if someone stole them; or left the door of the cage open?*

Then she shrugged and decided it was none of her business anyway. So she busied herself getting ready for school. This promised to be something of an ordeal as she had not done her homework and there would be all the social pressures.

Everyone will question me about what happened, she worried. And there was concern about Andrew and the Wildlife Ranger. *Is the ranger still alive?* she worried.

To try to find out she made a point of listening to the radio news while she had breakfast. As this was something she normally never did, her mother was surprised enough to comment. Tina replied, "I feel involved Mum. I helped save him, so I care what happens."

"Good. That is a normal and healthy reaction," her mother answered. "Now hurry up and finish your breakfast."

"Can you write me a note to explain why I haven't done my homework please Mum?" Tina asked.

Her mother frowned and hesitated but in the end she did. That eased some of Tina's anxiety. But all her normal anxieties remained as she prepared for school. Near the top of these was her appearance.

I must look really freaky, she thought. *My bum is too big; and my waist is too thick; and my boobs are way too big. Oh, I wish I was more shapely!*

But she knew it was no good voicing these ideas to her mother. She had in the past and all her mother had done was tell her to have some sense. 'You have a pretty face and a lovely personality and that is more important; and you can't change things anyway, so make the most of what you've got,' she had said.

What niggled at Tina was the somewhat depressing thought that she was doomed by genetics to end up looking like her mother. As her mother was quite short and stout and had enormous breasts, she felt quite anxious. But she also knew she was strong and healthy. The fact that she felt fit and well after the weekend attested to that.

Tina caught the bus to school as usual. Her little brother Garth, a Year 8, travelled with her. And as usual he acted the fool with his friends, to the annoyance of both Tina and the bus driver. She found it a relief to reach school. But then it was a sobering experience as she found that almost no-one at school knew she had been involved in the incident at Lake Koombaloomba. Being naturally a shy person Tina did not mention it, but it hurt her feelings a bit to find people did not know or seem to care.

The one person who did was also her best friend, Sarah. But that was because Sarah had been with her in the same canoe and had been equally terrified. The two girls hugged each other and then sat in their usual seats under the school.

Tina studied Sarah's face and saw that she looked pale and tired. "Are you alright Sarah?" she asked.

Sarah nodded but then trembled. "Yes, but I haven't slept very well for the last two nights. I keep having a bad dream about trying to paddle a canoe to get away from horrible men but the water seems like treacle and then I lose my paddle."

Tina nodded and managed a smile. "I've been worrying about that ranger who got shot," she said.

"Oh yes! How is he, do you know?"

"Still alive, Mum said," Tina answered. Then she voiced an idea she had been nursing for a few hours. "I was thinking of going to the hospital to see how he was this afternoon."

"That's a good idea, but are you allowed?" Sarah queried.

"I haven't asked my mum, but I will," Tina answered.

As the girls talked Tina kept watching other students as they arrived at school and she was again slightly miffed that barely any one even glanced at her and she was sure that not one in a hundred associated her with the weekend drama. Even the girls in their class did not seem to know. Nor did they care, beyond a certain level of curiosity. The only other student who seemed to know and care was Carmen Collins. As soon as she saw the two friends Carmen hurried over to ask how they were.

Carmen's concern touched Tina, but it was not Carmen Collins she wanted to talk to but Andrew Collins. "How is Andrew?" she asked.

Carmen smiled. "He's fine. He is at school today. He's a typical boy and thinks it was all a big adventure."

At that Sarah shook her head. "Not me! I was really scared. Sorry I let you all down," she said.

Tina reached across and squeezed her arm. "You were acting normal. It was all such a surprise none of us knew what to do. I mean, it isn't every day you get a man with a gun trying to shoot you."

"No, and I hope it never happens again," Sarah answered. Then she made a face. "Mum said she didn't know if she would let me go on any more canoe trips."

That was bad news to Tina. She said, "But what about next weekend? Are you still allowed to come with us?" Her family was planning a camping trip to the Gulf Country over the coming Easter Holidays and Tina was really looking forward to it. And she did not want to go with just her own family.

That won't be much fun with just Mum and Dad and 'Toad Face' little brother, she thought.

Sarah again shook her head and said, "I will have to ask."

"Where are you going?" Carmen asked.

"Out to Croydon and Normanton," Tina answered. "My dad and Sarah's want to go fishing."

"Oh you lucky things! I have never been out there," Carmen answered.

"Neither have we," Tina replied. "I'm not sure if I am looking forward to it though. I hear it's an awful lot of nothing much, you know, long, boring drives just so the men can go fishing."

Carmen laughed and said, "I wish I was going! I like fishing. And I've heard that the barramundi fishing out that way is great. Anyway, here's Andrew."

Andrew came over to them, smiling and apparently none the worse for the adventure. He looked from one to the other and asked how they were.

Tina smiled back and shrugged but felt her heart beating faster than normal. "I'm alright. How are you?" she replied.

At that moment the bell for classes went so Tina got no chance to talk to Andrew. He just grinned and said, "I'm a bit sore, but the doctor said I will be OK."

Carmen made a face and added, "His thick skull and tiny brain saved him from serious harm."

Sarah looked surprised. "Oh Carmen!" she cried.

Carmen laughed and said, "See you later." She hurried off to her class and both Tina and Sarah stood up and followed Andrew as he walked towards their first class. As they walked Tina noted that he had several dark marks on the back of his neck and on his left arm. Closer inspection revealed these to be small scabs with a circle of antiseptic on the skin. She badly wanted to check that he was alright but was afraid the other girls would tease her so instead she chatted happily about nothing much while they walked.

At the classroom they separated and Andrew moved to sit with his own friend Arthur Blake. Blake was another navy cadet and was a leading seaman in the same watch. He had been in another canoe on the weekend so was quite concerned about how they all were but his queries were cut short by the arrival of the teacher.

The lesson was Maths A with Mr Maclaren. He was a dry stick with a very pedantic manner and the nickname 'Sylvester' (After the cartoon cat). But Tina did not mind being in his class and she liked him even more when he came over to where she and Sarah sat and asked how they were. His concern was genuine, and he asked several very sensible questions about what they had done when confronted with the emergency.

He is interested because he is an officer in the Army Cadets, Tina thought.

It was another reason that she tolerated the teacher's mannerisms and foibles. Her school was one of the very few in North Queensland that had an army cadet unit and the army cadets were both the navy cadet's friends and their best rivals.

But Tina's next teacher had no interest in cadets of any sort and did not even seem to be aware that anything had happened to the girls. Miss Massey was a formidable woman with huge, jutting breasts. She taught Commerce and her nickname, because of her huge bosom, was 'Massive'. Tina did not like her at all and even feared her. But she knew her job and taught the subject very well, so Tina also respected her.

A period of English followed and the teacher was another officer in the army cadets. Mrs Standish was a lieutenant and Tina often wondered what she might be like in uniform because as a person she came across as being very warm and caring and gentle. She was very 'arty' and full of poetry and quotations.

Mrs Standish demonstrated this at once by asking how the girls were and then for details of the incident. They had to show their shotgun pellet wounds and that made them both feel quite special as others in the class looked at them with a mixture of interest, admiration and envy. The jealousy particularly came from Jessica and Nicole but that was no surprise to Tina as the girls had clashed often over the past few years.

And we will clash some more if that sneaky bitch doesn't stop making passes at Andrew, Tina thought, watching with a chill in her heart as Jessica touched Andrew's wounds and oozed sympathy and interest all over him. To add to Tina's concern Andrew smiled back and chatted cheerfully with Jessica.

Morning break was next, but it was equally as frustrating because Andrew and Blake went off to sit with a group of boys under another part of the school. Tina could only sit with Sarah and Lynn and watch wistfully from a distance as the boys talked, joked and skylarked. She was too far away to hear what they were saying but knew from other times that it was mostly good-natured teasing from the boys who were in the army cadets or air cadets, with a few crude jokes and typical 'boy' language thrown in.

The boys in that group were mostly Year 10s with a few Year 9s on the edges. There were other groups of boys who clustered together because they were cadets with age and year level the main determinants of who 'belonged'. It was a much more obvious grouping for the boys than it was for the girls and Tina always felt slightly annoyed and jealous when she thought about it.

I wish I was part of a big group of cadets, she thought. That was because being a cadet of any sort was not considered 'cool' and people who were cadets came in for a good deal of teasing and even taunting abuse.

Two of the male army cadets particularly held Tina's attention; one because he was so good looking and the other because he was so nice. Graham Kirk, a corporal in the army cadets, was the most handsome youth Tina had ever seen. He was fit and tough and had a reputation for being very brave. She also knew he was very loyal and good to his mates. In appearance Graham matched Andrew with fair hair and bright blue eyes but his hair was more 'mousy' than blond and he had a good sprinkle of freckles on his face. Graham was also shorter and had much broader shoulders.

The other army cadet was in her own class. He was Corporal Peter Bronksy and he was the 'brain' of 10A. Peter had plain looks and dark eyes and hair, but he was a very kind and considerate person and was Graham's best friend.

Graham had two other friends, neither of whom Tina particularly liked. Stephen Bell, another Year 10 and also an army cadet corporal, was a thin, freckled youth with glasses. He had a real reputation for being good with the girls, but Tina could not see why. From what she had seen he was fairly coarse and she did not trust him.

The other boy was Roger Dunning, a Year 9. He was only tolerated in the Year 10 group because he was one of the four members of the 'Hiking Team'. Roger was chubby and cheerful and frequently the butt of jokes or teasing.

But at the moment Tina could see that it was several air cadets who were the target of the jibes. She nudged Sarah and said, "Who is that boy talking to Graham Kirk?"

Sarah looked and then smiled. "That is Willy Williams, the 'Mad Professor'," she answered.

On hearing that Tina remembered several stories about Willy. "He is an air cadet, isn't he?" she asked. Willy was famous around the school for his gadgets: the rocket which exploded, the radio controlled plane which had buzzed the army cadets Passing-Out Parade, the man lifting kite which had crashed off the roof, the giant catapult.

"I think so. And so is that tall bloke next to him, the one they call 'Stick'."

Tina giggled at that because the description was so apt. Stick had long, thin, gangly legs and arms. Then she felt bad about laughing as she knew how important looks and nicknames were. The year before she had been nicknamed 'Tub' or 'Tubby' and she had hated it.

I hope I don't have a horrible nickname now, she thought anxiously.

Because she was so shy and because the boys stayed in such a tight group Tina had no chance to talk to Andrew during the morning break. All she could manage were a few friendly comments as they walked into their next class. This was Maths B with Mr Ritter and he made them work very hard and did not tolerate any talking or interruptions.

Music followed with Miss Wall. Tina loved music and she also intensely admired Miss Wall who was in her early twenties and was both very talented and very stylish in her dress and behaviour. The fact that Andrew seemed to be oblivious to music was a source of secret pain to Tina and she could only shake her head in puzzlement.

The period before 'Big Lunch' was Physics with Mr Holden. He was a very serious and strict teacher and Tina respected him. So did Andrew, who appeared to be deeply interested in the subject. But Andrew sat with Blake and Tina was much to shy to push in beside him.

It was during Physics she got another of those disquieting jolts that sent her anxiety level shooting up. There was another army cadet in her class, and she was a very attractive blonde, Gwen Copeland. Gwen was another corporal but she was much more. She appeared to have all the things Tina felt she lacked: beauty, a perfect figure, wit, charm, a style and grace to the way she dressed and the way she moved that could only inspire both envy and anxiety, particularly when Andrew kept talking to her and smiling!

But it wasn't that simple. Tina thought Gwen was a lovely person and she actually liked her enormously and had seen her being very helpful to other students. So even though she was afraid that Andrew might fall for Gwen Tina still admired her.

Nor did Tina get any real chance to talk to Andrew at lunch time as he went off with a group of Year 10 boys to play soccer on the oval. Tina could only wistfully wish she was more active. Instead she went to the library and helped as she was a Library Monitor.

The afternoon classes were no better for furthering Tina's romantic ambitions. There was Chemistry with Mr Feldt, a grey-haired stick of a man who had a very droll sense of humour and really knew his subject. Andrew was very good at Chemistry and had no time for social diversions during it. German with Mr Ritter was no better. So the end of the day arrived and Tina was left with a vague ache of longing and wishful daydreaming to leave her unsatisfied.

Then it was home on the bus and the routine of homework and

household chores. One of these was feeding the birds so she collected the seed and water and made her way out through the back gate. As she reached Beaky's cage she saw movement next door. It was the man who lived there, Neville (She never knew his last name), a thin man with a dark beard flecked with grey. Hearing her he looked up and nodded.

Tina felt shy but nodded back and said "Hello." Then, as he was obviously cleaning out the cages where the cockatoos had been kept, she plucked up the courage to ask what had happened to them.

Neville shrugged and said, "Sold them to pet shops," he answered. Then he turned away and left the cage.

Tina felt a bit awkward at the snub but decided it was her own fault. *It was none of my business,* she thought. So she fed the birds and then the dog.

Dinner and the TV news followed. That brought Tina a very unpleasant shock, the Ranger had died. It took a while for the meaning to sink in and then she began to cry. Her mother at once moved to comfort her but all Tina could think of was what a waste it was. "He was so young and handsome mum. It is just terrible."

She was so upset she could not eat anymore and went to her room where she lay quietly weeping. Thoughts of death and of what it might be like to die came to depress her and make her anxious. It was not a subject she gave much thought to normally but now it seemed to take over her mind and she became very sad and thoughtful. She knew she had to die one day but whenever she did think about it there was the hazy notion that it was sixty or seventy years away when she was an old granny.

Later Tina suggested to her parents that they attend the ranger's funeral but her mother was strongly against that, so she dropped the subject. It was only after the washing up had been done (Garth washed, she wiped and put away) that she remembered the holidays. These holidays, ten whole days of them, were now starting to loom as a bit of a black hole in Tina's life. She knew many of her friends were going off to do exciting and interesting places and she was quite unsure what a week-long family fishing trip might be like.

When the family was settled in the dining room for supper Tina asked about them. "Are we still going for this trip?" she asked.

By the surprised look on her parent's faces she knew the answer even before her father said, "Why of course. I am really looking forward to it."

51

Tina's mother frowned. "Aren't you keen on the idea Ti?"

Tina shrugged. "Yes, but I am a bit worried I might get bored, or that we might not get on with the Creswells," she replied.

"But I thought Sarah was your best friend," her mother said.

"She is Mum, but I don't really know the rest of the family," Tina answered.

"It will be alright dear," her mother answered. Tina had to be content with that but later As she did, her homework she thought, *I hope so!*

Later she watched the late news and this time the announcer stated that the police were now searching for three men for the murder of the ranger. *Murder!* she thought, *and we were witnesses.*

That got her wondering if she would ever have to appear in court and that idea did not appeal. But then another much worse thought crept into her mind. *If I am a witness, then those men might hurt me to stop me talking.*

It was a scary thought and she comforted herself by the thought that the men would have no ideas who she was or where she lived. But it was still an anxious girl who turned the lights out and went to bed that night.

Chapter 6

EASTER

Wednesday was similar. Tina woke up feeling anxious, and as soon as she arrived at school she sought out Sarah to check if her family was still planning to go on the fishing trip. Sarah nodded her head and replied that her father was really looking forward to it.

"What about you?" Tina asked.

"OK I suppose," Sarah answered. "Why? Don't you want to go?"

"I'm a bit anxious," Tina admitted. "I am worried we might all get bored or get on each other's nerves and clash."

"It will be alright," Sarah assured her.

At that moment Tina saw Andrew and all worries about holidays went out of her head. She thought, *I wish it was Andrew's family we were going away with!*

But she did not say this. Instead she began to chatter about her birds and how they were misbehaving. "Particularly poor old 'Beaky'. Since the cockatoos went from next door he seems to be doing a lot of moping," she said.

"Where did they go? Did they get away?" Sarah asked. She was a dog person and did not care about birds at all.

"No, they just weren't there one morning," Tina replied. "The cage was still closed."

"Maybe they gave them to friends, or sold them?" Sarah suggested.

Further discussion was interrupted by Lynn who arrived agog with the latest scandal concerning teachers. Apparently, the male art teacher had been sprung kissing the female art teacher in the art storeroom.

"Who saw them?" Tina asked. The subject of kissing was one she was very interested in and she could only wish it was her being kissed, but by Andrew!

The girls discussed the incident until the bell went. Then it was into Maths A with Mr Maclaren, followed by English with Mrs Standish. During this lesson they were given an assignment to research over the holidays to write a description of a place they were going to visit.

During the morning break Tina sat with her girlfriends and they talked. She could see Andrew in the distance, but he was with the usual group of boys and she pretended she wasn't interested.

Oh! I wish he would notice me, she thought with a mixture of exasperation and wistfulness.

The three lessons during the middle session were Maths B with Mr Ritter, Physical Education, and Computing with Mr Hamilton. Hamish Hamilton was a handsome young man with a moustache and Tina knew he fancied himself with the ladies. But she found that only mildly annoying and even laughed at his attempts to flirt with some of the girls. What really peeved her was that he made no attempt to flirt with her!

He must think I am too ordinary, she mused.

By coincidence Mr Hamilton was also an Officer of Cadets in the school's army cadet unit so she was able to relate to him fairly well. From time to time he made a dig at the Navy or Navy Cadets, but it was always a friendly comment.

Wednesday afternoons were when the army cadets did their 2-hour Home Training parade. This was at the school and they began with a company admin parade on the grass quadrangle at 1545hrs. Sometimes Tina would stay and watch, but usually only when Andrew or Carmen did so. This time she did not, even though she wanted to. Instead she went home as usual.

At home Tina fed the pets and then cleaned the bird cage. As she did, she chirped to Beaky, talking to him as though he was a human being. "Need to clean up old chap," she said. "We will be away for a week and you will be fed by dear old Mrs Norton from next door."

It was an arrangement that worried Tina, but she did not have much choice. Mrs Norton had minded the pets on previous occasions, but it had never quite been to Tina's satisfaction.

As she worked Tina glanced at the empty cage next door and made a wry face. "Poor Old Beaky, you must be a bit lonely now," she said. "I hope the neighbours get some more birds soon."

That evening Tina began packing. Usually she was filled with excitement about holiday trips but this time she felt quite anxious. Partly it was because they were going much farther out into the 'Gulf Country' but mostly she knew it was because she wanted to be with other friends.

Thursday was a wearing and slightly anxious day. At least half the students were absent, so most classes were just supervisions with no real teaching being done. Tina didn't mind that as she could happily read or draw or quietly gossip but it was still a frustrating waste of time. She did not like to just sit around.

The fact that Andrew still did not seem to notice her and the knowledge that he and Carmen were going off to camp on some island down near Cardwell did not help. Tina had heard the most amazing rumours of what had happened at that island the previous year. These included tales of nudity and pirates. It was the mention of a busty blonde nudist from Townsville that got Tina jealous and worried.

I hope Andrew doesn't have an affair with her, she thought unhappily.

Then it was 1500hrs and school was over for ten days. Tina sighed with relief and made her way home to flop onto her bed. The holidays had begun!

That evening Tina completed her packing. She then helped her mother with the evening meal and washing up before settling in front of the TV with some books. Among her personal library were such useful works as *What Bird is that?* and *A Handbook of Australian Birds.*

As she leafed through them Tina studied the familiar pictures and hope she would see many of those that were illustrated. Ever since Year 3 she had been a keen bird watcher and kept a detailed notebook of her sightings and observations. She also tried to take photos of them but so far with limited success.

I wish I had the money to buy a really good camera with a telephoto lens, she thought.

It was one of her strongest desires and for several years now she had been hinting aloud to parents and grandparents that such a gift would be very much appreciated. But so far several birthdays and Christmases had slipped by with no such present appearing.

While she was looking at her books her father knocked on her doorway and came in holding a magazine. "I thought this one might interest you. I had to do a bit of digging to find it. But if you want to see any bird, this is the one."

He handed the magazine to Tina and she saw it was an *Australian Geographic* and on the cover was a picture of the cutest, most beautiful bird she had ever seen. It had a brilliant purple breast and yellow undersides and a black face.

"A Gouldian Finch," she read.

She was instantly captivated and sat reading for the next half hour. The story quite gripped her but also saddened her when she read that the beautiful little creature was endangered and now quite rare.

It is just so lovely, she thought, noting that some of the species had bright red faces. She decided to make a special effort to keep a sharp lookout for them although her reading did not make her very hopeful.

And then there were three relatively boring and lonely days because Tina's grandmother insisted that they not go away during the Easter period. Tina found this irritating because she was not very religious, but she dearly loved her gran, so she accepted her wishes, as did her mother. Her grandmother came from a strict north of England protestant background, very dour and serious; all hard-working, God-fearing folk.

So Good Friday was spent quietly at home and with a visit to Gran. Saturday was a more normal day with lots of chores. These were the usual and numerous little things that had accumulated over the last few months and that everyone had been too busy to attend to. For Tina it meant a day of helping re-pack the garden shed in the backyard, plus a lot of sweeping, scrubbing and caring for pets. She also helped her mother with a back-log of laundry.

Sunday morning meant church and they picked up Gran and took her. Tina actually enjoyed that and was glad she went. *I should go more often,* she thought, knowing that she did not feel guilty enough and that idea spurring even more guilt. She also experienced a spasm of guilt at disloyal thoughts about her church. Over the last year or so she had attended church ceremonies with some of her friends of different denominations and had been quite impressed by the colour and spectacle they presented, particularly the Roman Catholic, Anglican and Greek Orthodox services. They were a stark contrast to the austere furnishings and drab clothing of her own strict church.

But at least the duty was done and after returning Gran to her home and enjoying a pleasant lunch it was home and final preparations for the fishing trip. With that came the rising excitement and anxiety and once again she wished she was with Andrew and his family on their tropical island.

But how can I compete with busty nude blondes? she wondered, experiencing yet again a spurt of intense dislike for such creatures. This was immediately followed by another bout of guilt for being jealous and for having unkind thoughts. But it did not help much. Once again she bewailed the fate that had given her a stout build and dark hair. And she knew she was too inhibited to deliberately use her most obvious assets to attract Andrew's attention.

The family was up early on Monday morning and Tina at once went to feed Beaky and the other birds. There were more doubts about whether the birds would be properly cared for but it was too late to change any plans like that so she had to just hope and she gave Beaky an extra serve of feed 'just in case'.

After breakfast came the complicated business of loading the Jackaroo 4WD. Tina knew her mother was very fussy about how this was done so she tried to stay right out of the way and could only shake her head when she heard her father getting into trouble for just shoving things in

"It is all in the vehicle," he said.

"But we need to be able to get things out easily and it has to be done neatly or it won't all fit," Tina's mother replied, scolding and pulling the items out for re-stowing.

Oh silly Dad! Tina thought. *When will you learn that Mum knows best?*

The loading and packing was all done by 8:00, which was apparently half an hour later than the time Tina's mother had planned on. The family then took their places in the vehicle. Tina's mother drove with her father in the front passenger seat. She went behind him in the left-hand seat and little brother Garth sat on her right. The boat was hooked on behind and with a last round of 'have we got everything?' questions they were off.

First they drove over to the Creswell's. They were also packed and ready and also had a boat trailer hooked on behind and a Canadian canoe lashed to the roof racks of the 'Patrol' 4WD. Mr Creswell was a big, burly man with a cheerful personality but Mrs Creswell always looked slightly anxious to Tina. Mrs Creswell was a slim woman with mousy-fair hair cut at shoulder length. Two younger brothers completed Sarah's family. Aiden was 9 Years old and a bright little fair-haired boy with a very inquisitive mind. Michael was 11 and in Year 6 and had glasses. He was a beanpole of a lad and looked awkward and gawky and always looked serious and slightly surprised.

After a brief discussion on the route and stops along the way the two vehicles set off, Tina's family leading. That suited her and she suddenly felt anxious as well as excited and she just wanted to quietly cope.

The first part of the trip was very familiar: south along the Bruce Highway to Gordonvale and then west into the Mulgrave Valley. Tina enjoyed that section of the journey, partly because of the scenery, which she thought the most beautiful in Australia, and partly because of pleasant memories. She had done canoe trips on the Mulgrave with the Navy Cadets and also numerous family picnics at lovely places like Ross and Locke.

But she didn't enjoy the next part, which was 20 kilometres of winding road up the side of the mountains along the Gillies Highway. The scenery was spectacular, but the endless curves soon had her feeling queasy. Only when they came out of the dense tropical rain forest onto the open farmland of the Atherton Tablelands did she start to relax.

Another 10 minutes' drive had them at the beautiful little town of Yungaburra. They stopped there for morning tea at a café and as soon as she climbed out of the vehicle Tina felt the cool nip of the mountain air. Both families sat around two tables and talked while they consumed food and rink. Tina had a chocolate flavoured milk and some biscuits and was content to chatter to Sarah and to take in the local atmosphere.

Michael sat to one side and made only a couple of shy comments, but young Aiden was an endless flow of questions of the why variety. At first Tina found it amusing but when it kept on she got a bit irritated. However Aiden's engaging smile and brightness made it impossible for her to stay that way and she soon became his chief question answerer, much to the obvious relief of his parents.

The suggestion was made that some of the people swap vehicles. Tina wasn't keen on this but then her mother swapped with Mrs Creswell and Aiden came to take her place. She ended up in the back of the Creswell's vehicle with Michael on the right, Sarah in the middle and herself on the left.

From Atherton they drove south and up into the mountains of the Herberton Range. Tina had been there a couple of times before but had never paid any particular notice. Now she noted that the road wound up the right-hand side of a deep but steadily narrowing valley. The vegetation was more open than she had expected and became a mixture of She Oaks growing on steep rocky slopes or larger trees standing in long grass.

Near the head of the valley Mr Creswell pointed to the left and said, "There is the old railway over there."

That surprised Tina and she looked and saw the line of a bench cut on the opposite slope. She had vaguely known that there were railways on the Tablelands but did not know there had been one to Herberton. That there had been was brought home more firmly after they crossed the saddle at the pass and went down a long slope to cross the railway at a level crossing. They re-crossed it again 2 kilometres further on.

From then on Tina kept glancing to her left to try to get glimpses of the railway but she did not see it. What she did see was a line of rugged mountains a few kilometres away. Through a gap in the low cloud she glimpsed a very rugged knoll standing higher than any other part of the range.

"That looks rough," she commented. "I wonder what it is called?"

Mr Creswell glanced and said, "Stewarts Head. I climbed it once, years ago, when I was a Boy Scout. It is on a long ridge that runs all the way to Herberton."

Herberton was next, a few kilometres further on. Of particular interest to Tina was the Catholic girl's boarding school, the Mount St Bernard Convent. She knew several girls who had been sent there and as she stared at the pile of big buildings on the hillside above the road she wondered what boarding school might be like.

The expedition did not stop in Herberton but drove on along a winding road through hills and a scattering of houses. At Wondecla they re-crossed the abandoned railway line and then went through the remnant of the tall timbers that once clothed the whole area. Another 30 kilometres of winding roads through hills covered with either tall trees or open fields dotted with cows brought them to the town of Ravenshoe.

This was a small town with one main street and a dozen side streets. Tina was familiar with it from previous trips, the most recent being the canoe trip to Koombooloomba. Shops were open so the expedition stopped for refreshments. Tina opted for a flavoured milk and then went outside to study the town. She was joined on the footpath by the others. To Tina it all looked very sleepy and it was just cool enough to make her shiver.

"Highest town in Queensland," her father commented in reply to her mentioning the temperature.

"And probably the coldest," Tina added. The sky was overcast and there was a hint of drizzle and looking up at it she had a sharp flashback to the previous weekend when she had been waiting beside the dam for the ambulance. That sent a shiver through her and she shook her head and wondered how any person could possibly shoot another.

Her thoughts were interrupted by young Aiden who came running back from the end of the row of shops. He called, "Hey Dad, Mum, there's a steam train here."

Mr Creswell replied that he knew that but at Aiden's urging they all had to walk to the end of the buildings to look. There was a toilet there and then a large open area. Beyond this was the old railway station and standing on the line was a blue painted steam engine. Men were busy around and on it and a feather of steam was visible issuing from some valve on top.

Aiden and Michael both wanted to go over and look. Mr Creswell looked at his watch and said they didn't have the time, but the boys were so obviously disappointed that the whole group walked across the grass to look.

"But only for 5 minutes," Mr Creswell added. "We've got a long way to drive yet."

"Aw Dad!"

Then the boys discovered that not only did the steam train work but that it was taking people for paid rides. "Can we please Dad!" Aiden cried.

"Sorry, not today. The train doesn't go for another hour and that will take even more time. We are late already," Mr Creswell said.

"Aw Dad!"

Mr Creswell sighed. "We will come here again and go for a ride on the train," he said.

"Promise?" Michael asked.

Mr Creswell nodded. "Promise, now let's go."

Reluctantly the boys followed the others back to the vehicles. It was 1125hrs by then and a misty drizzle was beginning. The vehicles were driven out of town on the south side and turned right at the Kennedy Highway. As they did Tina looked across the intersection and noted that it was the start of the road to Koombooloomba. That and the drizzle brought back another wave of intense memories and she shivered and thought of the ranger who was shot. Then she shivered again and wondered what death might be like.

Sarah noticed her shiver and hug herself and said, "Are you alright Tina?"

"Yes, just remembering last weekend at the dam."

"That's the road to the dam isn't it?" Sarah commented.

Tina nodded. Michael turned and said, "Did you see the man get shot?"

Tina nodded again. "Yes I did," she replied.

"Was it awful?" Michael asked.

Mrs Creswell turned in her seat and said, "That will do Michael. You don't ask people questions like that. I'm sorry Tina."

"It's alright Mrs Creswell. It is probably better to talk about it," Tina replied.

So as they sped west along the Kennedy Highway she recounted the events at Koombooloomba. As they travelled along Tina noted the sign to the Millstream Falls. That was as far west as she had ever been, so she divided her attention between telling the tale and looking at the scenery. What was immediately apparent to her was a dramatic change of vegetation, from the tall timbers and rain forests of the Wet Tropics to the open savannah woodland of the drier interior.

We are now in the sort of country where the Gouldian Finch lives, she thought, her eyes scanning the bush on both sides of the road. But she did not see one. All she saw were lots of hawks and peewees and the odd little sparrow or crow.

Midday found them at the small town of Mt Garnet. The expedition stopped there to refuel and to buy lunch and to go to the toilet. This took up another half hour and by then Tina's mother was getting fretful about the time.

From Mt Garnet the group drove on along the Kennedy Highway, now heading almost south. The country remained savannah but the road deteriorated to a single lane of bitumen which made the journey both less safe and slower as they had to slow right down and get off onto the gravel shoulders every time they encountered another vehicle coming in the opposite direction. As much of the traffic comprised huge ore trucks with three and even four trailers the need for caution was very evident.

After three quarters of an hour of driving the vegetation changed almost instantly to a very thick tangle of bushes, trees and giant prickly pear.

"What an odd place," Tina commented.

"It's called the Forty Mile Scrub," Mr Creswell replied.

At that moment a rest area and tourist sign came into view on the right. Michael pointed and said, "There's a toilet. I need to go. Please stop."

Mr Creswell pulled into the parking area and Tina's father drove in beside them. As he did, he indicated his watch but then shrugged when Mrs Creswell got out. Tina climbed out as well and stared at the wall of dense vegetation hemming them in on either side of the road. In places it was so thick that she was sure it would not be possible to push through the tangle.

"Quite spooky really," she commented. "I'd hate to have to try to get through this bit of country."

There was a sign explaining the vegetation which was in a small National Park. The other side of the sign explained the 'Savannah Way', the tourist route which ran right across northern Australia from Cairns to Western Australia. She read this with interest and decided that one day she would travel right along it.

The boys ran off along a walking track into the scrub and Tina went a little way, but she found it so claustrophobic and unpleasant that she soon returned to the car park. Mr Creswell bellowed to the boys to stop playing the fool and to get back in the car. They came scurrying back and clambered in. Tina did likewise, and as soon as Mrs Creswell was back aboard they resumed their journey.

After travelling for only another 10 minutes they came out into open savannah woodland again and arrived at a major road junction. Here they turned right and headed west. As kilometre of bush succeeded kilometre of similar bush Tina began to tire and grow bored. The only sighting that really gripped her interest was a fleeting glimpse of some emus.

"They are becoming quite rare," Mr Creswell commented.

"Why? Do people hunt them?" Tina asked.

"No. It is probably because feral cats eat the chicks, or maybe because of the Ten Eighty Poison baits laid for dingoes," Mr Creswell answered.

Those ideas bothered Tina as she had somehow thought that there were lots of emus. To find that such an Australian icon was under threat concerned her and she puzzled over what could be done about it. But she kept on hopefully scanning the bush, still hoping to see a Gouldian Finch or one of the other types of rare birds that the book said lived in that environment. She described these and asked the others to also keep a sharp eye out for them. This led to a discussion on why the Gouldian Finch was endangered.

Forty-5 minutes of 100kph driving along a good bitumen road had the party at the railway siding of Mt Surprise. The place was a surprise to Tina as there actually was a surprising looking mountain, one of the very few around. It was rough and rugged and stood up from the mostly flat bushland a few kilometres away. The small town did not impress her. It consisted of little more than a main street and a few scattered buildings beyond and most were devoted to the travel industry.

After a visit to the toilet Tina and Sarah made their way to the nearby shop. As she walked along the grassy footpath Tina studied the railway station on the other side of the road. "Is that the same railway we saw at Herberton?" she asked.

Michael answered that, his voice full of scorn for older people who were ignorant of basic facts. "No! This railway is the one that goes west from Mareeba to Almaden."

Feeling quite silly Tina bit her lip and nodded. Sarah asked, "So where does it go, Mr Smarty Pants?"

"Out to a little town called Forsayth," Michael replied, pointing off to the Southwest.

Mrs Creswell looked at the rusty rails and grass growing along the rail track. "It doesn't look very busy. How often do the trains run?"

"Only one train a week Mum," Michael answered. "A tourist train called the 'Savannahlander'. It is a rail motor really."

"Oh, I've heard of that," Mrs Creswell commented.

Tina had too but made no comment. Then, as she went into the shop, she saw advertisements and pictures all over the place for the train. But trains did not really interest her and she was more taken by observing a kingfisher in a nearby tree.

After some refreshments and a change of seating the party continued on its way. By then it was 1430hrs. Sarah moved to the front next to her father. Tina moved into the middle and had her mother beside her and Michael on her right.

The road was a good double lane bitumen one, so the average speed was still up near 100kph. The country remained open savannah and there were more small hills and undulations that Tina had expected. She had thought that all the country was just flat and very open and dry but most of it she found to be quite normal Australian bush. She was even more surprised when a range of mountains appeared ahead after they crossed the Einasleigh River.

"Newcastle Range," Mr Creswell informed her.

Tina found them quite attractive in a rugged sort of way. *More like pictures I have seen of Central Australia,* she thought as she studied the reddish rocks and yellowish grasses.

The view ahead from the top she found quite impressive. What particularly caught her eye was the flatness. Except for a few blue tinged hills in the far distance the level country seemed to extend on to the end of the earth. The sight caused Tina to experience an irrational shiver.

"We are a long way out now," she commented.

Mr Creswell looked and then laughed. "We are about halfway. In fact we are now getting closer to the sea on the other side."

It was that 'other side' that Tina found daunting for no obvious reason. She had never seen the Gulf of Carpentaria and had always had a vague fear of the 'Gulf Country' and now she was approaching it.

I hope everything is going to be alright, she thought, wondering yet again what this half mythical region of flatness and legendary fishing might be like.

Chapter 7

NOT WHAT SHE EXPECTED

2 0 minutes of driving through more fairly ordinary Australian bush brought them to a long concrete bridge which spanned half a kilometre of dry, white sand. 'Etheridge River' proclaimed a sign. On the other bank was the pleasant little town of Georgetown. Once again Tina was surprised. She thought it a nice enough little place, with half a dozen streets each way with the usual petrol stations, hotel, shops, shire council offices and police station. She was disappointed when they did not have time to visit the Gem & Crystal Museum.

To look at the place they drove up and down the grid pattern streets. As they did Tina glimpsed two grey and yellow coloured parrots flit past her and into a tree in the yard of a house.

"Was that a pale headed rosella?" she cried, pointing. But it was too late. The birds were gone and she was left puzzling over what she had seen. *Did they have a patch of yellow on the outside of their wings or not?* she wondered. A quick leaf through her books on birds did not help as her memory was now too uncertain. But she hoped it was and she increased her vigilance in case she saw more of them.

After 10 minutes of driving around the town Mr Creswell stopped at one of the petrol stations and they all climbed out while he refuelled the vehicle. Quarter of an hour later they were on their way again. This time Tina was seated in the front passenger seat. Michael sat in the back on the right, with her mother in the middle and young Aiden on the left while Mrs Creswell had replaced Mr Creswell as the driver and the two fathers were in the Jackaroo.

There was a short visit to look at an old brick chimney at Cumberford; all that remained of a rock crushing battery from a gold rush 150 years earlier. As always when she saw such places Tina marvelled at the tenacity and toughness of the early pioneers who came to such out-of-the-way places without any of the comforts or medical support the modern generation took for granted.

Back on the highway and speeding west again Tina sat and stared out at the seemingly endless bush. *I wonder what Andrew is doing now?* she mused. She tried not to be jealous but knew she was.

Suddenly a splatting sound drew her eyes to the windshield. What she saw made her cry out in horror. A bird had been struck and was caught in the windscreen wiper in front of her. Its eyes were open and its beak kept opening and closing.

A finch, her mind told her while she cried, "Oh stop! Please stop!"

Mrs Creswell brought the vehicle to a standstill at the side of the road. As soon as it stopped Tina jumped out and ran to the front, only to stop in horror. It was instantly apparent to her that the bird was beyond saving as the impact had ripped it open and its entrails were stretched and spread across the front grille and bonnet. The sight of the purple and pink intestines caused her stomach to churn but she managed to keep control.

Tina's mother joined her but Tina stubbornly persisted in doing the cleaning up. It took several tissues and half a bottle of water to wash most of the mess away, and even then a few spots of blood remained in the corners of the grille.

Garth did not help when he came to look and then said, "It could have been worse. What if it had been the last one of the only pair of breeding Gouldian Finches in the world?"

That was a horrible thought to Tina and she snapped, "Don't be awful, Garth!"

Their mother joined in, saying, "Don't tease you sister, Garth. Now get back in the car."

Tina shook her head sadly and went on cleaning. By the time she was finished the nausea had been replaced by sadness and slight shock. *Life is a very chancy business,* she mused as she climbed back into the vehicle. From that came a determination to live it and to enjoy it.

The expedition resumed its journey, driving west for another two hours along a mostly deserted highway through mostly flat country covered in savannah woodland of varying density. In all that time they did not pass a single house and only a couple of dirt side roads. The only hills were a small range of low, flat–topped ones which looked big but in fact were only about 20 or 30 metres high when they were reached.

Tina stayed interested by looking for birds but only saw a few crows, many finches and a couple of plain turkeys. She kept hoping to see emus but there were none visible.

Just after 1700hrs the vehicles turned off the highway onto a graded gravel road. They followed this for about 20 minutes before turning again and going through a wire gate onto a rough vehicle track. This was just two wheel ruts in the grass but was flat and easy to follow. By then the sun was low in the west and already the trees were casting long shadows. Tina found the flickering of the sunset through the trees a bit hard on the eyes. She also realised she had a headache.

Not drinking enough water, she told herself.

To her relief they came to a stop in a dusty clearing under some large trees. About 50 metres away she got a glimpse through a gap in the trees of a large lagoon. Both vehicles were parked side by side and everyone climbed out.

"Well, this is it: Pink Lily Lagoon," Mr Creswell announced. He then pointed towards the lagoon and said, "And you kids don't go and play near the water. There could be large crocs in there."

"Crocs!" cried Michael in disbelief. "We are hundreds of kilometres from the sea, aren't we?"

"A couple of hundred, yes," Mr Creswell replied. "But don't be fooled son. Big crocodiles love to live in lagoons like this one."

"But isn't the lagoon freshwater?" Michael queried, still obviously not convinced.

"Yes, but that doesn't mean that you won't find saltwater crocodiles in it. *Crocodilius Porosus* is quite happy to live in freshwater," Mr Creswell explained.

"But this is a lagoon isn't it? How do they get here?" Tina asked.

"Yes, it is," Mr Creswell replied. "But it is part of the river system and crocs are really just big lizards."

"Saurians, Dad," Michael said.

Mr Creswell snorted. "Don't be a smart-arse, Michael. They have four legs and they walk around. You find them hundreds of kilometres from the sea. So just be careful."

Tina stared anxiously at the now sinister looking waters of the nearby lagoon and noted the reeds and water lilies and shivered. *What lurks in there?* she wondered.

Resolving to be very wary, she turned and began helping her parents to unload their vehicle. Then there was the family tent to set up and here she had plenty of experience and was able to make herself very useful. It gave her mild satisfaction that they had their tent up with much less effort and well before the Creswell's had erected theirs.

Cooking was then begun. While the parents set up the camp Michael and Aiden both went to look at the lagoon. That got Tina anxious, so she strolled over to keep an eye on them, making sure to keep well back from the edge of the water.

While she stood there Tina admired the sunset and then scanned the water for birds. There were plenty but they had retreated away from the vicinity of the campsite. She observed various types of herons, mostly brolgas and Sarus cranes but also a few white ones and even a few pied herons and a blueish coloured one she could not clearly identify. There were ducks of several varieties and a couple of pelicans. To add to Tina's pleasure a black swan glided into view in the distance.

Then Aiden began wading into the shallows at a small sandy beach and Tina anxiously scanned the water for any tell-tale ripples. *But a real croc attack will just come without warning*, she told herself. *They swim underwater and just emerge with jaws open*. That thought got her worried as she noted how close the boys were to the water.

"Aiden! Come back away from the water!" she called.

To her relief he did and soon after that they were called back to camp to have their tea. This was mostly cold meats and bread but there was tinned fruit and cream and some fruit. Tina sat on a camp stool and relaxed. Darkness set in swiftly, with the added interest of dozens of fruit bats: 'Flying Foxes' as the North Queenslanders called them, flapping overhead. There was also the occasional swish of unidentified wings that Tina hoped were owls.

"There might be tawny owls or frogmouths," she commented as another large bird flew low overhead.

The families talked for a while but it had been a long day and the boys were both obviously tired, so bed was organised early. Tina set up her own bed, glad that the family tent had a floor and a zip-up door to keep out creepy-crawlies and reptiles. After saying goodnight she lay down and relaxed, or tried to as she knew they were a very long way from any sort of civilization. Even the station homestead was about 30 kilometres away and in the dark on bush tracks she knew that would be a long way.

Despite her fears Tina slept well. She woke just on First Light and lay in her sleeping bag listening to the bush sounds. The distant laughter of a Kookaburra told her what had woken her.

Cheeky bird! she thought.

Then the Kookaburra chortled again, closer this time. Tina grinned and slid herself out of her sleeping bag. She pulled on a dressing gown over her pyjamas and then slippers and quietly made her way out of the tent, taking care not to wake anyone else.

Outside it was cool and still and apart from the chatter and cackle of birds was very quiet. There was no sound from the Creswell's tent, so she tiptoed past it and stared carefully towards the lagoon. There were no tracks to indicate nocturnal visitors of any size and the water of the lagoon was as smooth as glass.

The Kookaburra cackled again and Tina moved to try to spot it. As she did, she stretched and felt a twinge of guilt at her sensations of loneliness. In her heart she sensed that the trouble was psychological. Like all Australian children she had been brought up to believe that 'The Bush' and rural life were the 'Real Australia'. But like 95% of Australians she lived in a city on the coast, so the bush was just a myth to her. Now she was in it and a long way from a city and that made her uneasy. That in turn made her feel slightly guilty for not being more at home in the bush environment.

But it was a beautiful morning and she stretched again and breathed deeply, then moved to try to spot some black cockatoos that had begun their raucous cackling further down the lagoon. Then a voice behind her made her turn. It was young Michael hissing to Aiden to get back in bed. A moment later Aiden's head poked out of his tent. He saw Tina and grinned, then slipped out to look at the view.

Michael followed and then Mr Creswell called in a grumpy voice, "Be quiet you kids! I'm trying to sleep!"

The boys giggled and then hurried off to look at the lagoon, prompting another reminder from Tina about crocodiles. But for the adults sleep was now impossible and soon the whole group was awake and bustling around the camp. Tina snuck back along the road to go to the toilet and then went to her tent to get dressed. First, she pulled out a white top, but then thought that might get soiled too easily so she chose a dark floral top with large red roses on green and purple.

Breakfast was cereal followed by bacon and eggs all washed down with Milo for the children and coffee and tea for the adults. There was also fruit juice and Tina had a cup of that. By 0730 the men were ready for fishing. The boat trailer was backed to the water's edge and the boat slid in. Mr Creswell got the motor working and the boat was loaded with fishing gear and then the two men and the boys climbed in and they set out. Tina had no real interest in fishing but did help the two mothers to clean and tidy up. Neither mother wanted to go in the boat so the females were left in camp.

"Typical silly males," Mrs Creswell commented as the boat stopped in the middle of the lagoon and fishing lines were cast in.

Tina agreed but the gender bias of it nettled her a bit. However she did not dwell on it and instead got her bird books and binoculars and moved to a safe spot where she could see along the lagoon. There she settled to see what birds she could spot.

In the next three hours she spotted many and was rarely bored. The most common birds were ducks of various kinds, but she again saw black swans and pelicans. A variety of water waders worked the shallows and both white and black cockatoos flew by in flocks that settled noisily in the trees before rising in screeching swirls when the boat with the fishing party got too close.

The fishing party returned to shore somewhat disappointed, with only three small fish to show for their efforts. The largest had been caught by Michael, much to the embarrassment of the men and the amusement of Mrs Creswell.

Mr Creswell grunted. "Last time we fished here it was full of big barra," he grumbled.

"Well your boozy mates have fished them all out it seems," Mrs Creswell replied.

Tina's mother then said, "Anyway, it is getting late. We are booked in at the Croydon Hotel tonight don't forget and I'd like to be there in daylight."

So they set to work packing the camp. Tina's mother had already been busy and all of the Babcock's bedding and personal gear was already tidied away and stowed. All they had to do was strike the tent and roll it up. This was soon done but then they had to wait while the Creswell's got their camp pulled down and loaded on their vehicle. They had such a litter of gear around that Tina and her mother finally went to help. Tina had already been a little bit annoyed by the Creswell's camping style: lots of gadgets and luxury items and very untidy. They weren't exactly grubs but it still irritated Tina's tidy senses.

The expedition set off after a late lunch with each family in its own vehicle. An hour of driving along dirt roads brought them back to the bitumen. Here they turned left and continued on west. Another hour of driving had them at the small and, to Tina, very isolated town of Croydon. She had often seen it on the map but as usual found that the reality had very little relation to what she had imagined. The town was laid out in a grid pattern on flat land to the west of a range of low hills. The first impression was of distance and space as the streets were very wide and the buildings were mostly widely scattered and with many vacant allotments between them. Only in the main part of the town were the buildings closer together.

The older buildings of the 'heritage' area at once caught Tina's attention and she studied them with approval. They were mostly made of timber and iron and were single story and obviously old. They gave the town a very 'historic' feel and Tina at once decided she liked the place.

Although it's a bit isolated and I wouldn't like to live here, she thought.

They drove straight past this part of town and on along a street with a couple of houses and a shed beside it and came to a timber building with a large curved iron roof attached to it. To her surprise Tina saw a sign informing her it was the railway station.

"I didn't know there was a railway here," she said. "Where does it go to?"

Her father answered. "Normanton, over near the Gulf."

"Is that a port?" Tina asked.

"It used to be, back in the old days. Now the town of Karumba is the port," her father replied.

Tina had seen these places on the map and nodded but was still puzzled. "Does this railway connect up with that one back at Mt Surprise, the one that goes to Cairns?"

"Nope. It just goes west to the sea," her father answered as he pulled the vehicle to a stop outside the station.

"Will they ever link them up?" Tina asked, thinking that a sensible thing to do.

"Nope. No chance. It would cost too much and there is no reason. As it is this railway only exists for tourism. There is just that one train and I think it only runs for one day a week."

Tina saw that the station was really just a big shed with a semicircular roof over two rail tracks. A couple of offices and platform took up the rest of the space on their side. Visible through the open doorway was a red painted rail motor with the word *Gulflander* painted in yellow on its side.

Oh, I've heard of that, Tina thought. She was feeling slightly embarrassed and foolish at her lack of knowledge and told herself to keep her mouth closed until she was sure.

Little brother Garth looked at the remains of an old steam locomotive and tender sitting beside the car park and said, "Can we get out and look please Dad?"

"Tomorrow. We are going to check out the dam while it is still light," her father replied.

"Dam?" Tina asked, immediately forgetting her resolution.

Her father pointed to the hills a few kilometres to the north. "Up in those," he said.

As he explained this the Creswell's, who had pulled in behind them, pulled out and drove back the way they had come. Tina was a bit upset by that because she could see that Garth really wanted to look at the trains but she told herself it was a fishing trip. Her father put the Jackaroo in motion and followed. They drove back to the main intersection and turned left. This took them past a couple of nice old buildings and to another intersection with a large old 'traditional' Australian hotel on the far corner. The hotel was made of timber and was the usual two-story structure with the upper level built out over the footpath and supported by posts.

As he swung the vehicle up the side street to the right Tina's father said, "That is our hotel."

Garth craned to look past Tina and said, "It needs some horses and hitching rails for the cowboys."

"Stockmen or ringers son, not cowboys, not in Australia please," Tina's father chided.

As they drove past the hotel Tina studied the building and felt slightly uneasy. She hoped they were not in one of the upstairs rooms but assumed they would be. One of her recurring nightmares was being trapped in a burning building and she knew it was one of her phobias.

Mr Creswell led them along one more block and then turned left and drove out of town. After half a kilometre they turned left onto a bitumen side road that ran across flat bush before starting to climb. The road at first did a couple of gentle curves through open bush on the lower slopes. On the first curve to the right Tina saw a parking area on the right. *Chinese Temple Site* read a sign. She looked but could only see a few pathways through the scrub. When her mother said she would like to visit that Tina could only agree and wished that the fishermen were more considerate.

The road then climbed straight up a steep slope and did a sharp right at a Council Depot. Then the road wound around the side of bare, open hills. They passed a lookout and Tina got fleeting glimpses out over the flat country beyond the town. The words 'endless plains' flitted through her mind and she again experienced that sense of isolation and distance that told her she was a long way from anywhere.

The road then curved left and wound through the open hills for a kilometre or so before coming abruptly to a picnic area on the shore of a large lake. Seeing that amount of water in such a dry area quite surprised Tina. *Oh! I didn't expect anything like this,* she thought.

The picnic area included a building and a shelter shed surrounded by a bitumen ring road. A boat ramp led steeply down across a small beach.

The vehicles were parked and everyone climbed out. Tina's priority was a toilet, but she did stand and study the lake for a minute or so. "Is it natural?" she asked.

"In this country? Not likely!" Mr Creswell answered. "It is here because they built a dam."

He pointed to the left and in the distance Tina could just make out the line of the dam wall. Beyond it to the right she noted a gravel road leading over the low hills and down to the water. After studying that for a few seconds she swept her gaze around to the right, taking in a series of bays and low hills which extended of to the southeast out of sight behind the spur they were standing on. She now saw that the lake was much bigger than she had thought at first glance.

By the time she had been to the nearby public toilet the boat had been launched and the vehicle was being driven back up to a parking area on the right. Spotting some distant water birds Tina went to the vehicle and collected her bird book and binoculars and moved to a clear area on the grassy slope. Here she sat and used her knees to steady her elbows.

Carefully and with practiced hands she focused her binoculars on the tiny shapes.

"Burdekin ducks, I think," she told herself. She squinted to refocus and studied the ducks. As she did, her eyes caught sight of the gravel road leading down to the water on the far side of the dam. *Looks like another boat ramp,* she thought. After a quick study of the distant landing space she went back to observing the ducks.

To her annoyance the boat with her father, Mr Creswell and the boys disturbed the ducks as it went roaring out across the water. The ducks flew away with a honking that mirrored Tina's annoyance. As no other birds were visible, she went and joined her mother in the shelter shed. Here she sat and talked or read her book while the males fished out in the middle of the lake.

They returned an hour later without catching anything. Mr Creswell shook his head. "Last time I was here I caught three big barra in half an hour," he grumbled.

"Maybe everyone else has heard about your luck and come here to fish," Tina's mother suggested.

Disgusted with their poor luck the men went to haul the boat out of the water. Once that was done, they drove back down to the town, stopping briefly along the way at the lookout to admire the vista of vast plains. Down at the town they drove to the hotel and parked outside. Tina's father went inside and returned a few minutes later with the keys to the rooms they had rented.

The rooms were in a long, prefabricated building on low stumps. This was located in the hotel yard beside the hotel. The building was double sided and the side they were in faced a high metal wall across a narrow driveway under trees. The building was some way from the old timber hotel and had other small buildings under trees between the two. Another pre-fabricated building stood at right angles to theirs beyond a small grassy car park at the rear of the layout.

The Creswell's vehicle and attached boat were parked out on the end of the grass and Tina's father drove their vehicle in between the fence and driveway and parked it close to the short flight of steps leading up to the timber veranda that ran the length of the structure. Unloading and unpacking then took place.

Tina now learned that the buildings were typical of the pre-fabricated types used on construction camps and mining camps, able to be moved by big trucks. The nickname 'Donga' entered her vocabulary. The rooms were small and cramped. Tina shared with Sarah. The two girls placed their bags beside the two small beds and then went to investigate the amenities. Finding a washing machine Sarah at once took an armful of dirty clothes to it and set to work. Once the machine was working Sarah re-joined Tina in the room.

By then was dark. Tina's mother knocked on the door of their room and said, "Time for dinner. You girls go over to the hotel dining room now please."

Sarah stood up and said, "I will just hang the washing out first Mrs Collins."

"I'll help," Tina offered.

"Don't bother. There isn't much. You go over and I will join you in a few minutes," Sarah replied.

Tina nodded and made her way outside onto the veranda. By then the adults and younger children had gone so she set off to catch them up. Then her troubles began. While she was on the veranda things were OK because light from the amenities gave some light but once down the steps in under the trees and between the darkened building and the high metal fence it was so dark she could hardly see. Carefully she made her way out past the end of the building to the footpath she knew was there.

Having arrived on the grassy footpath Tina looked both ways along the quiet street. Not a single vehicle was moving and there were big pools of darkness between the small islands of light from buildings and the few streetlights. Diagonally off to her right 100 paces away was a shop and petrol station on the other side of the street and the same distance to her left was the hotel. Across the street was just empty blackness of vacant allotments.

Just visible in the darkness across the street was a parked 4WD vehicle with a boat trailer behind it. Further to her left a streetlight lit up the intersection beyond the hotel and a few lights illuminated a 'heritage' house diagonally across from the hotel. Not a single vehicle was moving but there were a line of five or six parked outside the hotel.

Seeing no sign of the others Tina turned left and walked along the grass footpath until she came to the hotel. Three doors opened out onto the bitumen sidewalk under the overhanging second story. The first door led into the dining room. The other two led into the public bar which was crowded with rough looking men, mostly miners and stockmen by the look of them.

Knowing it was illegal for an under-age person to enter a public bar Tina went into the dining room and looked around. Three out of six tables had people sitting at them but there was no sign of the others and she was too shy to ask which table to sit at so she turned to study the array of old historical photographs of the town which lined the walls.

For the next few minutes Tina idly read the captions and studied the photos. From time to time to time she looked around to see if the others had arrived. As she did, she casually glanced at the people who were sitting eating. At the closest table was an elderly couple who were obviously tourists. Seated at the next table was a family with young children. At the third table were two men and as she glanced at them Tina experienced something like an electric shock. Seated with his back to her was a man with black curly hair and a short beard who looked vaguely familiar. The man wore a dirty khaki short with the sleeves cut off, shorts and rubber thongs.

But it was his companion who really caught Tina's attention. *I know him,* she thought. *Now, where have I seen him?*

The man had a long, narrow face, well-suntanned and had longish brown hair. He wore a grubby dark green shirt with the sleeves rolled up and dirty jeans and boots. Then, with a shock, recognition came to her.

That is Danny, the man who shot at us on Lake Koombooloomba!

Chapter 8

INSTANT DECISION

Tina stared in amazement. Then she realised that she must not let the men know she had recognised them.

They might hurt me; and I need to tell the police, her racing mind told her.

To her embarrassment she realised her mouth was hanging agape and she snapped it shut as she turned away. Facing the old photos again she tried to focus her eyes so as to observe the men in the reflection from the glass in the frame of a picture showing a very antique looking rail motor crossing a bridge almost covered by floodwaters.

What should I do? she wondered, very conscious of her racing heart and rapid breathing. For a few seconds searing flashbacks of Danny shooting at her and of him shooting the Ranger caused her to feel dizzy.

Don't be silly! Keep control of yourself, she thought. As her anxiety level shot up she contemplated hurrying out. Then she shook her head. *No, don't turn so they can see your face,* she told herself. She didn't think they would recognize her as they had only seen her from 50 metres away and then she had been wearing sunglasses and a cap and lifejacket. But she did not want to take the risk.

At last she managed to focus her eyes and saw that neither man was paying her any attention. They had both finished eating a meal and were drinking beer from bottles and talking. As the seconds ticked into minutes, Tina really began to fret. *Oh, where are the others? Where is Sarah?* she wondered. Anxiously, she kept glancing towards the front door or another doorway that led through to the public bar.

But there was no sign of her family or friends. Then Tina realised she had been staring at the same old photo for several minutes. *If I keep looking at the same picture the men might become suspicious,* she thought. She found herself faced with a difficult decision. To study the next old photo she had to move further into the corner and away from the door. *If they recognize me I will find it harder to escape,* she thought.

But she decided that was better than moving back to the door and out.

So she took a deep breath and sidled along to stand facing the next photo. Another anxious glance showed no sign of any of her family.

Oh, where are they? Why don't they come? she wondered.

Tina again moved to focus on the reflection in the glass. She had just done this when both men suddenly pushed back their chairs and stood up. The man with black curly hair and beard said, "Come on Danny. It's time we moved."

Danny nodded and lifted a beer bottle to his lips. "OK Marco. Just a sec."

With that he drained the beer and set the bottle down and both men headed for the door. Tina took the opportunity to slip around the angle to face the side wall, placing an empty table between them and her. To her mixed relief and frustration the men did not even glance at her but walked out onto the front footpath.

Oh, they are getting away! What should I do?

She was torn between rushing to a telephone, telling someone or waiting for her parents and friends. Then another worrying thought came to her: Were the men staying outside or leaving? And if they were leaving was it on foot or by vehicle?

And if it is by vehicle then I need to know what type and what its registration number is. That way the police can more easily track them down, she thought.

That meant taking a risk but she decided she must. *I can always run into the bar. They won't hurt me with all those people there,* she reasoned. So she turned and walked across to the front door and 'casually' glanced out.

What she saw at once told her she had made the right decision but immediately presented her with another dilemma. The two men were just visible walking across the street towards the 4WD and boat parked in the shadows across the street. She had expected them to get into one of the vehicles parked immediately in front of the hotel, but this gave her a more difficult problem: how to see the vehicle's number plate without the men seeing her.

Observing that the men had their backs to her Tina stepped outside onto the footpath. The footpath was brightly lit but there were several people seated there drinking and a couple of men were leaning on the tray of one of the vehicles. Tina decided to take the chance and turned right and walked quickly to the last vehicle in the line and around to its side where she was in the shadows. As she did, she glanced both ways along the footpath, still hoping to see Sarah or the adults.

But they were nowhere in sight and by then the men had reached their vehicle. They opened doors and climbed in, Marco in the driver's seat and Danny in the passenger's. The fear that the vehicle would immediately be driven off sent Tina into a lather of anxiety and she dithered for a few seconds over what to do next.

Then she made a decision she knew was very risky. *I must see the number plate,* she told herself. Afraid that if she dithered she might change her mind, she set off walking quickly across the street, thankful that she wore rubber soled trainers. As she did, she angled towards the rear of the vehicle. *Maybe they won't look in the rear vision mirrors,* she thought. She reasoned that if anyone did it would be the driver so she kept on walking across to the grass footpath behind the boat trailer

Here she paused, partly to get her breath back because she was almost gasping for air she was so anxious. Another glance showed her that her parents had not yet appeared over at the hotel. There was still no sign of them, so she took a deep breath and began walking slowly towards the left rear of the vehicle. She knew that she must be silhouetted against the streetlights behind her but still hoped the men weren't looking.

A few seconds later she reached the boat and ducked down to crouch beside the trailer. *I can always run back to the hotel,* she thought, hoping she could get away faster than the men could get out of the vehicle to chase her. By now her mouth had gone dry from fear and her hands were sweaty. Her heart was pounding so hard it seemed to make a booming, swashing noise. Even her eyes seemed to be hard to focus.

But despite being really scared Tina made herself creep forward past the trailer wheel at a low crouch. As she did, she heard Marco's voice. Very clearly he said, "Roger that Grey. We will be there. See you in ten. Over."

He is talking on a radio, Tina thought. That did not really surprise her as many vehicles in that part of the world carried CB radios and large antennae were quite common. Another man's voice answered amid the electronic crackle of static.

"Roger, Out," was all it said.

They are going to meet someone, Tina thought. *I must hurry.*

So she crouched in under the bow of the boat, a typical fisherman's 'tinnie', so that she could see the rear number plate on the vehicle. But it was dark and the plate was smeared with mud, forcing her to bend right down. Still finding it difficult she reached forward and rubbed at the number plate and tried to make out the letters and numbers.

F... I... Q... 5... Oh drat, is that a 3 or an 8? she puzzled.

Suddenly the small light above the number plate came on and she could read it. It gave her such a fright she flinched back, banging her head on the bow of the boat. Even as she wondered if the men had heard the noise, the vehicle's engine burst into life.

I must get out of here, Tina thought. But there was no time. Before she could reach behind her to hold the boat to steady herself, the vehicle's motor roared and it lurched forward. *I'll be run over!* she thought.

Unable from her crouching position to jump aside Tina grabbed the upright on the trailer. She was instantly jerked off her feet and began to drag on the gravel. A wave of fear engulfed Tina, almost paralysing her. Part of her mind told her to let go while she still safely could, but she could see the trailer's wheels and feared she would get caught under the trailer and be dragged along. She realised that whatever she did it would hurt. Stung by desperation she twitched her whole body up and got her feet onto the trailer frame just under the bow of the boat.

By then the vehicle had pulled out onto the bitumen road and had begun to accelerate. By the time Tina had recovered her grip and shifted her left buttock up onto the trailer frame the vehicle was going much too fast to safely jump off.

If I do, I could be badly injured or killed, she thought. Then the enormity of her predicament sank in. *Oh no! I am trapped!*

Now fear changed to terror as she began to wonder what the men would do to her when they reached their destination.

That is if I don't fall off first, Tina thought grimly.

Once again, she contemplated jumping off but by then the vehicle was going really fast. She clung on tightly and moved so as to get a better look around. She noted that they had left the lights of the town and that there was only dark bush on either side.

Then the vehicle turned abruptly right onto a gravel side road and Tina's fears all returned. *I will never be able to hold on long if they hit potholes or corrugations,* she thought.

Ghastly images of being mangled under the trailer and being dragged and torn to bits under it while the vehicle raced on unheeding at 100kph made her cringe. When the trailer bounced over a pothole she cried out in fright.

That first bump nearly did unseat her and she found she was crying and that her hands had become sweaty. To her horror she found it very hard to keep a grip on the smooth metal and her feet kept bouncing off, despite her attempts to brace them. All she could do was jam her boots in between the boat and its trailer but then a bump allowed the boat to move and that jammed the foot even harder and pinched.

I could get caught or have my foot broken, she thought. But what to do? *How long can I hang on?* she wondered fearfully.

Off to the left she noted the lights of a couple of houses but the vehicle was still travelling much too fast to safely jump off, so Tina had no choice but to cling on and hope.

Then another problem arose. Dust was billowing up off the dirt road and was being sucked in behind the vehicle to engulf her. She began to cough and blink and it became hard to breathe. Unable to stop herself she began to cough.

The men will hear me! she worried.

But the vehicle did not slow down. Instead it hammered over the potholes and corrugations, the trailer jerking and bouncing along behind with a terrified Tina clinging on for dear life. To try to keep the dust out she closed her eyes and tucked her nose into her shirt to try to muffle the worst of the dust. But it still got in everywhere and she continued to sneeze and cough.

Worse still, the dust mingled with her sweat to make her hands slippery and she had to repeatedly take one hand away at a time to wipe it dry on her clothes. *Oh how much longer?* she wondered, knowing that she was rapidly tiring. *The man said 10 minutes,* she remembered but she had no idea how long they had been driving.

To add to her fears the road began to cross dry creeks and low ridges and it became rougher. The driver at last slowed down a bit but only after Tina had been slammed and banged hard against the boat and upright several times. But at least the dust eased as they came onto a different gravel surface.

Then the moment that Tina had been fearing arrived. The vehicle began to slow and then came to a stop. The vehicle's lights were turned off. That left Tina clinging to the boat trailer in a state of rising panic. She knew she must be found if she stayed but feared to move lest the men hear her.

But I can at least try to run if I have to, she reasoned. So, rather than do nothing except hope, she eased her shoes down onto the gravel and began to twist her body around.

As she did, the passenger's door was opened and she heard Danny step out. As his boots crunched on the gravel near her, she experienced a spasm of terror. She had no doubt that if she was discovered the men would kill her. As he moved so did she, slipping into a crouch in against the back of the vehicle. In her fluster, she tensed to run.

Just as she was about to spring out, she heard Danny speak. He said, "Just wait till I have a look Marco. The plane might be here already."

With that Danny walked away past the front of the vehicle. For a few seconds Tina's mind grappled with what was going on and what to do.

Plane? she wondered. Then she understood. The crooks had used a floatplane at Koombooloomba. Hoping that the noise of Danny's boots and the noise of the vehicle engine would mask her own movements she acted.

Very carefully she crept out from behind the vehicle, moving at a crouch. As she did, she looked to her right and noted that Danny was now standing 20 paces in front of the vehicle and was on the edge of a lake. Seeing the water did not surprise her and she even guessed which lake it was.

We are at that gravel boat ramp across the lake from the picnic area we were at this afternoon, she thought.

But she also noted that the vehicle was stopped in the middle of a large open area and there was enough moonlight to make things clearly visible. *If I try to move they might still spot me,* she thought.

So she paused, then regretted it as Danny turned and came walking back. Once again, a spasm of panic gripped her and she felt bile rise into the back of her throat, causing her to gag. Sweat and shivering became dominant.

However Danny went to the driver's side of the vehicle and said, "Turn this thing around Marco and we will get this boat in the water."

Marco grunted a reply and the engine revved as he engaged the gears.

Tina gulped and knew she had to move now. *I can't stay with the trailer and my cover is about to drive off,* she thought.

So she edged further out, and as soon as the vehicle began to move she went the other way, keeping low and glancing anxiously back. 20 metres away was a wall of bushes at the base of a scrub covered hill and that became her objective. Now she was very glad she was wearing the dark floral top and not the white one she had considered.

As she scurried across the open ground, she glanced back and saw that Danny was watching the vehicle and not her and that he had turned so that his back was towards her. But it also meant that the driver's side swung around to be on the same side as her. Knowing she had to be hidden before the vehicle was around, she took a risk and scuttled across the bare gravel.

A couple of seconds later she pushed into the bushes, just as the vehicle swung to a stop on the other side of the clearing. For a few seconds she crouched, her heart beating so hard that she could not hear properly. Again she tensed, ready for flight. But no sounds indicated that the men had heard her, so she waited. Then the vehicle began to reverse.

A wave of intense relief swept through Tina and she broke into a fit of trembling. Almost sobbing with the release of tension, she used the sound of the vehicle's tyres crunching on the gravel to cover the rustling of the leaves as she pushed further back into the bushes. She found there was a ridge of soil half a metre high, obviously pushed up by the grader that had made the clearing, and she was able to crouch behind that and peek through the wall of bushes to watch.

Behind her were more bushes and then the dark shape of the scrub covered hill. *They might hear me if I try to move up that,* she thought. For a few seconds she knelt in safety to get her breath back and to recover from a fit of shivering. Then she thought hard and wondered what to do. *Now is the time to sneak away,* she thought. But then it came to her that the men obviously had no idea she was there. *I might be able to see what they do,* she thought.

With that in mind she edged forward to get a better view and then half lay, half crouched on the earth mound. She was aware that her clothes were getting filthy, but it was of so little importance that she just shrugged the thought off. Then she settled as comfortably as she could and watched.

Within minutes the boat trailer had been reversed down the ramp and the boat launched with speed and skill that suggested much practice. Then the vehicle drove forward and circled around to face the lake again. As it did, Tina caught Marco's voice saying, "Roger, over."

He is on the radio again, talking to the plane, Tina decided.

Suddenly the vehicle's headlights came on, shining out onto the lake. Tina reasoned that the lights were to assist the plane in landing. She was correct, but she was quite amazed when the white of wash around the floatplane's floats suddenly appeared on the edge of the headlight beams, then the greyish shape of the aircraft itself.

I didn't hear it land, she thought.

The headlights suddenly went out and it took her a few minutes to adjust her eyes to the moonlight. During that her ears detected the low buzz of the aircraft's motor. Then she saw it close offshore, a black silhouette against the moon-dappled water. Marco climbed out of the driver's seat and joined Danny. Both men moved to the canvas covered sides of the vehicle's tray. Tina guessed what would come next and she was right. The canvas sides were rolled up and then metal sides were unlocked and swung upwards and held up by metal rods.

From inside the back of the vehicle the men began lifting out cages of identical size. Tina could not see what was in the cages. Nor were there any sounds to give a clue but she guessed they contained birds.

Or maybe rare reptiles and mammals and so on, she thought.

The men carried the cages down and placed them into the boat. A sudden splash made Tina look towards the now stationary floatplane. She could not see anything but decided that the pilot had dropped an anchor. The aircraft remained about 20 metres from the shore. Marco and Danny walked back up to the vehicle and began pulling out more small cages.

Oh! They will get away. What should I do? Tina wondered. For a few seconds her mind raced. Then she made an instant decision.

Chapter 9

TINA ACTS

I must get the police, Tina thought. And there was only one way, by foot. *I wish I had brought my mobile phone,* she mentally wailed.

But she wasn't even sure if there was service in the hills, so she decided the next best option was the farmhouse she had seen a few kilometres back.

By the time she had decided what to do, the two men were back down at the boat and were busy stowing the cages into it. Tina had no idea how many cages there might be, but she reasoned there could not be many.

I won't have much time, she thought.

With that in mind she crawled carefully out of the bushes to the edge of the clearing. Then she realised she might have made a fatal mistake and lay flat in the dust and froze as Danny and Marco came trudging back up to the vehicle.

Tina tensed, ready to spring up and run but the men did not even glance in her direction. Instead they bent into the interior of the vehicle and began extracting more cages. Confident they were pre-occupied Tina rose to her hands and knees, her throat dry with fear and her heart hammering with excitement. As soon as the men moved away again she stood up and began walking as quietly as she could back along the road.

As she walked Tina kept glancing back towards the men. She could just make out the shape of the aircraft and could even hear the murmur of voices. *The pilot of the plane must be looking this way. He might see me,* she thought anxiously. The idea made her whole back seem to tingle and she felt very stiff and tense.

With an effort of willpower she mastered her rising fear and made herself keep walking. Several times she kicked small stones that chinked audibly against others and she was sure that the crunch of the sand and gravel beneath her joggers must be very loud. But there was no sound to indicate that she had been seen.

Then she heard the men start walking back up the ramp towards the vehicle. That meant they were facing in her direction, so she froze into a crouch in against a bush and looked anxiously in their direction. But they just went to the vehicle and again dug in the back. This time they extracted heavy containers that looked like jerry cans to Tina.

Fuel? she wondered.

As soon as the men had their backs turned, Tina rose and resumed walking. By the time they were at the boat she was at the back of the clearing, and within another half minute she was 50 metres along the gravel road and out of sight of the men. As soon as she saw she was around the bend and out of sight Tina gasped with relief and increased speed. Now she was driven by an intense urge to bring the men to justice.

Confident they would not hear her, Tina broke into a run. But however urgent her desire the running only lasted for about a hundred metres. By then she was gasping for breath and sweating. *Oh, I should do more exercise,* she berated herself as she reluctantly slowed to a fast walk.

She went down across a small dry creek and then up over a low ridge. Even that small rise got her puffing and perspiring. As she reached the crest Tina glanced back. *I wonder how long the men will be?* she thought. She did not want to get caught in the headlights of their vehicle when they drove back out again. With that in mind she began to study the bush beside the road, trying to pick places she could hide.

Tina trotted down the next slope and then up another low rise, slowing to a panting plod by the time she was halfway up. She pushed herself on to the crest and paused to again look back. Behind her all was silent and dark. By now she was gasping for breath and trembling with excitement and fear.

As she walked down the next slope Tina looked up and experienced a sense of awe at the brilliance and number of the stars. This was replaced almost immediately by a sense of her own relative unimportance and of the sheer immensity of the universe and of earth. Then she contemplated the vast size of Australia and how far she was from her home. This drove an intense feeling of isolation as she looked around the dark hills and bush. Never before had she felt so lonely and so far from civilization.

The whole eeriness of being alone in the dark bush caused her to tremble with apprehension and she felt her chest tighten up. To counter the anxiety she tried to estimate how far she had to walk. *We only drove along that gravel road for about 5 minutes,* she decided. From that she calculated that she might have at most 10 kilometres to walk to reach the town. *How long will that take?* she asked herself.

Something Graham Kirk, one of the army cadets at her school, had once said came to mind about walking 100 metres in 1 minute, a kilometre in 10 minutes, and 5 kilometres in an hour. That depressed her further.

That means two hours of walking! she thought with dismay. To cheer herself up she recalculated, estimating the distance they had driven to the picnic area as only 5 kilometres from the town.

But there was nothing for it but to keep going so she clenched her jaw and pushed herself on over another rise. This turned out to be the last one before the flat country and that cheered her up, even though she could see no sign of any lights anywhere.

Then a glow appeared ahead of her. For a few seconds Tina puzzled over it and then it dawned on her what she was looking at. "That is the glow of a car's headlights and it is coming this way," she muttered. But what to do?

Do I flag it down? What if it is more crooks? she worried.

Fear decided her. Just in case she found a gully beside the road and scrambled into it. She was only just in time as the vehicle came racing around the corner at high speed, its headlights lighting up the bush. Tina crouched and hid and only got a glimpse of another 4WD driven by a bearded man wearing a crumpled old hat. The back of the vehicle had the same square covered look and that made her glad she had not stayed out on the road.

If he is just a fisherman then he might run into trouble, she thought.

But she suspected the man was another crook. And there had been something familiar about him that niggled at her. However she could not place what it was, so she climbed back onto the road and resumed her rapid walk.

From then on she spent as much time looking over her shoulder as watching where she was walking. *I don't want to get caught by those men,* she told herself. But just in case they did, she tried to invent a plausible reason for a teenage girl to be walking a lonely bush road at night. Her feeble attempts at fabrication caused her to give a wry smile.

"Better not to get caught," she told herself.

About 10 minutes later she rounded a bend and saw the twinkle of distant lights. There were two off to her right but a dozen or more further along to the left. *Those lights are the town,* she decided. Which put her into a quandary. *Do I go to the first farmhouse? Or do I walk to town where I know my family and the police are?* she thought.

The lights of town did not appear to be much further than the farmhouse, so when she drew level with the farmhouse about 10 minutes later she opted to walk on. This turned out to be a mistake as the lights were actually much further away, but once she was past the farmhouse she had no intention of turning back. She was heartened to reach the main bitumen highway a few minutes later and she turned left onto this and stepped it out along the smooth bitumen.

Then another worrying thought came to her: if a car came from behind would it be the crooks; or was it coming from further west? She knew that towns like Normanton and Karumba were out that way, but she had no idea how much traffic there was along the highway at night. Not much, she decided after 10 minutes of walking without a single vehicle coming from either direction. But just in case she kept eyeing the scrub beside the road for hiding places, having resolved to take no chances.

It was about 2 kilometres to the first buildings of the town, and it took her over 20 minutes to walk it, even at a power-walk. As she entered the town, she found the streets deserted and not a soul in sight.

Now, do I go to our motel rooms or do I go to the hotel? she wondered. She opted for the motel rooms but when she reached the lane that led in beside the high fence a glance showed the building to be in darkness. *They aren't there. I will try the hotel,* she decided.

So she strode on along the footpath, moving as fast as her weariness and chafing would allow. Within a minute she had reached the well-lit veranda area in front of the hotel and she sighed with relief.

Safe! she thought.

There was no-one on the footpath and a glance in the door of the dining room showed it to be deserted. But voices indicated that there were people in the public bar, so she walked the 10 paces to the next door and looked in. To her enormous relief she saw her father and mother standing over near the back of the bar. And they were talking to a uniformed policeman!

"Oh thank God!" Tina gasped, relief washing through her.

She stepped inside, noting as she did that her little brother was sitting in the back hallway with Michael, Aiden and Sarah. Mr and Mrs Creswell were with them and they were talking to a big man who Tina thought was the publican. There were half a dozen other people seated at the bar on her right: tourists, miners and bushies by their clothes. A barmaid in her twenties was working behind the bar and was the first one to see her.

"Is this her?" the barmaid called.

Everyone turned to look and Tina saw her parent's faces light up with relief. "Oh yes! Oh Tina, where have you been?" her mother cried, rushing to embrace her.

Tina ran to her mother and clung to her. For a few moments she was unable to speak and could only sob and bury her head in her mother's shoulder. As she did, she heard a vehicle arrive and pull up at the front. The sound caused her to tense up and remember her mission.

But her mother spoke first as the pair moved to arm's length. "Oh Tina, where have you been? We've been so worried! We have been turning the whole town upside down searching for you. Where did you go?"

Tina looked over her mother's shoulder at her father and the policeman and then went to speak. But as she did, boots sounded on the floor boards behind her and she glanced over her shoulder, to freeze in shock. It was Marco! And close behind him was Danny. Both men headed for the bar and appeared to be quite unaware of anything unusual happening.

For a moment Tina could only gape and gabble as she wondered what to do. Then she saw that both Marco and Danny had stopped and were looking around. "What's the go?" Marco asked the men nearest.

The man, an 'old timer' in dark blue denim, pointed at Tina and said, "Bit of a flap because this girl went missing."

Danny turned to look at Tina and their eyes met. That sent a stab of fear though her but also loosened her tongue. She pointed and cried, "These two men have just been loading birds and reptiles into a floatplane up on the lake."

Danny's eyes widened and he swore softly. Marco looked even more alarmed. Then he frowned and shook his head. "What you say? What rot! We just been fishin', eh?"

"You were not!" Tina cried, louder than she meant and with a rising pitch as anxiety strangled her throat.

The policeman stepped forward. "Why do you say that, Miss?"

"Because I saw them," Tina said. "I have just walked back from there. That's why I am so grubby and sweaty."

The policeman studied her appearance and then glanced at the two men. "You'd better explain," he said to Tina.

Tina opened her mouth to start her story, aware that the whole bar was silent and listening. But she never got out the words she meant. At that moment Danny pounced, punching the policeman in the side of the head. "Run Marco!" he shouted.

The policeman went crashing to the floor. Marco turned and ran for the door. Danny turned to follow. But he was just there and Tina instinctively made a grab for him, forgetting her own safety in her desire to have the men apprehended. She managed to grab Danny's sleeve.

But it was only a fleeting hold as he immediately wrenched himself free. As he did, he lunged at her. "You little bitch!" he shouted. He tried to punch her, but she stepped back. In the process she stumbled over the policeman and into her mother. She and her mother went down in a tangle of arms and legs, her father grabbing at both.

For a moment Danny hesitated, his fists clenching and unclenching. Then he saw the men at the bar start to move and the policeman began to roll over and climb to his feet. Instead of attacking Tina, Danny lashed out at the policeman with his boot. The blow connected with his side and sent the constable reeling backwards into the arms of the publican. Again Danny hesitated, but by then Tina had regained her feet.

Danny glared hate at her and shouted, "You'll pay for this girl!"

Then he turned and dashed through the doorway.

Chapter 10

BAD DREAM

For a moment Tina was stunned by the violence and the speed of events. Then she sprang after Danny. "Catch him! Stop him!" she screamed at the men at the bar.

But they just stood and gaped or looked anxious. Behind her the policeman was being helped to his feet but he was doubled over in pain. Tina looked through the door and saw that Danny and Marco had run to their vehicle, which was parked further along the footpath in the darkness. She stepped out onto the footpath and then hesitated. Her father joined her and she pointed. "Quick Dad! They are getting away."

The vehicle's engine roared into life even as Danny jumped in. As he slammed his door shut the headlights came on, half blinding Tina. The vehicle roared into motion and swung out onto the road. It went past with a grinding of gears and shouted oaths. As it did, Tina saw Danny looking at her, his face a mask of hate.

Danny shook his fist at her. "I'll get you, you bitch! You'll pay for that!" he screamed.

Then the vehicle was gone, its boat and trailer in tow. Tina stood watching it until it swung left out of sight. Then waves of fear and shock hit her and she began to shake and sob. Her father and mother both held her. The policemen, still in evident pain, staggered out onto the footpath, his right hand working to draw his pistol.

Tina's father pointed and said, "They went that way, to the left, back along the main street."

Even in her distress Tina tried to work out which way that was. "That is back towards Cairns isn't it?" she asked.

"Yes, but there are a few side roads," the policeman gasped. He winced with pain as he tried to straighten up. Then he groaned and shook his head. Turning to Tina he said, "Did you get the vehicle type and number?"

That stopped Tina trembling. She nodded and stifled her sobs, then said, "Yes."

"Good girl!" the policeman said. He placed his pistol back in its holster and took out a notebook. Tina gave him the number and the names of the two men and a brief description. "And you say they were up at the lake putting caged birds into a floatplane? What were you doing there?"

Tina had calmed down a bit by then and she was able to explain how she had seen the men at Koombooloomba. "I saw them in the dining room here having a meal and when they left I followed them," she said.

Her mother was aghast. "Oh Tina! You silly girl! Those men are very dangerous. If they shoot Forest Rangers and hit policemen, what might they do to you?"

Her father and the policeman nodded. The constable said, "You are right there. Now, you saw them here and followed them out to their vehicle where you noted the number. How did you get to the dam?"

Tina described how she had nearly been run over by the boat trailer and had been forced to cling to it. "Then it was going too fast for me to jump off without getting hurt so I er.. I ..er.. I sort of went along for the ride," she explained.

Her parents were appalled. The faces of the listening crowd all showed amazement and some admiration. Her father shook his head. "That was incredibly silly thing to do Tina! Just imagine what might have happened if those men had caught you."

Tina had been imagining just that and she shivered violently with reaction and fright. All she could do for a minute or so was bite her lip and tremble. Her mother held her tight and stroked her until she calmed down again. Then she described what had happened at the lake and how she had walked back. "The rest you know," she finished lamely.

The policeman shook his head but with admiration. He then said, "Yes, well, very well done. But please don't place yourself at risk like that again. Now, let's see if we can catch these characters."

He took out a mobile phone and moved off along the footpath to talk on it. From time to time he looked towards Tina and her group.

Tina now had a real breakdown, sobbing and shaking as the reaction hit her. Her family and friends crowded round to comfort her and the other people went back into the bar. A vehicle turned into the street from the main street and pulled up and a 'bushie' dressed in baggy shorts, a blue singlet and battered hat got out. He gave them a curious look as he went towards the bar where a real buzz of conversation had broken out.

The policeman called to the man, "Hey Bill! Wait."

Bill did, obviously full of curiosity. The policeman walked over and asked him which road he had come in along. On learning that it was from the direction of the hospital he was asked if he had seen the vehicle. Bill shook his head and went on into the bar to ask his friends what the story was.

The policeman said, "I have called HQ and they are putting out an all points call. There is a good chance we will catch these characters. Now, I will do a drive around town and ask at the service station on the other side of town if they saw which way they went. I would like you people to stay at the hotel, and stay together and keep your doors locked."

Tina's father frowned. "You think there might be some danger?"

The policeman nodded. "I heard the man threaten young Tina. You had better be careful. Tina, stay with the group. Do not wander off on your own."

Tina felt a stab of terror deep down inside and she shivered again. The hate-filled image of Danny's face floated to the top of her mind and knew she was really scared.

Tina's father said, "It should be fairly easy to apprehend that vehicle shouldn't it? I mean there is only the one bitumen road and it is hundreds of kilometres back to Georgetown."

The policeman shook his head. "You would think so. There are really only three roads out of here: west to Normanton, east to Georgetown and the dirt road south to Julia Creek. But there are a few bush tracks going off to the north and south. Anyway, we will have roadblocks on all three main roads within the hour. I had better go. I will see you in an hour or so to take a full statement."

With that the policeman walked off to his vehicle. As he went, he pocketed his notebook and then held his side, which was obviously still sore. As he reversed out another vehicle arrived, this time from the direction of Normanton. It parked as the police 4WD drove off in the direction the smugglers had taken. A man climbed out of the vehicle that had just arrived and walked into the light of the hotel. As he did, Tina opened her mouth in surprise. It was their back neighbour, Neville.

As he reached them Neville's face also registered surprise Tina's father said, "Why Nev, fancy meeting you here! What are you doing in this neck of the woods?"

"I was going to ask you the same question," Neville replied. "Hello Mrs Babcock. Hello young Garth. Hello Tina. Are you alright Tina? What's happened?"

Tina looked at Neville with her mind swirling with suspicion. Her parents described to Neville what had just happened. As they did Neville looked concerned and several times asked Tina if she was alright. But she felt he was not being sincere. She felt herself to be in a state of heightened consciousness and that sharpened her perceptions.

Neville has all those caged birds; and he goes away for weeks at a time. Or at least we don't see him so I presume he has gone away. Is he the other man I saw driving to the dam? she wondered.

But she could not voice her suspicions and could only nod and hang her head as she hugged her mother. That allowed her to keep her face and eyes from betraying what she was really thinking and fearing. Neville then moved on into the bar and Tina's parents insisted that they go back to their room to clean up before they go to the dining room. The hotel management agreed to keep the dining room open as none of them had eaten.

Two hours went by before the policeman returned. During that time Tina had a shower and changed into clean clothes and her mother washed the dirty ones, muttering about the grease stains from the boat trailer. They all went to the dining room and had dinner. Tina found that she was too upset and anxious to eat much but she tried. Sarah was all admiration and sympathy and so was young Michael. Garth just played up, obviously jealous at not being the centre of attention.

While they sat in the dining room after eating Tina made a note of the fact that Neville was still there, drinking and chatting to some other men. Once or twice he glanced at her but she made sure their eyes did not meet.

Is he one of the gang? she wondered, remembering his evasive answer about why he was in the area.

Then the policeman arrived and began taking statements from people in the bar who had witnessed the incident. While he was doing this another vehicle drove into town along the Normanton Road. It was a police 4WD. Two more policemen came in, one a sergeant. He at once took over and Tina felt safer.

Now they will surely catch the crooks, she thought.

The police had driven from Normanton, 150 kilometres to the west. They said that a roadblock was in place there and that police in other districts had been alerted. Tina's father and Mr Creswell opened a map on the dining table and considered the roads the crooks might use. That lowered Tina's hopes considerably when she saw how many there were. At least three dirt roads led off to join roads leading to Cloncurry and Mount Isa.

The police will have trouble watching all of them, she thought.

Both families were then asked to come to the police station and Tina was interviewed at length. Statements were also taken from the adults about the assault on Constable Weatherly. They were then allowed to go.

"But keep together," Constable Weatherly reminded them, again raising Tina's anxiety.

"Where are you planning to go next?" the sergeant asked.

Mr Creswell named some lagoon, but the sergeant pursed his lips. He shook his head and said, "Might be better if you stay away from isolated fishing spots until we have these characters in the bag. I advise you to stay in public places until then."

Hearing that chilled Tina. *Oh no! What have I done to myself?* she thought as fear flooded in to almost reduce her to a trembling wreck. *Will that horrible Danny come back to get me?* she wondered.

That was the terrifying thought that stayed with her all night. Back in the rooms she was moved in with her mother and her father moved in with Garth and Michael. Reaction set in with more tears and shivering and she had trouble getting to sleep. For hours she tossed and turned and started up at very little noise.

Danny is a killer, she told herself, imagining him creeping back in the night to strangle her. *Or will he smother me with my pillow? Or will he use a knife?*

The awful possibilities filled her with dread and left her trembling and exhausted. Only after midnight did she at last drift off into a fitful slumber. But even that gave little rest as she had a nightmare, the classic bad dream where she was being chased. It was dark and something, someone, was after her, a horrible, black, shadowy shape that got closer and closer, and she couldn't run! Then she had the most vivid dream of being out on a lake in a small boat in the moonlight. Her boat somehow vanished and she was in the water. It was cold and she bumped something under the water. Then from underwater came this clutching hand, all silhouetted in the moonlight.

"It's alright little baby!" her mother said soothingly, gently wiping her face. "You are just having a bad dream."

"I was too!" Tina agreed. She sat up, soaked with sweat despite the air conditioning. "I dreamt that man was coming to get me."

Her mother looked very anxious but then said, "He won't. You are safe." But she did not sound too sure. Tina's rational mind told her that two crooks on the run from the police had better things to do than come back to try to get vengeance on her but that was cold comfort when the lights were out and her imagination was again filled with awful possibilities.

It was a very tired and sick girl who went to the bathroom at 6 o'clock next morning. Her mother looked at her anxiously and said, "You look very pale dearie. Would you like to go home?"

Tina did want to go home, but equally she did not want to spoil the holiday and said so. "I will be alright, Mum. We want the others to enjoy themselves."

"You are sure?"

"Yes, Mum."

So they agreed to go on with the holiday trip. A revised itinerary was organised over the breakfast table and Tina felt better after that. She even managed to eat a full breakfast and that picked her up even more. She found that the story was headlines on the local radio news and was thankful that her name was not mentioned. But she was also concerned that there was no mention of the smugglers being arrested.

While they were finishing their breakfast Constable Weatherly arrived. After a cheery 'good morning' he shook his head. "Haven't caught them yet," he said.

Mr Creswell was quite grumpy about this as it meant they would not be visiting his favourite fishing spots. He said, "Can we go then?"

"I'd like you to come to the station to look at some photos if you could," he said.

Tina's dad answered. "Sure. When? Now?"

"In half an hour or so. I am going to the railway station to watch the railmotor leave," Constable Weatherly replied.

On hearing that Garth cried, "Oh Dad! The *Gulflander*. Can we go and watch, please?"

When young Michael added his plea this was agreed to so the families walked back to their rooms to get hats and cameras and then piled into the vehicles and drove to the railway station. Tina was not really interested but she did marvel at the stamina of the early pioneers who built a railway by hand in such an isolated place and under such harsh conditions.

There were only six passengers, all tourists, on the railmotor. For 20 minutes nothing much seemed to happen with the policeman and driver standing talking in the shade and the tourists, Tina's group included, walking around taking photos. Michael, Aiden and Garth walked off along the railway and Tina's mother tried to call them back. Then she warned them about snakes. Tina watched and said, "I'll go with them Mum."

"Don't you go far. Remember what the policeman said," her mother reminded her.

"I won't Mum. We will only go to that old crane thing," Tina replied, pointing to where a piece of rusty machinery showed among the long grass on the edge of the bush a couple of hundred metres away. But even so she felt a chill despite the bright sun. So she strolled along the old railway line behind the boys.

By the time she caught them up at the old crane she was feeling the heat. She stood and looked back along the curving line to the station and suddenly felt quite isolated. Anxiously she looked around, but all she could see was bush with a few dirt vehicle tracks winding through it, and the railway vanishing around a curved to the west.

Now I'm being silly, she told herself. *Those men will be far way by now.*

Then the rail motor tooted and soon after that it came clanking and rattling past. Tina and the boys waved and the tourists waved back and then Tina called the boys and walked back to the station. Her father said, "Don't wander off so far next time please Bub."

"No, Dad."

The policeman reminded them to come to the station and then drove off. They climbed into their vehicle and returned to the cabins to load their belongings. As the families carried their luggage out to load into the vehicles Tina met Neville again. He was loading his brown Toyota 4WD which was parked up at the back of the yard. "Hello," she said, not really wanting to speak to him.

"Feeling better?" he asked.

"Yes thanks," Tina replied.

Neville smiled and nodded. "That's good. What are youse doing now? Are you heading home?"

"No. We are going to Normanton and Karumba," Tina answered. She kept on walking, noting that his vehicle had the same sort of square framework over the tray and that this was covered by canvas sides which were locked down. To her it looked very suspicious but she also knew it was a fairly common arrangement so she could only shrug and continue on.

An interesting hour followed at the police station. Tina sat and studied hundreds of photos on a computer, but she was unable to find any of Danny or Marco. The sergeant said, "That's a worry. It means they have been clever enough to avoid any sort of police attention."

Mr Creswell, who had also been watching, said, "These birds they are smuggling, are they worth much?"

The sergeant nodded. "Oh my word yes! A pair of sulphur crested cockatoos can fetch up to $10,000 on the black market in America."

Mr Creswell was amazed. "As much as that! Holy mackerel! I am in the wrong business. But how do they get them there? It's some sort of smuggling operation, right?"

"Yes, it is. But we don't know the links in the chain or we could shut it down," the sergeant replied.

Tina looked up from the monitor and said, "Well we can guess one link. They use a floatplane, so my guess is they fly to a rendezvous at sea where they land and transfer the birds or animals to a ship. The ship would then take them to wherever the market is."

The sergeant nodded. "Probably. But we don't know the range of the plane or whether it lands on water or on land."

"It is possibly an amphibian," Tina said.

Michael looked puzzled. "Aren't amphibians things like frogs, creatures that live on land or in the water?"

"Yes they are," Mr Creswell replied. "But we also call vehicles and aircraft that can operate on land or water amphibians."

"You mean the plane has wheels as well as floats?" Michael asked.

"That's right. It might have. There are several types that do," Mr Creswell replied.

Sarah, who had been standing next to Tina, said, "I read about these smugglers who had all these baby snakes hidden in their pants but they got caught by the customs people at the airport."

Both Michael and Garth thought the idea of snakes in their pants was very funny and both grabbed themselves and giggled until Mr Creswell gave Michael a biff under the ear and Tina's mother frowned at Garth. Tina had to smile at the boy's silliness, but she agreed.

The sergeant nodded. "That's right. Lots of smugglers try to sneak in at airports with a few reptiles or small animals. The trouble is the creatures often die in transit."

"Snakes!" Tina's mother cried. "Surely people don't smuggle snakes?"

"They do. Reptiles like amethyst pythons or green tree snakes can be worth thousands of dollars," the sergeant explained.

There was a general discussion about the types of living things that wildlife smugglers sold, and Tina was amazed and appalled at the sheer number and the prices. *That really could place some endangered species at risk,* she thought, baffled that anyone could pay thousands of dollars for blue tongue lizards or frill neck lizards.

The sergeant then said, "Anyway, can I now ask Tina to show us exactly where she saw these men? We have a team of detectives and wildlife specialists on their way from Cairns but they won't get here until about eleven. They want us to have the scene ready."

So Tina was driven out to the dam by the police. The two families followed in their cars. But well before they reached the area where the boat had been launched, they came to a barrier of police tape across the road. This was guarded by the other policeman who had arrived the previous night. The sergeant stopped the vehicles and told the others they would not be driving any further.

"We will go forward on foot," he explained. "But only Miss Tina is to come with us. You others wait here please."

Tina's parents weren't happy but she felt fine about it. *I have three armed policemen to protect me,* she thought. So she walked on along the road with them. As they went, they photographed wheel marks and kept very much to one side of the road. Tina was able to point out her boot prints and these were photographed as well.

As they got closer to the boat ramp she became a bit anxious but it was all so different in daylight, bright, clear, good visibility, that she soon relaxed and concentrated on showing the policemen exactly where the vehicle had been and where she had hidden. After more photos she was left standing to one side while the police scouted the edge of the lake. As they searched for clues she stared at the rippling water and felt a sense of unreality.

Did I really see a plane? she wondered. But she knew it was no dream. *That is twice now I have seen this gang and their floatplane.* That thought caused her to idly wonder if she would ever see it a third time. *I hope so. I want them caught,* she told herself.

She noted buildings on the far side of the lake and realised they were at the picnic area that the family had been to the previous day. She also noted how open the bush was, and how small the bushes. In the dark it had all looked very dense.

Four more men arrived, all plain clothes detectives and officials. They took more photos and the Detective Inspector in charge asked her several questions and then told Constable Weatherly she could go. Tina did not really want to, preferring to watch the investigation, but she had no choice but to walk back with him to re-join her family.

Back at the vehicles she thanked the constable and he smiled and said, "No. Let me thank you. This has solved something that has been a bit of a local puzzle for a long time, locals reporting strange humming noises at night. It must have been that plane's engine. We just thought they had had too much to drink!"

"Do you think you will catch them?" Tina asked.

Constable Weatherly shrugged. "Probably. Now that we know they exist we can at least keep our eyes open."

"Can we go now?" Mr Creswell asked.

"The Inspector asked that you hang around for another hour or so in case he needs to talk to you," Constable Weatherly replied.

"Then we will look around the sights," Tina's mother said firmly.

So they did. They visited the Chinese cemetery, which Tina found very interesting, then the main town cemetery and then walked around the old buildings, the 19th Century courthouse, police barracks and lock-up. The boys enjoyed this and played bushranger games and did a lot of hiding and chasing. Lunch time came and they went to the shop and service station on the edge of town for pies, hamburgers and soft drinks.

While they were having lunch Constable Weatherly drove up and told them they could go. After thanking them again he drove off.

After lunch the group set off for Normanton. It was only later, when they were halfway to Blackbull, that a horrible thought came to Tina. *If Neville is one of the gang then they will know who I am and where I live!* That was a truly terrifying thought which slowly grew in her mind until it dominated and gripped her.

She did consider mentioning her suspicions to her parents but then did not. *I have no proof. It might be just coincidence,* she told herself.

Then she bit her lip and mentally slapped her forehead.

And I have told him where we are going! Oh, what a fool I am!

Chapter 11

FISHING

This fear stayed with Tina for the next four days. It was always there, as insistent as a toothache but much more emotionally draining. This was worst at night, but she felt afraid even in places where there were other people. But she made no mention of her feelings to anyone, not wanting to spoil the holiday for the others.

She suspected that her mother guessed how she was feeling and there were a few emotional breakdowns when the tears just came and she needed to be held. The fact that the police did not catch the smugglers did not help. Knowing that they were at large and possibly hiding somewhere in the district was a cause of nagging worry.

The families visited Normanton but Tina was not impressed, even though the menfolk enjoyed good fishing. Apart from the garish, and Tina thought, ghastly, 'Purple Pub' the place had little to interest her. It seemed to be a flatter, drier version of Croydon, all spread out in a grid pattern.

They only stayed there one night and then went on to Karumba, the port at the mouth of the Norman River. Being back where she could see ships cheered Tina up, even if most were only prawn trawlers. Because of the police request they did their fishing off the wharf, the riverbank being a dangerous place because of the crocodiles that infested the muddy tidal estuary.

As she sat there, line in hand, Tina brooded over whether the crooks might seek her out to get revenge. She also thought frequently of Andrew and fretted about what he might be doing. Anxiety over him becoming emotionally entangled with the girls from Townsville added to her distress. Even catching the biggest barramundi caught by anyone in the two families did little to lift her depression. She just wanted 'it' over.

To her it was a relief when they set off back towards Cairns on the Saturday morning. They stopped in Croydon for refreshments and to check with the police. But Constable Weatherly could only shake his head and admit that the smugglers seemed to have slipped the net. No sign of them had been reported anywhere in the region.

"They either got out of the area before we could set up our roadblocks; or they have a secret hideout," he said.

Tina was inclined to think that they had a secret hideout. *They could fly food in and people out if it had an airstrip,* she thought. But where? That got her studying what maps they had. She looked for both airstrips and also lakes and large lagoons that a floatplane could use.

It was just before 1100 that they left Croydon, driving east along the main road. Lunch was in Georgetown and the vehicles were refuelled. Tina had cheered up a bit by then, her thoughts moving back to Andrew and her normal life. The closer they got to home the more her spirits lifted. She began to daydream, constructing romantic fantasies about how she and Andrew might get together.

By 3pm they were back at Mt Garnet. Tina now began to relax She was back in familiar territory and that gave her the 'I'm home' feeling. But she wasn't and it took two more hours to drive via Ravenshoe to Atherton. There was a half hour break there for a meal and then another hour and a half to Cairns. It was just after 1900hrs when the two vehicles parted and Tina's father turned the Jackaroo into the driveway of their home.

They were all tired but Tina at once hurried to the back yard to check on Beaky. He was fine and very pleased to see her, but while she was talking to him she noted the chatter of birds from Neville's aviary. She had forgotten about him but now she saw that there were lights on in Neville's house.

Is he home? Or is that his family? she wondered. *And what type of birds are these?*

In the dark she could not tell but she thought they were rainbow lorikeets. *Where did Neville get them?* she wondered. She knew there were all sort of laws restricting the trapping, sale and ownership of various birds. But she did not know enough and had no idea whether Neville had the required licenses or permits.

And if he is one of the gang, has he told them where I live? Will they come to get me? Suddenly her home ceased to be a sanctuary and became instead a potential death trap!

A shiver of fear ran through her and she looked anxiously around, then hurried inside, carefully closing and locking the back door behind her. Inside she paused and found she was gasping for breath. *Oh no! How long might this go on for?* she wondered. Then awful thoughts like having to move to another town and even to take on another identity to throw off any pursuers caused her to burst into tears.

Her mother found her in this state and calmed her and the family then discussed her fears. Garth poo pooed the concept but then looked very anxious. Both her parents were obviously worried, but her father said, "But how would these men learn who you are or where you live?"

That put Tina in a dilemma. She hesitated, then shook her head. *I don't have any proof that Neville is involved,* she told herself. Knowing she was possibly placing herself at risk and being foolish in the cause of justice she said nothing.

That meant a night of anxiety and growing terror, once she was alone in her bedroom and the lights were out. Because the house was low level, she knew that any prowler could just walk around the yard to her window. The fact that her window had a security screen was small comfort. She felt sure that determined murders would easily find a way to remove it without waking her. The best she could do was close the sliding window and then draw the curtains. That cut off any breeze and made the room hot and stuffy, but she opted for that and the fan in preference.

She had a bad night, and woke feeling drained and afraid. Nor did she feel like going to school. But equally she did not want to stay home alone. She was too scared to do that and yet not brave enough to mention her fears to her parents. So she went about her normal morning routine pretending that everything was well. The only change was to go out and check that Beaky was well. Her real motive though was to see what type of birds Neville now had in his aviary.

They were rainbow lorikeets and that worried Tina. There were about twelve of the birds, they fluttered about too often for an accurate count, but she was sure that keeping such native birds was illegal.

Do I report him to the authorities? she wondered. Then she thought, *If the police or whoever come then he will guess it was me and if they don't lock him up he might really do something to me.*

Biting her lip with anxiety she went back inside, casting anxious glances through the back fence in case Neville was watching. The 7:30 radio news was no help. There was no mention of the police catching the smugglers. Instead it was taken up with details of a murder in the Davies Creek area of some farmer who had been chopped up by a chainsaw. Tina shuddered at the idea and turned the radio off. To divert her mind she focused on plans to meet Andrew.

I mustn't appear at all pushy, she told herself. *But how do I get him to notice me?*

Trying to come up with strategies to achieve that aim kept Tina's thoughts off her other problems for most of the day. Just going back to school helped because there was all the news and gossip to exchange with her friends. She was a bit peeved to find that almost no-one had heard anything about the police manhunt in the Gulf Country. But it was not her classmates she wanted to talk to: it was Andrew and his sister Carmen. However she did not see either before classes and Andrew arrived late. So worry about how his holiday had gone gnawed at Tina all morning. All she could do was surreptitiously study Andrew while trying to guess. He looked normal and seemed happy but that equally might mean that he and the blonde had enjoyed a good holiday together.

It wasn't until morning break that Tina got a chance to ask Carmen how the holiday had gone. Carmen smiled and said, "Good, really good. We did lots of sailing."

Tina really wanted to ask about Andrew and the blonde but could not think of any way to casually introduce the topic without revealing her true interest. But she did walk with Carmen when she went over to where Andrew and Blake were sitting with a group of other boys. As they got closer she heard Blake say, "And you really saw the body?"

Blake was talking to Stephen Bell. Stephen nodded and looked very pale. "Yep. It was really horrible. The chain saw had nearly chopped him in half and one of his legs was cut off."

Tina realised with a shock that Stephen was talking about the murder she had heard about on the radio. But it was Carmen who asked, "Were you there Stephen?"

Stephen replied, "Yep. Me and Willy Williams and Stick Morton and his little sister Marjorie."

"Where was this?" Blake asked.

"Davies Creek. Willy's uncle's farm," Stephen answered.

"What were you doing there?"

Stephen laughed and pushed his glasses up his freckled nose. "Willy had secretly made an airship, a huge bag of balloons with a bicycle slung underneath and we went there to try it out. His parents didn't know and he and Marjorie nearly got killed when it just took off."

"What happened?" Andrew asked. He glanced up and his gaze met Tina's eyes and he gave a brief smile before looking back at Stephen. Stephen explained the construction of the 'airship' and then Blake asked about the murder again.

Stephen said, "It was the middle of the night. We went with Willy's dad to see where his Uncle Ted had gone and we found him down at the creek with a huge tree on top of him, all chopped up." He then described some of this and Tina felt quite ill at the images it conjured up.

Carmen frowned and said, "Do they know who killed him?"

Stephen shook his head. "Nope. The cops reckon there must have been at least two guys and they drove off across the creek in a 4WD before we got there."

When he said that Tina had a vivid image of two men in a 4WD and she was suddenly seized by frightened curiosity. She said, "Do they know why this man was killed?"

Again Stephen shook his head. "Nope. Uncle Ted apparently heard noises down the creek, the chain saw Willy said, and went to investigate. The cops thought that maybe the men were stealing rare orchids or perhaps wildlife or growing drugs."

Wildlife! Tina thought, her heart hammering with anxiety. She swallowed and said, "Do they know if it was wildlife, birds or whatever?"

"Nope. The cops searched the creek banks for kilometres, looking for marijuana crops or things like that but they didn't find any."

"Was there any bird netting?" Tina asked, remembering the mist nets at Koombooloomba Dam.

"Nope. The only theory they had was that the men were after rare plants, orchids and things. I mean, why else would they cut down a big tree in the middle of the night?"

None of them had any idea but it certainly provided Tina with food for thought. *Are they the same men? Was it Marco and Danny?* she wondered. She could imagine both of them committing murder and now death by chain saw was added to her mental list of possible endings. It was so horrific to contemplate she thought she was going to be ill.

Luckily the bell went, and they went to classes. Andrew walked with her part of the way, but they barely exchanged a word. So her plans were no further ahead. To help quell her frustration she immersed herself in her schoolwork. But even that did not fully work as in English they began drafting their essays, the topic being an account of their holidays. Just jotting the facts down as notes caused Tina severe flashback and she became all anxious and teary and suddenly couldn't hold back the sobs. Sarah joined in and then Gwen Copeland. It took quite a while for Mrs Standish to calm them and to extract the reason. She was then all sympathetic and agreed they could choose another topic.

But that wasn't much help as Tina had no idea what else to write about, so she resolved to go on with the same subject. The only good thing to come out of it was seeing Andrew cast sympathetic glances in her direction. He was at least interested in her story of the smugglers, particularly when he learned they were the same men who had shot him.

That at least got him talking to her during the lunch break. He followed her out to the port racks when the bell went. As he packed his books away, he asked her about the trip. After she had outlined the main events, he frowned.

"And you believe they were the same blokes?" he asked.

"Positive," Tina replied, looking into his eyes and wanting to melt. *Oh! Why doesn't he notice me?* she thought.

But he seemed more interested in the mystery floatplane and while Tina was glad the topic kept him in conversation she really wanted to scream with frustration. But again shyness held her back from hinting or flirting and she could only inwardly sigh and keep on hoping.

School soon settled into its grind until by the end of the day it seemed to Tina that there had not been a holiday break at all. She found it a relief to go home, until she remembered Danny's threats. That made her even scared to go into the back yard to look after the pets but she nerved herself to do it. Then she sat and did her homework and daydreamed about Andrew.

Tuesday and Wednesday were boring re-runs with more frustration and tears for Tina. By Thursday she was so exhausted from not sleeping properly that she felt ill and exhausted and her mother was worried about her. But she went to school anyway. One reason was the school Anzac Day ceremony. This was scheduled for a special assembly on the Friday and the cadets of all three services were to take part in uniform.

On Thursday there was to be a rehearsal and she did not want to miss that.

To her disappointment she was only placed as part of the tri-service group along one side of the hall. There was a tri-service 'cenotaph guard' of five, plus two navy cadets who were tasked to be the flag orderlies. Carmen was chosen for the guard along with an air cadet flight sergeant and two army cadet sergeants and an army Cadet Under-Officer. Cadet Petty Officer Gordon and Cadet Able Seaman Luke Karaku, a Torres Strait Islander, were chosen to do the flag duty. To her delight Tina found herself standing next to Andrew, who was the 'right marker' for the small group of five navy cadets who stood, by custom, at the right of the parade. On her left were Blake and Sarah and then young Recruit Milson, a Year 8. The next group to her left were the army cadets. There were about forty of them. Their right marker was Graham Kirk and next to him Stephen Bell and Peter Bronsky. The air cadets stood at the left of the parade. They were only a small group as well and Tina was interested to note that Willy Williams was there along with a couple of others.

For a few moments she studied Willy, knowing that he had attended his uncle's funeral the previous day. *Poor boy,* she thought. He looked wretched. With him were 'Stick' Morton and another Year 9 boy. *That silly 'Noddy' Parker,* she remembered.

Capt Conkey did the organising and led them through a full rehearsal. This included the school captains and band and choir. Tina enjoyed it all as a welcome break from classes and also as something that was a bit more real to her.

But the next day she was all anxious as she wore her best white uniform to school and she felt very self-conscious. This was partly because many students jeered at cadets and called them names or derided them. But the other cause had to do with the way the white uniform shirt seemed to emphasis her bust. *Heavens, it makes them look big!* she thought, glancing down and blushing. Then the wicked thought crossed her mind that maybe that wasn't a bad thing. *Andrew might actually notice me,* she told herself.

And during the day she was sure he did. Both before and after the ceremony she several times noticed his gaze flick to her bosom and then quickly away when he saw that she was looking. He even coloured a bit around the neck and ears and that caused her a secret smile.

Good, he has noticed, and he is embarrassed being caught looking, she thought. Then she got all ashamed at being so forward. A niggling feeling of guilt bothered her, along with an entirely feminine concern that he not view her too much from behind. *I don't want him thinking my bum is too big,* she thought. She was very conscious of how tight the trousers felt across her bottom.

But how can I get him to notice me and ask me out? she fretted.

Chapter 12

BREAKTHROUGH

Friday night was Navy Cadets and during the evening Tina continued to study Andrew while puzzling over how to attract his attention.

I don't want to be so pushy as to have to ask him, she thought.

Then an opportunity arose which she instantly grabbed at, even though she wasn't all that interested. After First Parade Lt Cdr MacNamara ordered all the cadets to be seated in the lecture room. Once they were ready Lt Cdr MacNamara moved to the front to speak.

"Five things," he said. "First is Anzac Day. We will spend the remainder of the evening practicing for that. Second is a challenge from the army cadets and air cadets to take part in a tri-service weekend field exercise. This will be in eight weeks' time, so we have a chance to do some training for that. The third is a call for volunteers to do the Duke of Edinburgh Scheme."

Tina listened with some interest to the plan for the Tri-service exercise, army versus air cadets with the navy cadets as the umpires and safety signals network. But she wasn't at all interested in trying to win a Duke of Edinburgh Award until Lt Cdr MacNamara said, "We need teams of four for each level. Four is the minimum number for safety on the expeditions which are part of the award. Now, who might be interested?"

When Andrew put his hand up for the Bronze Award Tina suddenly became interested. But there were only three people who volunteered in that level: Andrew, Blake and Stella Piermont, the lovely raven-haired AB in the Starboard Watch. When Andrew glanced at Stella and she flashed a big smile back Tina's mind was instantly made up. She put up her hand.

Lt Cdr MacNamara said, "Thanks Able Seaman Babcock. That gives us a team for the bronze award. Now, any of you who did this last year want to try for your silver award?"

There were but Tina barely noted who they were as she was taken up with looking at Andrew. When he turned and flashed her a smile and

110

nodded, she felt a wave of emotion sweep through her that left her feeling slightly breathless. *Maybe now he will notice me?* she hoped.

Lt Cdr MacNamara then went on to detail other events. "In June we have two things scheduled for the holidays. They both last a week so I do not expect people to attend both, although they may if they wish. The first is an invitation by 130 Army Cadet Unit in Townsville to take part in their annual Senior Field Exercise. That will be in the first week of the holidays. During the second week we are combining with other navy cadets from T.S. Coral Sea in Townsville and T. S. Pioneer in Mackay for promotion and specialist training. Can I have a show of hands for who is interested in taking part in the army cadet activity?"

Tina wanted to attend the promotion training as she aspired to be a Leading Seaman but did not really want to give up two weeks of her holidays. However, when Andrew and his sister Carmen both put up their hands to attend the army cadet 'Senior Exercise' she felt impelled to do likewise.

Lt Cdr MacNamara took their names and then said, "Ask your parents please so we can give the army cadets firm numbers. Let me know next week. Now, the promotion course; if you are interested in attending write your name on this list. It will be on the noticeboard. OK, now Lt Ryan will take over and we will do some training for Anzac Day."

For the next 40 minutes the whole unit marched around and did drill so that they could put on a good show the next day. It was hot and sweaty work, even though it was nighttime, but Tina still enjoyed it. She wanted the Navy Cadets to look good on the parade as she knew full well that the army cadets and air cadets would all be casting critical eyes on their rival's performance.

Especially the Air Force cadets, she thought, knowing that they placed great store on appearance and that they did a lot of drill.

And she was right. The following day was Anzac Day, Australia's national day of remembrance for its war sacrifice, and all the cadet units took part in the city's street march and commemorative ceremony, along with the navy, army and a multitude of community groups such as the Scouts and St John's Ambulance and many school groups. And the members of the other cadet units cast very obvious critical eyes over the dress, bearing and drill of the others.

Tina found this slightly stressful but not just because she was worried that her own unit's drill might not be up to standard but because of how her white uniform shirt emphasised her bust. Several times she noted male eyes studying her, most with admiration and interest but a few with the leering gaze that she particularly resented.

One male who did give her a very appraising once over, even as he said a cheerful hello before the march formed up, was Graham Kirk. His glance lingered on her shirt front and then lifted to her face and his bright blue eyes looked into hers in a way that left her unsure if she resented his male appraisal or whether she had enjoyed it. That got her blushing and yet again wishing she had a better figure.

Graham was in his army cadet uniform and she thought he looked very handsome and dashing. *He is very handsome,* she thought, then blushed and looked around to check that Andrew was better looking. Graham was with his friends Peter, Stephen and Roger. They were strolling around chatting to friends and teasing rivals and enemies while officers and marshals called on groups to assemble ready for the march. For several minutes they chatted to Andrew and Blake and made silly comments about the navy.

Tina watched them with interest and twice Graham glanced in her direction and their eyes met. Tina immediately looked away both times. *Oh dear, I hope he doesn't think I am interested in him,* she thought. But she did think he was good looking. *And brave and very fit and muscly,* she noted. Then he met her gaze again and this time he lifted one eyebrow and she blushed deep red and looked hastily away.

By seniority of service the Navy Cadets led the cadet part of the parade so she only glimpsed the Air Cadets as they marched past to their place in line behind the Army Cadets. As they went past, she could not help noting that their blue uniforms looked very smart, much neater than the Army Cadets, and also that their drill was of a high standard.

At least we are at the front, so they won't see us, Tina thought, noting Willy Williams marching stiff and erect in the ranks of the Air Cadets.

Then, when the parade began, it was Tina's turn to march erect and proud. She was very conscious of the watching crowds and felt very pleased when they clapped and called encouragement. For the next hour she tried her hardest to stand up straight and to do her best drill. As always with Anzac Day in North Queensland it was sweltering hot with a hint of rain, the sun blazing down and the sweat trickling down in uncomfortable rivulets between shoulder blades (and breasts). Several times Tina felt quite woozy and worried that she might faint but she managed to stick it out and was still standing at the end, even though a dozen others had fallen out or sat down.

After the parade she wanted to talk to Andrew but could only stand tongue tied on the edge of the group, listening to him and his friends until her mother arrived to collect her.

Oh drat! Why can't I make him notice me? she fretted.

From a few metres away she studied Andrew while her mother chatted with Carmen Collins and Sub Lt Mullion. Suddenly Andrew glanced at her and their eyes met. She saw his widen and then he looked away and bit his lip. She noted a blush mottle his neck and cheeks and felt her own start to burn.

He saw me looking then, she thought, worrying that she might scare him off.

Suddenly Andrew turned from talking to Blake and Luke Karaku and walked over to her. Their eyes met again and she felt herself go weak. Fearful she had annoyed him she swallowed and tried to think up an excuse. But instead he smiled and said, "Gee Tina, you look really nice."

Now Tina did blush. She bit her lip and bowed her head for a few seconds before her natural courtesy made her look up. "Thank you." she managed to utter.

For a few more seconds they looked at each other. Tina noted anxiety in Andrew's eyes and her own emotions went up and down. Then she saw him swallow and straighten himself up. He glanced around to see who was close and then blurted out, "Er. er... er. Tina... er... um... I'd like to take you out on a date, that is if you are allowed to go on dates."

For a few seconds Tina stood as though stunned. *He has noticed me! He has asked me for a date!* her mind screamed. Then she noted the beads of perspiration on his brow and the anxiety in his expression and she thought, *Answer him you nong, before he thinks you don't like him.*

With an effort she cleared her throat and nodded. "Er... I'd like that," she croaked.

Again Andrew glanced sideways, she presumed to check that his big sister wasn't within hearing. Then he broke into a grin as her answer registered in his mind. "That's great. Are you allowed?"

"Only with nice boys that my mum and dad approve of," she replied mischievously, certain that her parents would allow her to go out with Andrew.

But that got him looking even more anxious. "Oh... er... do I... er... Should I ask your father?"

Tina thought that was very quaint and old-fashioned but also appreciated the fact that he was brave enough to do so if he had to. She replied, "I think it will be alright. You can if you want to but they already know you so it shouldn't be a problem. Where did you have in mind?"

Andrew blushed deep red and again glanced towards his sister and friends. Then he shrugged. "Wherever you would like to go," he replied. "You choose."

They discussed several options but had not decided when Tina's mother turned and said, "Come on Tina, time we went."

"Yes Mum," Tina answered. To Andrew she said, "I'll think about it and we can decide at school," she said.

Andrew nodded and beamed with happiness. It dawned on Tina that he must have been worried she would turn him down. To reassure him she gave him her brightest smile and then waved as she followed her mother towards the car.

She barely noticed the drive home. *He has noticed me! He wants to take me out!* she told herself, smiling and hugging herself with a happiness that seemed to bubble out of her.

Her mother noticed and said, "What are you smiling about Tina? You look like you are the cat that got the canary."

That put Tina on the spot. *Do I tell my mother, or do I wait till Andrew has asked dad?* she wondered.

There was also the desire to avoid teasing and embarrassment from the family. But when she saw her mother's quizzically raised eyebrow reflected in the rear-view mirror she shrugged and said, "I have just been asked if I would like to go out on a date. May I Mummy?"

Before her mother could answer what Tina feared happened. Her little brother snorted and cried out derisively, "Date! You? The poor bugger must need glasses."

Tina blushed with hurt, but her father spoke first. "That is enough of that, Garth. You should be ashamed of yourself, saying hurtful things like that." He then turned in his seat and said, "And what if we think you are too young?"

"I hope you don't," Tina replied a little breathlessly, the first words giving her some hope as they were not a definite no.

Her father then said, "And who is this person? I may not approve."

"Andrew Collins," Tina replied.

Her father and mother exchanged glances, and both smiled. That both cheered Tina and peeved her. "May I?" she asked.

"Yes, but we need to know where and when and we have to approve the venue," her father answered.

Tina sighed with relief and was happy with that. She knew that her parents were really worried about her possibly getting in with the wrong crowd and that they did not want her involved in unsupervised parties where there was possibly alcohol or drugs.

"We haven't decided yet," she replied. "Andrew left it up to me and I think that maybe something simple like the movies might be suitable to start with."

"To start with eh?" her father commented with a laugh.

Tina blushed again and it was on the tip of her tongue to retort that she intended to marry Andrew one day but she restrained herself.

They left it at that but for Tina where to go for the date became all she could think about for the remainder of the day. It obsessed her thoughts that night and led to warm fantasies of them kissing and hugging and of her being deeply in love and of him treating her like a fairy princess.

Instead of just like another sister, which is how he treats me now, she mused.

The same topic dominated her thoughts on Sunday and she conjured up pleasant daydreams while she did her usual household chores. She was in the middle of washing the dog out on the side lawn with the help of her father when she got a real surprise. Her mother appeared, and behind her was Andrew.

Andrew! she thought, suddenly very aware of her straggly hair and the old T-shirt and baggy shorts she was wearing. *Oh! I hope I look alright,* she worried, using a soapy forearm to push a straggle of hair back away from her eyes.

Andrew was dressed in shorts and a white shirt and looked very anxious. He walked over and stood looking at her father, with a few glances at Tina. As he said hello it suddenly dawned on Tina why he was there. *He is going to ask dad if he can take me out!* she thought.

The notion that he was both that brave and that courteous sent a pulse of admiration through her and she knew she loved him for sure.

It was the reason. After licking his lips and looking worried Andrew said, "Er, hello Mr Babcock. I am Andrew Collins."

"Yes, I know," Tina's father replied, standing up and putting out a hand. As they shook, he added, "Tina has often mentioned you. And we have seen you at cadets."

Andrew nodded and then said, "I have come to ask if I can take Tina out on a date."

Tina's father smiled and nodded. "Yes you may. It is not common these days for young men to have the courtesy to ask and we appreciate it. Now grab a leg if you don't mind and we will get this pesky dog bathed and then we can sit in the shade and have afternoon tea."

Without hesitation Andrew knelt and helped hold the dog. As he did, he looked at Tina and their eyes met. Tina also noted with approval that her dog did not resist or bark but instead licked at Andrew's hands. The irrational thought that if her dog approved he must be alright crossed her mind, making her smile. She also smiled with happiness and admiration and he smiled back, looking so handsome she felt like swooning.

Later they sat with Tina's mother and had afternoon tea: cordial and biscuits, in the shade of the courtyard. Tina felt very self-conscious but also elated. Her admiration for Andrew had reached new heights. He added to this by talking to her parents in a relaxed and mostly mature way. The venue for the proposed date and the associated administrative details such as timings and travel were agreed on. Tina's mother was to drive her to met Andrew at his house and then take them to the movies. Afterwards she would pick them both up afterwards and take Andrew home first.

When it came time for Andrew to leave, he shook hands with Tina's dad and thanked her mother. To Tina's delight, her mother beamed back and obviously approved of Andrew. Tina stood up and shyly walked with him to the front door. There she felt quite tongue-tied although she boiled with things she wanted to say. She also ached to reach out, to take his hand, to hold him; to kiss him. But she did none of those things and just stood and mumbled a thank you and gave him a nervous smile. She felt unable to believe her good luck. Then she watched as he turned and walked out to where his bicycle leaned against the fence. As he pedalled away, he turned and waved and she waved back, her heart hammering with joy.

So elated was she that she had trouble thinking straight and difficulty concentrating. In bed that night she was a mass of nervousness and heated fantasies and lay awake for hours. She felt she could not wait till the following Saturday evening. She began to itch with impatience.

At school the next day, Tina was a tingling mess of emotions and uncertainties. She was unsure whether Andrew would want to be seen with her at school. As she did, not want to annoy him or make him regret asking her she stayed with her own friends and watched him from afar, all the while wishing they were together. Equally she was very reluctant to even hint to her girlfriends that Andrew was taking her out, at least until she was more confident of her position.

He did speak to her, but only casually when they met during a change of classes. That was enough for Tina. *He spoke to me. He wants to take me out. I'm in love!* she thought.

Her daydreams almost got her reprimanded for inattention in class but as she usually got very good marks and rarely gave any trouble it was not serious. She settled back to her work and then drifted into more reveries of romantic fantasy.

This set the pattern for the week. But Tina did yearn for Andrew to be seen with her at school, to sit with her in the way that other couples did who were acknowledged 'items'. She knew this was partly so that other girls would notice and be jealous and because it would boost her status. She did not want to be seen as just a 'frump'. There was plenty of the normal woman in her for those sorts of vanities.

But she was too shy to go and sit with him. Twice she did walk past where he was sitting with his friends but apart from some eye contact and him nodding a greeting there was no encouragement for her to join them. That peeved her a little, but she was too anxious about possibly annoying him that she did not push her luck.

He is taking me out on Saturday night, she reminded herself.

That had the effect of making time seem to drag. It seemed that Saturday would never come, and school became a mixture of pleasure and frustrating torment. Tina tried to smother her feelings by working hard and even by playing some games of handball and netball with other girls during the breaks but it was all still a trial of impatience.

Only on Wednesday during the lunch break was there an incident to break the pattern, and that did not involve Andrew. Tina was sitting under the school with a dozen other girls, nibbling at her lunch and chatting about nothing much when she noted Willy Williams walk past and stop to talk to one of the Year 9 girls seated further along. Out of idle curiosity she glanced to see who it was and saw that it was a red-haired girl she had often seen before. The red-head was big for her age, long-legged and with quite prominent breasts, but Tina did not know her name.

She did not hear what Willy said but it was obvious he was trying to win on. Tina noted that Willy looked nervous and embarrassed and assumed he was asking the girl for a date. The fact that he had plucked up the courage to do so in such a public place and in front of a dozen other girls raised Tina's estimation of him a notch. But she was only casually interested and was turning away when it all exploded into a major incident.

Tina heard Willy say: "I wanted to ask you for a date; to go to the movies on Saturday night."

There was a moment's pained silence. Then the red-head replied: "So ask me then."

Willy blinked and looked flustered and confused. There was a ripple of laughter. Tina felt quite sorry for him and decided she did not like the red-head. But Willy stood his ground, swallowed and said, "Er... Will you... umm. will you go out with me?"

"Not this Saturday night. I'm already going out then," the red-head replied.

"Oh! Er... Well. What about some other time?" Willy asked.

Seeing his embarrassment, but also his determination, Tina admired him even more. Then she saw a large Year 11 lad named Scranton stride across behind Willy. Scranton then reached out and grabbed Willy by the collar with one hand and by the waistband of his shorts with the other. Before Tina's astonished gaze Scranton reefed upwards, lifting Willy off the ground and giving him a wedgy when the shorts were pulled tight up into his crutch.

Scranton was bigger than Willy, and obviously stronger. Willy was lifted off the ground so that his feet scrabbled to touch. He struggled and tried to turn but was propelled along past a line of laughing faces. It was obvious to Tina that Willy was humiliated.

At the corner of the building Scranton let go and pushed hard. Willy sprawled on the concrete path, skinning both knees and an elbow. Instantly he sprang up, tears in his eyes and anger on his face. Tina expected him to run away when he saw Scranton, but instead he put up his fists and lashed out.

Scranton knocked Willy's blow aside with ease, grabbed his shirt front with his other hand, then struck him hard in the face. He snarled loudly, "Barbara doesn't want to go out with you, shithead. She's going out with me. Now piss off before I make that ugly face of yours even uglier!"

Willy struggled to free himself. He tried to break the older boy's grip and was punched again. He tried to duck but couldn't. His head jerked back, thudding into a concrete post.

Despite this, Willy lashed out again. But it was no good. Scranton was a head taller and his arms longer and Willy could not land a single punch. Willy was hit again, then abruptly pushed. He stumbled, fell heavily on his bum and landed flat on his back. Scranton tried to kick him, but he managed to roll aside and scrambled to his feet. By then Tina was on her feet, sickened by the unequal fight and the unfair fighting. She moved to intervene.

Scranton shook his fist in Willy's face and snarled, "Piss off Williams, or I'll knock your block off! And keep away from Barbara or I'll mash your nuts to pulp."

Willy sprang clear of another blow. "I'll talk to who I like, you bloody bully!" he shouted. He charged, fists flailing.

Thump! Whack! Willy reeled back from two hard blows, one to the left side and one to the head. He gasped in pain but raised his fists to attack again.

A boy stepped in the way. "That'll do Scranton. Pick on someone your own size," he said. Tina recognised Peter Bronsky, one of Graham's mates in Year 10.

Scranton hesitated. "Mind your own business. He was annoying my girl."

Willy looked hurt, but he shouted back angrily, "She can go out with who she likes. If she doesn't want to go out with me, she can tell me herself."

"Keep away from her, you little turd. If I hear you've been bothering her, you'll be sorry," Scranton threatened, adding, "Besides, she prefers real men!"

With that cruel jibe Scranton turned and walked back under the building. Willy stood, shaking and rubbing his bruised face. Tina stopped and stood uncertainly. It appeared that the ugly incident was over. She heard Peter ask Willy if he was OK and then advising him to wash the gravel rash.

As he did, a voice called, "Hey Willy! Come on!"

Tina saw that a Year 9 boy was waving from the veranda of the main building in front of the science lab. The two boys turned and walked away across the quadrangle towards the main building.

Chapter 13

FIRST DATE

Tina walked back to her seat, noting that Scranton was talking to Barbara. Squeezing back into her seat beside Sarah Tina whispered to her, "Who is that red-head?"

Sarah curled her lip and whispered back, "Barbara Brassington, a Year 9. I've heard she is a real tart."

"I don't like that Scranton either," Tina said, noting the Year 11 boy walking away. "He is a real bully."

"It certainly wasn't a fair fight. That poor Year 9 kid was in trouble then," Sarah agreed.

The two fell to discussing the incident and its main players. Tina decided she did not like Barbara at all and that she did like Willy.

He's got guts, she thought.

The girls were still gossiping about the fight when another even more dramatic incident suddenly unfolded. The girl next to Barbara suddenly grabbed her arm and pointed.

"Oooh! Look!"

Tina stared in the direction the girl was pointing. She saw that up on the veranda of the main building a large group of students had gathered. Among them she noted Graham Kirk and his friends. Then she saw what had excited the other girl's interest. A huge, grey, sausage shaped object about 3 metres long had appeared out of the door of the science laboratory and was floating above the heads of the crowd.

"What is it?" Sarah asked.

The girl next to Sarah cried out, "It's Willy Williams' model of a German zeppelin."

"What's a zeppelin?" the girl next to Barbara asked.

"One of those giant airship things they used in World War 1," the other girl explained.

Tina knew that. She had seen photos of them at navy cadets. There was one of the cruiser HMAS *Sydney* firing at a zeppelin. Now she stared in amazement. The huge model was actually flying over the heads of the people on the veranda. She could hear the buzz of tiny motors, even from across the quadrangle.

Holding the nose of the model to keep it under control was Willy. Another student Tina recognised as being the long skinny kid nicknamed 'Stick', held the tail. Stick's little sister Marjorie, a Year 8 with freckles and big boobs, was jumping up and down excitedly beside them.

As Willy tried to walk along the veranda towards the office Tina saw his path blocked by another student. It was Scranton. As soon as she recognised him Tina felt a stab of anxiety.

Oh no! What is he going to do now? she wondered.

What followed was hidden from her by the other students crowding on the veranda, but she heard later that Scranton took out a cigarette lighter and flicked it on. The result was all too evident, even at 50 metres. A flicker of flame engulfed the model. There were loud cries and then the whole centre section of the model exploded with a loud *whoof!*

Willy shouted a warning then hurled the blazing model out over the railings. Tina let out a cry of concern and ran out onto the grass with the other girls to watch. The model spiralled down, a ball of flame, to crash onto the lawn. Within seconds it was just burning embers.

Tina was torn between watching the model and the fight that erupted on the veranda. Willy was obviously furiously angry and was shouting at Scranton who had his fists up. Tina saw Mr Feldt, the senior Chemistry teacher, push between them and point towards the office. Then there were gasps from the other girls and Tina even heard Barbara say, "Oh no!"

She saw that Willy had started to collapse but had been grabbed by Mr Feldt. The teacher then helped Willy along the veranda. Stick's sister held him up on the other side. "Willy is hurt," someone cried.

Oh poor Willy! Tina thought. *He didn't deserve that!*

She turned and looked at Barbara and was mollified slightly by seeing the look of genuine concern on her face. She and her friends hurried off. Tina and her friends sat down and burst into chatter about the incident.

It at least gave Andrew a reason to talk to her in the next class. He had not been a witness to the scene but Peter had and he provided the details. Willy had burns to his hands, arms and face.

"Are they serious?" Tina asked.

"Don't think so, but his parents have taken him away," Andrew answered.

"What about Scranton?" Tina asked.

"Don't know. He was sent to the office," Andrew answered. He then said, "I wonder why Scranton did it?"

Peter answered that. "Willy had been trying to chat up Scranton's girlfriend."

"Who is his girlfriend?" Andrew asked.

Again it was Peter who supplied the information. "That red-head Barbara Brassington in Nine 'B'."

"Her!" Andrew cried. "I've heard she is a real moll."

That comment bothered Tina, making her wonder how Andrew knew Barbara and about her reputation. All she could say was she thought it was a terrible shame that the model had been destroyed.

Andrew agreed. "You are right there. It must have taken Willy hours and hours to make a model like that," he said.

Peter nodded. "And all gone in a flash," he added.

Tina found it all very sad and was not impressed with Scranton or Barbara. Now that she knew who she was she learned a lot more about her. Later when the boys weren't there Sarah explained, "She is two-timing. She is going out with Scranton but during the lunch breaks she is sneaking off with Nigel Cressly and going for drives in his sports car. The word is that they go parking and have sex."

Sarah blushed and giggled and was obviously very interested in sex. So was Tina but she did not want to admit it. Nigel Cressly was one of the school leaders, a prefect in Year 12 and owner of a red sports car that made him a very desirable catch in some girl's eyes.

Over the next two days Tina had opportunities to observe Barbara and what she saw did not impress her. *She is a flirt and a bitch!* she decided. Then she modified that and observed that Barbara did not appear very happy.

It all helped fill in the time until the weekend. At last Friday came. Friday night meant Navy Cadets and that gave her several chances to be with Andrew, even if it was in a group. She did not dream of doing anything at cadets as the officers were very strict about 'fraternization' and she did not want to cause any trouble.

And I would like to be promoted!

So Tina was just happy to be near Andrew and to be aware that he had noticed her. She was sure he would not want their relationship to become public knowledge at cadets as others would tease and make comments, so she was careful not to say anything that might lead to such a conclusion.

The training that evening included preparation for the Duke of Edinburgh expeditions and for the tri-service exercise. Those going on the D of E expedition sat through a period on expedition planning. Part of this was a discussion of when to do the practice expedition and when to do the real thing.

They soon agreed that the weekend 23, 24 May, three weeks from then, was suitable for the practice as all of the groups and some of the officers were able to go then.

Lt Cdr Hazard faced them and said, "Now we need to choose a period of at least three days for the actual expedition, four days for the 'Gold' team."

Blake studied the calendar and said, "What about the Queen's Birthday long weekend?"

Sarah at once vetoed this. "I couldn't go then. My family have booked a holiday site up at Lake Tinaroo."

"Surely you don't have to be with your family on holidays at your age," Blake commented.

Sarah looked hurt and said, "I do. My mum will be very upset if I am not there."

Tina spoke next. She wanted to soothe the situation. "What about the last few days of our camp in the June holidays. Could we do it then sir?"

Lt Cdr Hazard thought for a moment and then nodded. "Probably. In fact the promotion training and testing only takes four days so you could do that. We will look into it."

So the second week of the June school holidays was tentatively pencilled in as the time for the test expedition. Then there was a signals lesson on Morse Code for those who intended to go on the field exercise. The last period was on boat maintenance during which they sorted, checked and cleaned all the parts of one of the 'Corsairs', the small sailing craft the unit used. Tina enjoyed all of these activities and was glad she had volunteered.

After dismissal parade Tina got another little boost when Andrew walked with her to her parent's car and stood talking to her. A few others noticed this and she saw a few raised eyebrows and knew that gossip and speculation would now start to circulate. For her sake she did not mind, being glad to have her name linked with Andrew's. She just hoped he did not get hurt by it.

When Carmen came over to say to Andrew it was time to go home, she gave Tina a quizzical glance. Tina was both thrilled and puzzled. *Surely, he has told his big sister?* she thought.

But he hadn't. Carmen only learned when Andrew said in front of her, "See you tomorrow night then Tina. Sleep well."

"Tomorrow night?" Carmen queried with a raised eyebrow.

"We are going to the movies," Andrew explained as he turned to walk away.

Carmen gaped and then nodded. As she also walked away she looked over her shoulder at Tina and winked. Tina blushed with happiness at this gesture of approval and knew she wanted to go home with Andrew. As she stood and watched Andrew walking away she hummed and grinned and just could not help herself. Her mother also smiled and called, "Come on Petal. Tear your eyes from Prince Charming and get into the car."

"Mum!" Tina cried, blushing even harder but quite unable to stop smiling.

"I just hope he doesn't break your heart. He's only a boy you know," her mother replied.

Tina did not believe that. *He is the most wonderful man in the whole world,* she told herself as she climbed into the car.

But the waiting hurt!

That night she could not sleep properly and tossed and turned on the edge of wakefulness, her thought a swirl of romantic fantasies. In the morning she felt tired and fidgety and just wanted the day to end. But it didn't and she was set to work on chores. Beaky's cage had to be thoroughly cleaned and the bird's wings clipped. It was only while doing this and seeing the lovely Rainbow Lorikeets in the aviary over the back fence that her suspicions and fears returned.

Other chores and homework assignments helped fill in the day but there still seemed to be long periods of itchy impatience. Then it was teatime and time to get ready. By then the impatience had been replaced by ever increasing anxiety of the 'What if he finds I am boring? What if he thinks I am ugly?' type.

Tina showered with particular care, not wanting to smell wrong, and then she added dabs of her favourite perfume and powder. As she did, she gently fondled her own breasts. Holding them both she studied them in the mirror.

They are big, she mused. *But I like them, and I hope Andrew does too!*

She noted with pleasure that they were still firm and had not yet begun to sag. Again she squeezed and stroked them, enjoying the sensation and wondering if Andrew would try to play with them. She knew from overheard conversations and 'girl talk' that males were generally fascinated by them and that they had strong urges to touch them and to play with them.

Will I let him if he tries? she thought.

But she knew she would, her real doubts being about how gentle he might be and what he might think of her if she let him.

That led to another worry when she was dressing, how much of them to show. *Do I cover them up or wear something revealing?* she wondered. After some thought and more study of herself from various angles in the mirror she decided to cover up. *I have attracted his attention, now I want to make him enjoy the chase,* she thought, smiling at the fantasies that conjured up.

So she dressed in a button up cotton blouse and wore a print skirt and casual shoes. It was not a dressy event and she wanted to save her better dresses for other, more worthwhile occasions.

Having done that she again fretted in front of the mirror, turning this way and that and critically examining her shape from all angles. *I hope he doesn't notice that my bum is a bit big,* she worried.

By then she was almost trembling with nervousness. Thinking that what she had on was not right she considered changing. But a glance at the clock told her she did not have time and then her mother called and told her it was time to go.

Oh, I hope he likes what he sees! she thought.

Her mother did. When Tina came out into the lounge room her mother smiled and nodded with approval. "You look lovely Dear, and just right for this sort of a date."

"Thanks Mum. I just... just..." Tina said.

"Stop worrying Petal! We all do that. It is natural. I'll bet Andrew is a bundle of nerves right now as well. So let's go and pick him up and put him out of his misery."

So Tina gathered up her handbag and then stood for her father to look at her. She half expected him to say something about behaviour but all he did was smile and say, "You look beautiful Princess. Have a nice time."

Tina and her mother then drove over to Andrew's. As they did. Tina hoped that Andrew would be waiting outside as she did not want to add to her nervous stress by having to talk to Carmen or their parents. Luckily, he was, and her heart warmed to him. It also broke into a rapid pitter-patter when she saw how handsome he looked. He wore a smart casual open necked shirt with short sleeves and a neat pair of long trousers. It made him look a cut above the usual scruffs she saw around the town and confirmed her opinion that he was worth the effort.

After that the evening went well, but not as well as Tina had hoped. Andrew acted the complete gentleman. He opened doors for her, complimented her on her dress, said nice things to her and about her and looked at her with admiring eyes. But he did not whisper that he loved her, and he made no move to even hold her hand, much less try to put his arm around her or kiss her. As they sat in the darkness of the movie theatre, she felt quite peeved and curiously let down by his good behaviour.

So much for worrying about what bra to wear! she thought. When he made no overt moves she began to worry. *Is there something wrong with me?* she thought. *Am I unattractive? Or does he now regret having asked me and is just being polite until it is all over?* A hundred anxious thoughts crowded her brain: whether she smelt or whether she had said or done something to offend him; or whether his friends or his sister had teased him over taking her out.

No, Carmen is too nice to do anything like that, Tina told herself in an attempt to reassure her sinking confidence.

Later she could barely remember the details of the movie, except that it had been too loud and the smell of popcorn had made her feel nauseous. But she was hotly conscious of the fact that as they stood on the footpath afterwards while waiting for her mother to pick them up his hand had touched hers and then he had tentatively moved to hold it.

He does like me! she thought as a burst of joy swept through her.

It suddenly dawned on her that Andrew was very anxious and that he might be afraid of her reaction if he did the wrong thing. To help him she took hold of his hand (after a few nervous fumbles). He then stood and looked pleased and she felt even better. It made her feel even more valued when she noted a few others give them glances. To be holding the hand of the most handsome boy around made her feel good!

To cap her night he nervously licked his lips and said, "Thanks for coming out with me. Would you like another date?"

All Tina could do was nod and smile she was so happy. Then she squeezed his hand and suddenly got all coy as she realised she had started to snuggle against him. She realised that her right breast was pressing against his left arm. *I hope he doesn't mind,* she worried. But she kept herself close as it just felt so right and so natural, and also so nice.

"What about next Saturday night?" Andrew asked.

Tina began to nod and then remembered a conversation with her father. "Oh! Oh sorry. I'd love to but we are going bird watching at the Mareeba Wetlands and Mitchell River Lake next weekend."

"Who is we?" Andrew asked, his face struggling to hide his disappointment.

"My family and Sarah's," Tina replied. "The men want to go fishing as well."

"Can I come do you think?"

That seemed to be a wonderful idea to Tina so she said, "I will have to ask. We can do that when Mum comes to pick me up or you could you come over tomorrow afternoon and we can ask," Tina said.

"What about tomorrow morning? I think we are going for a drive after lunch and I have to finish an assignment and do my jobs at home," Andrew answered.

"I have to go to church and won't be home until after eleven," Tina said.

Andrew smiled and did not seem to sneer at the mention of church, not in the way she had seen others do when they learned that she actually did go to church. "Then I will call after that," he promised.

That really pleased Tina and she beamed her happiness. Then Andrew glanced over her shoulder and grunted then said, "There is that bully Scranton and his cronies."

Tina turned to look and saw that Scranton had his arm around Barbara Brassington's waist. Scranton and his two mates wore tattered jeans and trainers and loose shirts and the girls with them had a distinctly 'tarty' appearance. But she had to admit that Barbara looked very attractive and was better dressed than the others.

Better than that sour bitch, Karen, she decided.

Tina noted that Barbara did not look happy and that Scranton looked annoyed. At that moment her eyes met Barbara's and she quickly looked away. She held Andrew's hand tighter and began to discuss the incident of Willy's zeppelin model. Andrew was not impressed.

"Scranton is just a thug," he said.

Tina glanced back at Barbara and again their eyes met. This time a distinct look of resentment appeared on Barbara's face and Tina blushed with embarrassment and again looked away. She decided she did not like Barbara or her friends. But she and Andrew had no further chance to discuss things as her mother arrived and they had to get into the car. Tina was pleased that her mother saw them holding hands and regretted that they had to let go as they climbed in.

As they drove off Tina looked out at the people still waiting on the footpath and saw Barbara watching them. It appeared to Tina that Barbara was about to burst into tears. *She is not happy,* she thought, then wondered what Scranton might have done to upset her. That opened up a whole mess of speculation and she quickly shook her head and thanked her lucky stars she was with Andrew. She gave him an admiring glance and he turned and smiled at her, making her heart turn over with gladness.

During the drive to Andrew's he again reached out and took her hand, sending waves of warm affection through her. His hand felt nice, warm and smooth, and he felt nice and she happily snuggled against him.

Andrew then asked Tina's mother if he might join them on the weekend camping trip. She at once said yes, "As long as Tina approves."

"What if Dad says no?" Tina asked.

Her mother snorted and then said, "Your father wants to go fishing. Andrew can come," in a tone that seemed to imply that her father might not enjoy his fishing if he said no. Having watched her mother get her own way many times Tina was not surprised and had to suppress a giggle. Instead she smiled at Andrew and gave his hand a squeeze. He grinned at her and squeezed back.

She felt so happy that she wanted the drive to go on for much longer. When they drew up to the front of his house and he let go or her hand she sighed with regret. Now she worried about whether he might try to give her a goodnight kiss or not. She would not have stopped him if he had, although as a general principle she had decided she would not allow boys that liberty on a first date. There was also the potential embarrassment of such an act where her mother could see to worry her. But he just smiled and said nice things and then thanked her mother before standing and waving as they drove off.

As they turned the next corner Tina's mother met her gaze in the rear vision mirror. "Have a nice time Petal?"

"Yes Mum. He is wonderful. And he wants to take me out again," Tina gushed. Then a tear of happiness crept into the corner of her right eye.

"Good. I'm glad. He seems very nice," her mother replied.

At home there was pride, embarrassment and irritation. The pride was in having been on her first date and with Andrew. The embarrassment was in talking to her parents about it without revealing all her anxieties or any personal details. The irritation came from teasing comments from little brother Garth, who implied that Andrew needed glasses, or his head read.

Later that night, in her bed, Tina relived the date and then embellished it with fantasies. She even practised kissing, using her pillow to hug and embrace and she gave her own breasts a gentle fondle, imagining that it was Andrew. That caused her some very hot thoughts that she was then ashamed of and she stopped, to drop off into a deep sleep.

On Sunday after lunch, just when Tina was beginning to think that Andrew had changed his mind, she heard a car pull up out the front. Her mother glanced out and said, "It is for you Petal. It is the Collinses."

Tina got up and went to look, anxiously straightening her blouse and patting her hair into place as she did. To her surprise she saw both Andrew and Carmen get out of the car and come up the driveway to the front door.

I wonder why they are both coming? she thought even as she opened the door and smiled at Andrew.

Chapter 14

SCHOOL GOSSIP

It was Carmen who spoke first. "Hi Tina! We are going on a picnic. Would you like to come?" she called.

Tina was thrilled. "I'd love to, but I will have to ask my parents. Where are you going?" she asked.

Carmen hurried to the door and took her arm. "Only to Ellis Beach. Come on, let's ask your mum and dad."

Andrew was left standing on the doorstep while the two girls hurried in to where Tina's parents sat in the lounge room. When they learned that Mr and Mrs Collins would be in charge and that Carmen would also be there, they had no objection. Tina wanted to be alone with Andrew but was still happy to accept.

"Wait till I change," she said.

"Oh never mind that. Just grab a towel and a hat and your bathers," Carmen said.

"What about food?"

"We have plenty. We brought extra, just in case," Carmen explained.

Young Garth, who had come to the door, asked, "Can I come too?"

Tina did not want that and was relieved when Carmen answered. "Sorry. We'd like to but we don't have room in the car."

Garth scowled and suggested that they take their own car and come. But Tina's parents said no. Details of time to be home were agreed and Tina hurried to get her towel and bathers, sunscreen and hat, then went out. A minute later she was saying hello to Andrew's parents as she climbed into the car. When all were in they drove off with Tina happily squeezed in between Andrew and Carmen.

After that it was just cheerful chat all the way to the beach. Once there Tina went to the change rooms to put on her bathers and then she nervously joined the others on the beach. She was a bit anxious about Andrew seeing her in her swimming costume even though it was a plain dark blue one-piece. *It makes me look tubby,* she thought, wishing yet again that she had a slimmer waist and smaller behind.

Andrew did not seem to notice, and Tina was almost overcome with love when she saw him in just his bathers. He looked so muscular and attractive she just wanted to hold him. Instead they horsed around, and he did not even duck her in the surf. Despite that she was still happy to be there, even though they were not alone.

After a swim they all sat on rugs in the shade and had cold cordial, cake and biscuits. Tina sat next to Andrew and kept surreptitiously studying him, noting the fine, tanned skin, the good muscle tone, the laughing eyes and the straight nose. *He is just so good looking!* she thought. Even with his windswept, uncombed hair he looked handsome.

Then she noted Carmen staring out to sea with a pensive look on her face and she suddenly felt anxious and self-conscious. *Poor old Carmen. She must be having flashbacks,* she thought.

"Are you remembering those horrible crooks?" she asked.

The previous year, during a Navy Cadet sailing weekend off this bit of coast, Carmen had been taken hostage by a gang of crooks who were waiting at the beach to collect a shipment of drugs that had been smuggled in. She had been released after the crooks pirated another yacht and left her and the family from the yacht adrift in the disabled Navy Cadet motor launch. Tina had been in another sailboat with Leading Seaman Hayley Page and Anthony Simmonds. She had only witnessed the start of the incident from a hundred metres away and that had been enough to leave her shaken.

Carmen gave a wry smile and nodded. "Yes. I sometimes worry that some of those pirates that got away might come back for revenge."

Come back for revenge! thought Tina, a chill stabbing into her as she remembered the bird poachers. *Oh, I hope not!*

"They won't," she said. "They will be on the other side of the country now and lying low," she said, trying to reassure herself as well as Carmen.

Carmen smiled her gratitude at the attempt to cheer her up and then said, "Never mind that. Let's make sandcastles. I'll bet we can make a better one than Andrew."

They did, but Andrew denied it and protested that it took two girls to make one castle whereas he had to work on his own. His was actually more technically correct but the girls made a more spectacular 'pile', until the sun dried the sand and it began to crumble. But theirs outlasted Andrew's. He built his close to the sea so as to allow a moat with water in it and a small harbour for ships, but the incoming tide soon began to wash it away.

As the first wave washed part of the sandcastle away he laughed and did not seem to care and without thinking he reached out for Tina's hand. She took it and he pulled her to her feet. "Another swim," he said, indicating the sand sticking to his arms and legs.

They ran into the waves together and Tina thought she would swoon with delight. She would happily have held his hand all afternoon, but he let go and then pushed her over so that her head went under. She came up spluttering but happy and laughing. A water fight erupted and the others joined in until Andrew was driven off by sheer weight of numbers. He swam further out until Carmen warned him not to be silly and to remember there were sharks in the Coral Sea.

That worked but also made Tina very anxious. Andrew swam ashore and Tina joined him. They rinsed the salt off under a freshwater shower near the kiosk and Tina went to change back into her clothes. As she peeled off her bathers, she fantasised that it was Andrew undressing her and that got her all hot and horny and then ashamed of her wicked thoughts.

It was a very happy girl who was delivered home late that afternoon. She hummed and sang as she fed the birds and other pets and then she lay on her bed and listened to music and daydreamed. To her it seemed that all her wishes were starting to come true.

During the whole of school assembly that was held every Monday morning Tina was given another idea. The principal spent some time reminding the students that the school fete was coming up. The fete was held over two nights, Friday and Saturday. .As the fete was a major fund-raising activity as well as an important social event he asked for classes and interest groups to make a special effort to run stalls or other money making activities. That got Tina thinking about the school dance. This was a traditional activity held on the Saturday night after the main activities of the fete had concluded.

Into Tina's mind leapt an image of her walking in on Andrew's arm to a triumphant greeting by the school. For a few minutes she fantasised about the looks of malicious envy that would appear on the faces of girls who did not like her. She had an uncomfortable belief that others considered her to be 'frumpy', 'dowdy' and a tubby 'square.'

Walking in with Andrew will show them that I am not, she thought. Then another worry surfaced. *But I have to get him to take me,* she mused. But how to do that? She did not want to ask him outright and knew she would have to drop some subtle hints. *But not too subtle, he's only a male!* she thought.

She left the assembly feeling that her love life was definitely moving in a positive direction. But if hers was it was obvious that for others it was the reverse. During the lunch break Tina sat with Sarah and looked wistfully across the quadrangle to where Andrew sat with his friends. She would have loved to go and sit with him but was still very unsure of her position and did not want to offend him.

If I embarrass him in front of his mates, he might not like me, or I might scare him off, she told herself.

While she was thinking how to move their relationship forward, she noticed Barbara Brassington walk past and sit down nearby with her friend Gillian. They were discussing something and kept glancing across the quadrangle as well. This got Tina's attention, so she followed their gaze. She saw that the object of their attention was Willy Williams. He had not been at school on the previous Thursday or Friday, having suffered burns in the Zeppelin incident but Tina now saw him talking Stephen Bell.

As Tina watched she saw Stick's little sister run over to ask Willy how he was. From across the quadrangle Tina could see that Willy's hands were bandaged.

At that moment Barbara's other friend Karen arrived. Barbara stood up to greet her. She nodded towards Willy. "Who's that girl talking to him? The blonde with freckles whose brother is in our class?"

Karen looked then said: "Marjorie Morton. She a real little prick teaser. Never mind her, come and talk to the Year Twelves."

Marjorie, Tina thought. *I knew that.*

Then she saw David Scranton approaching Barbara, so she sat quietly and listened in. She didn't have to eavesdrop as they all spoke so loudly. Scranton pointed towards Willy and said with a sneer, "Bloody Williams is a poof. He's wearing make-up."

"Oh he is not," Barbara replied.

"He is so. You go and look. It's a wonder he hasn't got a handbag. I'll bet he goes in the Gay Mardi Gras."

"Oh don't be awful David," Barbara said. To Tina she did not look amused. Scranton shrugged and swaggered off towards Willy.

Oh dear! I hope he isn't going to cause more trouble, Tina thought. She felt sorry for Willy. *He is an odd-ball but he is also nice.*

Scranton was. Tina watched and saw Scranton stand with his hands on his hips while sneering down at Willy as he spoke to him. Then Scranton stepped closer and raised his fists. Tina found her heart beating very fast with concern. *Scranton is a real bully,* she decided. Feeling unhappy and somewhat helpless she watched as Scranton pushed at Willy as he stood up. Willy put up his bandaged hands to defend himself.

Tina was sure there was going to be another fight but to her relief she saw Graham Kirk, Peter Bronsky and Stephen Bell, walk over and speak to Scranton. Whatever they said caused Scranton to scowl and walk away, calling taunts about homosexuality as he went. This was echoed by Martin and Larry. It all made Tina feel quite upset.

She watched with distaste as Scranton walked off, pointing to Willy and telling groups of boys, who all went to look, then to jeer and laugh. Then she heard Barbara ask her friend Fiona, "What's it all about?"

Fiona, who had just joined them, answered. "Willy's eyebrows were burnt off in the fire and his mother put false ones on with make-up. Now those horrible boys are all teasing him and calling him queer."

"Oh he is not!" Barbara cried.

"How do you know?" Karen teased mischievously.

Barbara snorted. "I just know. He asked me out. Oh, poor Willy!" She looked very annoyed with Scranton who was walking around obviously spreading the story. Tina also felt annoyed as she could see that Willy was getting teased and was plainly upset.

But worse was to follow at lunch time. Once again Tina sat with Sarah in their usual seats. They quietly ate their sandwiches. Then she saw Barbara walking towards her usual seat. Then she stopped and looked anxiously around. Tina heard the Year 9 girls who sat to her left whispering and overheard the names Barbara and Scranton several times, and then the word sex. That got her interested but also made her feel uncomfortable. It was obvious that Barbara was the object of the gossip.

While Barbara stood on her own, apparently deep in thought, Willy appeared and walked over to her. Tina was just too far away to hear what they said but she got the distinct impression that Willy was apologizing.

To begin with Barbara gave him a cool stare but then she smiled. Willy listened to her, nodded and then walked away, looking a bit happier.

That evening Tina forgot all about Barbara and Willy and their problems when Andrew appeared at her house just before teatime. "I came over to check on the details for the bird watching next weekend."

Tina was thrilled and once again glowed with happiness and admiration. Andrew was shown in and at once asked her parents. Her father at first frowned but her mother smiled and immediately gave him the times and other details. That sent Tina into raptures of anticipation and she had to resist the urge to run over and throw her arms around him. As it was, she walked back to the door with him and tried to convey her feelings through her eyes and face. But As she did, she was overcome with shyness and the fear that, if she was too forward, she might scare him off.

That night she could hardly sleep for her heated fantasising and happy thoughts.

At school next day it was all she could do to keep her secret to herself. Her desire was to shout her joy to the whole world but fearing teasing and gossip of the wrong sort she stayed silent. And there was plenty of malicious gossip, but luckily not about her. During morning break as she sat under the school eating, she heard a group of Year 9 girls discussing an alleged sexual incident between Barbara and Scranton at the movies the previous Saturday night. It sounded improbable and disgusting to Tina, but she had to admit she had not even known Barbara and her friends were there until afterwards.

This exploded into another incident a few minutes later at the drink taps when Barbara arrived and overheard one of the girls. Tina did not hear what the girl said but saw her look at Barbara and then blush and look hastily away.

Barbara obviously heard the girl as she looked very hurt. She had a drink and then walked over to where her friends sat along the seat to Tina's left. Tina watched out of the corner of her eye and noted that they also looked like they were talking about Barbara.

Barbara stopped a few paces from them and said angrily, "People are talking about me. What are they saying?"

Her friends looked embarrassed and obviously did not want to answer. Barbara loudly insisted, "Please tell me what people are saying."

A Year 9 girl named Fiona, a pretty blonde who Tina thought was rather nice, met her eye and said, "It isn't very nice Barb."

"Whatever it is, it isn't true and I want to know," Barbara cried.

Fiona nodded. "Apparently David Scranton is boasting to all his mates that he had sex with you in the movies on Saturday night."

Gillian nodded. "Except I heard it was in the park and that you had to run away with no clothes on when the cops came," she added.

Tina winced inside and thought, *Ouch! I hope no-one ever says things like that about Andrew and me.*

She saw Barbara go red with embarrassment and anger, who cried angrily, "But that's not true! We didn't leave the theatre at all." She turned to Karen. "You know that. You were there."

Karen looked embarrassed. "Not all the time. I went outside with Martin for a while," she said.

"But we didn't do anything. Gillian, you were there too. You know that," Barbara cried. She was now looking very hurt and upset.

Gillian shrugged. "He had a good grip on your tits when I came back."

Once again Barbara flamed with shame. "That's all he did, and I wouldn't let him go any further. Oh, the bastard! Who does he think he is?" she shouted.

None of them answered this. It was all very hurtful and upsetting. Barbara stood defiantly in front of her friends. "Who told you anyway?"

Nicole pointed. "Donovan," she said. Donovan was a boy in their class. The gaze of every girl there followed Nicole's finger and saw Donovan talking to Willy and his friends on the far side of the quadrangle. From the body language it appeared that Donovan was taunting Willy.

What's going on? Tina wondered.

There was a follow up during the lunch break. Tina had just sat down to eat her lunch when a disturbance over past the end of the building attracted her attention. She could just see what was going on because the building was held up on concrete posts and had no side or end wall. Only a few people obscured the view, at least until the shouting started. Then a crowd quickly began to gather, making it hard for Tina to see.

It was Barbara again. She had marched up to Scranton and confronted him. "Hey Scranton, I want to talk to you," she called.

"And I don't want to talk to you," Scranton retorted. He went red in the face making Tina think, *He's guilty alright!*

But Barbara confronted him. "I've heard you are saying we did things at the movies last Saturday night."

"So?" Scranton put his hands on his hips and sneered at her.

"So stop saying things that aren't true," Barbara snapped.

"I'll say what I like," Scranton replied.

Barbara glared at him. "You do and you will regret it," she said.

"Oh yeah! What will you do little baby?" he said with a curl of his lip. "Run along and play with your dolls little girl."

"You don't have to be nasty just because you didn't get your own way," Barbara snapped back.

"Get my own way! I wasted all that time and didn't get anything. You are frigid, you stuck up little bitch!"

Under the lash of his insult Barbara's anger flared. She waved her finger under Scranton's nose and shouted: "If you were a decent man you might have gotten more but you just wanted to use me. You don't care about me at all. You are just a selfish bully!"

That obviously enraged Scranton as he swore at her in a disgusting way and called her horrible names. At that Barbara exploded. She shouted angrily: "Don't you call me a troll, you foul-mouthed pig!" She waved her clenched fist at him and went on: "Clear off! I don't want anything to do with you ever again! And don't go around spreading more lies about what you claim to have done to me, you filthy toad!"

At that Scranton lost his temper. His hand shot out and grabbed Barbara's wrist. "Don't you call me a toad, you stuck-up moll!"

"Let me go!" Barbara shouted. She pulled back and tried to break free. Scranton held on and twisted her arm. She cried in pain then swung her free hand in an attempt to slap him. But he fended off the blow and then punched her hard in the face. Tina was appalled and stood up, thinking to intervene. As she hurried towards them, she saw Barbara struggling to break free. Barbara tried to kick Scranton in the shins but failed. To Tina's horror Scranton punched Barbara again, the blow almost knocking her off her feet. Then Tina saw Scranton draw back his fist for another punch and she screamed both as a warning and because of her own helplessness, still being 20 paces away.

At that instant, another shout distracted Scranton. He glanced, pushed Barbara aside, and turned to defend himself from the new attacker. Tina saw a boy run across and crash into Scranton so hard that both boys went sprawling on the ground. Only as they separated and sprang to their feet did Tina see that Barbara's rescuer was Willy.

As Scranton scrambled up mouthing obscenities Willy lashed out at him. The punch connected but it did not knock the bully down. It just made him angrier. Scranton swore vilely and lunged forward, fists flying.

Whack! Willy was struck a hard blow on the side of his head and reeled back. Thud! Another punch by Scranton stuck his shoulder. Tina could see that it was a most unequal fight. Scranton was bigger, stronger and had a longer reach, and he was wild. He seemed to have completely lost control and was shouting and punching like a madman. Willy reeled back from another blow to the face. Then he sprang forward and punched hard with his bandaged right hand.

The blow took Scranton full on the nose. He stepped back and yelled in pain. Fury glittered in his eyes.

Tina was dismayed. *Oh my God! He will kill Willy!* she thought.

She stepped forward to help but was blocked by others. As she tried to move forward, she saw Mr Conkey step between Willy and Scranton. Mr Page, the Geography teacher, also appeared, as did Graham Kirk and Peter Bronsky. The fighters were separated and Barbara suddenly burst into tears. She looked stunned as she wiped blood from her face. Fiona appeared and wrapped her arms around her.

"It's alright Barb. You are safe now," she said.

Karen also joined them and began to comfort her. Barbara buried her face in Fiona's shoulder and sobbed with reaction. Tina stood and watched, feeling both angry and helpless. Never in her life had she witnessed such a brutal assault and it left her feeling shaken and nauseous. She hated violence, especially brutality to women by bigger males and she felt quite sick. She also now felt quite sorry for Barbara and she even admitted to a grudging admiration.

The teachers now took control. Willy and Scranton were ordered to the office and Barbara was sent of to the sick room with her friends. Tina stood and discussed the incident with her friends but was still feeling breathless and upset when it was to me to go back into class.

Oh, I hope nothing like that ever happens to me, she thought.

Then she thought of Danny's threat to get her and she was gripped by a spasm of terror so strong it temporarily paralyzed her.

Chapter 15

MITCHELL RIVER

O ne result was that when Tina went out to feed her birds after school she felt quite anxious. She did not want to admit that she was scared but she suddenly felt very alone when she went into the back yard. As she fed the finches and budgerigars, she kept looking at the back of Neville's house and into his aviary. But there was no sign of anyone, only the birds. Tina saw that there were still a dozen rainbow lorikeets but that there were also a couple of new parrots she could not identify.

To study them more closely she stood and pretended to talk to Beaky. Still unsure she went back inside, after carefully locking the back gate to the courtyard, and took out her copy of *Australian Birds Field Guide*. After some searching, she decided that the unusual parrots were Australian King Parrots.

Is it legal to have them as pets? she wondered.

But she was still so unsure that she took no action, not wanting to cause trouble. Instead she settled to her computer to do a homework assignment. Later she sat and watched TV but was barely aware of it, her thoughts being mostly about Andrew, with some worry over the Barbara-Scranton incidents.

When she met Andrew at school the next day, she learned that Scranton had been expelled from the school. That relieved some of her fears but did make her wonder whether that would be the end of it.

Classes then ground on with their usual routine and Tina settled to studying, and daydreaming. *A weekend camping must offer some romantic possibilities?* she decided. So she imagined various incidents that would all help to help the romance flourish.

During the breaks she sat with her friends, and yearned to sit with Andrew. She listened to the gossip and noted that Barbara was not at school and heard that she and a girl named Nicole had been involved in a fight in class the previous day. "What over?" she asked Sarah.

"I heard that some of the girls were being really bitchy and were passing notes accusing her of all sorts of horrible things," Sarah answered.

"I'd fight too in that case," Tina said.

She tried to imagine what it might be like with people making accusations and whispering gossip about her. *It would be horrible,* she thought. But she couldn't help thinking that Barbara had brought it on herself by her behaviour. *The way she and her friends act; flirting and flaunting themselves,* she thought.

Thursday dragged slowly and Friday even more. Only the knowledge that she had Navy Cadets, and then the weekend camping trip to look forward to, made the waiting easier to bear. Tina threw herself into her work to try to blot out the ache of impatience and soon had all her homework and assignments done and she was left fidgeting and wondering what to do next.

That night at Navy Cadets the D of E teams were given another lesson in preparation. This was on navigation on land, somewhat different from navigation at sea and with different technical terms for the same thing ('Triangle of Error' instead of 'Cocked Hat'). There was another lesson on Morse Code including an introduction on how to send messages by signal lamp. There was also lesson on knots used in sailing. Tina enjoyed them all and tried her hardest.

Before dismissal parade there was a discussion on training expeditions for the D of E. Lt Ryan suggested that all the groups go together for one weekend to practice the various skills with instructors to help them.

"But where sir?" Andrew asked.

"Over the mountains somewhere. I will ask the army cadets for ideas. They do more of that sort of thing," Lt Ryan answered.

Andrew put his hand up. "I know some army cadets who go hiking all the time sir. They go to our school. I will ask them if you like."

"Yes please."

Tina looked quizzically at Andrew and he said softly, "Graham and his mates."

"That's a good idea," Tina agreed. Graham, Peter, Stephen and Roger went hiking at least once a month and always seemed to be getting into some sort of a scrape or adventure.

Dismissal parade followed. Afterwards Andrew walked with Tina to her mother's car. He did not seem to be bothered by the looks they got from several other cadets and that gave her hope. "See you tomorrow then," he said.

Tina nodded and stood close with her face upturned. She had to suppress a strong urge to reach up and take his head in her hands. The impulse to give him a kiss was so strong she trembled. "Yes," was all she could croak. *Tomorrow,* her mind cried, even as her body seemed to ache in need of his embrace.

But there was the night to get through and she could not sleep. She tossed and turned and fantasised, sometimes in quite naughty ways. Then her dreams were just frustrating; with Andrew about to kiss her or about to do other things and then the situation would change, or she would wake up. It was all very tiring and annoying!

Saturday morning was more fidgety waiting as the vehicle had to be packed and the main chores done. Tina quickly packed her own bag and carried it and her hat and sleeping bag out to the vehicle. Then she fed the birds, once again looking anxiously at the house at the back. As she did, she had the niggling beginnings of a worrying idea but did not want to organize it into proper thoughts lest it spoil the weekend.

It was not until nearly 1000hrs that the boat was hooked on and they could set out. By then Tina was almost in a fever of impatience. *Oh come on!* she fretted. *Andrew will be worrying and wondering if we are coming.* But she said nothing and tried to act calm.

Andrew was waiting at his front door. He wore baggy old blue trousers and a long sleeve blue shirt and baseball cap. To Tina he looked very rugged and handsome and she wished she was going away to camp with just him. Andrew's mother and father and his sister Carmen all came out to say hello. Tina climbed out to greet Andrew. In her fantasies she hugged and kissed him, but in reality she just gave him a shy hello and showed him where to put his gear.

She then climbed back in next to Garth and Andrew sat on the outside. Farewells were said, Tina noting a delighted gleam in Carmen's eye. "Have a good time!" she said, her voice dripping with double meaning. Tina blushed at those thoughts and then sat and barely spoke a word to Andrew. He also remained silent much of the time except to comment on the scenery. Garth kept glancing at Andrew and then smirking at Tina, but he soon tired of this game and became a typical bored little nuisance instead.

It was lunch time when they reached Mareeba, so they parked in the main street and walked up and down and then purchased pies and hamburgers. Tina enjoyed a chocolate milkshake while she and Andrew sat and looked self-consciously at each other. To her relief her parents just seemed to accept Andrew as 'the boyfriend' and they took it for granted that they would sit together.

Tina liked Mareeba. It is a busy town of about 10,000 with sufficient variety of people and shops to make it interesting. But she had been there a dozen times, so it was no novelty. They waited until Sarah's family arrived and had some refreshments. After lunch they drove on northwards. That took them into territory that Tina was unfamiliar with. She was struck by how straight the road was and how flat the country. Then she noted that there was a very gentle slope on both side with mountains in the distance. Those on the left were further away and looked much more rugged.

Tina's father pointed out the window and said, "This road runs along the Great Dividing Range. You are on it now."

Garth did not believe this and disputed it until his father said, "This gentle rise we are on is the watershed between the rivers that flow east into the Coral Sea and those that flow west into the Gulf of Carpentaria. To your right is the Barron River, down among those trees there; and to your left is the Mitchell. You can't see the river from here but later we will pass a lake where its waters are impounded."

On reaching the small town of Biboohra they got their first disappointment. They stopped at the turn-off to the Mareeba Wetlands and found a sign saying that they were closed. After a short conference with the Creswells it was decided to go on to the campsite and start fishing and bird watching.

The drive after that was northwards along a good bitumen road with open savannah woodland on both sides. After 10 kilometres or so this gave way to more swampy and scrubby country on the left. They passed through a small range of hills at Carr Creek and then along a few long straights in open country.

Suddenly the view opened up on their left to reveal the lake and as soon as she saw it all of Tina's vague thoughts crystallised into a solid theory that sent chills of excitement through her. Ever since the incident at Croydon Dam she had considered all large lakes in North Queensland as likely places for the wildlife smugglers to operate their float plane, and as soon as she saw the Mitchell River Lake she thought, *This is the ideal place for them. It is big. It is well away from any houses or settlements;*

it is right beside a bitumen road with dirt roads going off to it at various places to give easy access.

When she saw the teeming bird life on and around the lake she was even more certain it was just the sort of place the crooks would operate from. A feeling of tense anxiety began to grip her and she felt sure that some sort of malevolent fate would lead to her encountering them that weekend. But when she thought about it rationally she shook her head. It would be too much of a coincidence. Despite that, the idea lodged and she felt uneasy.

I hope I don't meet those crooks again, and not in a place like this. Danny and Marco might not be very nice to me if they catch me alone.

What that 'not very nice' might entail was the sort of dark nightmare she preferred not to dwell on. But when the vehicles slowed and turned left onto one of the gravel roads in a very lonely stretch of apparently uninhabited bush her anxiety went up a notch.

There was a gate with a lock, but Mr Creswell had a key and opened it, then closed it behind them. "We have permission from the owners to be here," he explained. "So we should have the place to ourselves."

Oh, I hope so! Tina thought, looking at the bush on both sides of the road. Apart from the road and a barbed wire fence, there was no sign of settlement. To ease her fears she asked, "What do we do if there is an accident? Do we have mobile phone communication?"

Her mother answered that, checking her own. "Yes, we do."

Feeling slightly easier Tina sat back and studied the bush as they drove away from the highway. After a kilometre or so they came to some low hills and then drove across a low causeway with water on both sides to another low hill.

Her father gestured at the hill in front of them. "This is an island joined to the mainland by a causeway," he explained. "We are camping on the island."

That sounded nice to Tina but when they got there instead of unloading and setting up camp at a nice little beach all they did was drop both boat trailers and then her father turned the vehicle up a bumpy rough track to a level area a hundred metres up on the side of the rise. "Why don't we camp down at the beach?" she asked.

"Because there are crocodiles in the lake. You kids keep well away from the water and when you are near it keep an eye open for them."

"But isn't the lake freshwater?" Garth queried.

"Yes, it is, but *Crocodilius Porosus* is quite happy to live in it," he said.

"How did they get here?" Garth asked.

"They just walked up the river. They had hundreds of years to do it. They have always lived here and after the dam was built they have multiplied," their father explained.

"Up from where?" Garth asked.

"The Gulf of Carpentaria."

"But that is hundreds of kilometres away isn't it?" Garth said.

His father nodded and said, "Yes. But they are just big lizards remember. They can walk on land. So just believe me and be careful. Now, hop out and help us set up camp."

Tina and Andrew climbed out and Tina looked around. Almost at once she revised her negative opinion of the camp site. From the level area she could see out the other side of the island as well and the view was most impressive. "Oh, you can see for ever!" she cried.

Andrew joined her with a map and they studied the scene. The lake stretched off to the south, west and northwest for many kilometres. There were other similar islands, including a big one a few kilometres to the south which was also connected to the mainland by a long causeway. In the far distance was the rugged line of mountains which Andrew now named as the Hann Range.

"The lake isn't very deep," Tina commented as she observed large tracts or reeds in swampy bays and inlets. There were also hundreds of dead trees sticking out of the water. "And lots of birds," she added.

The next hour was taken up with setting up camp. This included four tents, a 'fly' between four trees, tables, folding chairs and a barbeque. Only when all was ready did the group prepare for fishing and bird watching. Then they walked back down the hill to the boats. These were prepared and then launched. Andrew was able to assist with this and quickly showed himself to quite skilful. "I have a boat licence," he explained.

"And years of training as a navy cadet," Tina's father added. The evident approval in his voice really pleased Tina.

Dad must like Andrew, she decided.

But then Andrew wanted to go fishing with the men. That disappointed her but she realised that she had never explained that she did not particularly like fishing. They had not discussed bird watching either so she did not know if he would be interested. Rather than deny him the chance to go fishing she hid her feelings, and when he asked if she was coming she said yes.

Reluctantly she climbed into the motorboat and moved to sit beside Andrew. Garth took up a seat in the bows and began splashing his hand in the water as they floated out from the beach after launching. Tina's father at once called out, "Garth! Get that hand in the boat before a big croc grabs it; and do up your life jacket."

Garth pulled his hand back smartly enough but then scowled and fiddled with his 'Personal Floatation Device'. Both Andrew and Tina had theirs on and done up and Tina was about to speak to Garth again when Andrew beat her to it.

"Sailor, do what the captain says. Do up your PFD or you will be given fifty lashes and keelhauled," he said in a firm, no-nonsense voice.

Garth looked at him in astonishment and for a moment sulky rebellion showed on his face. Tina braced for a scene but then Garth just nodded and bent to clip the PFD up. Then he said, "What's keel hauling?"

Andrew began explaining while Tina looked at her father in astonishment. A feeling of warmth swept through her as she realised that Garth both liked and admired Andrew and was willing to listen to him. Her father smiled back and turned to start the motor. A minute later the boat puttered out onto the glassy lake with a crew of happy people.

Tina remained sort of happy for most of the afternoon but after a couple of hours of sitting in a small boat in the sun she began to get a bit peeved. Adding to her discomfort was the fact that she had not caught any fish and that Andrew seemed to be devoting most of his attention to Garth. That was all very well because it kept Garth contented with a lot of boy talk and fishing technicalities, but it was not what Tina had hoped for.

To occupy her mind Tina used her binoculars to observe and make notes on all the types of birds she saw. Luckily there were many and of a dozen different types. She noted the usual magpie geese, pied herons and brolgas plus a number of types of ducks. As well there were Australasian grebes, royal spoonbills and several types of ibis. Overhead circled a number of hawks and kites. Each time she spotted what she thought was a new variety she would consult her *Fieldguide of Australian Birds* to check on the distribution of that species and on details of their colouring and so on.

The birds at least gave her some interest and enjoyment as the fishing and hot sun did not. She actually found it a relief when her father said it was time to head home. They had drifted a few kilometres by then and the other boat was a few hundred metres away. As they motored back to shore her father kept the speed to slow as there were a few dead trees and snags showing and from time to time they ran across muddy patches that were so shallow that the propeller churned up a swirl of mud. In other places they skirted patches of reeds growing in the shallows.

"You could probably wade halfway across this lake," Andrew said.

Tina's father nodded and said, "You probably could but I wouldn't like to try if there are crocs around."

That idea lodged in Tina's brain and she looked anxiously around. The water was very calm. The waves were barely bigger than ripples, but it was just enough of a disturbance to make it difficult to detect a crocodile as it surfaced for a look or as it swam towards them. *I hope there aren't any,* she thought, taking her hands off the gunwale. For a few seconds she experienced the distinct impression that the boat was not big enough to be safe.

Then she shook her head and told herself she was being silly. *Crocodiles don't attack people in boats,* she told herself.

She had heard of them dragging people out of canoes, but could not ever remember hearing of that happening to people in power boats. But it still made her glad when they reached the beach and she was safe on dry land.

The boat was dragged up by Andrew and her father so that its bows were beached. To do this they stood in knee deep water. That got Tina all anxious again and she wanted to warn them about crocodiles. But rather than appear to be a nervous girl she said nothing and instead just carefully watched the lake. But she knew that was not liable to work.

Crocs attack from under water. You don't see it till it lunges out at you, she thought. All she could hope to see was a swirl of mud or a ripple on the surface to indicate that the creature might be swimming fast in the shallow water.

But nothing happened and the males seemed oblivious to her fears. Andrew looped the anchor rope around a tree and then went to help heave the Creswell's boat up as well. So Tina could only really relax after they were all ashore and walking up the hill towards the camp.

Her mother and Mrs Creswell were at the camp talking and reading. They looked very relaxed but also fairly bored. Seeing them sitting there Tina hoped that her future husband wouldn't just abandon her while he went fishing but she suspected that he might.

Men don't seem to even be aware of things like that, she mused.

Then she glanced at Andrew and wondered what sort of a father he might be. It was the way he was talking to Garth that prompted that idea and she knew instinctively that he would be a good one. Then she blushed, remembering what had to happen before she could become a mother.

I hope he is good at that too, she thought. Then she blushed again as she tried to imagine what it might feel like.

A barbeque tea of steak, fish and sausages was enjoyed and then everyone sat around and talked as the sun set. Tina enjoyed that as it looked very beautiful with the reddish reflection across the still waters of the lake. Her happiness was increased by the way Andrew seemed to be accepted with no problems. He sat and chatted in a very relaxed way. She could only admire his easy manner and confident, mature way of speaking to the adults.

As dusk settled in she glanced at the clear sky and noted that the stars were coming out. It was cool and promised to be cold later. She stood up and strolled over to the edge of the level area to watch the last of the sunset and to enjoy the still of the evening. As she stood there gazing out over the lake, she hoped that Andrew would join her and wished that she and he were alone on the island.

That would be very romantic, she thought, hugging herself and hoping.

But he didn't join her. Instead he set to work lighting lanterns and washing up and generally making himself useful. From the edge of the darkness Tina watched him with a mixture or exasperation and affection.

Then a sound caught her attention that at once drove thoughts of romance from her mind. It was an aero engine. She stiffened with fear and looked around.

A plane! Is it the crooks? she wondered.

Chapter 16

FEAR IN THE FOG

For several seconds Tina seemed to freeze up as anxiety swamped her emotions. Then her questing gaze located the plane. It was coming from the north and sounded like a small twin engine aircraft. A flashing strobe light on the plane helped her eyes to detect it. Then she noted the green starboard wing light and other lights. Seeing the lights caused her to shake her head and relax.

No, the crooks won't have any lights; and their plane's motor is much quieter than that, she told herself.

The aircraft flew almost directly overhead and a few thousand feet up. It appeared to be heading due south and Tina turned to watch. *Heading for Mareeba maybe?* she thought, knowing that Mareeba was the nearest major airfield in that direction and that it was a busy place for light aircraft. With that in mind she looked out across the lake and noted the distant twinkle of a couple of lights and the glow in the sky that indicated where Mareeba was.

Then another unpleasant idea came to her. Apart from these few lights many kilometres away there wasn't another light to be seen. The entire shore of the lake and the mountains on both sides were in darkness.

We are certainly in an isolated place, she thought. She walked a few paces further from the camp and kept scanning in all directions, hoping to see a light. *There must be a station homestead or a farmhouse or something,* she told herself.

Then a tiny moving light came into view away across the lake to the southeast. *A car, on the highway,* she noted. Then the car's headlights went out of sight and she experienced a peculiar sense of foreboding. *If the crooks know we are here they could come and get me,* she thought. The knowledge that there was a locked gate was no comfort as she had already seen the crooks cope easily with such a thing.

At that moment Andrew came walking towards her from the camp. "Tina? Are you OK?" he asked.

Tina wanted to run to him, to hug him, for him to hold her. But she was too inhibited and could only croak an affirmative and then say, "I was just looking at the stars and the lights."

Andrew stopped next to her and she yearned for him to take her hand, to hold her, to show affection rather than just friendship. Instead he just said, "We are going down to the lake to look for crocodiles."

"Look for crocodiles!"

"Young Garth's idea," Andrew replied.

"Isn't that dangerous at night?" she queried, walking with him as he started down the slope.

"Yes, a bit. But we aren't going far," Andrew answered.

Tina did not want to go near the water but everyone else, including her mother and Mrs Creswell, was walking down the track so she felt compelled to go. But she certainly did not want to go out in a boat. This feeling was reinforced when she stood at the lake shore 5 minutes later and looked out across the blackness. The water was rippling in the gentle breeze but to her it had an evil, malevolent feel to it.

Garth and Mr Creswell did not help as they used torches to scan the water looking for the reflection of crocodile's eyes. As the torch beams swung back and forth Tina looked but she saw nothing. But she could imagine the slimy saurians sliding quickly towards her through the inky ooze and she shuddered at the idea and moved back a couple of paces from the beach.

The rush of wings attracted Tina's attention and she glanced up, hoping to see the bird against the sky. *If it was a bird,* she thought, knowing that the fruit bats, Flying Foxes as they were locally called, would also be abroad.

Then the very distinctive sound of a Tawny Frogmouth Owl sounded from behind her. She turned and listened. At that moment young Garth began throwing stones into the water and the splashes interfered with her listening. To get away from the noise she walked a few more paces back along the road. This brought her to the end of the causeway and she stood and looked into the darkness.

The swampy lagoon behind the causeway looked even more sinister than the lake on the other side. The water was quite still and the skeletons of the dead trees sticking up looked spooky. Tina shivered and wished she had brought her torch. But she stayed there listening as she heard the owl twice more.

Over among those trees on the far bank, she decided.

She strained her eyes to see but then wondered if her eyes were playing tricks as the dark mass of distant trees seemed to blur and fade, then come into sharp focus again. A sudden waft of cool air caused her to shiver and she noticed a white haze drifting by.

What is that? she wondered.

Plop!

The sound caused the already tense Tina to twitch. Then she relaxed. *Only a frog or a fish,* she told herself. *Crocodiles would not go plop!* But it was enough to scare her. So was a glance along the narrow causeway and the thoughts that followed. *The crooks would have to come that way,* she told herself.

She did not believe they would come by boat in the dark. Thinking of that caused her another tremor of anxiety and she turned to go back to the others, knowing she was being silly and irrational by imagining such a thing.

Only to get a shock. She knew she was only about 50 paces from where the others stood on the beach but all she could see was white!

Fog!

It had rolled in off the lake in just a few minutes and now completely surrounded her. The sound of the other's voices could be heard but they were quite muffled and indistinct. Then she noted a faint glow and the shadowy shapes of tree trunks and knew that was the glow of their torches. At that moment there was a bigger splash in the swamp behind her and the whole of her neck and arms prickled into instant goose bumps. Anxiously she glanced back over her shoulder and then started walking back to join the others.

But it wasn't that easy. Almost at once she found herself off the road and walking in knee high dry grass. Sticks crackled underfoot and she barked her shins on a log. A tree blocked her path and she came to a standstill and peered anxiously in the direction she thought the others were. She found that her heart was beating fast and she knew that she was scared.

"Don't be silly!" she told herself.

Then a swish of wings close overhead made her cringe and when this was followed by a loud splash she actually jumped with fright. Then the mournful and creepy cry of a curlew sounded and shiver ran up her back.

Another noise came to her and her heart hammered even faster. *Are they footsteps I can hear?* she thought. She looked behind and was sure she could hear boots on gravel and into her mind's eye leapt an image of dark shapes, human shapes. And there was one just off to her right!

"Tina?"

Tina jumped with fright and then gasped with relief. It was Andrew. "Here I am," she croaked.

A torch came on and shone in her direction. Even though it was only 10 metres away the fog was so thick that it was just a glow. Andrew walked over, lowering the torch beam to the ground so as not to shine it in her eyes. "What are you doing?" he asked.

Tina was trembling with emotion by this time: fear and relief, but she was also ashamed of being scared of nothing. Not wanting Andrew to think she was a coward she said, "Just listening to the birds. I was just on my way back."

Andrew joined her and reached out and took her hand. Her whole impulse was to throw herself into his arms, but she resisted this. He felt her hands and said, "You are trembling! Are you alright?"

"Something went splash and gave me a fright," she admitted. But her mind screamed for him to hold her, to love her. To her intense disappointment he didn't.

Instead he shone his torch at the swamp. "Looks pretty spooky in the mist," he said.

"It came in very quickly," Tina commented, silently agreeing with the spooky bit. In the beam of his torch all the shadows in the reeds and dead trees and snags seemed to hide things of menace. The unspoken thought of what those things might be caused Tina to tremble again.

Andrew felt this and switched his torch off. Turning to face her he put his arms around her and held her close. "Why Tina, you are shaking!" he said, his voice full of concern

Tina was and she snuggled close and held him tight, relishing the comforting feel of his arms around her. Suddenly she felt safe, and she wanted to be kissed.

Kiss me now! Kiss me now! Now is the moment, she thought. She even turned her face upwards in readiness. But even then instinct made her hold back. *He must do this,* she told herself. *He has to really want me. I mustn't give the lead. If he really wants me he must show it.*

For a few seconds it seemed as though he would. She could feel his heart beating strongly and his grip tightened. His eyes looked into hers and she saw him lick his lips.

Now! she thought. *Now! Kiss me!*

A voice called, "Tina! Andrew! Are you there?"

It was her father. The spell was broken. Tina could have wept with frustration but only allowed it to show in a sigh. Andrew looked worried and drew away from her. "We are over here," he called.

"Well when you two have finished smooching come back. We are going back to camp," Tina's father called back.

He was only about 25 metres away, but the fog was so thick that Tina was sure he had not seen them. Even so a spasm of guilt and embarrassment coursed through her and she called back indignantly, "We are only listening to the birds."

Tina's father chuckled and made some comment about 'When I was a boy!' which Tina didn't hear properly. But she did hear her mother say, "Henry, stop teasing the children; and don't boast."

Tina stepped back but kept hold of Andrew's hand, still hoping. "We had better go," she said, not wanting them to be teased any more.

Andrew agreed. He turned on his torch and led her out to the vehicle track and along it. As they walked away from the swamp Tina had one last shiver of irrational anxiety about what might be lurking in the fog and then tried to push it out of her mind. She went up the hill thinking about kissing and how she might get Andrew to make the move.

Back at the camp Andrew released her hand and they re-joined the others. They toasted marshmallows on a fire and sat and talked, but with the fog came a chill and it wasn't long before pullovers became the standard dress and then the sleeping bag became an attractive place to be.

Tina would have loved to have Andrew share her sleeping bag, and blushed deeply at the things she imagined might then go on, but she gave no hint of this and reluctantly organised her own bed in the same tent as her mother. Andrew moved to share another tent with her father and Garth. Tina lingered for a few minutes, hoping for a good night kiss, but it was in vain. Andrew just gave a cheery goodnight and then crawled into his tent.

Oh drat! Tina thought. She slid into her own sleeping bag and then lay back and let her mind fantasize about Andrew being with her.

* * * * *

Sometime later, Tina woke to find herself sweating and gasping for breath. She knew she had just experienced a horrible nightmare, the details of which were even then fading from her consciousness. But she knew there had been men chasing her in the darkness and fog; big, evil men who wished to harm her. Then she had found she was no longer on the causeway but was wading in shallow water full of reeds. The reeds dragged at her ankles and snared her feet as she ran. Then she fell and had trouble getting up and the men came closer. They loomed as monstrous black shapes in the mist.

They are going to kill me and throw my body into the lake, her terrified mind told her, and she redoubled her frantic efforts to escape.

But suddenly she was lost in the fog, with no idea which was the closest shore to make for. And the water was deeper, waist deep, then chest deep. And there were ripples arrowing towards her and long dark shapes in the water and the men behind and -and she could not bear it any longer and woke up, trembling and perspiring.

What a horrible nightmare, she thought, wondering if she had screamed of if that had just been part of the dream too.

For a few minutes she lay and looked anxiously out of the tent. Outside was still very dark and shrouded in thick fog. It was so dense that she could barely make out the other tents and the vehicles were just black blobs.

Anyone could just sneak up, she thought. Then she shook her head and told herself not to be silly. *Don't be paranoid,* she told herself. Her rational brain told her that the crooks would be far more likely to do something to her at her own home. *If they know where I live.*

That got her speculating about Neville again and then she tensed. *What was that noise? Was it an aircraft?*

No. It was just the wind in the trees. She shivered and then snuggled further into her sleeping bag as an icy wind began shredding the fog, pulling it into swirling streamers. Within a quarter of an hour the fog had all gone and a clear sky showed, dotted with the brilliance of millions of stars. The only sound was the rather eerie whistling of the wind through the trees.

Tina lay and watched this, too scared to go back to sleep until she had calmed down. Instead she lay and thought about her life and how to get Andrew to kiss her.

And to take me to the dance.

She fell asleep eventually, but it was so cold that she did not sleep well. She woke in the morning feeling stiff and slightly ill. But she had not forgotten her plan and twice during the morning she 'casually' mentioned the fete and the dance. But Andrew did not seem to take the hint and made no contribution to discussions about how Tina's class could make money at the fete.

It was a clear, cold sunny day but the wind had whipped up waves as much as half a metre high and these threw up showers of spray when the boats were taken out for more fishing. The attempt did not last long before the boats were back. Nor were there many birds to observe, just a few high-flying skeins of storks and ducks which vanished to the northwest.

By mid-morning the group were busy dismantling their camp and packing up. As she helped load the Jackaroo Tina kept glancing at Andrew, hoping they might get away on their own. But no opportunity or excuse presented itself and he made no moves toward intimacy. He did give her several very approving looks, but Tina put that down to the fact that the sweater she was wearing really emphasised her bust and that made her blush and feel very self-conscious.

The expedition headed home at 1100hrs and was in Mareeba by 1130hrs. There was a stop to have refreshments and at that point the Creswells went off on their own. By the time Tina's family started off again she was beginning to feel anxious about whether Andrew would ask to see her again. All the way back to Cairns Tina sat beside him and kept up a bright and happy chatter and commented on every bird she saw.

I hope he doesn't think I am just an empty-headed 'bird brain', she thought, aware that most of his conversation was single words or short sentences.

But she was rewarded when they reached Andrew's house. He thanked her parents very much, said a cheerful goodbye to Garth, who had by then become his firm admirer, and then turned to Tina.

"Thanks for asking me," he said. "I would like to take you out again, if your parents don't mind."

Tina blushed and felt very pleased, even as she said, "What if I mind?" Her parents both laughed and said they were happy, and Tina then nodded and could hardly speak.

Andrew said, "I will see you at school then and we can work out where to go."

"Yes please," Tina answered, hoping he meant they might sit together as well. She also hoped for at least a goodbye peck on the cheek, but he just stood back and waved and she was left unsatisfied again. Still she was happy.

I am making progress, she told herself. *Mum and Dad accept Andrew as my boyfriend, and they like him and trust him. I just hope he isn't too honourable.*

Chapter 17

AT THE SWIMMING POOL

On Monday morning there was another assembly and yet again the principal reminded the school about the fete, now only three weeks away. Tina immediately thought of the dance and glanced along the line of students to where Andrew sat. She hoped to catch his eye to give him a hint but instead she saw he was looking the other way and whispering to Blake. It must have been a joke or smart comment as Blake nodded and chuckled.

Oh, silly boys! she thought in exasperation.

The dance began to loom larger in Tina's imagination and hopes, and while sitting in class she constructed fantasies about it. She saw herself gliding into a huge ballroom on Andrew's arm, he dressed in a smart, white, full-dress naval uniform with medals and she in... in what?

What will I wear? she thought. Quickly she made an inventory in her head of the gowns and dresses that she owned that might be appropriate. *Or that might still fit me,* she thought ruefully. With something of a shock she realised she did not have a dress to match her expectations.

Despite that she continued to picture the scene; the other students, the girls who looked down on her first looking jealous and then spiteful; the young men looking awe-struck at her beauty (Well, maybe just admiring); the crowd parting and every head turning and her taking Andrew's hand. It was all nice fantasy, but she had to give a wry smile every time she remembered that Andrew still had not asked her to be his partner.

Not that you need a partner, she reminded herself. It was, after all, just a school dance and most students would go on their own or with groups of friends rather than as couples. But it was nice to dream about.

She did not see Andrew during the breaks, only in class and between classes. Then he was friendly and spoke to her but only in a seemingly casual way.

He doesn't want to be teased by his mates for taking me out, she thought gloomily, knowing that some of the crueller males (and females) considered her to be a bit of a joke. She had once overheard Vincent and

Price talking, and it had clearly been about her. Vincent had said with an unpleasant snicker that she was 'Built for comfort, not for speed'. Quite apart from its crude sexual overtones the comment had really hurt and Tina felt tears prickle at the thought of it.

I'm not that fat! she tried to tell herself.

On Tuesday Tina saw Andrew and his friends talking to the army cadets during the morning break. Later, just before they went in to class, Andrew came up to her and said, "I've just been talking to Graham Kirk and his mates and have a good idea for where to go for our Duke of Edinburgh hike."

"Where?" Tina asked, not particularly interested but pleased that Andrew was talking to her.

"From Davies Creek over the mountains to Lake Tinaroo," Andrew replied.

Tina knew where Lake Tinaroo was but wasn't sure about Davies Creek, so she asked. Andrew said, "It is off the main highway between Kuranda and Mareeba. Graham is going to bring me some maps so we can plan it in detail. It sounds good."

"Has he done it?"

"Yes, last year," Andrew answered.

At that moment the bell went so they had to leave it at that but it was also progress of a sort. Tina went off to class and sat alternately doing her schoolwork and sketching gowns and dresses.

I will ask Mum if I can try to make one, she thought.

She had the basic skills from school Home Economics but knew she would need help. She also knew that there was no way her parents would pay for a new ball gown just for a school dance in Year 10.

I will only get that for my Year 12 Formal, she told herself.

That evening at home she checked her wardrobe and found that her conclusions were right; there was nothing suitable that fitted her. Feeling fairly fragile she took the problem to her mother and then floated the idea of sewing her own gown.

Her mother looked surprised but after some persuading warmed to the idea. "Do you have a design and colour in mind?" she asked.

Tina had vague ideas so mother and daughter spent an hour or so studying pictures of gowns and her mother promised to see what patterns she could buy the next day. That put Tina into a good mood, but she went to bed with the depressing thought that Andrew still had not mentioned the dance.

But he had at least thought about their next date, and when he found her alone in the library at lunch time he again suggested the movies. "You choose which movie," he added.

Tina agreed at once, happy just to be asked. Then he went on, "I have the maps for the hike. Would you like to see them?"

"Yes please," Tina answered. So Andrew sat down and opened the maps and showed her. They were army topographic maps and she was unfamiliar with them but after a while began to understand what she was looking at.

Andrew pointed to a thin red line that wriggled over the brown contours indicating a large mountain. "Graham said that this road doesn't exist here, but he has told me how to get across this bit. All the rest is either a good road or an old timber track."

"And we have to carry everything we need," Tina added. She was a bit worried about that, not being sure of her own strength and stamina.

"Peter Bronsky said he would give us one of the 'What to Take' lists that the army cadets give to their people for hikes," Andrew answered.

As they talked Tina kept thinking, *How can I hint about the dance?* But she was too shy to openly ask to be taken. *Oh! How can I make him see it?* she wondered.

No plan came to her, but that afternoon the dance was on the top of her mind as her mother had brought home a dozen dress designs that were of the type she thought suitable. Tina didn't agree with her in a couple of cases, but she found one she particularly liked and her mother then measured her and promised to take her shopping on Thursday evening to buy material and thread. That night, as she lay in bed, Tina was able to clothe her dreams in the dress she wanted, a pale blue silk one that was nearly full length and which did not emphasize her bust too much (Just enough cleavage to be respectable and to attract some attention; and which took the viewer's attention away from her waist and behind).

On Wednesday during morning break Tina sat under the school in her usual place with Sarah and other friends. She ate her food and hoped that Andrew would appear. But she saw no sign of him and was left to observe the goings-on of Barbara and her friends.

What a mob of little teasers, Tina thought, noting the top buttons of blouses undone and the skirts pulled up as high as they could go without showing their knickers. *But Barbara has lovely long legs,* she conceded.

At lunch time Tina again sat in hope but finally gave up and took herself off to the library to do some research for an assignment. While she was sitting in a quiet corner Andrew finally appeared. "There you are," he said. "I looked everywhere for you."

That mollified Tina a bit and she felt happier when he sat next to her. He had the 'What to Take' list and she quickly scanned it. It was the sorts of things she expected: clothes, packs, water bottles, food and bedding and so on but there were a few items she did not understand and had not thought of so she discussed these with Andrew.

"Can I make a copy for Sarah?" she asked.

"Of course," Andrew replied. They made their way to the student photocopier and made four copies. While they stood there Tina glanced around the room, hoping that some of her friends (Or her enemies!) might see her with Andrew. But there were only a couple of Year 8s she did not know and one Year 11 girl who was a library monitor.

The meeting was over all too soon for Tina. She thanked Andrew and went to give a copy of the list to Sarah. During the afternoon classes she returned to day-dreaming about school dances, dresses, dates, and whether a hike over the mountains offered any scope for romance. Then she sighed and shook her head.

No. It will be a Navy Cadet activity, she told herself, knowing that the rules forbad any fraternization at cadets.

That evening Tina sat with her mother and they worked on the details for her new dress. More measurements were made and calculations about how much cloth was required. But Tina was still anxious. "Mum, do you think I have time to make this?"

"How long to this dance?" her mother asked.

Tina did a quick calculation. "Only seventeen days," she replied.

Her mother smiled. "We will make it."

A relieved Tina went to bed with more happy fantasies, and a gnawing sense of frustration at Andrew's inaction. *He hasn't even kissed me yet,* she thought. That got her fretting that perhaps he found her so unattractive that he did not want to. Her rational mind told her that was nonsense; that she was quite pretty, but in the dark of the small hours of the morning it was cold comfort.

Thursday was a better day, not at school, which was ordinary, but afterwards, when she went shopping with her mother. Tina found it a delight to see all the types of cloth and to feel their textures. When they finally selected the blue silk for her dress, she thought it was the smoothest, nicest cloth she had ever felt.

At home she and her mother set to work, her mother commandeering the dining room table and banishing dinner to side tables and kitchen benches. Garth as usual had to comment. "I thought we weren't to eat while watching the TV," he muttered.

"Don't you be a Mister Smarty-Pants, or you won't get any dinner at all," his mother retorted. "Tina needs a new dress more than you need to sit at this table."

Garth snorted. "Huh! An old garbage bag will do," he replied.

The jibe hurt and Tina wished yet again that she was slender and beautiful. The work of measuring, pinning the paper patterns to the cloth, and then carefully cutting the pieces went on for several hours and Tina went to bed satisfied that real progress had been made, and dissatisfied with Andrew.

He must get the hint soon, she thought.

But when she saw him on Friday all he mentioned was the arrangements for the date the following night. Exasperated she finally said, "Are you going to the school fete?"

"Yes, but we have Navy Cadets on the Friday night," Andrew replied.

"What about the dance on the Saturday night?"

Andrew shrugged and replied, "I suppose so. Are you going?"

"I'd love to go," Tina answered. But she could not bring herself to say, 'with you'.

In response to that Andrew just nodded and said, "OK," which left her wondering if he had understood. But she did not want to push it at that moment. *At least the idea has been accepted,* she told herself. With two weeks to go she thought she could persuade him to do what she desired.

That evening at Navy Cadets there was a long discussion with the officers and the other D of E candidates about possible expeditions. Andrew presented the plan suggested by Graham Kirk and once they had studied the maps and measured the distances (about 30 kilometres) there was general consensus that it would do. Lt Ryan noted the details and said he would do the checking and paperwork with the Department of Natural Resources as most of the area was in a World Heritage Area.

There was then more Morse Code training, this time of a more practical nature with cadets in pairs spaced along each side of the parade ground sending short messages to each other by flashing light. Tina enjoyed it but found it harder to do than she had imagined.

She was also interested to note that Lt Ryan was adamant that when using a torch they not click the torch on and off. "It is not how they do it on ships, and it tends to make the bulb blow," he explained. "On ships they turn the light on and leave it on but it is hidden behind the shutters. To send a message they open and close the shutters. That is how we will do it, except that we don't have proper signal lamps so you will just hold a piece of thick cardboard in front of the torch, then turn the torch on and take the cardboard away and then put it back over the front again."

That made sense to Tina and it actually worked quite well. What was difficult was having the torch pointing in the right direction and in being able to read the pattern of short flashes and long flashes, the dots and dashes. They found it took two people at each end, one to read the dots and dashes and the other to send. At the receiving end it needed one to read the pattern and the other to write it down. The cadets also found they needed to write out the complete messages. It all provided an hour of quite amusing activity.

At the end of the night Tina was drawn into a conversation with a group of others including Andrew, Blake, Jennifer Jervis and Carmen. The discussion was over a planned social gathering for a swim at the Tobruk Swimming Pool the following afternoon. Andrew liked the idea and turned to Tina. "Would you like to come?" he asked.

Tina had already thought about it. "We are going out that night," she reminded him, not wanting to be tired for the main event.

"That will be OK," Andrew replied. "A swim will be relaxing. I'd like to go, and I'd like you to be there."

Tina flushed with pleasure at that and to divert the embarrassment she said, "You just want to see the girls in their bikinis."

Andrew grinned. "Too right I do!" he replied, "And you. You look really attractive in your bathers."

The compliment sent a warm glow of pleasure and embarrassment through Tina. She blushed and knew she was looking coy. "I will have to ask mum and dad," she replied.

"We will do that now," Andrew said. He at once turned and walked over to where the parents were waiting outside the gate. Tina was so surprised that she was left behind and had to hurry after him. She did want to go with him and got all anxious when he asked her mother. As he did, his own mother said, "You haven't asked me."

Andrew smiled and said, "I am going to the swimming pool tomorrow afternoon Mum."

"Don't be cheeky!" Andrew's mother replied, but she smiled and then Tina knew it would be alright. Her own mother smiled as well and said, "As long as you young people don't tire yourselves out before you go out."

"We won't," Andrew assured her. He then turned to Tina and for a moment she thought he was going to kiss her. But he just took her hands and smiled.

That put Tina in a good mood for the remainder of the night and she slept very well, with happy dreams. The next morning she was a-squirm with impatience and set to work on her chores without being prompted. Cleaning the bird cages was the main task and she did this quickly, only remembering Neville when she noted two more cockatiels in his aviary. But she was too happy and it was too nice a day for her to spare thoughts on what were only vague suspicions.

After lunch she put on her dark blue one-piece bathers and then dressed in shorts and T-shirt. Her mother drove her to the swimming pool at 2pm and told her she would pick her up at 4pm. "Two hours will be long enough. It is winter so the water will be cold and you need time to get ready to go out," her mother said.

Tina did not disagree. She waved as her mother drove off and then made her way inside, but not without some anxiety. She had half hoped some of the others might be waiting outside but none were to be seen.

Andrew could have met me, she thought.

Once she was through the office and kiosk at the entrance Tina stopped and looked around, hoping to see Andrew or her friends. There were plenty of people there, even though it was supposedly a winter day. In Far North Queensland that only mattered when it was overcast or raining, which wasn't very often. She saw there were people in the pool, on the grandstands on the far side, and sitting or lying in groups or singly on the lawn among the garden beds.

To her relief, she saw Andrew siting on his towel over near a garden bed. He waved and she hurried over. "Where's Carmen?" she asked.

"Not coming. She has too much homework," Andrew answered.

"What about the others?" she asked, looking around.

Andrew shrugged. "Haven't seen them yet," he said.

Tina spread her towel and then somewhat self-consciously peeled off her T-shirt. She was immediately aware of her breasts. The tops of them filled the lower periphery of her vision and when she glanced down there seemed to be altogether too much exposed.

Oh dear! Have I made a mistake wearing these bathers? she wondered.

But a glance showed Andrew looking at her with apparent interest so despite a hot blush of embarrassment Tina bent over and pulled down her shorts. She knew that when she bent forward Andrew was granted an eyeful of bosom but that just made her blush some more, even as she smiled inside.

I want to get his attention, she told herself.

But she didn't want him to look too much at her waist and behind, so she sat down quickly and then dug out a tube of sunscreen. "Would you rub some on my back please," she asked.

Andrew nodded and she noted that he licked his lips and appeared nervous. His eyes kept glancing to her bosom and he hesitated. Then he carefully and gently began to smear the cream over her shoulders and the exposed part of her back. Just for a moment Tina had the wicked wish that she could roll the top down so that he could rub it over her breasts as well but then she blushed with shame at her own shameless thoughts and could only ask him not to miss anywhere.

She then did the same for him. It was the first time she had really felt his skin and she enjoyed the experience. It was smooth and tanned and the muscles felt firm and good. *He is very fit and handsome,* she thought, smiling at him and wondering what to talk about. She was secretly thrilled that the others hadn't arrived yet and that she was alone with Andrew. But she could not think of what to talk about.

Andrew saved her from embarrassment by saying, "What about a dip?"

"Good idea," Tina replied. But she then deliberately waited till Andrew was standing before holding up her hands. He smiled and took them and pulled her to her feet. But he then let go as they walked across to the water. Tina tested the water and found it a bit chilly. To get it over with quickly she held her nose and jumped in. For the next few minutes she and Andrew swam lazily around before coming to rest against the side. Tina turned on her back and hooked her elbows into the drain along the edge and paddled with her feet, talking light chatter and looking idly around as she did.

Then her gaze settled on a group in the water on the other side of the pool. "There is that Barbara Brassington and some of her friends," she commented.

Andrew looked and nodded, then said, "With some of the Year 12 boys."

Tina saw that he was right. She noted Nigel Cressly, Warwick Grey and then Mike Masters. With them were two Year 9 girls: Karen Hart and Fiona Davies. Fiona was an attractive blonde.

Mike is very handsome. I can see why the girls want to be with him, Tina thought.

Andrew then said, "Here comes Willy the Mad Scientist and Stephen Bell."

Tina looked and saw Willy and Stephen walking in through the entrance. They stopped and looked around and then walked over to join a group that she had not noticed because they were almost hidden by another garden bed. It included Stick Morton and his Year 3 sister Marjorie. With them was another Year 8 girl. She had glasses that looked like the bottom of a coke bottle. The other boy Tina recognised as an air cadet in Year 9.

As Willy and Stephen walked across the lawn Tina heard a peal of laughter from across the pool. She glanced that way and saw that Barbara had climbed out and was now standing on the edge looking down. She wore a white one-piece swimsuit and Tina had to admit that she was very shapely with a trim waist and nice curvy hips.

And big boobs too, she noted, comparing them with her own but feeling smugly confident. She then looked back towards the group on the lawn.

As Willy and Stephen sat down, Tina noted Willy cast several lingering glances towards Barbara. *He fancies her,* she decided. Then she watched the by-play as the two boys sat down. She noted that Marjorie wore a polka dot bikini that looked very skimpy. *Heavens, she has got big boobs for a Year 8!* she thought. Then she saw Marjorie lean forward and wobble her bosom in the loosely tied top. *She is doing that deliberately,* she thought. *Oh, what a little tease!*

Stephen sat and said something to Marjorie which made her peal with laughter. Tina saw her put her hand on Stephen's arm. Then laughter and shouting from behind her drew Tina's attention back to the other side of the pool. She saw that the Year 12 boys had pushed Barbara and her tarty friend Karen in and were ducking them. In the process they put their arms around the girls and appeared to give them both a good grope. Tina saw Cressly put his arm across Barbara's breasts, causing her to shriek and giggle. The sight aroused a conflicting mix of emotions in Tina. Part of her did not approve at all and made her purse her lips. But she also felt a strong sense of arousal and jealousy and wished it was her with Andrew. That thought made her burn with shame and desire.

Andrew nudged her. "Never mind them," he said. "Let's have an ice cream."

Tina readily agreed, so Andrew heaved himself out. He then leaned down and took her hands and helped her to climb out. They then walked back to their clothes. Andrew took out his wallet and led her across to the kiosk. As they did, Tina noted Stephen looking at them, so she looked away and felt both pleased and self-conscious.

I wish there were other Year 10s here to see me with Andrew, she thought.

Andrew smiled and waved to Willy and Stephen. They both waved back.

After buying ice creams, Andrew and Tina strolled back across the lawn to their towels and lay down side by side and continued talking to each other. But despite their apparent intimacy, Tina felt restless.

I wish Andrew would hold me; and when is he ever going to kiss me? she worried.

Chapter 18

FIRST KISS

For 10 minutes or so, Tina lay beside Andrew in the pleasant winter sunshine. She chattered and pretended to be happy but was actually fretting about their relationship and how to move it forward.

How can I suggest he take me to the school dance without making it too obvious? she wondered. Then, seeing another couple embracing and kissing over on the lawn, she sighed and again wondered when Andrew would kiss her.

She idly noted Willy, Stephen and their group make their way to the pool. She noted that Willy looked quite normal, but that Stephen looked gawky and was quite hairy. They all jumped in and began horsing around. Tina noted that Willy stayed on the sidelines and that he spent much of the time looking hungrily towards Barbara and her group, until they left the pool. That confirmed her suspicion that Willy was sweet on Barbara.

The others splashed water on each other and Tina several times saw Stephen duck Marjorie; and in such a way as to get a good handful each time. She appeared to enjoy this and laughed and made comments to encourage Stephen even more. Tina pursed her lips and again felt confused and embarrassed. She also noted Willy watching this with a sour look on his face.

Either Willy doesn't approve of that sort of behaviour, or he is jealous, Tina thought.

Andrew touched her arm. "What about another swim? I need to have some exercise. I'm getting unfit."

"Oh you are not!" Tina cried in disbelief, eyeing his rippling muscles with approval.

"I am, and good divers need to be very fit," Andrew answered.

Tina knew that Andrew was a qualified diver and that he had been involved in some dramatic adventures out on the Great Barrier Reef. She said, "You look pretty fit to me."

"I'm not," Andrew replied ruefully. "I used to be able to swim the whole length of the pool underwater but now I feel like I would be flat out getting across."

"Oh you could not!" Tina said, wanting to believe but finding it hard to do so. She had never seen anyone swim that far underwater.

"I could," Andrew replied shortly, nettled at her tone of disbelief.

"Show me then," Tina challenged.

Andrew nodded. "OK, I'll try. We need a swim anyway. I'm starting to get hot," he said.

Tina was happy to do that but again she waited until Andrew was standing before she put her hands up for him to help her up. This time though he did not let go and to her delight held her hand as they strolled over to the edge of the pool. Andrew led the way and went to where Willy stood in the shallows.

Willy looked up and Andrew said, "Hello Willy, having a good day?"

Willy nodded and said yes but his answer did not sound very convincing to Tina. Andrew let go of Tina's hand and she bent down to sit on the edge of the pool. As she did, she realised that she was granting Willy a good view of her cleavage. She blushed and felt both the heat of her embarrassment and of the thrill of being naughty. But when Andrew just stood talking, she decided to challenge him. She said to Andrew, "Well, go on! You said you could, now prove it."

"Prove what?" Willy asked.

Andrew looked embarrassed and did not answer, so Tina did. "Swim the length of the pool under water," she said.

Stephen, Marjorie and Stick joined them, and Stephen called, "Well go on Andrew, have a go."

Andrew made a face and said, "I'm a bit out of training."

Stephen looked at Tina and a grin spread over his face. He said, "Tina will give you a kiss if you can do it."

Tina opened her mouth to deny this, but the idea seemed to explode in her head and she felt a surge of delight. *I don't need that sort of incentive to give Andrew a kiss,* she thought.

She instantly knew it was a good idea so did not say no. To her secret joy the others all joined in, daring Andrew and teasing them both. Tina smiled at Andrew and he gave an embarrassed smile back, and then said, "Will you?"

Tina nodded, drawing loud cries from the group. After more teasing and encouragement Andrew shrugged and walked off to the far end of the pool. As he did, Tina studied his physique and knew she was in love. He looked very fit and with his broad shoulders, slim hips and good muscles she knew he cut a handsome figure.

Andrew spent a minute or so flexing muscles and taking deep breaths before he dived in. Tina watched with anxious interest, hoping Andrew could do it but doubtful. *I hope he makes it,* she thought. *And not just because he might give me a kiss. I don't want his pride hurt and him humiliated.* She began to wish she hadn't dared him.

The pool was a standard Olympic size, 50 metres long, and she knew she would not even be able to swim half that underwater. *I might get across if I dived,* she thought.

Anxiously, she watched his dim shape go past. At that point he looked to still have a long way to go and her anxiety shot up. She started to breathe deeply with worry and chewed on her knuckles. The others began to call encouragement, which she thought was silly as Andrew could not hear them.

But he did it. As Andrew surfaced at the other end, they all cheered. Andrew climbed out and walked back, water dripping off rippling muscles and a smile on his face. Tina felt both embarrassed and excited. She stood up and Stephen called, "Now give him his reward Tina."

Tina blushed some more but stood and waited for Andrew. He stopped facing her and took her hands. For half a minute or so they just stood and looked at each other, both breathing fast. To Tina it seemed that time had slowed down and her whole focus narrowed down to just Andrew's face, and particularly his eyes. They seemed to be huge pools of sparkling blue that peered deep into her very being. She waited with her heart pounding with hope. But still he hesitated so she decided to give him just a tiny bit of encouragement. She closed her eyes and puckered up.

Andrew leaned forward and gave her a gentle kiss on the lips but kept his arms by his side. As they drew apart Stephen called, "That wasn't a kiss! Have a proper one. Do you need me to show you how?"

This drew more cheers and jeers and made Tina blush. Andrew raised an eyebrow and Tina gave a tiny nod and stepped forward and put her arms around his shoulders. The pair came together in a proper embrace and this time there was real passion in the kiss.

He does like me! Tina thought as she savoured the experience, the skin on skin, the scents and tastes and the feel of his strong arms and muscly chest.

He can kiss me for ever and ever, she thought, tightening her muscles and pressing her body hard against his.

His breathing increased and she felt his body responding. Knowing that she was succeeding as a woman made her feel even better. They kept on kissing. This caused the watchers to call encouragement and to tease.

I don't care who is watching; or what they think, Tina thought, the arousal surging in her body and making her want even more.

But out of curiosity she did open her eyes. The first person she saw was Barbara. She and her friends were watching from the other side of the pool and Tina noted that she had an arm around Cressly's neck and appeared to be snuggled against him. For a moment their eyes met and Barbara smiled.

By then others were calling either encouragement or teasing jibes. Stephen called, "Come up for air you two!"

Then Stick yelled, "They need cooling down!" he began to splash water on them.

Others joined in and cold water and the knowledge that they were a public spectacle broke the spell. As Andrew and Tina at last drew breathlessly apart she saw a look of wonder in his eyes.

Delightedly she thought, *I really am in love.*

Without a word Andrew took Tina's hand and started walking away. Tina happily went with him, but she blushed at the mostly good-natured laughter that followed them. This developed into a noisy water fight when Noddy asked who would give him a kiss if he could swim the length underwater. Tina glanced back and saw him look hopefully at the other Year 8 girl but she curled her lip and moved away. Stick and Stephen both jeered and proceeded to splash Noddy.

Tina did not care. She lay down beside Andrew on their towels and just wanted him to hold her and to kiss her again. But he didn't. Instead he kept looking at her with a look of surprised wonder on his face. Once she thought he was going to apologise, which she knew would have disappointed her.

I want him to kiss me again. Can't he see that, the silly boy? she thought.

It was obvious to her that he was aroused and that he had enjoyed the kiss and that he was pleased. But he was also shy and she suspected that the incident had given him a bit of a shock and that he was pulling back emotionally to regain his self-control. She decided to give him the space.

I don't want him to think he is being pushed, she told herself.

So they lay and chatted. It was very relaxing as the sun was just warm enough to not feel like it was burning and there was gentle breeze. After about half an hour their peace was disturbed by the others as they climbed out and returned to their towels. Willy trailed along at the rear, looking unhappy. After some discussion with the others he and Stephen went to the kiosk. Tina took the opportunity to go to the toilet.

When she returned a few minutes later, Tina noted with some disapproval that Marjorie was lying on her front and had undone her bikini top. When she reached up to take a packet of crisps from Stephen, she showed most of her breasts. Tina shook her head and noted that even when Marjorie was lying down her breasts bulged out from under her in a most enticing and provocative way. She also noticed that Willy was pretending not to look but was actually flicking glances at Marjorie every few seconds.

So, does he fancy Barbara or Marjorie; or is he just being a male? Tina wondered.

Stephen sat beside Marjorie and she leaned against him while they ate and chatted. Marjorie kept raising herself up on her elbows so that almost all of her breasts could be seen; and that irritated and embarrassed Tina as she sat next to Andrew because she could see that he was also watching. Marjorie appeared to be giving all of her attention to Stephen and even rested her hand on his thigh. Tina began to mentally call her unkind names, then stopped. *I am just being catty and jealous,* she thought, knowing that she wanted to snuggle against Andrew in that way.

When the food was consumed, Stick suggested another swim. Most of the group went back into the pool but Stephen and Marjorie stayed on their towels and began to caress and kiss. That made Tina feel uncomfortable (or was it jealous?), so she suggested another swim to Andrew. He agreed and they made their way the pool and jumped in. While they swam lazily up and down, Tina yearned for Andrew to grab her, to play games with her, to kiss her. She watched with envy as the others indulged in a lot of horseplay that involved ducking and grabbing the girls in their group.

They began a game of tiggy, and Tina saw Willy pursue the other Year 8 girl and tag her. Then he clung to the edge to get his breath back. At that moment, Stick called out: "Come on you two. Stop that and come and play."

Tina raised herself to look across the lawn. She saw that Marjorie and Stephen were still lying on their towels behind the garden bed with Stephen lying on his back and Marjorie half on top of him. She still had no top on so her bare breasts were resting on Stephen's chest. They were kissing.

Stephen stopped kissing and turned to look at them. "We are playing," he said with a grin.

"Not that sort of game," Stick replied. "Come on gang, let's throw cold water on them."

Willy joined in the scramble out of the pool and raced across the lawn with water cupped in his hands. Marjorie cried out and raised herself to run. She seemed to forget she was topless so that her breasts hung fully exposed. Tina was scandalised and also peeved that Andrew was watching.

From nearby, where Barbara's group sat, Nigel Cressly cried out, "Holy mackerel! Look at the knockers on that that little Year Eight! They are nearly as big as yours, Barbara."

Tina was shocked. She glanced at Barbara and saw an embarrassed look on her face. This changed to obvious hurt when Warwick Grey said, "Well, you'd know, Nigel!"

Tina could not decide which way to look and kept glancing from one group to the other. She watched in amazement as Marjorie ran around for a few seconds with her breasts bouncing while she chased Stick. Then she appeared to notice her state of undress. She covered her breasts with her arms and bent to pick up her towel.

Tina shook her head. "What a rude little exhibitionist," she muttered.

"Not so little either," Andrew replied with a chuckle.

"She's a cheap tart!" Tina snapped.

But then she felt guilty as she knew she did not really mind Andrew seeing. She knew for certain that one day she would want Andrew to see her breasts. *But not in public and showing off like that,* she told herself.

Andrew blushed at her rebuke. "She will be in trouble with the management," he suggested.

"They will all be in trouble if they keep acting like that." Tina commented.

The group were now running around the garden beds and flicking at each other with towels. Stephen managed to hold off their attacks for a time, but then Noddy yelled, "Let's chuck Steve in the water and cool him down properly."

Stephen was grabbed and hustled to the pool and tossed in. When that was done the boys returned to their towels. By then Marjorie had put on her bikini top. She and her friend went off to the toilet and the boys lay down, laughing and joking.

Tina next noted an unhappy looking Barbara walking towards the change rooms with her bag and towel. *She looks a bit upset. I wonder if that relationship is not working either?* Tina thought.

Andrew glanced at his watch and said, "It is nearly four. Time to go mate."

Tina was not sure if she liked being called mate or not. Certainly she wanted to mate with Andrew, but she did not just want to be another friend. But she agreed and reluctantly she pulled on her T-shirt and shorts, gathered her things and then walked with Andrew to the front entrance. As they did, she hoped he would hold her hand, but he didn't and she began to worry that he had been put off by the display of emotion.

Oh, I hope he kisses me again tonight, she thought.

Chapter 19

HIGH HOPES

Three hours later, Tina sat beside Andrew in the movies. She was watching the film but with no particular interest. Her main focus was on Andrew. After their first kiss she had gone home in a state close to euphoria. During the time at home while she had tea, showered, dressed and prepared, she had been imagining the evening with high hopes.

I must get him to kiss me again, she thought.

She was aware that she was in an unusual mood, that the events and sights of the afternoon had aroused her in unfamiliar and unsettling ways so that now she felt as though her whole body was tingling with anticipation. She yearned to be held, to be touched.

He can even touch me in some naughty places if he wants, she thought.

But so far he had been a perfect gentleman. Too perfect, she decided. He hadn't even held her hand as they walked from the car to the theatre. Now at last he had taken her hand, but only in the darkness and privacy of the theatre.

Maybe he doesn't want others to see him with me? she thought, the old nagging worry about her appearance resurfacing. *At last he is moving his right arm in preparation to put it around my shoulders,* she thought as Andrew changed position.

To her immense relief, he did place his arm around her shoulders. Then there was no more movement for another few minutes. *Do something!* she thought, knowing that the movie only lasted another hour or so. Tina sensed that she was perhaps being a bit unreasonable, but her instinct was to leave it to the male. *If he isn't brave enough to find out what I like, then he is not good enough for me,* she told herself.

Then he held her close and rested his head against hers. She felt that wonderful sensation of closeness and of being held and allowed her head to rest on his cheek and shoulder. *It feels nice. He feels nice,* she thought.

To her delight, he squeezed her shoulders a few times and then moved his body slightly sideways. Tina was now attuned to every slight change and every nuance and hoped he was preparing to kiss her.

To check she glanced in his direction and saw he was looking at her with a very intent expression on his face. He was plainly anxious, and she assumed he was mustering his courage to make a move. She saw him lick his lips and then his left arm reached across her front and took her right hand. She was delighted and quickly took a firm grip. Their clasped hands ended up in her lap.

Then suddenly he was kissing her. She could not quite remember how it came about but she seemed to just melt in his arms and their lips met. A tingling wave of excitement swept through her and she savoured the feel, the scent and the sensations. *He smells nice, and he tastes nice,* she thought.

That was a real relief as she had heard some horror stories from her friends about boys that they had kissed who had bad breath or body odour.

As mum says, a girl's got to kiss a lot of toads before she finds a prince, she thought.

That made her smile and she opened her eyes and saw he was smiling too. They kissed again, for longer and with more heat. Tina became aware that her heart was hammering rapidly and that her breathing was rapid and shallow. She felt suddenly weak and flushed and a curious tingling, itchy sensation coursed through her body and down to her thighs.

Oh this is nice! she thought. She returned his kisses with pleasure and pressed herself against him. After about 10 minutes of this they were both flushed and panting. She knew she was becoming aroused and part of that knowledge aroused her more. The other part began to scare her. *We don't want to get out of control,* she told herself.

Then the movie came to an end. Tina could have wept with frustration. *Oh! Drat!* she thought. Andrew released her and sat back to rearrange his shirt and hair before the lights came on. Tina did likewise but already her mind was plotting the next move. *Another date, or perhaps meeting after school?* she mused. Then an impish thought crossed her mind: *Or at school!* She knew that boy-girl stuff was against the school rules and that added another level of delicious dare to the idea.

Or the dance, she remembered. But how to remind him and manoeuvre it so that they went together?

When her mother arrived to take her home, Tina was very happy. Andrew stood holding her hand and this time, before he climbed out of the car, he leaned over and gave her a kiss. She put her arms out to hold him and kissed him again and then blushed when her mother, who was watching in the rear-view mirror, said, "That is enough, children! You've had hours for smooching. Poor Andrew won't be able to sleep."

I hope not, Tina thought. She giggled and said goodnight. As they drove away and she waved, her mother said, "It was a good night then?"

"Yes, Mum."

"Good, but don't rush it. You have plenty of time."

Tina answered "Yes, Mum" but she didn't believe her. Now that she was starting to experience romance she wanted more and felt an intense desire explore the other aspects of love. Dimly she understood that this could lead to her and Andrew doing some very naughty things but that did not bother her.

That is what couples do, she told herself.

In her mind it was all so romantic, and she lay in bed fantasising for several hours. She wanted to see Andrew on the Sunday but that was no to be. So it was a frustrating day of church and chores and she got all grumpy and irritable.

Her mother was not sympathetic. "You need to get more sleep and then you won't be a grizzle puss," she said.

Tina was sent to feed the birds. It was only then, when she was in the cage and changing their water that she noted that Neville had four strange birds in his aviary. And only as she returned to the house did she remember her suspicions. But in her romantic mood she just shrugged and brushed them mentally aside as being silly. Back in her room she frowned and then dug out several reference books on birds to try to identify the ones next door.

They turned out to be Blue faced Honeyeaters. That made her frown even more as she was sure they were protected birds and that it was illegal to have them as pets. *Or maybe you need a permit?* she thought. For a few minutes she sat and considered checking with the Wildlife Department.

However on Monday morning she quite forgot about this as her mental focus was on seeing Andrew. She went happily to school knowing he would be there. *He might even sit with me now,* she thought.

But he made no move to do so and Tina was too shy to go and sit with him. He continued to sit with his mates on the other side of the quadrangle. So Tina sat with Sarah and her other friends and tried to pretend she was happy. She was, but in a frustrated sort of way, wishing the relationship was more complete.

Her anxiety about the dance was also increased during assembly that morning when the Principal again reminded them about the fete. *And the dance. How can I get Andrew to take me?* she thought. Until he said something, she did not even want to hint to her friends that she was making a new dress.

At least the dress kept her busy at home because her homework did not. Assisted by her mother she began the cutting, sewing and fitting and by that evening had the main pieces assembled enough to put on for a trial fitting.

Tuesday and Wednesday were the same. The only things that caught Tina's attention were seeing Barbara and her friends flirting with the Year 12 boys and watching Willy moping around, casting wistful glances in Barbara's direction. From the body language Tina deduced that Willy wasn't really on speaking terms with Stephen, who was busy chatting up Marjorie at every opportunity.

By Thursday morning Tina was starting to feel a sense of desperation. She was also anxious about the arrangements for the weekend expedition. She decided that this provided her with a reason to speak to Andrew so at lunch time she excused herself and went looking for him.

He was with Arthur Blake and Luke Karaku down near the oval. When she approached him directly, he looked a little anxious and said, "Hi Tina. How are you?"

"Good. But I am a bit worried too," she admitted.

"Worried?"

"About the expedition on the weekend," she explained.

Blake snorted. "Huh! Nothin' to worry about. It will just be a hike."

"Easy for you to say," Tina replied. "But I have never been on a hike before. I just hope I have the right things and that I can carry it all."

Andrew gave her a reassuring smile. "You will be alright," he said.

At that moment Luke said, "There they are. They are coming in now."

Tina looked in the same direction as Luke, which was out over the school fence. "Who are?" she asked.

"Nigel Cressly and that Barbara chick from Year Nine," Luke replied.

Tina now saw Nigel and Barbara getting out of a red sports car that had just parked among a row of other cars. Barbara looked a bit anxious and Cressly seemed to walk with an exaggerated swagger. "Where have they been?" she asked, then felt foolish at asking such a silly question.

Blake answered her. "Where do you think! Parking somewhere to have a pash."

As he said 'pash' Tina's eyes met Andrew's and she blushed and knew she was blushing. He looked poker-faced and not amused. Tina shook her head. "They will get expelled if the teachers catch them," she commented.

And Barbara will get herself into trouble, she thought.

For a few moments she wondered how Barbara could take such a silly risk. Then she blushed again as it occurred to her that if Andrew wanted her to sneak off for 'a bit of a pash' (or even more) she would probably say yes. She had heard about girls sneaking out to be with boys, but this was the first time she had ever witnessed it. And she doubted if she would be brave enough to take the risk.

But I can live in hope, she thought, and blushed again.

They watched Cressly and Barbara jump the fence and then wander off in different directions. Tina again shook her head and did not know if she felt jealous or sorry for Barbara. But it occurred to her that Andrew was acting as though he did not want her there, so she said a cheery farewell and strolled away as though she didn't have a care in the world.

So her dress progressed but not her relationship. Andrew had not even suggested another date and she did not know what he now thought of her.

Does he regret taking me out? Was I so horrible to kiss that he did not get any pleasure from it? Have I scared him off? she worried.

* * * * *

Thursday and Friday crawled by with no advancement of her cause. She could only hope that he might say something during cadets or on the hike. Friday evening arrived at last and with it a good deal of excitement. On Thursday evening she had gone shopping with her mother to buy the recommended foods and other small items such as torches and batteries and so on that the 'What to Take' list suggested. The plan was for them all to bring their gear to cadets for an inspection.

When Tina tried to cram it all into the pack and the few pouches on her belt she was dismayed. It just would not fit. Her mother did not help by suggesting that she take all sorts of things that were not on the list like pyjamas and an umbrella and a pillow.

"But what will you sleep in?" her mother asked.

Tina knew that much and thought her mother was being a real fusspot. It was on the tip of her tongue to say, 'In the nude' but instead she said, "In our clothes."

"But you can't sleep in dirty clothes!" her mother cried.

"The army cadets do it all the time. They go for three or four days without a bath and they wear the same clothes all the time," Tina replied.

"Urghh!" her mother visibly shuddered. "Oh well. Keep packing dear."

When it was all crammed in Tina got another shock. She stood up and tried to swing the pack on. It was so heavy she almost lost her balance and fell over. *Hmm. This might be more of a challenge than I thought,* she decided.

Her mother drove her to cadets, and she lugged the pack and belt in and got another surprise. Standing talking to the officers were two army cadet officers in uniform: Capt Conkey and Miss McEwen. Miss McEwen was a pretty young lady teacher in her mid-twenties and Tina now saw she was wearing lieutenant's pips.

Tina saluted and said, to Capt Conkey, "Hello Sir. What are you doing here?"

"We are here to help get you people ready for your weekend hike," Capt Conkey answered.

"I thought the army cadets had a weekend... biv... er camp this weekend," Tina replied.

"A bivouac, a camp without tents. Yes, we have. The company has already gone. Lt MacLaren is looking after them with the other officers. We will join them after we finish here," Capt Conkey explained.

Tina rather enjoyed having different instructors in different uniforms. It added both novelty and expertise. After the first parade the D-of-E teams were grouped and their gear all unpacked and inspected. This turned out to be both embarrassing and hilarious. Dimity Bates had packed a pair of pink fluffy slippers ("For wearing in the tent") and Davidson had a rolled-up stretcher that looked to Tina to be quite heavy. Most had extra food and some had frying pans and gas cookers. Hayley Peters had a raincoat and a rain hat and Clinton Evans had three changes of underwear and a set of pyjamas. Anthony Simmonds was found to have a large box of mosquito coils.

"My mother made me!" was his plea.

Tina's moment of embarrassment came when Lt McEwen found a can of hairspray, and a jacket as well as a pullover. "Choose one, but don't take both," Lt McEwen said.

Once the gear had been culled of unnecessary items everything remaining was packed. Then they were instructed to put the packs and belts on. Once again Tina found this a difficult thing to do and she knew she was going to hurt. *I should have followed advice and done some training for this,* she thought. For a moment she contemplated pulling out but then shook her head. *That would mean my group couldn't go. Andrew will not be impressed,* she considered. So she said nothing.

Next, they walked around the hall and the yard for 20 minutes. This drew some humorous or sarcastic jibes from those cadets not going and who were doing normal training, but Tina just shrugged and put up with it. But she was very worried by how quickly her shoulder muscles tired. She found it a relief to swing the pack off.

The straps and stow were then adjusted as seemed necessary after the short walk. Tina made only fractional changes. *My problem is weak muscles, not the way it is packed,* she told herself. The balance had felt alright to her. They then pulled the packs on again and walked for another 15 minutes.

After a 10-minute rest break, the groups assembled for a safety briefing and to check their navigation. As the four groups were all going by different routes that sometimes crossed each other the officers wanted to co-ordinate for the positioning of safety vehicles and radio relay stations. Mobile phone numbers were checked and each group was issued with a small hand-held CB radio. These were on loan from the army cadets and they were cautioned to take spare batteries as well. Each group was issued with a small First Aid Kit and to Tina's relief Blake opted to carry this.

Following a final check that all was prepared they joined the remainder of the unit on the parade ground for dismissal parade. Then Tina lugged her gear out to her mother's car. It was only as she called goodnight to Andrew that she remembered that she had not hinted at the dance. *I must do it during the weekend,* she told herself.

By the time she got home Tina felt tired and some of her shoulder muscles ached. That filled her with a sense of foreboding. *Oh dear! I hope I'm not going to break down so that we don't get over the mountains,* she thought.

She knew that part of the trip, about 3 kilometres, was on a compass course through the jungle and they had been cautioned that if they had an accident or injury during that leg that a vehicle could not drive in to help them. The worry that she might not be able to carry her pack on that part of the hike began to nag at her.

As a result she slept poorly and woke feeling tired. But she had to be out of bed by 0600hrs as they were due to meet at 0730hrs. There was so much to do that Tina could only push her anxieties aside and hurry to get ready. As she did, she began to feel sick in the stomach. She was so upset she could hardly eat the breakfast her mother insisted she have. She was also conscious of a few small aches and twinges in her shoulders.

But she was ready and in the vehicle by the appointed time and all she could do then was hope she was up to it. Her mother drove and they went around picking up the others: Andrew, then Blake, then a very nervous and drawn looking Stella. Seeing Stella made Tina feel slightly better.

She looks more of a wreck than I do, she thought. *So maybe it will be her that breaks down.*

Even so that was small comfort as Tina really wanted the expedition to be a success. So she pretended she was well and happy and chattered cheerfully away as they were driven out to Smithfield and then up the Kuranda Range. From there they went southwest along the Kennedy Highway for about 20 kilometres to the Davies Creek Road. Turning left there they drove south along a bumpy gravel road for 3 kilometres.

As they passed a turn-off on the left, Andrew said, "That is where the army cadets are having their bivouac."

Tina glanced and saw a gate and a road leading down through the bush and a State Forest sign. Her mother kept driving and another 5 kilometres on they came to the Davies Creek National Park. After a brief toilet stop they drove on up over a mountain.

Tina had never been to this area before and she saw that some quite huge mountains towered up ahead and on both sides. As the vehicle rounded a bend, a particularly rugged outcrop appeared through a gap in the trees. She heard Andrew say to Blake, "That is Kahlpahlim Rock and the rocky knob next to it is Lambs Head. That is the mountain Graham and Peter are trying to climb."

"What, this weekend?" Blake queried.

"No. They are at their army cadet bivouac this weekend. I think it is the weekend after the fete," Andrew answered.

The fete! Tina thought. It was only a week away! *Oh, how can I arrange things?* she wondered. It was beginning to look increasingly like she would have to be direct and ask.

The gravel road levelled out and ran through a forest of tall she-oaks and then entered dense tropical rainforest. Tina had known this was where they were going, but once they entered the gloomy shadows in under the trees she felt oppressed and a gnawing sense of anxiety began to chew at her insides.

All too soon the vehicle stopped at a small concrete bridge. Andrew had been doing the map reading and now he said, "Well, this is our start point. Everyone out!"

Tina climbed out and looked at the dense jungle on all sides and felt her heart sink. She bit her lip and thought, *Oh, I hope I can do this!*

Chapter 20

IN THE JUNGLE

Tina had never really been in the jungle in her life. The closest she had ever come was to stroll along a nice walkway to a tourist site like the Curtain Fig Tree near Yungaburra, or a short nature ramble along a path when she was in primary school. Now she knew she was a long way from the nearest civilization and that, once her mother had gone home, they would be very much on their own. Her mother was staying for the next three hours but after that the nearest help would be Lt Ryan and Sub Lt Mullion waiting on the other side of the mountain.

The fact that they had no mobile phone service and that the radios got no answer made her even more anxious. She had known this would be so even before they had started but the reality of it was quite different.

Andrew just shrugged, and said, "We should get coms once we are higher up the mountain. OK, packs on. Let's go."

Reluctantly Tina heaved her pack on. It was so heavy that she staggered under the weight and her mother helped steady her, then gave her a peck on the cheek.

"Have a good time dear," she said.

Tina felt like bursting into tears and was so anxious she was nauseous. But she lacked the courage to say so and just gave a smile and a nod and set off after the others.

Within a hundred paces Tina's fears had intensified. The road was muddy and went up a steep slope and she was gasping for breath and falling behind even before they had reached the first bend. A last glimpse of her mother wrung her emotions another notch.

I am a fool, Tina told herself.

But she kept walking, gripping the pack straps with both hands to help ease the weight. After a few more minutes she was breathing so hard she was hyperventilating and felt giddy.

"S... s... slow (puff) d...d... (gasp) down!" she cried.

Andrew and Blake looked back with puzzled expressions on their faces. "What's the matter?" Andrew asked.

"I... I'm... not (puff) very (puff) fit a... and... m... my (puff) p... pack is very heavy," Tina gasped.

Blake gave her a look of disbelief, and said, "We've only just started."

His tone of voice annoyed Tina. She stood panting for a few seconds, then snapped, "And if you want to get over the mountains take it slow so I can keep up."

Andrew looked thoughtful and nodded. "OK, we will," he agreed.

They resumed their walk at a slow plod. But Tina noted an exchange of looks between Blake and Stella that she interpreted to mean they did not think much of her. That hurt, but it also fired her determination.

I'll show them, she told herself.

The road quickly deteriorated and became rutted and muddy and partly overgrown. Tina knew it had once been a 'timber' road, used to haul logs out of the forest in the days before the whole area became part of the World Heritage Wet Tropics and the logging was stopped. Now it was disused by vehicles. Around the next bend was one of the reasons why, a large tree had fallen across the road and blocked it. This had obviously been many years before as the log was rotten and covered with moss and lichen. But it was still an obstacle.

To get around it the group had to snip a path through the weeds and the edge of the jungle. To do this Andrew had a pair of garden secateurs. Graham had advised them to carry these and Tina now saw the wisdom of it. She also met what one of the things she had been warned to avoid, 'wait-a-while'. A tendril of the vine snagged her forearm and sleeve, bringing her to a sudden, painful stop.

"Ouch!" she cried, amazed and annoyed.

Then she saw that the tendril was only a thin green thing with tiny, barbed hooks on it. She pulled to try to break it off. But it did not break. Instead it dug in deeper, dragging another cry of pain from her.

Andrew came back and said, "Don't pull at it. Graham said the tendrils are stronger than you are. Either back up and ease it off or let me cut it."

Tina tried to back up but another tendril caught her hat from behind and she cried out again. For a minute or so she was snagged and anxious and by the end of it she knew that Graham had been right. The 'wait-a-while' was stronger than a person.

They all got snagged by more wait-a-while over the next hour or so and soon started to fear it. They began keeping a watchful eye out for it.

Tina learned that the tendrils grew off the lawyer vine which grew out of a stand of spiky palm fronds. The tendrils varied from old dead ones nearly 5 millimetres thick to large green ones 3 millimetres thick with yellow barbs to really thin green ones less than half a millimetre thick. They were all bad news. The easiest way was for Andrew to snip the tendrils off with his secateurs.

"Graham said the machete or jungle knife is useless as it doesn't cut the tendrils and just makes the whole bush jump around so that more of them snag you," Andrew explained.

By then Tina was hot, panting and irritated. "Well he should be here to cut a track for us," she grumbled.

The reason they met more wait-a-while was that it overhung the track and in places fallen trees had dragged whole clumps of it down to form an almost impenetrable barrier. In those cases they had to detour through the edge of the rainforest, where there was usually more of the stuff.

Then they encountered another, equally painful pest, wild raspberries. Along stretches of the old road where the sunlight had good access it grew in dense thickets. The plants were head high and had vicious thorns which were even worse than the wait-a-while. The easiest way to progress was often to detour into the jungle. Unfortunately this was not always possible, usually because the bank on both sides was too steep.

Andrew swore and sweated as he led the group. As he pushed through some vines he called back, "Watch out for stinging trees."

"Is there one there?" Stella asked.

"No, but we don't need anyone really hurt," Andrew replied.

Tina knew what he meant. They had been warned that the stinging tree could cause an allergic reaction in some people that was potentially fatal. She had seen a photo of a stinging tree but there were so many leaves of different shapes in the jungle around her that she doubted if she would spot one in time. She began to have serious doubts about the wisdom of the whole expedition.

We should have done a canoe trip, she thought.

After battling past another clump of wild raspberry they came to what looked like a road junction. By then Tina was gasping and her shoulders ached so badly she just wanted to flop down and go back.

To her relief, Andrew said, "Packs off while we study the GPS and the map."

It was such a relief to drop the pack that Tina almost cried. As she stood rubbing her shoulders, she noted Stella doing the same and decided that she didn't look very happy either.

Maybe we are all suffering? Tina thought.

After studying the GPS and working out the grid reference it gave Andrew pointed at the map. "I reckon we are here, at this is track junction at the top of Varch Creek."

Tina looked and then made a pencil note on her map photocopy. To her dismay, she saw that they had only walked about 2 kilometres. *And that took an hour!* she noted as she glanced at her watch. It was almost 1100hrs. She estimated that they had another 5 kilometres to go before they met up with the officers and a vehicle. *Can I do it?* she wondered.

All too soon Andrew ordered packs on and set off again. Tina heaved on her pack and then made another painful discovery as she started walking. She found that during the 10-minute halt her muscles had stiffened up and that all of the chafing that was beginning to hurt was now twice as painful. Then she noted that the others were groaning and complaining as well, even Andrew.

"Bloody hell!" he moaned.

"Keep walking," Stella said. "It won't hurt as much when you warm up again."

Easier said than done! Tina just wanted to flop down, and she noted with dismay a sort of leaden throbbing in her left shoulder. Using her left hand she gripped the pack strap and tried to hold it in a better position. Then she gritted her teeth and kept on plodding.

The beauties of the rain forest were mostly lost on her. She later had vague recollections of big blue butterflies and of various brightly coloured fungi but apart from the birds she noted very little. There were birds, mostly white cockatoos that set up a hideous cacophony in warning to others of the human intruders. Tina also saw a topknot pigeon and heard a whip bird calling down in one of the ferny gullies.

I'd like to see one of them, or a rifle bird, she thought.

The road improved a bit, being mostly clear with only a few logs across it and occasional patches of undergrowth. The road was matted with a thick carpet of dead leaves and sticks and this made walking fairly easy and silent. Apart from the weight of her pack Tina realised it wasn't that bad, mostly being just one long, uphill slog.

There was a section of road where red clay showed through and Andrew commented that it would be no fun walking on it if it was wet. That made them all glance at the sky and Tina noted that it was a clear blue. The jungle was so dry that twigs crackle underfoot and dust rose as they walked.

There were patches of dug up soil which Blake said were pig rootings. That got Tina all anxious again. She had heard stories about wild pigs, and knew that if one attacked she would be too terrified to even run away.

Blake did not help by describing a wild boar he had once seen. "It was all black and hairy and had huge, curved tusks and it was as big as me, must have weighed a hundred kilograms; and it could really run! You should have seen it go!"

Stella wasn't impressed. "Shut up, Blake!" she snapped as she wiped sweat from her face.

Andrew gave a chuckle, then said, "It is the cassowaries I am more worried about."

Tina, who had been casting anxious looks into the jungle on either side, now felt another stab of fear. She really wanted to see a cassowary but also knew they could be dangerous. For the next 5 minutes the friends discussed cassowaries and what to do if they met one.

Tina commented, "I'd love to see one, but I think they are now so rare there isn't much chance of that."

"Are they rare?" Stella asked.

"Yes. They are endangered," Tina answered. By now she was almost sobbing with the effort of keeping up. Finally she said, "Let's have a break. I need to adjust my pack."

Andrew nodded and gave her a worried glance. Then he stopped and swung off his pack. "Good idea. In fact it is nearly midday. Let's have lunch."

Thankfully, Tina swung off her pack and undid the top. Not wishing to sit on the leaf mould, she took out a plastic groundsheet and spread it, then sat down. That drew a groan from her as sore and tired muscles protested. For a few minutes all she wanted to do was ease her limbs and massage them while she got her breath back. Then she realised she needed to do a pee.

"I will just go back along the track a bit," she commented.

"Why?" asked Blake.

Tina blushed with embarrassment. "To powder my nose," she replied.

"To unload a bit of extra weight," Andrew added, making her blush again.

She walked stiffly back along the track, flexing and stretching sore muscles as she did. Once she was around the bend out of sight, she stopped to relieve herself. While she did, she was struck by how quiet it all was. *And how isolated we are.*

Suddenly a skittering, rustling noise behind her made her tense. Unable to get up and run she glanced anxiously around. To her great joy she saw it was a Victoria's Riflebird. Even as she watched the bird raised both its black wings into the characteristic arch, allowing Tina to see the green feathers of its abdomen. The bird gave its loud 'yaas!' call and pirouetted in a dance. Suddenly it saw Tina and quickly scuttled off into the undergrowth.

The wonder of it held Tina for several minutes and she dressed and moved quietly to look over the edge of the slope, hoping to see it again. But she didn't. The only other bird she saw was the all too common Brush Turkey. Pleased with her sighting she walked back to tell the others. Then she moved to her pack and dug around in it for some food.

She took out some biscuits and a tin of peaches. Then she began digging in her pack for her can opener. Seeing Andrew using one she said, "Andrew, may I use your tin opener please?"

Andrew nodded. "Here, pass me the can," he said. He finished opening his own can and placed it down. Tina passed him the peaches. Andrew studied the label and said, "These look nice. Hmm. Oh, here's why your pack weighs so much, Tina."

"What do you mean?" Tina asked.

Andrew turned the can and pointed to the bottom of the label. "Packed in heavy syrup," he read.

"Oh very funny! I'm just unfit," Tina replied. But she did laugh at the feeble joke.

Stella added, "So am I. I don't know if I can make it over that mountain."

"Mt Tiptree," Andrew said as he opened Tina's can. He passed it back and Tina used her spoon to start eating.

Stella pulled out her map and looked at it. "Where do you think we are now?"

Blake and Andrew both leaned forward to point, an action which peeved Tina. *They don't both have to fall over themselves to help her!* she thought.

Stella nodded and said, "Is it far to the top?"

Andrew shook his head and pointed at the map. "That is the crest. It is only about another kilometre."

That was good news to Tina and she resolved to keep on trying. But she already felt tired and her shoulder muscles ached. Worse still there was chafing under her armpits and on her shoulders and hips that was starting to really hurt. "We will do our next expedition by water, in a boat," she commented.

"From where to where?" Andrew asked.

Blake answered, "Mulgrave River, from Goldsborough to Deeral?"

"Bit dangerous. The lower part of the Mulgrave has some big crocodiles," Andrew replied.

"Koombooloomba then?" Blake suggested.

Hearing that gave Tina searing flashbacks: the ranger being shot, the chase, Danny shooting at her and his angry expression. This was followed by the image of Danny's face at Croydon as he swore to get her.

"Oh no! Not there!" she cried. A wave of fear so intense that it made her feel faint swept through her.

Blake did not appear to notice her reaction, but Andrew did. "You OK, Tina?" he asked.

"Just having some bad memories," she answered. She trembled and found she was perspiring and breathing fast.

This is silly, she told herself. *It was months ago.*

Blake said, "What about Tinaroo then?"

As the question seemed to be directed to her Tina nodded. "That will do," she replied.

Blake fell to studying Lake Tinaroo, which was on the 1:100 000 scale topographic map he was holding. The discussion of when to do the 'test' expedition and of where to go kept them occupied for the next 10 minutes. Tina ate her peaches and then nibbled a couple of biscuits. She also drank deeply, emptying a plastic bottle of cordial.

That should make my pack lighter, she thought hopefully.

But when she hoisted it on 10 minutes later, she was dismayed to find that it actually felt heavier. Clenching her teeth she pulled the pack into position then bent her head to hide the hurt and tears which prickled in her eyes.

Then it was on up the overgrown track. This section she found to be not too bad. The old road was in under the overhanging trees and because of the lack of sunlight very little undergrowth had grown up. *Amazing, even after all these years!* she thought when it was commented on by Blake. The gradient was reasonably gentle and the road went around a slope on a bench cut with a very steep drop down into a jungle choked creek line on the right.

After 15 minutes of sweaty plodding they came to another log across the road. Andrew ordered another halt while they checked their navigation. He used the GPS and then said, "Someone else check my readings please."

The GPS was passed around and Tina had a go with it, then marked the grid reference on her map. Andrew then compared his with hers and nodded. "That's what I get. So we are only a few hundred metres from the crest of Mt Tiptree. This is where Graham said we had to be very careful or we will end up going off along the wrong track."

After a break packs were hoisted on again and the march resumed. After climbing over several more logs they reached an area where the ground was definitely levelling out. The slope on their left became nothing more than a gentle rise with sunlight showing through it.

"This looks like the top of the mountain," Tina said.

But it was hard to tell because their visibility was only about 50 metres. At no time had they got more than a tiny glimpse out through the tree canopies and that was starting to induce a claustrophobic feeling in Tina. The group continued on and came to an obvious fork. The better track went left so they took it and that put the low rise on their right and the downhill slope on their left.

After another 10 minutes Stella called on them to stop. Tina saw she was holding her compass in her hand. "This road is going nearly east. Shouldn't we be going south?" she queried.

Andrew also had his compass out and he nodded. "Yes. What does the GPS say Blake?"

Blake checked the GPS and marked the location on his map. Tina leaned over and saw that it was clearly to the east of the track they were supposed to be on. Andrew nodded and pointed back the way they had come. "I was getting worried. Thanks Stella. We need to go back to that last junction."

Tina badly wanted a rest and was also peeved that Andrew was paying attention to Stella. Then she became angry at herself. *You need to push yourself forward and not just be a wagon on the train,* she told herself. So she bit her lip and trudged back without complaint.

Her reward came 10 minutes later when they returned to the track junction and Stella said, "Oh, let's rest. I've had it."

That gave Tina a tiny spurt of malicious pleasure, which then made her feel guilty. With relief she shrugged off her pack and sat on it, then had a big drink. To her surprise she found she had almost emptied her second water bottle. "We will need to find water soon. I am nearly out," she commented.

"So am I," agreed Blake.

Andrew checked one of his bottles, swilling the remaining contents around. "None on top of the mountain. We should find a creek when we go down."

At that moment, a movement caught Tina's eye and she looked up in time to see two reddish parrots flit past along the clearing and into the trees. "Oooh! Crimson rosellas!" she cried with delight. She looked hopefully but saw no more. The only other birds she noted were some tiny finches that she could not identify.

After the break they pulled on their packs and moved to the right-hand track. It was badly overgrown by a thicket of thin trees and was hard to push along. But the track ended after about 50 metres at the lip of a very steep slope. Tina stood beside the others looking down through the thick jungle. *I don't see any sign of a road here,* she thought.

Blake thought the same and said, "The road is marked on the map as being the same as what we have been walking along. Where did it go?"

Andrew answered. "Graham said it doesn't exist and probably never has. The map is wrong. This is the way he went, down here. Look, see these small trees that have been slashed or blazed?"

He pointed to a small dead tree which had obviously been cut off by a cutting tool. Tina then spotted several more further down the slope. "There's some more," she said.

"This is where we go down and at the bottom we should find old overgrown clearings and more timber roads," Andrew explained.

Stella looked apprehensive. "Do we just walk through the jungle?"

"Yes, on a compass bearing if we lose these cut off saplings," Andrew answered.

"How far is it?" Stella asked.

"About 2 kilometres before we come to a road," Andrew answered.

They had all known that from the planning session, so Tina was surprised by the questions. She now saw that Stella was looking distinctly uneasy.

Stella looked anxiously at the jungle. "What if we get lost?" she asked.

Andrew shook his head. "We won't. We've got compasses and a GPS and if they all fail we will just walk downhill and we will come to Emerald Creek. If need be, we could follow it down to the Emerald Creek Falls Picnic Area."

Stella still looked anxious. "What if someone has an accident?"

"Then we do First Aid and call the rescue chopper if we can. If not, we carry them," Andrew answered.

That gave Tina a cue. "Test the radio and the mobile phone," she said.

Andrew unclipped his hand-held radio and called Lt Ryan. There was no answer, so he tried twice more. There was still no response, so he hooked his radio back to his shirt and took out the mobile phone.

"We have service, but not very strong," he said.

But he was unable to call Lt Ryan. The system answered saying that the other phone was switched off or in an area where it did not have service. "Oh well, standing here isn't solving the problem," Andrew said. "It's after 2 o'clock and this could take an hour or two. Let's go."

He led the way down the slope. Feeling more anxious than she cared to admit Tina followed.

Chapter 21

EMERALD CREEK

The slope was so steep they had to lower themselves from tree to tree. Tina found her boots continually slipping on the thick carpet of dead leaves and twigs. Despite the coolness of the air at that altitude she started to really sweat. Slippery hands then made it hard to grip the tree trunks, some of which were too thick to hold.

They went down quickly as there was very little undergrowth. "No wait-a-while here," Andrew commented.

Tina looked around and saw that the rainforest on the slope was mostly just tall trees with very straight trunks. She noted that there were very few vines and almost no small bushes. But she still found it dark and gloomy. Through tiny gaps in the canopy she got glimpses of another jungle-covered mountain ahead of them.

Mt Haig, she told herself.

And she was becoming very thirsty. When they halted to allow Stella to regain her feet after slipping and falling Tina had a drink and drained the last of her water. That got her really worried as she knew heat exhaustion was a real danger.

Even in winter, she thought.

That caused her a wry smile as winter in North Queensland could sometimes be quite cool, even below zero up in the mountains, but at that moment it was sunny and hot.

After a short rest they continued on down. As they moved Tina felt more and more apprehensive. She knew that if they had an accident that every step down meant they must carry the casualty forward.

It would be a nightmare trying to carry a stretcher back up this slope, she thought.

Half an hour of careful but steady descent (and much slipping) brought them into deep shadow with Mt Haig looming above them, its presence felt more than seen. Tina became anxiously aware of her thirst and she hoped they would find water soon.

They came into a different type of vegetation. The undergrowth thickened up, but it was all ferns and cycads and was still easy to move through. Tina also found it reassuring to see old cuts or blazes on tree trunks from time to time.

At least we aren't lost, she thought.

It was damp here, the dead logs and tree trunks covered with soggy moss and lichens. While climbing over a large log (and trying to keep her clothes clean and dry) Tina heard the distinctive sound of a whip bird. She also heard a bird call that she knew she should recognize. It niggled at her that she could not remember what it was. 'Whoo-crk, whoo-crk, whooo-crk,' it went.

But the only birds she saw were some scrub turkeys and they did not particularly interest her. Three of them scurried about, scratching among the leaf litter for grubs and then hurrying away as the group got closer.

The going was slower, but the slope began to level off. In the cycad forest Tina thought it was quite spooky it was so gloomy. *We are in the shadow of the mountain as well,* she thought, noting that it was now 1500hrs. The day seemed to be slipping away very quickly, adding another worry to her already anxious mind. *We don't want to be in the jungle when it gets dark,* she thought.

Andrew led the way onto a flat area that was mostly clear of trees. The ground was deep in dead leaves, but it was at least more open, about 25 metres across.

"I reckon this is an old timber cutter's camp," he said.

Tina looked around and noted a rusty old 44-gallon drum in the undergrowth. She pointed this out. Blake then pointed to the right and said, "That looks like a bench cut."

By common consent they dropped their packs and walked over to look. And there was no doubt. An old, overgrown road went off around the side of the ridge they had been coming down. They followed it for a short distance. "We should follow it," Stella suggested.

They returned the 100 paces to their packs and hauled them on and set off to follow the old road. Tina found it a real effort to get her pack on and knew she was exhausted and weakening. Andrew checked their position using the GPS. A study of her map told Tina that they were now close to the bottom of the slope and to Emerald Creek.

Only about a kilometre to the road where the officers are, she told herself.

The old road quickly became a disappointment. Not only was it blocked in many places by fallen logs but there were a lot of thin trees growing up. Then it went upwards around the slope. Andrew stopped after a hundred metres of this and studied the map. "This is no good. It is going back up the mountain."

Blake nodded and said, "I think it is only an old snig track."

"What's that?" Stella asked.

"The timber cutters used to cut a narrow road in to the big tree they wanted and then they would cut it down and trim it, then they would haul it out to the clearing where they could load it on a truck,' Blake explained.

"How would they drag it out?" Stella queried.

"With a steel wire rope and winch or with a bulldozer," Blake answered.

Tina tried to imagine that and decided it would have been very hard and dangerous work. She said, "So what do we do now?"

Andrew pointed back and said, "I think the road we want will lead out of that camp clearing. The one we want goes down to cross the creek and then along the other bank."

Tina liked that idea. "We need to go to the creek. I am out of water and getting very dry," she said.

Andrew nodded. "We will do that," he said. He led the way back to the clearing and they scouted around for a few minutes. They now found several old roads led away from the clearing but the best went fairly steeply down in the same direction they had been going earlier. They took this and within a minute Tina heard the murmur of flowing water. The sound cheered her up enormously.

The old road was quite straight for about 50 metres and it was mostly clear of smaller trees so that it ran in a sort of tunnel through the jungle. A dense growth of ferns grew on either side and there were more vines and undergrowth. Tina climbed carefully around a washout, noting that the soil was a sort of damp, slippery clay. Then she helped Stella down before turning to follow the boys.

As she did, a movement caught her eye and she glanced up to see a bird flit across the clear lane. *What bird was that?* she wondered. It had been black but she and only caught an impression of yellow. *But was that the beak or on the feathers?* she wondered.

About 10 metres on she glanced up again, hoping to see another of the birds. She suspected they might be the ones making the *Dook! Dook! Dook!* noises she could hear. More movement caught her eye and she looked up. For a few seconds she could not work out what she was looking at. Then she saw it was a big bird twitching and struggling.

That is a crimson rosella and it is caught in something, she decided.

She pointed and even as she opened her mouth to speak she got a shock as she recognised what was happening. *That is a mist net! That bird is caught in a net!* she thought.

As a host of possible reasons for the net being there flitted through her mind. She pointed and said, "This is a mist net. They are not legal, except for people with a special research permit."

Stella frowned and looked at the net, the lower corner of which was secured to a tree trunk near them. "Maybe that is why it is here, a university project or some study by a park ranger?"

Tina was not convinced. "Might be, but I don't like it. It seems fishy to me."

At that Blake laughed, and said, "That is a bird, not a fish."

Andrew stepped over and gently felt the nylon mesh. As he did, he looked at Tina. "Do you think it might be more of those bird smugglers, like we ran into at Koombooloomba Dam?"

"That's what I am afraid of," Tina replied.

She was now feeling very uneasy. Her emotional state was added to by concern for the parrot, which was now struggling strongly to try to free itself. As she studied it she became aware of a tinkling sort of noise. Guided by her ears she looked and saw that several tiny bells were attached to the net and it was these that were making the noise as the parrot struggled in the net.

Her mind tried to grapple with the implications of this and as it formed the idea that the bell was to warn whoever had set the net that something was caught in it she heard a squelching noise behind her. She glanced over her shoulder and almost fainted with shock.

It was a man

And not just any man. It was Danny the bird smuggler!

Danny! her mind shrieked.

Memories of his threat to 'get her' swamped her with paralysing terror. Danny was looking very grubby and unshaven and was wearing an old jungle green shirt and grimy shorts. In his hand he had a bird cage. As he came up over the lip of the creek bank, he saw them and stopped. His mouth dropped open and he swore.

Tina could only gasp and croak. The others turned to look and as they did Danny turned and bolted. He went back down the slope at a fast run and was lost to sight among the ferns and undergrowth along the creek bed.

Blake spoke first. "Who was that?" he asked.

"Danny!" Tina croaked. "The man who shot the ranger at Koombooloomba and who shot at us," she replied.

"You sure?" Blake queried.

Andrew hurried forward to look down into the creek. "Yes. That was him. I won't forget his ugly mug too quickly."

"So the net was set by bird poachers," Stella stated.

Tina nodded. "Definitely. Come on, we must get away from here."

Stella frowned. "Why? There are four of us," she replied.

"That won't stop him," Tina said with conviction, terrifying images of Danny shooting at them in their canoe swamping her mind.

Andrew nodded. "You are right. We are witnesses to a murder committed by him," he agreed. "And this might be a good opportunity to get rid of us."

That idea so terrified Tina she felt nauseous. *Oh my God! He will come back and kill me,* she thought. She gasped and realised she was breathing very fast and sweating.

"He said he would get me," she added.

"When?" Andrew asked.

"During the holidays at Croydon, when I told the police about their plane landing on the lake there," Tina explained.

Andrew nodded. "I remember you telling us. But is he alone I wonder?"

"Doesn't matter. He will have gone to get his gun and he will be back in a few minutes. We must get moving," Tina said, her voice almost a wail.

Stella looked around and the pointed back up the slope. "Do you mean go back up the mountain?"

Tina nodded. "If need be."

Stella looked appalled. "Oh! I don't think I can do that."

"Then we must take to the jungle," Tina said.

A very anxious looking Blake pointed down the valley and said, "What about going around him through the jungle?"

"Not a good place to try," Andrew replied. "We are at the top end of a very steep gorge here and I think the country will be truly awful to try to get through if we go that way. I think we need to try to creep past him much closer."

"But isn't that dangerous?" Stella asked.

Andrew nodded. "Yes, but the officers are meeting us just over that way at a road. They will be able to contact the authorities."

At the mention of the Officers of Cadets Tina calmed down a bit. "Try the phone and call them," she suggested.

Andrew took out the phone but then shook his head. "No service down here in this valley," he replied. Before Tina could suggest it he unclipped the radio and called on that. But there was no reply and Tina's hopes slumped. She was now nearly hyperventilating and was almost twitching with fear. But her brain was working and so were other emotions.

"We must try to reach the officers," she said.

"Why?" Blake queried.

"They might run into trouble too. We must warn them," Tina replied. That notion had only just come to her but had instantly firmed into a moral duty that overrode her own fears.

"But they are adults!" Stella said.

That childish view annoyed Tina. "So was the ranger that Danny shot," she retorted.

Stella looked sulky at that but Blake said, "We should dump these packs in case we need to run for it."

Andrew nodded as he clipped the radio back on. "Good idea. We will hide them, and we can always come back and get them later."

He suited his actions to his words and swung his pack off, then walked into the jungle back up the track and pushed the pack out of sight behind a log. The others followed his example. Tina was so relieved to get rid of the weight that she almost sobbed. She kept glancing back along the track and her ears strained for any sound of Danny returning.

Then she glanced up at the struggling crimson rosella and two thoughts melded in her head into a desire to free the bird: out of pity for it and then from the fierce desire to deny Danny his prey.

C.R. Cummings

I won't let him get it, she thought. That urge helped calm her and she found herself pulling out her pocketknife.

"What are you doing?" Blake asked.

"I am going to set that bird free," Tina replied.

"Why? Let's go!" Stella cried. She was now clearly on the edge of panic.

"So that mongrel can't get it," Tina replied.

Driven by a sharp spasm of anger and a desire to hurt that later made her feel ashamed she went over to the net and slashed at the ropes holding it up. As she did, she knew she was being silly and that her actions were placing the others at risk. But she felt compelled to do it so she cut and sawed at the thin nylon ropes, while frequently glancing over her shoulder to watch for Danny.

Then another idea came to her. "Blake, use your camera to take photos please, lots of them."

Blake nodded and pulled out his camera. He began snapping shots using his flash, changing distance as he did.

Andrew moved to help Tina, even though Stella hissed at them to get going. Within a minute the whole net slid down in a tangle of slithery nylon. Tina pulled at the net and was amazed at what fine fibres it was made from, but how strong they were. Then she got tangled in it and frustrated. However she persevered and soon she had the bundle of net which contained the terrified parrot in her hand. Careful not to further injure the crimson rosella she took a firm grip and then very carefully eased and teased the net away from it. Andrew helped by holding parts of the net and by cutting bits that snagged on things.

Within a minute Tina had the bird free of the net but held firmly in her grasp. The terrified parrot immediately nipped at her, clamping onto the web of her left hand. The bite really hurt and the beak drew blood. She cried out softly in pain but was not diverted from her plan. After turning the parrot over to check it for injuries, she held it close and whispered, "You will be alright now fella! Fly away!"

With that she held both hands up and opened them. It took the parrot a few seconds to realise it was free and during that time Blake snapped two more photos. Then the parrot released its bite, flapped its wings and flew away. Within seconds it was lost to sight among the tree trunks and shadows.

Seeing it go gave Tina an intense feeling of pleasure and she smiled. Then Andrew took hold of her wrist. "Your hand, it's bleeding," he said.

Tina glanced down and was shocked at the amount of bright red blood that was flowing in thick trickles down over her hand and fingers. Trying to make light of it she said, "It's nothing. We will wash it when we find some water."

She was now focused on hiding, and on reaching the officers to call the authorities. She turned and began walking slowly down the slope towards the sound of running water.

The others followed: Andrew, then Blake and Stella at the rear. Tina glanced back to check and then focused all her attention on the jungle ahead. As she moved cautiously along her fear level went up again and she found she was sweating, dry in the mouth and that her heart was pounding so loudly it made it hard to hear.

A few minutes later she reached the creek. The old vehicle track dipped into the shallow water and then went up the other bank where it curved to the right out of sight. The creek was only a metre wide and ankle deep, so she was able to step over it.

As she did, Andrew whispered, "You wash that hand and put a bandage on it. I will keep watch from up on the bank."

Tina nodded agreement. She could feel blood dripping from her fingertips and she was worried about how bad the bite might be. Andrew went up the slope and Blake followed while Tina turned and knelt on some moss-covered rocks to reach the water. The water was crystal clear and so cold it gave her a real surprise when she plunged her hand into it.

Stella joined her, still looking very fearful. Tina sighed with relief and then rubbed off some dried blood. She kept washing until she could see that the bite was really only a surface nip that had torn some skin. Watching the thin streamers of blood swirling away in the water reminded her of her First Aid lessons.

Only capillary bleeding, she told herself.

She had a small bandage in a pouch on her belt and she got Stella to bind this over the wound. Stella did her best but she was shaking so much that she made a bad job of it. That annoyed Tina but she managed to bite back the angry words that formed in her mind. Instead she said, "Thanks."

Then she bent to have a drink and to wash her face. Stella did likewise. To Tina that mountain stream tasted better than anything she had ever drank in her life. It instantly refreshed her and she was able to think more clearly. After another drink she took out her water bottle and filled it. Stella followed her example. When she had drunk her fill and replaced the now full water bottle Tina made her way up the bank to where both boys crouched in the edge of the jungle.

"Go and have a drink and fill your water bottles," she said.

"But what if the man comes back?" Blake asked.

"All the more reason to have a drink now. We might have to run off into the jungle and who knows when you might find more water. No. Do it now," Tina replied.

Andrew nodded and made his way down past Stella. Blake followed. Tina crouched behind a big tree and peeked out to look along the overgrown road. She saw that it now ran parallel to the creek on an old bench cut, with the creek on the right and the hillside on the left, a dismayingly steep looking slope.

What was now bothering her was where Danny was. *What is he doing?* she wondered. *Surely he has now had time to run back to the road to get his gun?* she thought, remembering that Andrew had said it was only about a kilometre.

From the depths of her memory she dredged up something Graham had said once about soldiers marching a kilometre in 10 minutes. She glanced at her watch and saw that it was 1550hrs.

That is nearly 20 minutes since we saw him. He could appear at any moment.

She tensed, ready to run for her life and fearing that the jungle would make it impossible to escape, particularly from bullets. *Oh hurry up!* she fretted as the boys drank and filled their water bottles in the stream behind her.

Several more minutes went by before the boys re-joined the girls. Tina sighed with relief and realised she had almost been holding her breath from anxiety. Andrew at once set off through the jungle between the creek and the road. Luckily it was mostly ferns, cycads and vines with no wait-a-while so they were able to push through it fairly easily.

Until Stella discovered the leeches!

She gave a little shriek that made them all turn and glare at her and hiss for silence. Stella gave them a guilty but panicked look and pointed.

It was Tina's turn to gasp. Two slimy, fat leeches the size of her little finger were attached to Stella's forearm.

Blake wasn't impressed. "They are only leeches. Here, just pull them off."

"Aren't you supposed to burn them off or put salt on them?" Andrew commented.

Tina answered that. "That works but I have read that it is very cruel as it causes the leech to die in agony."

"So what?" Blake replied with a shrug.

"So it is cruel. Just pull it off," Tina said.

Then she discovered a leech on her own left arm up inside the sleeve. It had latched on to the veins on the soft flesh under her wrist. She at once lost all interest in Stella's minor problems and scratched at the thing until it came off. But then it bled worse than the parrot's bite and more blood quickly stained the now crumpled and wet bandage.

Blake looked at the blood and nodded. "They spit an anti-coagulant onto you so that your blood thins and flows more easily."

Stella was horrified. "Spits! Ugh! Will it get infected?"

Blake shook his head. "Shouldn't. In the old days the doctors put them on to take out blood."

"They still do," Andrew added, searching his own clothes for leeches and plucking one off his trouser leg.

It took a couple of minutes for them to deal with the leeches, all finding a couple. Andrew then pointed to others that were wriggling their way towards them. When Tina saw one of the tiny things making it way across a leaf with a head-tail-head-tail movement she was both fascinated and appalled. Then it stopped and stood up, its whole body waving.

"It is sensing your body heat," Blake explained. He flicked the leech away and grinned.

"Never mind the leeches, let's get past this bird poacher," Tina replied. She was dismayed that for a few minutes they had lost focus on the deadly danger they were in.

They moved on as cautiously as they could without actually creeping. Luckily, there was a flattish area beside the creek and they could move along that. There was plenty of cover behind twisted tree trunks and rotting logs all covered in moss. The moss was soaked with water and Tina found her clothes and hands were soon grimy as well as slimy. The bandage became disgustingly soiled and began to unravel.

Another 10 minutes careful movement brought them to a section of the valley where some of the afternoon sunlight was able to penetrate. That made it less gloomy but added a shadow problem to the fieldcraft. Now Tina found it harder to see. And with the creek gurgling and tinkling along beside them she could not hear anything.

1615hrs came and went. Tina began to fret about the officers walking into trouble. *If they aren't already there,* she thought anxiously. But she did not suggest using the radio in case Danny heard it. So she just kept on creeping from tree to tree, now ignoring the leeches and the wet moss.

Suddenly Andrew stopped and pointed. Tina crouched and then peered ahead to try to see what it was he was indicating. Then she saw it was a tent fly strung up between four trees. Underneath it was a jumble of boxes and gear. From the far side a faint column of wood smoke was rising through a band of sunlight.

"Their camp," Andrew whispered.

Tina looked around and bit her lip. The camp took up most of the flat and was only a few metres from the creek. "We will have to go around it on the uphill side," she replied.

As she was closest she led the way, still moving with extreme caution. Every nerve was now alert and she knew she was quivering with tension and that she was sweating despite the chill mountain air that was now flowing down the gorge. 30 paces had her at the base of the hill and another five had her up beside the old road on its bench cut.

We will have to cross this, she thought, knowing that could be risky.

For a few seconds she studied the slope on the other side. It was steep but covered with small trees. *We can pull ourselves up by them,* she told herself. After another cautious glance along to her right she rose to her feet and went to step out onto the old road. As she did, she glanced to her right again and the flicker of movement caught her eye. Fear coursed through her and she tensed and then felt she was going to die with shock.

Just 50 metres away, hurrying along the old road towards her was Danny, and he was carrying a gun!

Chapter 22

JANGLED NERVES

For a second Tina froze. Then she realised that she was still half hidden behind a big tree and that Danny's body language did not indicate that he had seen her. She began to ease herself back behind the tree, while at the same time gesturing frantically with her right hand to those behind her to stop and get down. To her relief they did.

"What is it?" Andrew whispered as Tina lowered herself to a crouch behind the tree's buttress roots.

"He's coming back, and he's got a gun," Tina croaked.

Heart in mouth she pressed herself in behind the mossy tree roots. She was terrified that Danny would walk past and see her and the thought of what he might then do to her almost transfixed her with paralysis. But she knew she had no other option but to try to hide, and hope.

We have made a terrible mistake! she thought as she strained her ears to detect his approach.

Then she heard a scuffling noise on the other side of the tree. This was followed the sound of hurrying footsteps crunching soggy deadfall. To her immense relief, the noise went away from her. *He's gone to their camp,* she thought.

By moving her head only a few centimetres she was able to see around the other side of the tree. *Yes, there he is,* she told herself. Danny had gone hurrying to the camp and was now bending over and shoving things into a Hessian sack. Her mind told her that he could probably see part of her and possibly the others, if he looked their way. He did in fact glance in their direction a couple of times, but his attention was focused up on the old road, not down on the creek bank.

Tina swivelled her head further and met Andrew's eyes. He was watching Danny from where he lay pressed flat behind some bushes. Just behind him was Blake, peeking through a bush. Stella lay behind a rotting log and her hands were white-knuckle clenched and she was visibly trembling. Tina could not see her face but was sure she was near to panic stricken.

So am I! she thought, realising that she was gasping so fast and so deep that she was getting dizzy from hyperventilating. With an effort she slowed her breathing. *Concentrate on Danny. What is he doing?* she thought.

After shifting cautiously to a more comfortable position that put her more behind the tree, she focused her eyes on Danny. She saw that he had now slung the gun over his shoulder using a piece of rope and that he was finished stuffing the sack. Next, he picked up the sack and then a box with a carry handle on top. Tina now saw that it was a bird cage and that it contained a white cockatoo. This began to squawk and shriek in protest. From the jungle in the distance arose answering cries from more white cockatoos.

"Oh, poor bird!" Tina muttered to herself as Danny swore at it and banged its cage against a tree.

For a fleeting moment she pictured the bird being cruelly treated. *I wish I could let it go,* she thought. But that was plainly impossible. However the scene did give her an image of 'Beaky' back in his cage. *I wonder if that is how Beaky was caught?* she thought. She had never considered that before and now, for the first time, she felt real doubt about whether it was right to keep such birds in cages.

Danny again swore at the bird and then turned and hurried back up to the old road. Again Tina tensed to run. But Danny just glanced to his left along the old road, then turned right and hurried away from them. Twenty seconds later he was lost to sight around the bend. Tina let her breath out with an audible sigh and managed a smile at Andrew.

Blake looked up. "What's he doing now?" he whispered.

"Gone away along the old road," Tina hissed back.

Even As she did, this she heard the sound of a vehicle door being slammed. A few seconds later another door was closed. *Is he getting into a vehicle?* she wondered.

Up until now she had assumed that there were two smugglers and she had been expecting Marco to appear at any moment. But when the sound of a vehicle's engine starting up reached her ears she decided that Danny had been alone in the camp.

Then another thought came to her: she did not know what type of vehicle. *I won't be able to report it to the police,* she thought.

On an impulse she stood up and a moment later was hurrying along the old road as fast as her cramped and stiff muscles would allow. She realised it was a frightful risk and that put her heart in her mouth, but she was determined to see the vehicle.

If I can get the registration number that will be even better, she told herself. It was only about 50 metres to where the old road curved left and she was close to that when she heard the vehicle's engine note change. *Oh no! He is driving away!* she thought. At that she pushed herself into a run, throwing caution to the winds in her determination.

As she reached the bend an instinct made her slow, but even as she did she heard the vehicle driving off. She looked around the bend and got another unpleasant disappointment. The road went straight for about 50 metres to where sunlight showed a good gravel road, but there was a hump in it and all she could see was the top of the vehicle!

Muttering swear words under her breath Tina dashed around the bend and up the rise. It wasn't much of a slope, but it hid the bulk of the vehicle and by the time she was able to see over the crest the vehicle was turning left onto a good graded gravel road. All she had time to note was that it was a small, muddy-brown, utility type truck with a covered in cabin constructed on the tray. She did not have time to read the mud-spattered number plate.

"Oh blast!" she cried in frustration.

Despite the risk she kept on running but by the time she reached the junction of the gravel road the vehicle had vanished around the next bend. Tina stopped and almost wept with relief and frustration. She stood there gasping and trembling while Andrew and Blake joined her at the run.

Andrew was angry. "Bloody hell Tina! What the hell were your thinking of?" he snapped.

"I wanted to –puff, get the-gasp, ve, vehicle's nu-puff-number plate."

Andrew nodded but still shook his head. "You took a risk."

"I know. I'm sorry," Tina replied. She looked back along the old road and saw a frightened and nearly hysterical Stella hurrying over the rise. "Why did you leave me?" Stella wailed.

Tina bit back the sharp re-joinder that came to mind and did not reply. She left it to Blake to calm Stella and was considerably peeved when Andrew also began to console and comfort her.

At that moment the radio on Andrew's shirt sounded loud and clear.

"Cutlass this is Blackbeard, over."

Tina's heart leapt. "Lt Ryan! Quick Andrew, ask him which way he is coming from. Warn him."

Andrew nodded and called back, "Blackbeard, this is Cutlass. over."

Again Lt Ryan's voice sounded clearly as he said, "Cutlass. where you trying to call us earlier?"

"Yes Blackbeard, we were. We need help, over," Andrew replied.

"What is the problem? Over."

Tina had been standing with her fingers twitching. She itched to do the talking and Andrew saw this. He passed the radio to her. Because it was tied to Andrew's shirt that meant she had to stand touching him, but she did not mind, in fact barely noticed.

"Sir, there are crooks, bird smugglers. They are the same ones we saw at Koombooloomba Dam and they have guns. Over," she said.

"Bloody hell! Are you in danger?" Lt Ryan asked.

"No sir, but you might be. They have just driven off in a brown truck with a covered in tray. Watch out you don't run into them. Over."

"Where are you?"

Andrew answered this. "At our RV on the B-road sir. Over."

"Which way did the vehicle turn? Over," Lt Ryan queried.

Tina had to think for a moment. "Left, I mean east," she answered.

"That's alright. We are coming in from the west, from Mareeba. We are only buz... ccrrraackle... buz away. We should be with you in crackle... crackle.... shhh..."

The radio transmission faded and became unreadable. Stella grabbed at Tina. "What did say? When will he be here?"

Andrew and Tina looked at each other. "He's not far away," Tina answered.

"A few minutes," Andrew added.

Tina sighed and shook her head. Then she smiled ruefully and said, "I'm glad that radio didn't start talking when we were hiding."

Blake laughed as well. "My oath! That would have cooked our goose."

Then the sound of a vehicle came to them. It was difficult to determine which direction it was coming from and the friends looked anxiously at each other. Andrew pointed back along the track. "Let's hide, just in case it is the crooks coming back."

Stella gasped and cried, "Oh they wouldn't, would they?" But she moved with the others.

They had only just reached the edge of the jungle when it became clear that the vehicle was coming from the west. Andrew said, "You guys wait here under cover. I will go out and flag it down. We don't want them to go driving past."

Tina was stuck by admiration for Andrew's courage and simultaneously appalled at the possible danger. She wanted to cry at him not to, but held her tongue. Instead she shepherded Stella behind a tree while Andrew walked back out to stand on the road.

It was less than a minute before the vehicle appeared but for Tina it seemed much longer. Then a white Navy 4WD roared into view and pulled up with a scrape of gravel under locked tyres. Tina saw Sub Lt Mullion and Lt Ryan and gasped with relief. Followed by Stella and Blake she hurried out to join Andrew.

For the next few minutes there was a babble of excited talk with each of them adding bits of the story. Lt Ryan and Sub Lt Mullion listened with evident alarm. Then Lt Ryan said, "This vehicle, you say it went that way?" He pointed east along the road.

"Yes sir," Tina answered.

"That is bad. The other 'Bronze' team and our 'Gold' team are both coming from that direction," Lt Ryan replied.

Tina felt a sudden stab of apprehension and went cold with worry. The other 'Bronze' team were rivals from the Starboard Watch but they were friends.

"Do you know where they are?" she asked.

Lt Ryan nodded. "Yes. We've been along this road twice and we passed the Starboard Watch team near Mt Edith about an hour and a half ago. They should be almost here by now."

"What about the 'Silver' team sir?" Tina asked. She was now feeling guilty with a half-formed notion that the whole crisis was her fault.

"Coming along the other way behind us," Lt Ryan said. "We saw them about 20 minutes ago. They are close to their night camp site." He looked at his watch and muttered, "Nearly five. Only an hour to last light. We had better go and check on the other teams. You people had better hide in the jungle until we come back, just in case."

"Yes sir," Andrew replied.

As the Officers of Cadets climbed back into their vehicle Tina said, "Sir, please phone the police and also the wildlife rangers."

Sub Lt Mullion held up a satellite phone and said, "We will do that right away."

"Thanks ma'am."

Stella then said, "Can I come with you please ma'am?"

Tina was amazed at Stella's apparent selfishness, but she said nothing. Lt Ryan shook his head. "No. You people stay together."

"But we are going home, aren't we?" Stella cried. She looked very pale and was trembling.

The officers looked at each other and Lt Ryan said, "We will ask the police for advice on that. Probably not. We will also call your parents and see what they want."

"But we must!" Stella cried.

Both Andrew and Blake tried to reassure her. While they were doing this the sunlight went from the road and it became quite gloomy. Tina looked up and noted that there was still sunlight up on the treetops across the road but even that was fading fast.

"We had better collect our packs," she suggested. "Or we will be spending a very cold and uncomfortable night."

Stella looked appalled. "Oh, we aren't camping here? Surely we are going home?"

Lt Ryan looked uncomfortable. "First we will gather everyone together and make sure you are safe. Then we will consider getting people home. Besides, I am sure the police and rangers will want you to show them where these nets are. Tina is right. Go and get your packs and we will meet you back here."

The vehicle sped away and the cadets walked back onto the old road. Stella was clearly reluctant to go into the jungle. Andrew tried to reassure her. "It is alright now Stella. The adults have things in hand. The police will arrive soon. We will be quite safe. Besides, we can't leave our packs there."

"Oh I can!" Stella said with vehemence.

Blake looked annoyed. "You might be able to but my mum spent a lot of money buying that gear and I need it. I'm going to get my pack." With that he set of back along the old road.

Tina hesitated for a moment but then followed him. To her annoyance

Andrew dithered and tried to reason with Stella. That really needled Tina's already jangled emotions.

"Leave her here Andrew. She can hide in the jungle if anyone comes."

Stella let out a little whimper and that irritated Tina even more. *Silly cow!* she thought. Her own response was to walk even faster. But as soon as she rounded the bend she was almost overwhelmed by a sense of dread. *What if there are more crooks here in the jungle?* she thought.

That worry began to oppress her as she strode along. It caused her to continually glance into the jungle on both sides and ahead.

At the bird poacher's camp she found Blake standing and contemplating the place. He gestured, "Should we have a look?"

Tina shook her head. "No. Leave it as it is. The police scientific people won't be happy if we mess up any clues."

Blake nodded and continued on. Tina followed him. As she did, she glanced back and saw that Andrew was not far behind and that Stella was now hurrying to catch up. The going was relatively easy as the bird poachers had cleared tracks around all the big fallen logs and bushes. But it was now quite dark and gloomy in under the rainforest canopy and Tina began to fret that they might not find their packs and be back at the road before it got dark.

As it was, they just managed it by the last of the twilight. It was further back to their packs than she remembered, and she found it a hard puff up the hundred metres or so to where the packs were hidden. They were there but pulling them on was a cruel little shock as all the sore muscles and chafing instantly complained. Tina bit her lip and swung the pack on but Stella whined and complained until Blake snapped, "Well I'm not going to carry your pack for you."

They set off back at 5:45pm, pausing at the creek crossing to refill their water bottles again. Then it was just a slow and painful plod in the dusk back to the road. To Tina's enormous relief the Officers of Cadets were back and so was the 'Bronze' team. As soon as she had dropped her pack Tina hurried to Lt Ryan and asked if the police were coming.

Lt Ryan shook his head. "They say they will arrive tomorrow morning about 0900hrs. They want us to stay here."

"Is that safe sir?" Tina asked. She was now torn between fear and the desire to help the police.

"They said to keep in contact, but they believe so. The 'Bronze' team saw the vehicle you described. It skidded to a stop when it met them but then accelerated past and the driver gave them a filthy look. I think he thought we were police. They wear dark blue work uniforms when they are doing scrub bashing."

"Scrub bashing!" cried Blake. "That's what we've been doing. I've done enough to last me a long time."

"Me too," Andrew agreed. "No more jungle for me. Our next expedition will be by water."

Lt Ryan laughed with them but then held up the satellite phone. "Now we will call your parents to check what they want, but they will have to come and get you. Just remember that they will have to find their way up these jungle roads in the dark if they do."

This was done. Each cadet was allowed to talk to their parents after Lt Ryan had explained the situation to them. Both Andrew and Blake told their parents they wanted to stay. Hearing that made Tina give a wry smile. *Andrew thinks it is a big adventure,* she thought. But she didn't. She was really scared. But nor she did not want to worry her parents or have them trying to drive the jungle roads in the dark, so she said she was fine and that she wanted to stay. Only Stella asked to be taken home, but her parents said they couldn't as they had no car. That got Stella crying and pleading but in the end she had to stay.

Once that was done Lt Ryan pointed along the old road and said, "You can set up camp along there. I will park the vehicle here to block the entrance so you will be quite safe. You boys go last in line so that the girls aren't on the end."

"Oh sir!" Andrew cried in mock horror.

Stella looked back along the old road, which was now just a tunnel of darkness. "But what if more crooks come out of the jungle."

Blake snorted with derision and said, "Look at it! Nobody is going to be pushing their way through that stuff in the dark, not without lights and an awful lot of noise."

Andrew said, "Blake's right. Anyway, we will protect you. Come on, let's set up out tents and then have tea."

So they did. Tina found that Andrew was right. In under the trees it was so dark that she literally could not see her hand in front of her face and they had to use torches to set up their tents. Then they joined the others out on the edge of the road in the slightly less dark starlight. The officers lit a lantern and that at once cheered her up. The others wanted to know all about the meeting with the bird poachers so there was plenty of talk over the next couple of hours. Tina had to recount her meetings with Danny and Marco and the floatplane at Croydon and that got her feeling very apprehensive.

Danny said he would get me, she thought.

But had he recognised her that afternoon? She did not think so but it was still a niggling worry. It made going to bed an anxious experience and once all the lights were turned off and there were just the jungle noises in the utter blackness fears began to crowd back in.

What if he comes back to get me tonight? she thought.

Chapter 23

LOOKING OVER HER SHOULDER

That thought came to dominate Tina's mind as she lay there in the darkness. Her rational mind told her it was ridiculous.

The crooks will be trying to get away. They won't come back here in case the police are here. And even if they do, how will they know which tent I am in? she reasoned. But it was no use. Irrational fears gripped her until she was shivering with emotion.

Then a sniffling, whimpering noise beside her attracted her attention. It was Stella and she was crying. Tina reached out and touched her and Stella twitched convulsively and cried out. Tina was shocked at the reaction and got a fright herself but said, "What's the matter Stella?"

"I... I'm... sniff... sc... scared...sniff. I... sob... j... j... just w.w.w..want to g... g... go h... home!" she answered.

I can identify with that! Tina thought.

But she reached across and put her arm around Stella's shoulders. She tried to calm her by using all the same arguments. But even as she said the words her mind conjured up images of Danny and Marco sneaking stealthily past the parked vehicles and then past the other tents. The images had the effect of causing her to tense up and hyperventilate until Stella's clinging grasp reminded her of what she was trying to do.

We should have organised a watch, she thought. She knew that wasn't quite the term she wanted and thought of how the army cadets might guard their camps. *Sentry roster,* she thought. That was the term she wanted. While she hushed Stella and comforted her, she wondered if she should even now wake up the others and try to organize a guard.

But she didn't. Even though she was terrified she was too scared of what she imagined the others would say. *They will sneer and tell me I am being silly and get annoyed,* she thought. So instead she lay back, miserable and afraid and tried to stay calm. But her eyes kept probing the darkness outside the tent and her ears, allied to her imagination, added to the mounting terror. The jungle seemed to be alive with sounds. Some, like the creek, she recognised but cursed because it made it harder to hear. Others were mysterious scuttlings and dripping noises. Once a rotten tree or branch fell with a crash. It was a long way off, but it still caused her to stiffen up and Stella to bolt upright.

"What was that?" she cried.

It took Tina more time to calm Stella. Then another frightening necessity developed. Stella tugged at her sleeve and whispered, "I need to do a pee."

The moment Stella put the idea in her head Tina felt the need too. She had been several times during the day but it was one thing to walk around the bend of the track in daylight and to listen to the birds but quite another to contemplate going out into that hostile blackness! But there was no help for it. She realised she urgently needed to go. So she pulled on her boots and picked up her torch.

It took some persuading before Stella would join her outside the tent. Tina even contemplated doing it just beside the tent but the knowledge that the boys were in their tent only two metres away stopped her. Even in the extremity of her fear she was too inhibited to do something so shameful.

So the two girls made their way 20 metres until they were around the bend in the old road. Then they turned their torches off out of modesty's sake. That was scary. Without even the thin beam of light the jungle seemed to envelop Tina and she experienced the sensation of it pressing in on her. And the jungle noises seemed louder and closer.

I hope there are no snakes, she thought as she squatted. She even opened her mouth to warn Stella but then clamped it shut. *She may not have thought of them and that might send her into hysterics.*

It was only after she had finished and pulled her trousers up that Tina remembered there might be leeches. The thought of one of the slimy creatures worming its way up into her private parts horrified her.

I will look later, she told herself.

But she forgot to. She and Stella used their torches to make their way back along the old road. As she moved cautiously Tina had the eerie sensation of feeling that they were being followed and it took all her willpower not to bolt back to the camp. Her whole skin came out in goose bumps and she found she was gasping each breath and that tears were trickling down her face. She knew she was terrified.

It did not get much better. Back in the tent she could not sleep and lay awake thinking about what to do and imagining death sneaking closer. Several times she fell into an exhausted slumber but each time she had a nightmare and woke with a start. One of the dreams had her out on a large lake at night in a canoe and there was mist and dark shapes were swooping low overhead and then hands, clawing, grasping hands, reaching up out of the water to grab at her. She woke up trembling and drenched with perspiration.

It was a long, miserable night and when the first grey of dawn showed she felt exhausted. She fell into a deep sleep for another hour until woken by the others as they got up to do their morning camp tasks.

As she crawled out of her tent Tina was greeted by a very cheerful Andrew. He said good morning and then frowned. "You OK Tina? You look a bit of a wreck."

"I didn't sleep very well," Tina admitted.

Suddenly she was gripped by a desire to be in his arms and she burst into tears. That put her there. Andrew stopped cooking his breakfast and hurried to hold her.

"Here, steady on kiddo," he muttered, hugging and patting her.

Dimity Bates and Grace Rushbrook from the other Bronze Group both hurried to join them. Tina didn't want their help at all but had to pretend she was grateful. After a minute or so she stopped crying and shaking but still had fits of shivering. As Andrew held her, she looked over his shoulder at the jungle, and then trembled again. The jungle now was a malevolent environment full of menace and threat.

A pale and drawn looking Stella joined them and then the officers. When Andrew saw them, he tensed up and made moves to release Tina. She was reluctant to let go. *He can hold me all day long,* she thought.

But he did take his arms away. After a few minutes Tina had calmed down enough to stand on her own and then she felt ashamed of her weakness.

Blake, all male cheerfulness, said, "You'll be alright after a good breakfast."

Tina managed a weak smile and did not argue. *No I won't be,* she thought, *not while those men are still out there.*

It was that idea that occupied her thoughts while she prepared and ate her breakfast. She pretended that everything was normal but inside she was churning with fear. *Danny said he would get me,* she told herself.

Will I have to spend the rest of my life looking over my shoulder? The notion that the 'rest of her life' might actually be a short period of time crept in to chill her some more.

The sun came out. The other cadets were cheerful and chatted happily about their expeditions or the bird poachers. But even though it was a perfect North Queensland day, clear skies, cool breezes, bright sunshine, Tina felt ill and depressed.

Despite that she did not ask to be taken home. When the police at last arrived with two wildlife rangers in two vehicles at 0930hrs she was able to answer questions clearly and then went with the others when they went to show the police and rangers the poacher's camp and the mist nets. The other bronze group went with them as they were hiking the opposite route that day.

Even with three policemen, two rangers and two officers Tina still felt apprehensive walking along the old road through the jungle. They did not stop at the camp but were asked if they had been into it. When Andrew replied that they had not so as not to muck up any clues the police all nodded with approval.

At the creek crossing the opportunity was taken to fill water bottles. Andrew said to the other group, "You won't find any water at all until you reach the bridge on the other side of the mountain. Drink as much as you can or you will be very thirsty."

While they did that Tina and Blake led the police and rangers on up the slope to the mist nets. The rangers were quite excited. "We know nothing about these," said the senior of the two. "Nobody has any permission to be using them and certainly not in this area."

"Who pulled it down?" a police sergeant asked.

Tina put up her hand. "I did. There was a crimson rosella trapped in it and I wanted to set it free."

"You cut it?" asked the sergeant, holding up the end of the net for her to see.

"Yes," Tina replied. She reached out and touched the nylon and was again astonished at how milky and light the net felt. She could only marvel at the technology that could manufacture such a thing.

Tina now noticed movement off to her right and looked up to see a small bird caught in another net. It was one she had noticed before and she wondered how many more nets there might be. So did the rangers, and they asked that question. They then untied the net and lowered it and tried to free the struggling bird.

It was a brightly coloured finch and it looked terrified. *That's how I feel,* Tina thought.

The ranger got the bird free but when he went to release it the bird flopped to the ground with its wings fluttering wildly. "Broken wing," the ranger said. He bent down and picked the bird up and held it for a moment. Then he used both hands and very quickly twisted its neck. Tina was simultaneously horrified and relieved. A bird with a broken wing had no chance of survival.

The ranger shook his head and Tina could see he was a bit upset. He said, "Lots of wildlife gets injured or dies when it is being smuggled. It is a very cruel activity. Much of it is waste but the prices are so high that people keep doing it."

Tina could not imagine how anyone could harm such beautiful creatures, but she realised that there were people who did. A shiver ran through her at the sickening reality that some humans would also kill and injure other humans. *Danny shot the ranger, and he said he would get me,* she thought. That sent her into a fit of trembling and more tears came.

Andrew again held her and helped calm her. Then the other group arrived from the creek and Andrew released her and joined Blake in giving them instructions on how to get over the mountain without getting lost. The other group all set off up the mountain and Blake said, "Rather them than me. We at least didn't have to climb any steep slopes."

That led to a discussion with the officers and others as to whether they would continue with their expedition. Tina did not really want to and nor did Stella but both boys did. Tina doubted if she could carry her pack and was also worried about Danny. "Is it safe?" she asked.

The officers looked worried and asked the police sergeant. He nodded. "Should be. We've got a roadblock at both ends of the Danbulla Road and that will stay in place for the rest of the day. And we will be here for quite a while."

Lt Ryan nodded and said, "Well, you can go on with your walk if you like. We will follow along, catch you up and then wait 10 minutes and then catch up again to stay with you if you like."

Tina brightened up at that because she did not want to disappoint Andrew. "That would be good," she said.

After answering a few more questions from the police and rangers they made their way back down to the creek. Here they followed their own advice and filled water bottles and drank deeply. Then they walked back to the junction. As they did Tina kept having flashbacks and a sense of gloom enfolded her again. She kept glancing over her shoulder and at the thick jungle on both sides. It was a relief to come out into the bright sunlight on the main road.

Their gear was already packed so there was no excuse to delay and it was already nearly 1100hrs so Andrew swung on his belt. "Packs on!" he called.

Tina picked up her pack and swung it on. There was immediate pain as sore muscles protested and she could feel the chafing. It hurt so much she nearly cried out and her immediate reaction was to take the pack back off and drop it. Stella did but then Tina saw the look on Andrew's face and she stiffened her resolve.

I don't want him to despise me, she thought. Instinctively she knew that pity and sympathy were no grounds for a serious and loving relationship. *That needs respect,* she told herself. So she kept her face neutral and pretended it did not hurt.

Stella's pack was placed in the vehicle and the group continued. Within minutes Tina regretted carrying her pack. The march was uphill and her shoulders ached. The energy seemed to drain out of her and the chafing began to rub and sting.

This hurts! she thought. But she did not want Andrew to think less of her, so she clenched her teeth and said nothing.

That was how it was for the next five hours. The only time she did object was when they stopped at a track junction 20 minutes later and Andrew pointed to a peak just visible through the trees. "That is Mt Edith," Andrew said. "Kirk reckons that there are a lot of World War 2 trenches up on it."

Blake looked surprised. "I didn't know they fought World War 2 here," he said.

"They didn't," Andrew answered. "The troops did their training here before going to fight the Japanese in New Guinea."

"And the trenches are still there?" Blake asked.

"That's what Graham said. He recommended we look at them. It isn't far, only a few hundred metres. We can leave our packs here," Andrew said.

They had all dropped their packs and both Andrew and Blake started walking up the narrow foot trail that led into the jungle. Andrew glanced back, then stopped and said, "You coming, Tina?"

Tina was torn. She did not want to stay there with Stella, not with Danny and Marco still on the loose and possibly still hiding in the jungle. But nor did she want to drag herself up what looked to be quite a steep little mountain peak. So she shook her head. "No. You can go some other time. Go with Kirk one weekend," she said.

"But it's just there," Andrew said.

Luckily Tina had thought of a very good answer. "It will take half an hour or more, an hour all up. We are already late and it is half past eleven. We are due to be picked up at three and still have to walk down the mountain. That is at least 8 or 9 kilometres."

"Aw, we can do that in three hours," Andrew answered.

"Well you can go but I am going to keep walking," Tina said. She knew she was being stubborn and she was actually half interested in climbing Mt Edith. But she was feeling both exhausted and scared. She actually had no intention of walking along that road on her own but was determined.

At that moment, the officers arrived in their vehicle and that made Tina feel safer. It also decided Andrew. "Alright. We will visit it another day," he conceded.

"We can drive to here to start," Tina replied as a sop to make it easier.

"We could have driven here this time too!" Blake said ruefully. He picked up his pack and hoisted it on. Soon the four were walking again.

The road was narrow and in places muddy. It wound around the side of the mountain top in a tunnel of jungle. The air was quite cool at that altitude and the rainforest would have been pretty if Tina had been of a mind to admire it. But instead she kept looking back over her shoulder to check that the officer's vehicle was following and the rest of the time she anxiously scanned the jungle and wondered where Danny was.

They stopped at 1230hrs to have lunch. The officers joined them, parking the vehicle just off the side of the road at a point where it was wide enough for another vehicle to pass. One did. When Tina heard it coming up the mountain she got all tense, but it was just a family car with some sightseers. As it went past she relaxed, but then shook her head.

I am getting paranoid, she told herself. She tried to concentrate on her food but felt so ill she could barely force the baked beans down.

At 1445hrs they reached the junction with the Danbulla Forest Road near Robsons Creek. The officers joined them. Tina was sharply disappointed that her mother was not there to meet them and she just slumped down on her pack, ready to cry. She did cry when her mother arrived 20 minutes later.

Her mother parked the car and hurried over. "Oh you poor dear!" she cried.

Tina hobbled to meet her and they embraced. All Tina could do was sob for several minutes. "I was so scared Mum," she said. *And I still am,* she thought. But she did not want to worry her mother, so she did not say that.

There was half an hour of animated talking. The incident was discussed at length. For Tina the telling did not give closure or comfort as she kept thinking about the poachers and their threats. The police had not caught them.

As long as they are free, I will feel threatened, she thought.

It was a very miserable and exhausted girl who climbed into the vehicle. And it was not only the poachers who were causing her distress. When Andrew climbed in to sit next to her, she thought, *I still haven't managed to get him to ask me to the dance and it is next weekend.*

How to arrange that occupied her mind during the drive back along the Danbulla Road. The Danbulla Road ran around the northern and eastern sides of Lake Tinaroo but for most of its length it was in thick jungle and too far from the lake to see it. There were occasional glimpses of sections of the lake but otherwise it was just a wall of trees and vines that were visible. Tina had been along it once before on a weekend drive but barely remembered it. It was a good two-lane gravel road and with plenty of traffic.

Tina's mum took the shortest way home going south past the old forestry settlement of Danbulla and through extensive stands of plantation pines. There was more jungle and a number or road junctions where side roads led off to the lake. None of it really interested Tina. She just wanted to be home and to be safe. She did not even pay attention when Andrew pointed out the turnoff to School Point.

"That is where we paddled our canoes to last year," he pointed out.

Tina had a vague recollection of a very pleasant little backwater ringed by pine forest and with a grassy lawn leading down from a picnic area to the water's edge but she only nodded and grunted.

Andrew wasn't put off. He went on, "We might make that one of our ports of call when we do our real expedition."

Blake laughed and added, "And definitely by water. I've had enough jungle."

They passed the turn-off to Fongon Bay, another picnic area, but much larger. Tina just glanced and then looked away, her mind dwelling on Danny. Nor did she pay attention to other turn-offs or to the tourist attractions of Lake Euramo or 'The Chimneys' as she was driven past them. The vehicle went on past an old ranger station and up a steep hill and past another turn-off to the right. Then it wound through the jungle for many kilometres until she felt car sick.

The only other vehicles they passed were obviously families on Sunday drives or tourists. There were three cars at the Mobo Crater car park and two at the Cathedral Fig Tree. Then they came out into open country and Tina felt a bit easier. After winding through open, hilly farmland for a few more kilometres they came to the junction with the Gillies Highway. Tina expected to see a police roadblock there but there was nothing visible. That bothered her as it seemed to her to indicate that the police did not take the situation very seriously.

Danny has got away and will come back to get his revenge, she thought miserably.

She was so unhappy she just brooded for the remainder of the trip. She barely noticed the 16 kilometres of winding mountain road as they descended into the Mulgrave Valley. Even though she thought that places like Little Mulgrave were among the prettiest places she knew she just stared at the scenery without really seeing.

Only when they arrived back in Cairns at Andrew's did another unhappy thought surface. *I still haven't got Andrew to ask me to the dance and it is only next weekend,* she thought. But despite being annoyed with him she gave him a smile and tried to pretend that she was alright.

It was when she was at home with her mother and father and was recounting the story that she finally unravelled emotionally. Suddenly the bottled-up fear became too much and she began to sob uncontrollably. It took her parents a good 20 minutes to calm her.

"You will be fine Little Baby," her mother said soothingly.

That just annoyed Tina even more. "It may not be mum. Those men are still on the loose. Now I am really scared they will come and get me out of revenge."

"Oh they won't. They wouldn't even know you were involved," her mother said.

That was a ghastly doubt Tina had. *Did Danny recognize me?* she worried. She said, "Do you think we should shift; you know, go to another town to live, even change our names?" She had seen such things on TV crime programs and now wondered if it was an option.

Her parents were visibly shocked. Her mother shook her head emphatically. "Of course not! Well, not unless the police advise it. We will ask. But I am sure things will be alright."

"Oh, I hope so," Tina replied. "I don't want to go around looking over my shoulder all the time."

Chapter 24

BOYS!

Tina had a feverish and exhausted sleep that night and felt so ill the next day that her mother allowed her to stay home. Her mother insisted on staying home as well. That comforted Tina but upset her even more as it meant her mother could not go to work. Her mother cleaned and bandaged Tina's hand but seemed satisfied. It was healing well and only weeping a tiny amount of pus.

For much of the day Tina lay in bed and dozed. But even when half-asleep she could not stop being scared. Worry about Danny and Marco dominated her thoughts and she felt ill and helpless.

The police can't protect me, she reasoned. *They can't guard the back of the house and the front at the same time; or keep me safe while I go to school, or to the shops or whatever. And even if they tried it would only be for a few days.*

Anxiety over the future kept her in a fever of worry all day and far into the night. She did hope that her friends might call. *Or Andrew, and I could tell the silly boy to take me to the dance,* she thought, with the dreadful concept of 'If I am still alive' lurking on the edge of her conscious thoughts.

The other thing she hoped for was learning that the bird poachers had been caught by the authorities. But there was no phone call from the police and no mention of them on either the TV or radio. That depressed her even more.

She also had the very uncomfortable experience of going out to feed her own birds and having doubts about whether it was right to keep them in cages. Images of the struggling crimson rosella in the mist net flooded in as she fed Beaky and she bit her lip and felt bad.

Would Beaky really like to be free? she wondered.

Intellectually she understood that birds reared in captivity had trouble surviving in the wild but that did not ease her gut feeling that she might be being cruel.

On Tuesday she went to school. Her mother drove her and promised to pick her up. That made Tina feel a bit more secure. When she had woken up she had felt so ill and sick in the stomach that she had not wanted to go but nor did she want to be the reason her mother lost another day's pay so she lied and said she was well enough.

As she walked through the school looking for her friends, Tina regretted that action and began considering spending the day at the sick room, until she saw Andrew. He came hurrying across to her and asked how she was. Suddenly Tina could not control her emotions. She burst into tears and stepped forward. To her great comfort he met her and put his arms around her. She held him tight, pleased that he had acted so spontaneously and regardless of the looks and comments from the many watching students.

Andrew patted her and then gently wiped the tears from her cheek. "What's the matter Ti?" he whispered.

With an effort she controlled her sobbing and told him, between sniffles, of her fears. Andrew nodded and looked serious but shook his head. "I think you are OK. I don't think that Danny bloke recognised you, or that we were navy cadets. I heard the officers saying to the police that they thought that Danny had the idea we were police in their blue work clothes."

"Oh I hope so!" Tina cried. Then there were more tears and she held him tight. He patted her and murmured soothing words and for a moment she thought he was going to kiss her. But he didn't and she rested her head on his shoulder and wiped away the tears.

Then she saw Barbara Brassington walk past with her friends and some of the Year 12 boys. That jolted her. *The dance,* she thought. But she could not just ask. The words seemed to stick in a throat that suddenly constricted. She burst into tears again.

"What's the matter?" Andrew asked.

"You," she croaked.

"Me! What have I done?" Andrew asked.

"It's what you (sob) haven't (sniffle) done," Tina replied.

Andrew looked surprised and then worried. "What's that?" he asked cautiously.

That exasperated Tina. "Oh boys!" she cried. "I've given you enough hints! Saturday night."

For a few seconds Andrew looked puzzled and slightly foolish. Then the light bulb came visibly on and he turned to look into her eyes. "I would love to take you to the dance on Saturday night, if you would like to come of course," he said.

Oh at last! Tina thought.

She sobbed yes and then grabbed his head and kissed him full on the mouth. That conjured up cheers, catcalls and cries of advice from the watching students. Tina saw Marjorie grinning at her and another girl named Naomi holding her hand to her mouth in delighted surprise. It all made Tina feel good.

I am not such a frump after all! she told herself.

Andrew kissed her back and then went all tense. He eased his head away. "We are breaking the school rules. We will get into trouble if a teacher comes along," he said.

Tina could not have cared less. To her school was unreal and she knew that there was a much bigger world out there, one with love and hate. But she was suddenly happy and she smiled as he reluctantly released her. Andrew turned to answer a smart jibe about coming up for air from Stephen. Tina saw that Stephen, Graham and Peter were there.

Graham spoke first. "What happened to your hand Tina?"

That jolted Tina. Vivid images of those terrifying moments in the jungle swamped her and threatened to turn her into a blubbering wreck. But she managed to say, "A bird bit it."

Stephen curled his lip. "Serves you right for keeping them locked up," he said.

That hurt and tears prickled but Tina managed to say, "No. I was freeing one from a mist net."

She did not really want to talk about it but Graham said, "Was that during your hike?"

"Yes," Tina replied.

They then discussed the incident. Graham was very interested and she sensed that he was even jealous that he had missed out on an adventure. He said, "So are you going hiking again Andrew?"

"Nope. You can have the jungle. No more for me thanks."

The army cadets laughed and the conversation turned to hikes and jungle adventures the boys had been on then to the weekend army cadet bivouac. As they talked, Tina found she was studying Graham. *He is very handsome,* she thought. Then she experienced a guilty jolt. *I shouldn't be looking at other boys,* she told herself. But she had to admit there were some very handsome males around. *And some gross grots!* she added as a group of grubby Year 8 boys went by.

In class Tina found it hard to concentrate. Her mind and emotions were in a whirl, a mixture of happiness and fear that left her feeling worn out by lunch time. By the time the day finished she just wanted to lie down. But when her mother took her home, she hurried to her wardrobe and took out her dress and held it against her in front of the mirror.

Later she did some adjustments and then tried it on. When she studied her image in the mirror, she bit her lip and wondered if it was the right dress. *I still look a bit tubby,* she mused unhappily. *And heavens, it emphasizes my bust!*

Turning side on did not change her opinion. She was very aware of how the dress caused her bosom to jut out. She shook her head and then bent to straighten the hem. As she did, she glimpsed herself in the mirror and was at first appalled at how that action revealed her cleavage.

Good heavens! I nearly spilled out then, she thought.

But even as she straightened up an impish thought crossed her mind. The idea made her blush with shame but would not go away so, feeling very daring she deliberately bent over a few times to study the effect.

"That will keep Andrew's attention, I hope," she murmured.

Still hotly aware she was being very naughty she removed the dress and went to make a small adjustment to the waist. She wanted to discuss her dress with her mother but was too embarrassed.

I hope it will be alright, she worried.

That night she slept better. Her dreams were a mixture of romance and anxiety but in her waking moments she was able to push the dark shadows of fear aside by fantasising about being with Andrew at the dance. She pictured herself as a princess and he as her 'Prince Charming.'

Next morning her mother examined her wound and decided that it no longer needed a bandage. "Healing well. You are lucky," she said.

The next three days went slowly. Tina wanted to be with Andrew every second of the day but didn't. Instead she watched him from afar while sitting with her own friends. She was still afraid he might resent her if she was pushy or clingy. Her anxiety about the bird poachers abated and she even forgot about them for hours at a time as preparation for the fete and the dance came to dominate her thoughts.

As a fete task Tina's class had been allocated the running the 'White Elephant' stall and a quite astonishing quantity of bric-a-brac and otherwise useless objects had been donated. These were sorted during school time on Friday and very little class work was done. Tina thoroughly enjoyed helping sort, clean and carry the objects to where benches had been set up under the main building. She was one of the students who had volunteered to staff the stall, but only on Saturday.

That was because Navy Cadets was on Friday evening. Tina was keen to go but it also revived her memories of the previous weekend and got her all anxious again. Because of the fete numbers were down a bit but the training went ahead as normal. There were more practice lessons on sending signals in Morse code by signal lamp and another one on the destroyers of the RAN; their characteristics, weapons and likely roles and tasks. There was also a period during which the Duke of Edinburgh teams did more planning and wrote up their reports.

During this Blake showed them his photos of the birds caught in the mist net and that got Tina all emotional and upset. Seeing the photo of the crimson rosella latched onto her hand made her rub the scab and then struggle to hold back tears. For a few seconds she was deeply angry at the people who were so cruel to birds, but this was soon replaced by the nagging fear.

This only remained at an intense level for a few minutes before subsiding to be like a dull, niggling ache. Tina consciously pushed it down by thinking about the fete and the dance. Another worry came to take its place: would Andrew be with her at the fete during the afternoon? Tentatively she hinted at this by mentioning that she was going to be working on the stall from midday onwards. "What are you doing tomorrow Andrew?" she queried.

"I have to work at home in the morning and we are going to visit Aunty Ida after lunch. I won't get to the fete until after tea," Andrew replied.

That was a sharp little disappointment for Tina but she managed to hold her smile and to prattle on in apparent cheerfulness. Andrew then smiled and said, "Don't worry. I haven't forgotten the dance. I will be ready on time, and suitably dressed."

"What do you mean by suitably dressed?" Tina asked as suspicious anxiety sprang up.

"Oh, you know, the usual old shorts, torn singlet with holes in it and rubber thongs," Andrew replied airily.

"Oh you won't! Don't please," Tina cried.

Carmen had overheard this, and she said, "He's teasing you Tina. He will be respectable, or else!"

Tina hoped so and she went home to fantasize about whirling around the dance floor in the arms of her handsome prince with all the other girls looking enviously on.

Saturday morning dawned clear and cool and Tina felt very refreshed and happy. Only when she went out to feed the birds did the nagging worry resurface. This was added to when she saw that Neville now had several black cockatoos in his aviary and that the coloured finches were gone. She bit her lip and wondered if she should report this to someone but then hurried inside lest he come out and see her. She did not want to remind him she existed.

After an early lunch the whole family went to the fete. Tina wore a skirt and bright cotton top and took her dress on a hanger. On arrival at school she took the dress and her bag to the 'cloak room' being run as a stall by 10D. Then she made her way downstairs and helped her parents to set up their 'Lucky Frog' stand. This was a small plastic wading pool full of water on which floated polystyrene frogs. To win a prize people had to toss coins. If they landed on a frog, they won a chocolate frog. If the coin went in the water, then the school got the money. Raising money for the school was one of the main aims of the fete but Tina wasn't interested. At the first opportunity she walked off with Fleur, the first girl in her class to wander past.

For the next half hour the two girls wandered around looking at the fete. Various school groups had set up displays: Folk music, Drama club, Bushwalking club, Marine Studies, and so on. There were also displays of academic work: maps, essays, photo sets and the like.

The photography display held Tina's interest for a time.

"Some of these are really good," she commented, bending forward to read who the photographer was. "Stephen Bell," she read.

That caused Fleur to give a scandalised giggle. "Remember those photos he took earlier in the year?"

Stephen had become notorious a few months earlier by taking several sets of photos of teachers and students. Some of the photos had been of people with no clothes on, taken without their knowledge or permission. He had also taken some of a girl named Elli, posed nude, which had been a sensation. Something had then happened and rumour had it that Stephen had been in trouble with the police over them. Whatever it was Stephen had been much quieter since then.

While Tina and Fleur were studying the photos Stephen actually appeared. Tina was surprised to see he was holding the hand of Marjorie Morton. *I thought she liked Willy Williams,* Tina thought. *Oh dear! I wonder what happened? Poor Willy!*

A few minutes later Tina saw another pair that made her shake her head. It was Barbara Brassington with Nigel Cressly. He was strutting around with a very smug look on his face and Barbara was glowing with pleasure and snuggling up to him. Tina wasn't impressed. For no apparent reason she did not like Nigel. *But at least Barbara has her boyfriend to hold hands with,* she thought, wishing Andrew was there.

Later Tina and Fleur reached the army cadet stall. There were a dozen cadets there including Graham and Peter. Graham gave her a big smile and teased her about being a navy cadet.

"You should transfer to the army cadets," he said.

He is a spunky hunk, Tina thought, as she teased him back.

As they talked, she glanced at the stand. It was a mock camp with camping gear spread around and tubby little Roger lying on a sleeping bag. On the walls were several coloured diagrams of badges and so on, plus photos of the cadets at some of their activities. She was interested enough to go and study these and Graham came and stood close beside her to explain them.

His obvious interest in her made her feel a warm glow of satisfaction and she wasn't even nettled when he kept glancing at her boobs. *They've at least got his attention,* she thought. *And he is nice.* But she wished it was Andrew she was with. That thought caused her a twinge of guilt at being unfaithful, so she gently ended the conversation and strolled on to look at the next stand, a display of floral arrangements and hand crafts.

After walking around for another half hour, Tina had seen everything so she went to the class stand. Even though she was rostered on there was no need for her as several mothers had also arrived and were busy bustling around running the stall. So Tina and Fleur sat outside in the quadrangle where rows of chairs had been set up. They watched the groups performing on the stage in the quadrangle. She found that interesting enough to amuse but all the time she kept looking around for Andrew.

Instead it was Graham who came and sat beside her. "G'day," he said. "You look a bit bored. Can I cheer you up?"

Tina felt a surge of emotion: warm pleasure at being flirted with (she was sure he was flirting) and anxiety lest Andrew saw them; then guilt that she was enjoying the company of another male.

She said, "I am waiting for Andrew."

Graham laughed and said, "Never mind him. I am better looking."

Tina was surprised but pleased at the obvious attention. "Watch out the wind doesn't get up and blow those tickets off you," she replied, but she said it with a smile.

Graham laughed. "I am more fun," he said.

Tina had a sudden awful feeling that perhaps Graham was right. But she had also heard some whispered scandal about Graham and that sent her heart rate up as well. "Dream on!" she said, then laughed with happy embarrassment.

Graham still wasn't put off and he asked, "What are you doing tonight?"

"Don't be fresh!" Tina cried, but secretly she was flattered.

Fleur watched and giggled and looked jealous and that made Tina feel good too. She turned to face Graham and began to talk. As she did, she decided she did like him and that he was very handsome. Then a look on his face caused her to glance over her shoulder. It was Andrew.

Andrew was smiling but there was a little frown on his brow. "You trying to cut in on my girl Graham?" he said. It was in a joking tone, but Tina sensed that it was no joke at all.

He is worried and a bit jealous, she told herself. Then another idea came to her. *Good! Maybe that is what he needs to make him appreciate me!* she told herself.

Graham nodded and said, "Yes, I was. You want to be careful mate. She is too pretty to leave on her own for long."

"I will be, now go back to your jungle hideout," Andrew retorted, plainly nettled.

Graham laughed but stood up and left. Andrew sat down and looked a bit anxious. Tina said, "You are early. I wasn't expecting you till later."

"Obviously!" Andrew said.

His tone annoyed Tina but she also felt a surge of guilt. She knew she had been flirting with Graham. She said, "What do you mean by that?"

"You were flirting with Graham."

"I was not! He was flirting with me," Tina replied.

"Well you shouldn't encourage him," Andrew said.

That annoyed Tina even more. "Why not? You don't seem to be very interested. Anyway, you don't own me. I can talk to whoever I please," she snapped.

She sensed that they were having a row but could not bring herself to stop. Instinctively she knew that if the relationship could not stand some plain speaking and home truths then it was no good.

If he really loves me it will be for the best, she thought.

Andrew seemed at a loss for words and just looked anxiously at her. Then his facial expression changed to surprise as he saw something behind her. "Oooh look! It is Willy Williams' new Zeppelin."

Tina opened her mouth to tell him not to change the subject but everyone around her was also turning to look so she did as well. It was another model Zeppelin and it looked so impressive that Tina let out a gasp of admiration. Willy was holding it by a cord up on the veranda of the main building. The model was three or four metres long and actually flew.

"Come on," she said. "I want to get a better look." She stood up and without thinking took Andrew's hand and walked towards that side of the grass quadrangle.

Andrew followed. "It's only Willy Willy Williams the mad scientist," he grumbled.

Willy handed the cord to Stick Morton then ran downstairs onto the quadrangle. Stick then tossed Willy the cord, which Tina now saw was nylon fishing line. The model's electric motors were then started and Stick pushed it so that it flew slowly out off the veranda and over the heads of the crowd. Tina stared at the huge model in fascinated admiration.

"Willy is very clever," she said.

Andrew nodded. "He is a real brain, that's for sure," he agreed.

As the model Zeppelin purred slowly out over the heads of the crowd, held by the nylon cord, there was a ripple of applause, which Tina joined in. She found herself standing next to Nigel and Barbara.

Nigel sneered and said, "Williams is just a stupid little kid. He's as mad as a cut snake."

His words caused Tina to purse her lips with dislike and she glanced and saw that Barbara wasn't looking very happy either.

Well, you chose him! Tina thought.

A gust of wind caused the model to slew around but Willy held it and reeled it lower, before starting to walk across the quadrangle through the crowd. The model began to buzz along at walking speed. Willy walked past close to where Tina stood and as he did he looked at Barbara. Tina saw her give him a smile and he smiled back. She also noted the way his eyes flicked to Nigel and the look of pain which crossed his face.

He really must have a crush on Barbara, she thought.

Willy walked the tethered model over towards the end of C Block. As he did, Tina saw some sort of disturbance. "Oh no! It is that bully Scranton," she cried. Scranton was blocking Willy's path. Tina was too far away to hear what was said but the look on Scranton's face caused her concern. Scranton tried to grab the nylon line holding the model. Willy stepped back and avoided this but Scranton suddenly produced a cigarette lighter and flicked it on. It was one of the butane gas ones and Tina saw a jet of flame roar out for twenty centimetres.

Barbara again cried loudly, "Oh no! Stop him Nigel! Do something." She let go of Nigel's hand and began thrusting her way through the gathering crowd towards Willy. At the same time Andrew let go of Tina's hand and began pushing towards Willy. Tina followed, noting that Graham and Peter Bronsky, both in their cadet uniforms, had joined Willy and were speaking to Scranton. But they were too late. Scranton suddenly jumped up and the gas lighter flared.

There was gasp from the crowd. The flame had cut the nylon cord and the model suddenly floated upwards. Tina felt a surge of sick dismay and continued pushing forward behind Andrew and Barbara.

The model was seized by the wind and, as its electric motors were still running as well, it was driven against the building. For a while it looked like it might snag or be caught, but then a gust slewed it round and it blew off towards another building. Tina could not get closer because of the press of people but did get glimpses of Willy's anguished face.

Oh poor Willy! she thought.

The model scraped along the upper part of M Block before sailing off out over the school fence, 10 metres up. It snagged briefly on the power lines before being blown off across the street. Some students followed it, including Willy, Stick and his little sister Marjorie, Stephen, Peter and Graham. Barbara followed them but Andrew stopped and took Tina's hand. He watched the model floating away and shook his head.

"They won't catch it now," he said.

"What a terrible waste," Tina cried.

A deep anger at Scranton's cruel act made her wish she was big enough to hit him. But all she could do was stand and watched as the model drifted higher and higher. It dwindled rapidly in size as the wind carried it off over the rooftops across the street.

They watched until the model had dwindled and vanished. Then they turned and made their way back to the fete. Tina looked around for Scranton but there was no sign of him. She felt very sorry for Willy as she knew the model must have taken him many hours to make. As she walked she gripped Andrew's hand but was aware that virtually nobody was noticing. They were all talking about the Zeppelin model or were busy with their own affairs.

But they will notice me at the dance, she told herself.

Chapter 25

EMOTIONAL TURMOIL

For Tina the afternoon now seemed to drag. She and Andrew went around to all of the stands and displays again. The real interest for Tina was in watching the other people. Several times she noted other girls look at her and Andrew and that gave her satisfaction. There were also several little incidents that added variety. Graham and Peter returned and Andrew asked them if they had caught the model Zeppelin.

Graham shook his head and said, "No chance. It just flew off into the mountains."

Tina met his smiling eyes and felt a twinge of warmth she did not want to admit to. "Is Willy very upset?" she asked.

Graham nodded. "He is. But I think he is more upset because Barbara Brassington is walking around holding Nigel Cressly's hand."

"Does Willy like her?" Tina asked.

"I think so. He hasn't actually said it but you can tell by the way he looks at her. And he did ask her out. That was why he had the fight with Scranton," Graham explained.

"Where is Scranton now?" Andrew asked.

Graham shrugged. "No idea," he said, but he kept his eyes on Tina's as he said it.

Andrew obviously noticed this as he sounded quite abrupt when he said, "See you later," and almost wrenched Tina around and led her away.

"What was that all about?" Tina queried, a bit peeved by his action.

"I didn't like the way Graham was ogling you," Andrew replied stiffly.

"Oh he was not!" Tina replied. But she also glowed with egotistical pleasure and admitted he had been giving her very appraising and admiring looks. *Maybe he likes me,* she thought.

"He was, and if he keeps doing it I will snot him one," Andrew snapped.

She liked that. "Would you fight over me?" she asked.

"If I had to," Andrew replied. "But only if that was what you wanted."

She liked that too, particularly the implication that it was her choice. She snuggled against him and strolled happily along. Soon after that she saw Barbara and Nigel in the distance, and they were obviously having a disagreement.

I don't think that relationship will last too long, she decided. *Cressly is too full of himself and he is just taking her out for what he can get.* Then she sighed, secretly wishing Andrew would try to get 'a bit'.

Later, while she and Andrew were enjoying a cup of hot chocolate, Tina saw Barbara walking around on her own. She looked quite unhappy and that got Tina speculating that Cressly had given her the brush off.

Andrew suggested something to eat and led the way to a hamburger stall where he bought them both a hamburger. While seated at the nearby tables eating Tina saw Barbara again. This time she was with Karen from her class. Tina also noted a dejected looking Willy standing there talking to Stick. To Tina's surprise Barbara went over and placed her hand on Willy's forearm. Willy looked surprised and then pleased as Barbara said, "Hello Willy. I'm sorry about your model. It was really marvellous."

Willy appeared tongue-tied but after a few seconds stammered, "Th... Thanks."

Karen tugged at Barbara's sleeve. "Come on, I don't want a hamburger either. It will make me ill."

Barbara gave a shrug. "See you later," she said to Willy, then followed Karen. As the pair walked past Tina Barbara said to Karen, "You could have waited a sec. I only wanted to cheer Willy up. It was a great model."

"He's just a stupid kid," Karen sneered, "playing with toys at his age!"

"He's alright," Barbara replied defensively.

Tina did not hear any more as the two girls moved out of earshot. But it did make her feel sorry for Willy. *He might have a crush on Barbara,* she thought, *but if her best friend is that negative, he doesn't have much chance.*

Andrew then spoke to Willy. "That was a great model Willy," he said. "The best I have ever seen."

"Thanks," Willy replied. He then turned and Tina met his eyes. To her they looked full of misery and she was worried lest he burst into tears. To save him the shame she added, "It was really good."

"Thanks," Willy muttered, nodding. But it was very obvious to Tina that he was deeply dejected. *Poor boy,* she thought as she watched him walk away with his friend Stick.

It was a fairly thoughtful Tina who finished eating her hamburger. She and Andrew then wandered around looking at all the stalls again. After that they sat and watched some of the displays on the stage. This included Scottish Highland dancing and musical items. Tina thoroughly enjoyed both and Andrew at least pretended to be interested.

Later they went upstairs to the coffee shop run by the Year 11 French class. Tina managed a cup of coffee and some bread, but she felt a bit tired and down. Despite being with Andrew she felt that the fete was not nearly as exciting as the previous year.

Never mind. Only a couple of hours to the dance, she consoled herself.

After the coffee they strolled around again and then went and worked in their class stall for an hour. Tina began to count down the time until the dance. But even that got her all anxious.

I hope Andrew likes my dress, she worried.

Then she fretted about the bust being too revealing. But the only other option now was to make some excuse and not go so she nerved herself to face the event.

To fill in more time she and Andrew went and sat and watched more displays: Irish dancing this time, followed by some ballet by a group of Year 8 girls. Tina pointed to the girl leading the dancing and said, "That dark haired girl in the lead is Graham Kirk's sister, isn't she?"

Andrew looked and nodded. "Yes. Kylie is her name."

Tina admired her trim legs and good muscle tone and style and said, "She's very good."

Andrew nodded and said, "If you like ballet."

"Don't you?"

"Not particularly."

Tina thought about this for a second and then said, "What if I said I wanted to go to the ballet, would you take me?"

Andrew hesitated and then said, "I suppose so."

That bothered Tina so she replied, "I suppose I could always find someone else to go with."

That made Andrew look uncomfortable and he muttered about it being alright. But Tina was still a bit worried.

If he really loves me, he should just make a sacrifice sometimes, she thought.

For the second time that night she wondered if in fact Andrew was the man for her. She realised that she really knew very little about him and also began to appreciate that learning about the other person and adjusting to their likes and dislikes was a basic part of any relationship.

That seemed to end the conversation for a while. Then at 2100hrs Andrew touched her arm. "All those cadets have closed their display. Look, there are Graham and Peter."

Tina looked and saw the army cadets carrying things back to their Q Store. "Yes, nearly time for the dance," she said.

Andrew nodded. "We'd better go and get changed then."

Tina experienced a sharp little thrill of anticipation mixed with anxiety. They both stood up and she said, "Will you meet me here or at the dance?"

"Here," Andrew replied firmly.

That cheered Tina up a bit as she had fantasised about walking through her admiring and jealous school fellows in her best dress and with Andrew. So they separated and went to the change rooms. A change room for the girls had been set aside in one of the Home Economics classrooms so Tina made her way upstairs and proceeded to change. The place was being run by some Year 10 girls and Miss Hackenmeyer so their belongings had been quite safe. Small, screened cubicles had been set up and Tina used one of these to change. But as she struggled into her tight dress and saw how it displayed her bosom her emotions were swamped by anxieties over whether it was too daring, or too overdone.

Then she discovered another problem: she needed someone to zip her up at the back. Biting her lip with anxiety she looked out. As she did, she saw Barbara and Karen arrive. Tina hesitated and then decided to ask.

"Excuse me Barbara, would you zip me up please?" she asked.

Barbara gave her a quizzical smile, then said, "Alright."

Tina turned and Barbara walked over and carefully zipped her up. As she did, she said, "You are in Year 10 aren't you?"

"Yes, I'm Tina Babcock in 10A," Tina replied.

Barbara nodded and said, "Let's have a look then."

Tina did not really want to but could not think of a good reason other than embarrassment, so she stepped out and turned around. She noted Barbara's eyes widen as they took in her cleavage and that sent her anxiety level shooting up.

Barbara nodded and smiled. "You look great! It is a very nice dress."

"Thanks," Tina replied.

She was tempted to ask if she thought the bust too revealing but could not bring herself to. Instead she moved to study herself in the mirror. It seemed to her that her whole front was creamy mounds of flesh and for a few seconds she contemplated going back to change. But that would need someone to unzip her and she was too afraid of mocking comments to admit to being scared.

I will just have to brazen it out, she thought, aware that her neck and cheeks were mottling with embarrassment.

Barbara nodded approval and then went to a change cubicle, leaving Tina alone in front of the mirror. Tina tidied her hair and checked her make-up then went back to pack her other clothes. Feeling very self-conscious she made her way to the counter to check them back in. She certainly drew some glances but they seemed to be more admiring and envious than censorious, but they still made her cheeks burn. With her heart fluttering with anxiety she made her way downstairs.

At every step Tina was conscious of her bobbling bosom. It filled the lower half of her vision and she was appalled at how much it quivered.

Oh dear! I hope I haven't made a real blunder, she worried.

But Andrew's reaction was all she had hoped for. He was smartly dressed in slacks and long-sleeved shirt and the moment he saw her his eyes widened in surprise and admiration.

"Gee! You look really great, Tina!" he cried.

A warm feeling of daring and appreciation caused her to glow inside. Then she blushed and felt a mixture of desire and shame as she knew he was looking. She could see he was trying to pretend he wasn't looking but noted his eyes continually flicked to her bosom.

I've got his attention at least, she told herself.

Wicked and naughty thoughts flitted through her mind and she had to smile, even as she blushed. Arm in arm they strolled across the quadrangle. As they walked through the crowds, Tina noted many people glance at them. Some stared, or ogled if they were boys. Her face scorched but she was also aware of a deep thrill that she knew was naughty but which she was enjoying. To her it suddenly all seemed worth it.

Tina and Andrew strolled across the quadrangle and under the school. Their route took them past the cadet Q Store, and she noted that Peter and Graham were still there in cadet uniform. They were helping to pack things up. Capt Conkey and Lt Hamilton were supervising.

Tina noted a tubby little brown-haired girl with a cheerful, freckled face helping Graham. As Tina passed, she was amused to see Graham's eyes pop open with interest, obviously at her. She smiled at him and walked on, aware that the young girl was giving her a jealous, hostile stare.

"Who's that chubby little chick next to Graham Kirk?" she asked.

Andrew looked and sniffed. "That's his pet dog. Margaret is her name. She's only a Year Eight."

"That was a bit unkind. Why did you call her that?" Tina asked as they passed out into the darkness again.

"Because she follows him around all the time. She thinks he's wonderful."

"He is handsome," Tina replied.

She was aware that she said that to make Andrew jealous and to put him on his mettle and she was also vaguely aware that she had suffered a sharp little pang of disappointment when she had learned that there might be a girl in Graham's life.

I am being silly, she thought. *I love Andrew.*

But she was also aware that she was attracted to Graham. Not only was he obviously very handsome and virile but he had a reputation around the school for being good fun with girls. Tina remembered whispers of a scandal the previous year. Allegedly Graham and a girl named Mandy had been doing something very naughty ('It', rumour had it) when they were caught by Mandy's father. Tina had even heard that that incident was why Graham was now in the army cadets. Mandy's father was a regular army warrant officer and he had insisted. Apparently, he had said that either Graham joined the cadets or he went to jail.

Tina had only heard this as rumour and was not sure if such a thing were possible but thought it was a good story. *So Graham probably knows what girls like. And Mandy got sent to a convent, so she isn't on the scene any more,* she mused. Then she bit her lip at the direction her thoughts had been taking. *I'm being disloyal to Andrew,* she told herself.

But the images crept back in and caused her to wonder It also reminded her that it was against the law to have sex under the age of sixteen. *But you have to get caught,* she thought. For a moment she imagined doing it with Andrew. *I wonder what it will be like?* she thought.

Then she blushed and felt hot. She was aware that it was both the heat of desire and the heat of shame and it left her tingling and with vague hopes of something happening. *But nothing too serious,* she told herself, glancing hopefully down at her breasts as she did.

By then they had reached the school assembly hall. The dance was already in full swing. Dozens of students and a few teachers and parents stood around outside. Tina scanned their faces, all her daydreams flitting through her mind to make her heart beat faster. To her delight she noted quite a number of people giving her and Andrew what she thought were admiring looks. Images of pleasurable anticipation swirled in her mind as they paid for their tickets and went in.

The band was playing a slow, old-fashioned tune, a foxtrot, Tina recognised. She knew the old dances because they still learnt ballroom dancing in Phys Ed. and the teachers insisted that the dance be more than just a disco. So the types of dances alternated between traditional ballroom and modern. That suited Tina as she actually quite enjoyed most of them.

Just inside the door she and Andrew stopped and looked around. The hall was in semi-darkness, lit up by stroboscopic beams of coloured laser light and by the sparkling shards from a rotating mirror 'light ball'. It all looked very pretty, and Tina's romantic hopes soared. She was already conscious of the effect her dress was having.

To her delight Andrew swept her into his arms and led her into the dance. A warm glow coursed through her and she wanted to cry aloud with joy. Around and around they went, and she thrilled to his embrace. It was wonderful. All too soon the music stopped and then the tempo changed to a disco beat. They stayed on the dance floor and Tina danced happily on her own. She deliberately put on a show for Andrew by wriggling her hips and making her bosom bounce and quiver so that his gaze was riveted to them. As she did, she burned with a mixture of lust and shame but the thrill of it kept her moving.

By the time that dance was over Tina was excited and perspiring. She found it a relief to go back to an old-fashioned waltz. Andrew stepped forward and held her. They rotated and twirled, and Tina knew she was happy. She sighed and embraced him and savoured every moment. The next dance was fast and again she showed off, hotly aware that she was becoming the object of some catty comments and scandalised behind-the-hand whispers, and also a centre of attention.

Then it was another slow dance. This time Tina melted into Andrew's arms and pressed herself hard against him. She deliberately held him tight so that her breasts bulged up and she felt his body responding. His male hardness pressed against her stomach. That made her feel both excited and satisfied. *Good! I can get him aroused,* she thought. More wicked thoughts flitted across her mind and she rubbed her stomach against his hardness. Then she rested her cheek against his. He felt so good she just wished it could go on for ever.

But there were other people and she could not help looking and noticing. As she looked over Andrew's shoulder, she saw that the couple next to them were Nigel Cressly and a blonde girl from Year 11. Into Andrew's ear she whispered, "I thought Nigel Cressly was going out with Barbara Brassington."

"So did I," Andrew replied. He swung her round to see what she was talking about then whispered in her ear, "Sallyanne, from 11C."

Then he looked over Tina's shoulder and went tense.

"Oh ho! Here is Barbara now. Get ready for some fireworks."

Chapter 26

DOUBTS

Tina turned so she could see more clearly what was happening. She saw that Cressly and Sallyanne looked very intimate. Sallyanne was snuggled up against Cressly's chest, her arms around his neck. He had his arms around her waist.

Then Tina shifted her gaze to find Barbara and saw her at once. By chance a gap had opened up in the dancers allowing a clear view. Barbara and her friend Karen stood just inside the doorway looking around and Tina saw that Barbara was smiling. Tina was also struck by how attractive Barbara looked. She wore a form-fitting green dress that really accentuated her shape and displayed her bosom in a very revealing way. Previously Tina had noted that Barbara had breasts that were nearly as large as her own, but now she saw with a twinge of envy that they were firmer and jutted out more.

Andrew chuckled and murmured, "She is certainly outstanding."

More anxious jealousy caused Tina to snap, "Why do you say that?"

Andrew blushed and stammered and then said, "Because of her red hair. You can always pick her in a crowd."

Tina suspected he was not telling her what he had really been thinking, but before she could reply she saw Barbara's gaze settle on Cressly and Sallyanne, both of whom were still unaware she had arrived. For a moment Barbara appeared stunned and her mouth gaped. Then she closed her mouth and Tina saw a look of fury appear on her face. She grabbed Karen's arm and pointed.

A moment later Barbara stormed out onto the dance floor, pushing dancing couples aside without even noticing them. She halted in front of Cressly and Sallyanne, hands on hips. Angrily she snapped at Cressly,

"I thought you were taking me to the dance?"

Cressly let go of Sallyanne and stammered something back. Tina did not hear clearly what it was, but she watched with anxious fascination. Cressly shook his head but Sallyanne kept her arms around his neck and gave Barbara a shocked look.

Then Cressly said, "I didn't say I was taking you, Barbara."

That statement obviously enraged Barbara. "You bloody well did!" she cried. "Only this afternoon at the fete. I asked you."

"I did not!" Cressly replied.

"You lying bastard!" Barbara shouted. At that Sallyanne let go of Cressly and stepped aside, looking anxious. Barbara pointed at her. "Who is this then? Your little bit on the side? You've been taking me out for weeks. Have you been seeing her too?"

Cressly's face changed and Tina saw him look worried. He shook his head. "No," he replied.

Sallyanne didn't help. She looked at Cressly in hurt surprise. That glance obviously confirmed Barbara's worst suspicions and she exploded, telling Cressly exactly what she thought of him. Tina was dimly aware that the music had stopped and that they were the centre of attention.

Barbara's face went as red as her hair. "You cheating rat!" she snapped. "You are a two-timing turd! Well, that's it!" She glared at Sallyanne, who looked frightened and on the edge of tears. "You can have him, for what he's worth! Good luck to you. You'll need it."

Barbara paused and then glanced around. Her eyes met Tina's before moving on around the hundreds of gaping faces. Abruptly she spun on her heel and strode to the door. People moved hastily aside to give her a clear path.

Tina watched her go with a mixture of relief and sympathy. *Poor girl!* she thought, imagining the humiliation she must be feeling. As Barbara went out through the door, a great hubbub of chattering and gossip broke out. Tina could only shake her head and hope such a thing never happened to her.

Andrew chuckled and muttered, "That told the mongrel!"

"Poor girl! She must be so upset," Tina replied.

She looked towards Cressly and met his eye. Cressly looked very embarrassed and guilty and Tina was instantly sure he had been lying. She glared at him and he looked hastily away. Then he tried to make an explanation to Sallyanne, but she began to cry and hurried sobbing off towards the toilets, pursued by more behind-the-hand snickering and scandalised chattering.

Tina watched her go as well and felt another surge of sympathy as it was obvious she had also been deceived. Then Cressly also left, pushing red-faced to the door. Tina turned to Andrew and said, "I hope nothing like that ever happens to me."

Andrew nodded and replied, "Nor me. Anyway, you are safe with me. I won't ever cheat on you."

At that Tina was engulfed by warm emotion and she almost burst into tears. She flung her arms around his neck and hugged him. "Oh, you are wonderful!" she cried.

As she kissed him, she heard another voice guffaw and add, "Just bloody lucky really. Give the poor bugger some air."

It was Blake, and Tina's response was to poke her tongue at him. Andrew started to discuss the incident, but the band started playing again so she firmly moved him into motion and resumed dancing. As they danced, she relaxed and allowed her emotions to ease. After a few minutes she forgot about the unpleasant incident and gave herself over to her own pleasure at being in Andrew's arms. They danced three more dances, two fast and one traditional before Andrew suggested a drink.

Feeling very happy and pleased Tina walked hand in hand with Andrew across to where there was a drink stall near the door. As they did, she saw another group come through the door. These were led by Graham, now dressed in smart civilian clothes. With him was the little, anxious girl from Year 8, Margaret. Behind them came Peter, Graham's little sister Kylie and several Year 12s who were army cadets. These included Mike Masters, Warwick Grey and Ian MacAlistair, one of the school captains. On his arm was Gwen Copeland from Tina's class. Gwen was a very attractive blonde and her dress was blue and white silk with gold trimmings which perfectly matched her blonde hair and gold accessories.

A twinge of jealousy smote Tina and she knew it. It was the sort of entrance she had hoped to make but wasn't sure if she had achieved. Her envy increased as Gwen and Ian began to dance. As they did others moved back to give them room so that they became the centre of attention of the whole room. As Gwen twirled and danced, the lights sparkled off her jewellery and glinted off her hair. The words 'fairy princess' formed in Tina's mind and she knew she was jealous. The scene was exactly how she had pictured it being for herself.

It got worse. As soon as that dance was over, Andrew muttered an excuse and left Tina standing. Next time she saw him he was dancing with Gwen. Tina was so stung and hurt that for a few moments she could only stare and feel the pain. When Andrew returned, he was happy and cheerful and seemed quite oblivious to having hurt her feelings. Tina experienced a tiny stab of doubt which in turn made her feel guilty.

She was diverted from this by the return of Barbara and her friends Karen and Fiona. The three walked in side by side. At the door no-one tried to ask for payment, but they certainly got some the curious looks. They had entered during a break between dances and it seemed to Tina that every face in the hall swivelled to stare at Barbara. Then hands went over mouths and tongues began to wag. Barbara took a deep breath and walked on, head held up and eyes glinting.

Mike Masters and Warwick Grey both walked over to her at once. "Great! That's the spirit!" Warwick said.

He took Karen's arm and hugged her as he did. Fiona stood and smiled up a Mike who leaned forward and very gently kissed her. Tina was aware that the whole school was watching and she felt a great surge of emotion: jealousy, hurt, affection. It was so romantic! It was what she had wanted.

Warwick gave the MC a nod. He stepped to the microphone and announced the next dance. The crowd dissolved in movement and a buzz of voices. A smiling Graham moved to speak to Barbara. Tina saw Graham bow in the old-fashioned way.

"May I have this dance please, Barbara?"

Tina experienced another stab of envy as she watched Barbara return his smile and give Graham her hand. Her dislike for Barbara was now tinged with admiration. *I wouldn't have had the courage to return after a scene like that,* she thought.

The music was suited only to a modern wriggly stomp type dance, but Graham put his arms out in the classic dance pose and she took them. Without being conscious of it they began to dance, a slow, swaying waltz. This caused another buzz of conversation. A few seconds later, Mike and Fiona moved out and began waltzing beside them. Warwick and Karen joined them, followed by Ian and Gwen. They were the only couples on the floor and everyone else seemed to ebb away to make room for them.

The band got the message and suddenly changed beat to suit the dancers. Suddenly the crowd cheered, a huge spontaneous roar of noise. Tina saw tears form in Barbara's eyes, but she managed to smile and kept on dancing. She kept her head up and twirled in Graham's arms. Tina watched enviously and thought that Graham was very brave. *He is like a knight in shining armour,* she thought. But that thought also caused her to look around and she noted a very anxious little Margaret standing there, smiling but obviously deeply worried.

At the end of the dance Graham bowed again in the old-fashioned way. He said, "Thank you Barbara. That was lovely but I must now leave you. Perhaps Peter will dance with you?"

Tina saw Peter Bronsky step forward and bow to Barbara. Barbara nodded and allowed herself to be led out again. She also noted that Graham had taken little Margaret's hand and that her eyes glowed with adoration as he did.

Lucky girl! she thought. *I hope he loves her as much.*

During all of this Tina had been hoping Andrew would sweep her out onto the dance floor with them but he was nowhere to be seen. That not only made her feel anxious, but she also again experienced little niggles of doubt. Then her anxiety level shot up another notch when she spotted him dancing with Sarah.

My best friend! How could he? she thought.

But she knew she was being jealous and unreasonable. It was quite normal for the boys to dance with more than one girl. But when he danced with a pretty Year 9 for the next dance Tina could only stand and feel miserable. Tears prickled in her eyes and she bit her lip.

Suddenly Graham's smiling, freckled face appeared in front of her. "May I have this dance?" he asked.

Tina felt her heart leap. She experienced a mixture of pleasure and anxiety. But she was also peeved at being abandoned by Andrew. So she smiled back and said yes. The dance was a fast one and almost at once Tina was torn between anxiety over how her bosom began to heave and bobble as she wiggled and a deep thrill at being naughty. She could tell by the way Graham's eyes continually moved to look at her bosom that he was enjoying the view and that he was admiring her. Those thoughts caused more scorching waves of shame and sheer pleasure.

She saw him stare and then lick his lips and shake his head in wonder. There was anxiety that others might label her tarty or sluty but the knowledge that she was being naughty merely added a thrill to a sudden desire to show off to Graham.

He at least appreciates me, she thought.

Graham again shook his head and dragged his gaze up to meet hers. "Geez, Tina, you are really something. You are really attractive," he said.

Tina glowed and felt a pulse of heat she could only label as desire. "Thank you," she murmured.

Graham grinned and said, "I would love to take you out. How about a date?"

Tina was completely caught off guard. For a few seconds she was so flustered she could not answer. It was only with an effort that she bit back the yes that was hovering on her lips. *Andrew,* she thought. *Think of Andrew.*

"Sorry," she managed to say. "But I am going out with someone at the moment."

Graham laughed. "Never mind Andrew. I am more fun than him. Let me show you a good time."

The impish thought that it wasn't just a good time that Graham wanted to show her flitted across Tina's mind and she was again sorely tempted to say yes. *He would be good fun too,* she thought. But she managed to say no.

Graham took the rejection in good humour and said, "When you realise I am the better man, maybe."

They left it at that and at the end of the dance Graham took her back to where she had been standing. He thanked her and left. Soon after Andrew re-joined her and chatted away about nothing but then she noted him casting worried looks in Graham's direction.

He must have seen us dancing, she thought. Then she pursed her lips and nodded to herself. *Good, that will make him more careful. He might realise he can't just take me for granted.*

But she mentally forgave him the moment he took her in his arms for the next dance. She was even pleased to see Graham dancing with little Margaret. Then Graham's eyes met Tina's and he winked at her. She was so surprised she gaped, and she knew it. He grinned and went on dancing and Tina experienced another little stab of doubt.

Later Tina noted Graham dancing with Gwen Copeland. Once again, the 'fairy princess' idea floated across her consciousness and she knew she was jealous, both of Gwen's beauty and, she realised with a shock, that she was dancing with Graham. Seeing them together caused Tina to look around for little Margaret. She found her standing beside Graham's sister Kylie, again looking anxious but smiling in spite of it.

She's a good kid. I hope he does love her. Then she shook her head. *I shouldn't be thinking about Graham. I am in love with Andrew,* she told herself.

Soon after that another small incident occurred which caused Andrew to comment to her. During a break between dances a couple walked in the door: Stephen Bell and Marjorie. From the look of the grass in her rumpled hair and on the back of her dress Marjorie had been out having a tumble on the lawn.

Tina saw Fiona point and heard her say, "I thought Marjorie was Willy Williams' girlfriend."

"So did I," Karen agreed.

Tina remembered seeing Stephen and Marjorie together earlier in the evening. But she still felt a spurt of sympathy. *Poor Willy! He must have been dumped!*

Worry over possible rivals and over being dumped gave her much food for thought and took some of the shine off the evening. But Tina still enjoyed it and it was with real regret she danced the last dance with Andrew. During that he held her tight and then waked with her hand in hand when she went to collect her belongings.

As they waited for her mother to collect her Andrew stood with his arm around her waist. That made her feel good and the fact that other girls were seeing it was nice ego food too, but she yearned for more. *I wish he would kiss me,* she thought. And she badly wanted him to ask for another date.

Does he love me? Will he take me out again? she worried.

Chapter 27

ANXIETIES

But Andrew did not ask and Tina went home hopeful but disappointed. Nor did she see him the next day. Sunday she spent at home. Most of the time she rested, dozing or reading, but there were also chores to be done and a visit to Aunty Flo. Tina had to clean out the bird cages and while she did that she chattered to Beaky and the budgies. She also cast frequent anxious glances through the back fence. Not knowing was what nagged at her.

Is Neville involved in this bird poaching and smuggling? she wondered, noting that there were now six black cockatoos and a dozen red breasted finches in the aviary next door.

Once again, she wondered if she should tell someone in authority about how frequently the birds in Neville's cages changed. Not having acted made her feel guilty. But she was also afraid.

If I tell and he has not broken the law it will make for a very unpleasant neighbourhood, she thought. *And it could cause a great deal of distress to his family and harm to him if he is innocent.*

Then the more chilling thought came to her. *And if he is and he gets away then he might come to get me too.* She vaguely understood that most people charged with some crime were let out on bail. *They only keep them locked up before their trial if they are accused of some really serious crime,* she told herself.

And once again she wondered if Beaky minded being locked up too. *He is in jail. But would he be better off free?* she wondered.

Monday was better. Andrew actually came over to where she sat at school and sat down next to her. That both embarrassed and pleased Tina as it caused a wave of smiling chatter and gossip among the other girls.

Andrew seemed to be oblivious to them. He talked in a relaxed way and Tina was able to relax too. She kept hoping he would ask her for a date or at least to hint he might visit her. So she got a shock when he casually mentioned that he and his family were going to Townsville for the long weekend. That sent Tina's anxiety level shooting up.

That blonde girl who is a nudist lives there, she thought.

After Andrew had wandered off to join his mates Tina sat and worried about how Andrew felt about the girl in Townsville and about what might happen. That made her feel guilty because Andrew had promised not to cheat on her, but she was a normal human and experienced doubts. It also made her wonder what to do during the long weekend. Her own family had made no plans that she was aware of other than visiting Aunty Ida.

She turned to Sarah and said, "Is your family still going camping up at Lake Tinaroo?"

Sarah nodded. "Yes, but we have had our campsite changed. We were going to School Point but the Forestry people have changed it because they are cutting timber along that road and they have closed it off. We have been relocated to Fongon Bay."

Tina had once been to Fongon Bay and was able to conjure up a vague image of the place. She nodded and said, "You are lucky. I don't think I am going anywhere."

Sarah at once took the cue. "Why don't you join us for a day, or maybe even two days?"

"I'd love to. You are very kind," Tina said. She felt a gush of gratitude for her friend. "But will your parents mind?"

"I'll ask them tonight," Sarah promised.

She did and phoned Tina to tell her it would be OK. Tina then went to ask her own parents. Her mother was happy for her to go but her father said, "You will have to ride your bike up. We will be too busy."

For a second Tina thought about the many kilometres of winding mountain road up the Gillies Highway and she quailed at the thought. Then she saw the grin developing on her father's face. "Oh, Dad! You don't mean that?"

"No. I was teasing you. But we will have to think about our movements," her father replied.

Garth then piped up, "What about me?"

"You are staying home to mow the lawn and sweep out the courtyard," Mr Babcock replied.

This time it was Tina's turn to grin at the indignant look on her little brother's face. He began to angrily protest then their father burst out laughing. So the family weekend was planned.

The remainder of the week then dragged by. Andrew spoke to Tina every day, but not once did he suggest a date. It was Graham who kept hinting at it whenever he met her when Andrew wasn't there. Tina was both pleased and annoyed.

He knows I am going out with Andrew. He shouldn't put me under that sort of pressure, she thought. But it was very nice to be asked and she realised she was looking forward to their meetings.

She also noted that Barbara was moping around looking very unhappy. Every time Tina saw her she was reminded of the scene at the dance and that caused her little twinges of regret. The dance had not been the success she had hoped.

The only other incident of note was on the Thursday when she and Sarah went to the library to do some research for an assignment. Tina had just settled with a reference book when Sarah came hurrying over, her face alight with scandalised excitement.

"Tina, come and look! Quick!" Sarah squeaked.

Tina was so intrigued by Sarah's excitement that she did as she was asked. She stood up and followed Sarah along between several rows of bookshelves. When Sarah stopped and pointed through a gap in the books Tina peeked through. Sarah leant close and whispered, "It is Willy and that Year 8 girl, Marjorie."

It was. Tina saw that they were sitting close together and that Marjorie had her left hand in under the desk and was obviously doing something naughty as Willy was looking embarrassed.

"I thought they had broken up," Tina whispered to Sarah.

Sarah nodded, her eyes alight with interest. "So did I, but it looks like they have made up."

Tina nodded but then overheard Willy say, "Marjorie! Stop that! We will get into trouble."

Marjorie had a wicked grin on her face and Willy looked distinctly flustered and embarrassed. He glanced anxiously around and hissed, "Stop it, Marjorie!" He then took her hand away. Marjorie put it straight back.

Sarah gave a scandalised snicker and whispered, "She's trying hard to get his attention."

"She's succeeding," Tina replied.

She was both deeply embarrassed and fascinated. She saw Willy speaking earnestly to Marjorie, who finally removed her hand. From what she could see Tina could tell that Willy was both embarrassed and aroused.

Sarah then embarrassed her more by adding, "Boys like that."

"Do they?" Tina replied, trying to sound disinterested, although she blushed fiercely at the thoughts that now raced through her mind.

Would Andrew like that? Would I do it to him? she wondered. But she knew instantly that she would. *And more, if he wanted it,* she thought. That got her all ashamed and anxious but also excited.

Tina felt so guilty at her hot thoughts that she glanced around. She was horrified to see that Barbara and another Year 9 girl were also watching from the other end of the bookshelf. For a second their eyes met, and hot shame flooded through Tina. She hastily turned away and moved back to her books.

As she tried to settle back to her work, Tina got all worried and confused about what romance and love might really entail. It was very serious food for thought and she didn't know whether she was disgusted or excited. After a while she shrugged and told herself that if the man truly loved her and she him then it would all just happen naturally.

At that moment she noted Graham come into the library and she felt another surge of guilty emotions. *But who is that man: is he Andrew or Graham?* Once again, she briefly contemplated what it might be like to go on a date with Graham. *He will be more hot blooded and earthy,* she decided. That thought got her aroused and guilty but also made her very curious.

Her hopes for being asked for a date remained high but were not fulfilled. Andrew spoke to her in a friendly way but made no comment about taking her out again. That annoyed Tina and made her feel resentful. So the remainder of Thursday and then Friday slipped by, leaving Tina feeling rejected and frustrated.

Friday night was Navy Cadets. Tina went but it was a dull and depressing event. The numbers on parade were right down because many families had left early for the long weekend. Among these were Andrew and Carmen. The thought of Andrew being in Townsville with the blonde nudist caused Tina to have frequent sharp bouts of jealousy and doubt. She tried to tell herself she was being silly.

He may not even see her, she thought. Then she imagined Andrew 'seeing' her and the hurt was repeated. Even having Sarah chirping happily about their camping holiday was a source of irritation to her. *I don't want to be with Sarah,* she thought. *I want to be with Andrew, or is it with some other boy?* Graham's face came to mind and she shook her head in annoyance at her own weak will.

So the Queen's Birthday long weekend began. That Friday night at home after Cadets Tina felt lonely and miserable and several times became so emotionally fragile that she wanted to cry. *Why doesn't Andrew ask me out? Doesn't he like me anymore?* she worried. Anxious doubts about her looks or her mannerisms and personality were crowded out by even worse ides: that she had bad body odour or bad breath. *Or maybe his friends think I am a frump and have teased him and he is afraid to be seen with me. There must be something that has turned him off,* she fretted.

On Saturday morning she packed her camping gear and some food and the family then drove up to Yungaburra to see Aunty Ida. They went via Gordonvale and Mulgrave Valley, then up the winding Gillies Highway. As always Tina enjoyed the change in climate and scenery between the coastal plain and the Tablelands. But the views of the jungle-covered mountains also brought back sharp memories of the trek over Mt Tiptree and of the mist nets and Danny.

I wonder where he is now? she mused. The worry was enough to cause her shortness of breath and a tingling sense she knew was fear. *Oh, I hope the police catch them soon. I can't stand much more of this,* she worried. For a few seconds she wondered if she should be going to join Sarah at Lake Tinaroo. *That is just at the base of the Lamb Range,* she thought. But then she shook her head. *No, he will be far away by now.*

At least she hoped so, but the fear stayed with her as a nagging ache in the back of her consciousness and took the edge off her enjoyment of the drive and of meeting her aunt. She thought Aunty Ida was a dear old soul and was always touched by her obvious gentleness and love. That brought her anxiety into sharper focus and left her puzzling over how some people could be so evil.

After lunch and a long talk they said farewell to Aunty Ida and set off to take Tina to Fongon Bay. This meant driving back along the Gillies and as the Lamb Range was clearly visible away off to the left Tina was again beset by anxieties. She tried to work out if she could see Mt Tiptree but reasoned she could not as it was north of the range. But she thought she could detect the sharp little peak of Mt Edith at the eastern end of the mountains.

At Mt Nomico they turned left onto the Danbulla Forest Drive and Tina became even more anxious as now they were heading towards the Lamb Range. At first, she did not feel more than a general anxiety but after the first few kilometres of open farmland when the road entered dense tropical rainforest she became progressively more upset. This was exacerbated by a feeling of claustrophobia as the road wound its way through a gloomy tunnel with the tree canopies meeting overhead.

She became so anxious she started to hyperventilate and found she was sitting on the edge of her seat and gripping the seat belt tightly. Several times she tried to pluck up the courage to ask her parents not to keep going but she couldn't.

I don't want to worry them, she told herself.

But her mother noticed and said, "You are very pale dearie. Is something wrong?"

Tina sucked in air and shook her head. "Just a bit carsick, I think."

Her mother did not press the issue, but Tina could see she was worried. To set her mind at rest she forced herself to chatter brightly about the jungle, the butterflies and the birds. This helped and by the time they crossed Mobo Creek she felt a bit better.

The road wound its way uphill until they came to the Mobo Crater car park. There were no other vehicles there and to Tina's dismay her father pulled the car in and switched the engine off.

"I've never seen this," he said. "It is only a few hundred metres so we can spare the time."

Tina did not want to go walking in the rainforest, not even with her own mother and father to protect her, but she could see that the others were happy and enjoying the expedition, so she kept silent and followed. Garth set off at the run down the path and then her father and mother. Tina came last. The path was mostly steps down a steep slope and the rainforest was quite open compared to some she had experienced but it was still enough to give her a hemmed-in feeling.

As she walked down the path, she kept getting glimpses of the others ahead and could hear their happy voices but she knew she wasn't enjoying it. *I don't like rainforest,* she decided. But she kept walking, anxious not to be left on her own.

But she was and she almost tripped and fell in her anxious hurry to catch up. She began to get prickling sensations up her back and that got her glancing over her shoulder to check that she wasn't being followed.

This is stupid! I'm being paranoid, she told herself. But it was one thing to try to be reasonable and quite another to control her emotions. Flashbacks of Danny and the mist nets did not help, and she found herself looking through the trees for mist nets.

When she reached the bottom of the steps, she found she was beside a small creek but still out of sight of her family. Even their voices were dulled by the roar of a waterfall and the noises of the creek. She knew it was a beautiful place and that she should ordinarily have enjoyed being there but even the sight of a flight of brightly coloured parrots did not move her.

Suddenly she could take it no longer and tears misted her eyes. Unable to see clearly, she grabbed at a tree to keep her balance. For a minute or so she shook with sobs, her whole body shaking and shivering. But even in that situation she did not want to make her parents anxious, so she began gulping the cool mountain air and wiping the tears with her sleeve.

But she was not quick enough. Her mother appeared, hurrying back around the bend in the track. When she saw Tina's state she hurried over and hugged her. "Are you alright Ti? Oh you poor dear! What's the matter? Is it those men?"

This time Tina really broke down. "Y... Y... Yes," she blubbered. She clung to her mother as she was wracked by sobbing.

Her father reappeared and joined in trying to comfort her. To both of them Tina blubbered out her fears. That helped and she slowly calmed down and the tears stopped. After a time she steadied her breathing. Her mother said, "You are safe little Ti. Do you want to go home?"

Tina did but she also did not want to let Sarah down. "I do," she replied as she wiped her face, "But Sarah is expecting us. I will be alright."

"You are sure?" her mother asked anxiously.

"Yes mum. Anyway, we will be sailing and canoeing so it should be fine," Tina assured her.

By then Garth had re-joined them and she did not want to endure his scorn, so she knelt and rinsed her face from the crystal clear water of the creek beside the track. The water was ice cold and the shock helped. She managed a sickly grin and started walking.

Garth ran on ahead and her parents followed, their heads together as they anxiously discussed her condition. Tina half expected them to over-rule her decision, but they accepted it and tried to act normally as they visited the pool in the crater at the bottom. Then they walked back up to the car. Tina was anxious lest the men arrive and she knew such thoughts were silly. Even so, she was very glad to be back in the car.

They drove on up the winding forest road for another 5 kilometres, until it began to descend. At a very sharp bend back to the right she noted a gate and a side road off to the left. For a moment she wondered where it went. The main road then wound down a steep hillside and came out in pine forest with clearings. They passed the old brick chimneys and then the car park at Lake Euramo. Here they again stopped but there was no jungle path. They stood at the lookout and were unimpressed. It was a small 'crater' lake but was hard to see because of the surrounding vegetation and it looked to be half filled with reeds. It was certainly a poor relation to the big crater lakes of Barrine and Eacham.

After passing the old schoolhouse and driving through several more kilometres of tall pine trees, they turned left along the Fongon Bay Road. Tina had forgotten just how far it was and the drive seemed to be interminable. It was all through pine plantations. Most of there were old and had a dense undergrowth of ferns and long grass. Several other side tracks went off but they all looked overgrown and muddy.

It was nearly 4pm when they came out into the open beside the lake at Fongon Bay Picnic Area. Tina was instantly appalled. The whole place was a vast clutter of tents, vehicles and boats on trailers. There seemed to be tents and people everywhere. Tina had only ever been there when it was not a holiday and now she both amazed and disgusted.

This looks awful, she thought.

But she held her tongue and could only shake her head sadly as they drove slowly along looking for the Creswells. The Fongon Picnic Area was on a long, narrow peninsula several kilometres long. The nearest and narrowest end was a flat, grassy area about a hundred metres wide and a kilometre long. This was where the tents were. Beyond that was a dense stand of mature pine trees.

They found the Creswells on the south side halfway along and Sarah came running happily out to greet her as she climbed out of the vehicle. Sarah's obvious delight in her presence pushed Tina's residual fears aside.

Besides, there are lots of people here, she told herself. In fact the impression she had was of a fairground. *Or a refugee camp,* she added as she saw the litter and garbage on the grass.

The sight of some of the camps astonished her. Some had three or four tents linked up with tarpaulins between or in front of them and many had chairs and tables and a few had portable stoves or barbeques and even a couple of fridges.

It is not really camping, she thought. *More like moving home!* It seemed to her to be an awful lot of trouble for just a couple of nights.

There was half an hour while the adults talked and Tina knew by the glances they cast in her direction that her mother and father were informing the Creswells of her emotional state. That made her blush with shame and regret that she had broken down. She had to reassure her parents that she did not want to go home. This decision was firmed up by seeing Sarah's obvious disappointment when it was suggested.

"I will be alright mum," Tina assured her.

But half an hour later, when her parents and Garth said farewell and drove away, Tina felt a sharp stab of anxiety. She tried to tell herself she was being silly as she was there with the Creswells and hundreds of other people, but it didn't help much. It was when the sun went down and Tina found herself surrounded by dark shapes of tents, boats and vehicles that the anxiety returned in such force that she almost experienced a panic attack.

To her shame she was too afraid to go to the nearby toilet block on her own and waited until Sarah suggested they go. Later, as the family settled down for bed, Tina looked out across the dark waters of the bay at the even darker line of pines on the opposite shore and she began to shiver.

"I must be safe here with all these people around," she told herself. "The smugglers wouldn't come here."

But it was no good. She became so scared she could hardly speak. Not wanting to alarm or bother her hosts she said nothing and gratefully unrolled her sleeping bag well inside the tent next to Sarah.

Then she lay down and after the lantern was turned off tried to calm her racing heart and trembling limbs.

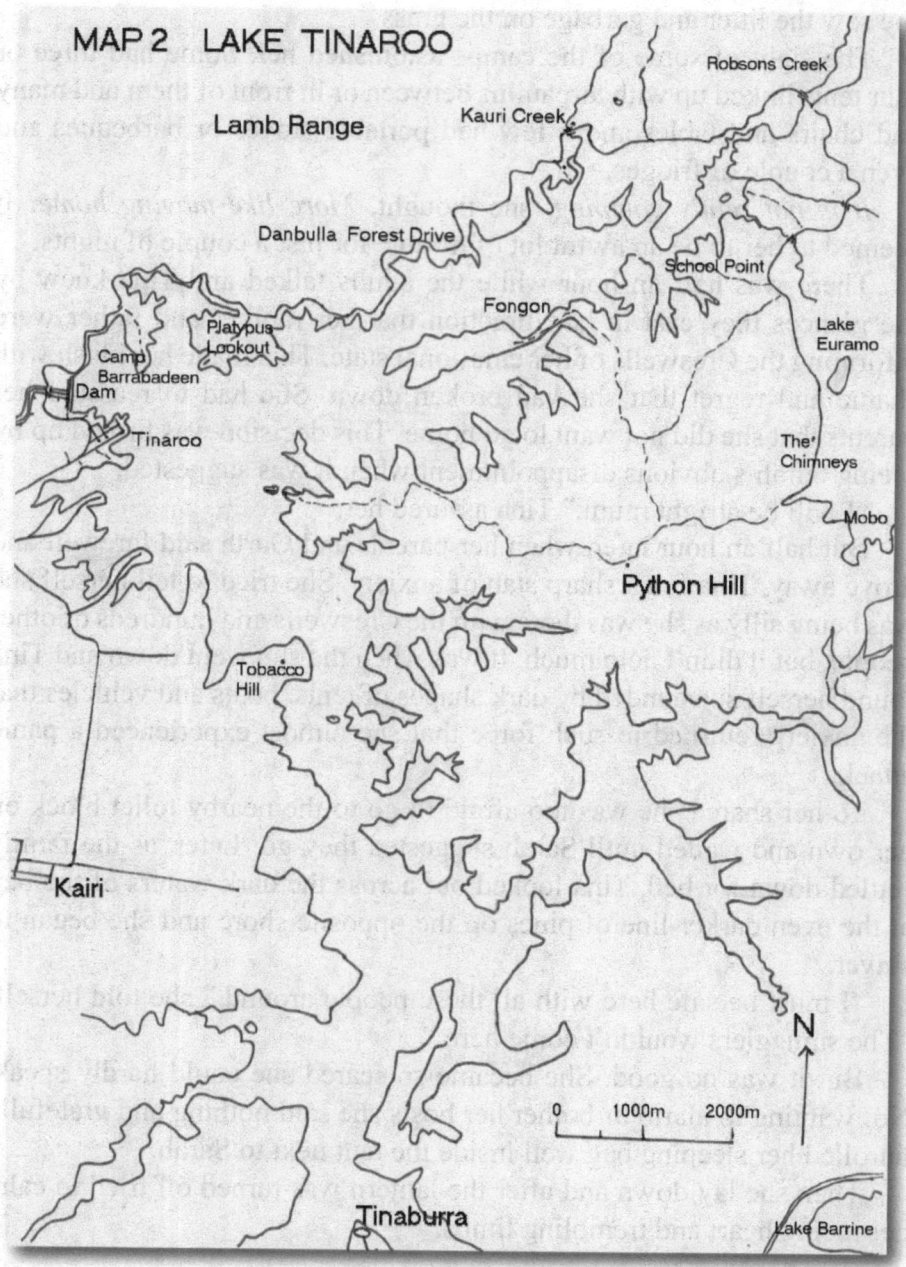

MAP 2   LAKE TINAROO

Lamb Range

Robsons Creek

Kauri Creek

Danbulla Forest Drive

School Point

Fongon

Lake
Euramo

Platypus
Lookout

Camp
Barrabadeen
Dam

The
Chimneys

Tinaroo

Mobo

Python Hill

Tobacco
Hill

Kairi

N

0   1000m   2000m

Tinaburra

Lake Barrine

Chapter 28

PYTHON POINT

It took a long time for Tina to relax and even longer for her to drop off to sleep. Not only was she tormented by vague fears of the bird poachers but there was nagging worry about whether Andrew loved her. When she did slip into a restless sleep it was to suffer an awful nightmare that involved the lake. She and Sarah were out canoeing and the water was calm and it was a bright sunny day. But suddenly Tina found herself alone in the canoe and it was dark and there were waves. Worse still, there was a current which was dragging the canoe along and her mind kept dredging up some fear that made her paddle frantically. But she was not strong enough. And then a ghastly, clutching hand came up out of the water. Tina stared at it, quite paralysed by fear, until the hand suddenly grabbed at her paddle and snatched it out of her hand.

She screamed, or tried to, only managing a strangled groan. Then she began to use her hands to paddle with. But every time she went to dip her hands into the water it took a huge effort of willpower as she was gripped by the terrible thought that The Hand would reach up and grab her. Frantically she cast around, trying to locate it in the dark waves and rippling current. But it was, yes, there it is! It is coming to get me!

She woke, trembling and all tangled up in her sleeping bag. For a few seconds she lay, gasping for breath and looking anxiously into the darkened corners of the tent. Only after about 10 minutes did she stop trembling and get her breathing back to normal.

Just a silly nightmare, she tried to tell herself. But then another much more horrible thought, crept insidiously in: *Is it a premonition? Am I going to die? Or is Sarah going to drown or be murdered?*

It was a dreadful thought and Tina tried hard to banish it from her consciousness. After all, there was Sarah sleeping peacefully right next to her.

I must be extra careful tomorrow, Tina reasoned. *Perhaps we shouldn't go canoeing or sailing?*

Then another, more shameful problem arose. Tina found she urgently needed to go to the toilet! But she knew she could not wake Sarah or her mother without revealing her worries. For nearly an hour she lay there, wrestling with her fear and trying to summon up the courage to go. Finally both pain and shame at her own cowardice forced her up. Trembling with both fear and cold she slipped on her sneakers and used her torch to help pick her way silently to the entrance to the tent.

Here she stood for a few more minutes, studying the now silent tents, boats and vehicles. Distant lights showed the location of the toilet, but it seemed a long way. Trembling with anxiety and continually glancing in all directions she cautiously ventured out. For her that hundred metres was a real test of courage. Under every vehicle was a pool of darkness that could hide a lurking attacker, or behind every tent or boat trailer.

Even inside the lighted toilet block Tina did not feel safe as she was all alone and she had the frightening thought that the men might have seen her and followed her. But it was cold so she finally had to pluck up the courage to leave. Shivering with both cold and fear she hurried back to her tent, losing her way twice and getting even more upset and panicky.

She found the tent at last and was just going to slip inside when she heard the sound of an aero engine. That caused her a sharp stab of alarm and she looked up. It was only a small plane and it took her a minute or so to spot it against the stars. When she did, she saw it was heading southwest almost directly overhead.

But it's got navigation lights on, and it doesn't sound like the smugglers' plane, she thought. But she still watched it out of sight and conjured up memories of the smugglers' floatplane. Then she told herself she was being silly and paranoid. *They wouldn't come near a place like this, not during the holiday season anyway,* she rationalised.

Still wondering what had become of the smugglers she looked anxiously around and then slipped quickly inside the tent. Her torch revealed only the Creswells sleeping. All was quiet and she felt ashamed of her weakness. Still shaking she slid into her sleeping bag and tried to compose herself for sleep.

In this she was successful as she dropped into a deep and dreamless sleep from which she was roused by the noises of voices, motors and cooking. She rubbed her eyes and looked out to see that the front of the tent was open and that it was daylight. Mr Creswell was outside cooking sausages on a portable barbeque. Sarah and her mother were nowhere to be seen.

As Tina emerged from the tent, she met Sarah and her mother returning from the toilets. Smiling and attempting to conceal the fact that she felt dreadful and also very apprehensive about the day. To set her mind at rest, she asked, "What are we doing today?"

Sarah smiled and said, "We are going to go sailing."

That was exactly what Tina had both feared and expected. In a faint hope of avoiding this she gestured to where a large power boats was revving its engine, the sound shattering the morning stillness and setting the cockatoos screeching in the pine forests. Several other power boats were already tearing across the lake in the distance.

"Do you think it will be safe?"

Mr Creswell heard this and nodded. "It will be OK. We will keep the canoe close inshore and you should be alright out in the open water on the sailboat."

Tina was dismayed but managed to hide this. "I hope so," she replied as calmly as she could. It was not power boats like the large one that was even then accelerating away in a welter of foam that she was worried about. Sarah did not seem to notice her lack of enthusiasm and prattled on instead about breakfast.

Tina stared out at the lake and through her mind flitted images from her nightmare and she shuddered momentarily. To divert her thoughts she said, "Where are we going?"

"Exploring," Sarah answered. "We will look at birds and check out an access road and a campsite dad says might be useful if we do our canoe expedition in the June holidays."

Tina remembered discussing with the others where they might paddle to and where they might camp and a check on a map that Sarah produced showed a road leading over Python Hill and down to the end of a long peninsula.

"That one over there," she said, pointing across the lake to a long, tree-covered peninsula.

Having set her mind at rest Tina set out alone to go to the toilet. In daylight the bustling fairground feel of the place did not bother her at all, although she thought it was strange place to camp for a holiday. Her steps led her across to the northern shore of the peninsula where half a dozen boats were being prepared or launched. Several were sailboats and there was even a canoe but most were power boats and already several of these were roaring up and down the lake.

She stood for a few minutes and looked northwards across the lake. There was a long arm of the lake to the north of the peninsula and much narrower and smaller one to the south. From where she stood she could see 5 or 6 kilometres of the north shore, which was a kilometre or so away. There were several other picnic areas crowded with tents, vehicles and boats at points along that shore. Beyond the wall of jungle or pine plantations that backed the shore rose the rugged, jungle-covered mass of the Lamb Range.

That is Mt Haig. Mt Tiptree is on the other side of that, she mused, suffering vivid flashbacks to the mist net incident. She was even able to make out the sharp peak of Mt Edith at the eastern end of the range. *That is where the road comes down that we walked along,* she thought.

With an effort of willpower, she forced thoughts of bird poachers and negative thoughts about the rain forest out of her consciousness and she went to prepare for the day. But those thoughts came crowding back later when she discovered where they were going to walk. Lake Tinaroo has a very distinct northern and southern section. The northern section is divided up by three large peninsulas. The two main peninsulas have in addition, dozens of small peninsulas or capes protruding into the lake. It was the largest and longest of the three that the expedition was to explore.

After breakfast, the group set about preparing their boats and gear and the sailboat and canoe were then launched. There was a small 'Laser' sailboat and a Canadian canoe. It was decided that Tina, Sarah, and Michael would go one way in the sailboat and come back in the canoe while Mr and Mrs Creswell and young Aiden would go in the canoe to begin with. Despite feeling very apprehensive Tina got ready, fitting on her personal flotation device and smearing sunscreen cream on her face. She made sure her belongings like bird books, camera and binoculars were in plastic bags in her backpack and added to that the sandwiches Mrs Creswell handed to her.

The expedition got under way just after 0900hrs. They launched off the sandy beach on the south side of the peninsula and, as Mr Creswell had feared, the first half hour was not very pleasant because of all the powerboats roaring around. Tina counted a dozen and could see more in the distance which had come from other campgrounds.

But in spite of her initial trepidation Tina was a very competent sailor and knew how to handle a boat. She soon became engrossed in the technicalities and forgot about her vague fears. In this she was helped by it being a beautiful sunny day with a good crisp breeze that made it feel good to be alive and which made sailing fun.

The pleasure of sailing was added to by the fact that the wind was from the Southwest and was just strong enough to throw up a chop. To make headway they had to do frequent tacks. Sarah acted as captain and Tina looked after the mainsheet. Young Michael just sat at the bows and kept up a running commentary. He appointed himself as lookout. The canoe went straight across Fongon Bay and hugged the southern shore, keeping it in the lee of the land out of the way of both the rougher water and most of the power boats.

The first tack took the sailboat right into a bay on the southern shore and they passed quite close to the canoe. As they passed, they waved and exchanged smart comments. The next tack took them slightly north of west and they did not turn until they were close to the pine trees on the tip of Fongon Peninsula. Then it was southeast again into another bay, passing the canoe as it cut across from one cape to the next.

Tina began to really enjoy herself and she felt like singing with happiness. Except that she was still bedevilled by nagging fears and the vague worry that Andrew still did not love her. To push such thoughts out of her consciousness she took out her binoculars and studied the birds. There were plenty of water birds in the sheltered waters of the bay; ducks of several different species and two black swans. She loved seeing them and had to comment that they were a long way from Western Australia. There were a variety of waders in the reeds and shallows, and in the jungle she saw both white and black cockatoos.

Their next tack took them Northwest right out across the lake past the tip of the Fongon Peninsula and close to the north shore behind the Platypus Lookout peninsula. While they crossed, they encountered some quite rough water and the bows threw up showers of cold spray that made Michael grumble, but which only made Tina shelter her binoculars and feel exhilarated.

Another long tack took them back close to the southern shore. This time they found that the canoe was half a kilometre ahead, but they could not point any closer into the wind so had no choice but to go back across the lake again. Once they got out of the lee of the pines the wind freshened and Tina found the speed and spray mildly thrilling. She leaned out and looked ahead and tried to match what she saw to her memory of the map.

Some parts were easy to identify. The tree-covered peninsula that had Platypus Lookout on top and a large and crowded campground at its base stood out clearly. So did another forested peninsula a kilometre to the west of that. This had many tents and huts in under the trees and Tina remembered it was the Scout Camp, Camp Barrabadeen. The sailboat shaved close past the western tip of this and into the large bay beyond. In doing so they passed close to a dozen canoes full of happy and enthusiastic Scouts.

Because the wind appeared to have shifted more to the south Sarah held on her course and Tina looked around to check their progress. Over her left shoulder she noted the cluster of buildings that comprised the town of Tinaroo. Then she noted an unusual black line almost dead ahead of them. For a moment she puzzled over it but, as it became silhouetted against the sky, she suddenly realised what it was.

That is the wall of the dam, she thought. She knew that the lake was held back by a huge concrete dam.

Then she noticed that there were rapidly approaching a line of bright orange buoys and she felt a sudden spurt of alarm. Turning to face Sarah she pointed and cried, "Sarah! Those buoys are the warning markers. Don't go any closer to the dam wall."

Sarah's face registered her alarm. The dam wall was still half a kilometre away but suddenly it seemed to be getting closer very fast. Michael had heard what Tina had said and now looked alarmed. "Is that the dam?"

"Yes, it is," Tina agreed as she shifted position ready to go about.

"Are we going to crash over it?" Michael cried, fear clear in his voice.

"No. Now come about Sarah," Tina answered, trying to sound reassuring but feeling herself suddenly gripped by apprehension.

The images from her dream swirled to the top of her mind and she was suddenly gripped by terror as she remembered the images of being dragged along by the current towards.. towards what? Her rational mind told her that there was no way they would go over the lip of the dam. It appeared to be at least a metre above the lake.

"And there is no current," she muttered. But even so she was almost paralysed by fear.

At that moment Sarah cried, "Stand by to come about. Ready… About!"

She put the tiller over and the sailboat swung sharply around. Tina scrambled nimbly across under the boom as it swung and quickly tightened the sheet as the boat settled on the new tack. As they sped away from the dam Tina looked back and let out a deep breath that she did not realise she had been holding. Then she trembled and shook her head, trying to shake the nightmare images out of her mind. For a few minutes she watched the wake as it swirled and gurgled around the transom.

Satisfied they were safe she relaxed and looked around, trying to pretend she had not been frightened. Luckily neither Sarah nor Michael appeared to have noticed so she was able to get herself under control and appear happy and interested.

Tina saw that they were now heading almost directly towards the point that was their objective. From a kilometre off the town of Tinaroo she was able to see right down the long, southern arm of the lake.

"We will start our expedition down there," she suggested, pointing south.

Sarah looked and nodded and then pointed out another campground on the next cape south of Tinaroo. Tina looked and nodded, noting a dozen small sail boats milling about off the place. Brightly coloured tents dotted the open areas. "This lake is certainly busy during holidays," she commented.

They now crossed the widest part of the lake and Michael became quite anxious about the size of the waves. These were about a metre high and had been built up by the wind blowing along the southern arm. Until he commented Tina had not really noticed as she was so used to sailing and was at ease in much larger waves than that. She reassured him and when he saw how well the sailboat rode over the waves he became more relaxed.

The crossing was about 2 kilometres of open water and took about 15 minute to sail. As they got closer to the cape Tina had to tell Sarah to make a couple of course corrections as she was aiming for the wrong point. It was clear to Tina that there were at least three points near the end and once again she was amazed at how indented the shoreline of the lake was. It was the sight of the bright orange canoe with three people standing on the bank beside it that gave them their destination. This was right on the tip of the peninsula.

As the sailboat drew into the shore Tina was amazed to see that the Creswells were standing on a bitumen road that ran down into the lake. As Mr Creswell helped her out, she pointed to it and said, "What's this? Where does it go?"

Mr Creswell grinned and pointed back across the lake. "Nowhere now. But before the dam was built it was the main road through the township of Danbulla. The town is under water. You must have sailed right over it."

Michael was even more fascinated by this idea, so they stood and looked back at the rippling waves and discussed the drowning of a town to make a lake. He shook his head in disbelief and wonder. "So they just flooded a town," he asked.

"That's right," Mr Creswell agreed.

"When?"

"Back in the 1950s," Mr Creswell replied.

Sarah turned to her father. "Were there farms as well or was it all forest?"

"Farms mostly and a bit of forest," her father replied.

"How could they!" Sarah cried.

Mr Creswell shrugged. "The government decided that we needed water more than we needed one little town and a few farms I guess."

Sarah was even more horrified that governments could do such a thing; that they could just flood people's homes and farms. Her father explained that there would have been compensation, but she was not convinced. Nor was Tina. She tried to imagine what the buildings might be like now they had been submerged for so many years. For a few seconds she imagined being a diver swimming among the ruins but then she spooked herself by a fleeting memory of that grasping hand.

Mr Creswell said, "Never mind. What is done is done. And you enjoy sailing on the lake so it's not all bad. Anyway, I brought you here to see if you like it as a campsite. It is an island."

"An island!" Sarah cried, turning to look around.

Tina did likewise and she saw it was true. The road ran up over a gentle rise but 100 paces further along it dipped down into water again, only to re-appear another 50 paces away. The road then curved out of sight into open savannah woodland and long blady grass. The island was fairly clear of undergrowth and with a gentle slope into the water in all directions. There were a number of small sandy beaches. The whole thing was shaded by tall trees and she decided it was very pleasant.

"This is a great spot. Andrew will love this," she said.

"How did you find it dad?" Sarah asked.

"On a canoe trip with the Scouts when I was a boy," Mr Creswell answered, gesturing towards Camp Barrabadeen which was clearly visible across the lake.

Mr Creswell pointed along the road and held up his map. "This road connects with the Danbulla Forest Drive. We need to check it out as well to make sure you can get a safety vehicle in to here, just in case there is an accident or some emergency."

"Is it far? Sarah asked. That comment surprised Tina as even a glance at a map showed her it was quite a few kilometres.

Mr Creswell did a quick count and said, "About 7 kilometres each way."

"That won't take long to drive," Sarah said.

Mr Creswell shook his head. "No can do. There's a locked gate and I haven't done the paperwork to get a permit. We will have to walk."

"Could we walk that this afternoon?" Tina asked.

"Maybe. We will see how we feel when we get back to camp," Mr Creswell answered. "Now, let's check the place out."

They explored the island in a few minutes and it was decided that it had to be one of the campsites for the expedition. The thought of camping there made Tina keen to do the trip and she felt much easier as they set out on the return journey.

It took an hour to return to the camp at Fongon Bay. This time the sailboat was able to scoot back and forth on fast reaches. This allowed them to pace the canoe but still have some sailing fun. It was only 1100hrs when they returned so an early lunch was organised and then a discussion on whether they would do another expedition by boat, perhaps in the other direction, or go for the walk.

"It will be a long walk," Mr Creswell commented.

"That's alright Dad," Sarah said. "We need to be fit for our expedition."

But Mrs Creswell said that she doubted that either she or young Aiden could walk that distance. At that Sarah said, "What if you only walk one way and we meet you with the canoe at our secret island? Then you could paddle back."

Mr Creswell nodded. "That sounds like a good idea, and if you want exercise for your expedition you and Tina can paddle the canoe there."

Going on the lake in a canoe was not what Tina wanted to do but she could think of no sensible thing to say to change the plan. So it was agreed and preparations begun. At 1230hrs they set off. Mr and Mrs Creswell and Aiden went by vehicle to where the Python Road turned off the Danbulla Forest Drive while Tina, Sarah and Michael launched the canoe.

As she climbed into the bow of the canoe Tina felt physically ill. She was gripped by an intense sensation of dread and kept trying to think up a reason to abandon the trip. But she could not think of one that would sound plausible.

They will think I am going crazy, she thought.

Reluctantly she dug her paddle in and began paddling as Michael settled behind her. *We have to go,* she told herself. *Mr and Mrs Creswell will think we have drowned if we don't arrive at Python Point.*

Fearing that might very well be the case, she turned her head to look across the lake.

Chapter 29

UNEXPECTED DRAMA

There was no problem on the way. It was only 4 kilometres and they covered this distance in an hour with no real effort. The course they took was straight across to the south shore of that arm of the lake and then westwards, cutting directly across the mouth of each bay from point to point. The waves were small and apart from the wash of a few passing powerboats they had no stability problems. Tina even began to relax and enjoy herself.

It was only after they had rounded the most westerly point that her anxieties returned. First, she stared across the lake at the town of Tinaroo and at where she knew the dam wall was. At that distance she could not see it but once again she remembered the dream and felt irrational fears about being drawn over the spillway by a mysterious current.

But there was no mysterious current, just a few large waves as the canoe headed south across the half kilometre of open water to their secret island. About halfway across, Tina saw what she mentally called 'The Secret Road'. It was a tiny strip of bitumen coming down to vanish in the lake a few hundred metres to her left.

Pointing towards it she called over her shoulder, "There's that old bitumen road again. Let's go and have a look at it."

Sarah looked doubtful and said, "What if mum and dad are waiting at the point?"

"We would be able to see them," Tina replied. "Besides, they won't be there yet. They have to walk 7 or 8 kilometres and that will take a couple of hours. We've plenty of time."

Sarah agreed so they changed course and paddled southeast across that arm of the lake to where the old road ran back into the water. As they got closer, Tina began to doubt the wisdom of her request as she saw that the water in that bay looked black and stagnant and the shoreline was all lined with reeds and long grass. Once again, she suffered images from her dream

A sudden splash nearby made Tina cry out in fright and flinch. Sarah cried out as well, but happily. "Did you see that?" she said.

"What?" Tina answered, her eyes scanning the water for signs of a grasping hand.

"Huge fish! It must have been nearly half a metre long. It jumped right out of the water," Sarah answered.

Tina had trouble calming her racing heart and found she was trembling. She wanted to go back but again knew she would look silly if she came up with a lame excuse. So they paddled in and beached the canoe on the bitumen. Thankfully, Tina climbed out and hauled the canoe higher, then walked a few metres away from the water and looked around.

She saw that the old road went up a gentle rise and then curved to the right out of sight among savannah woodland and long blady grass. That matched what she had thought it would do.

Sarah pointed to the side of the road. "Lots of people must land here. Look at all that rubbish."

Tina saw empty drink cans and bottles and a litter of picnic waste. It disgusted her and she wondered how people could be such irresponsible grubs. Michael pointed to wheel tracks in the grass beside the road.

"Cars come here too," he commented.

The trio walked along the old road for a hundred metres or so and Tina noted the remains of several campfires and more rubbish. They found where a rough vehicle track, just two wheel ruts in long grass, came in on the left at the point where the road curved to the right. From there they could see right along to where the road dipped underwater again before re-emerging on their secret island.

Michael then suggested seeing if they could paddle the canoe right around the secret island. But Tina did not want to get back in the canoe, again being seized by emotions she labelled premonitions but which she feared might just be ordinary funk.

But this time several reasons occurred to her and she said, "You might have trouble getting through those trees there on the right. And this is a better place to wait. If we land on the island, we will have to wade that bit of road and will get our shoes wet. Your parents have to come along this vehicle track. If we wait here, we stay dry and so do they."

Michael wasn't happy with that, but Sarah saw the logic and agreed. So they stayed at the junction and waited. Tina took the opportunity to go along the other track out of sight to go to the toilet. But no sooner was she out of sight of the others than she regretted it. All around her was bush and she began to peer anxiously into it. As quickly as she could she finished relieving herself and then hurried back to join the others.

Michael quickly became bored and went exploring and then began tossing sticks and small stones into the water. Tina sat and watched birds but there were none she hadn't seen before and she kept wishing she would spot an unusual one. Her eyes became tired from peering through her binoculars. It was a relief when the Creswells appeared just after 3pm.

Mr Creswell greeted them cheerfully and said, "It's a nice walk but it will test you going back up some of the hills."

Mrs Creswell and Aiden were helped into the canoe and sent on their homeward journey. As soon as they were well out on the water the others began walking.

It turned out to be a harder walk than Tina had expected. The first kilometre or so was mostly along a fairly level ridge but the track was just two wheel ruts in sandy soil amid dry scrub and weeds. It then curved left and went down a steep slope through a stand of very old, tall pines until it reached the shore of the lake again, or at least the thick belt of reeds and grass that fringed it. The road then went along beside the lake for a few hundred metres before turning uphill. At this point it became a proper graded road and entered jungle.

For the next 3 kilometres the road continued uphill. In places it was so steep that Tina found herself puffing and falling behind. The road was mostly in good condition with a sandy surface, but some parts were washed out and rutted and there was a fair litter of deadfall. In places where the sunlight was able to get through there was long grass growing along the sides and in the centre between the wheel tracks.

It was on one of these sections that they had their first minor drama. Michael and his father were walking in front along the wheel tracks, Michael on the left when Mr Creswell suddenly sprang into the air.

"Snake!" he yelled.

Both he and Michael appeared to dance and jump back. Tina looked down as fear surged through her. Into her flustered gaze flitted an image of liquid black and a flash of red. Even as her mind registered the words 'Red-bellied black snake' the reptile slid between her legs. She shrieked in fright and tried to spring away. But she was so flustered and the snake so quick she could not work out which way to jump and ended up dancing up and down.

"Oh! Oh! Where did it go?" she sobbed.

Sarah had also jumped but was able to point over behind Tina. "There! It has gone into the jungle."

Tina was just able to focus her eyes in time to glimpse the snake's tail vanishing into the leaf litter on the edge of the rain forest. She stopped dancing and stood trembling and sobbing.

Mr Creswell and Michael both burst out laughing and that made Sarah angry as she had also burst into tears. "It's not funny!" she shouted.

"Yes, it is," Mr Creswell replied. "Nobody got bitten."

"I nearly stood on it!" cried Michael. He spread his hands wide apart and added, "It was this big!"

Tina doubted that but did concede that it had been more than a metre long. *Certainly big enough to be deadly,* she thought. Apparently, it had been coiled up in the grass between the wheel ruts and had slid between Mr Creswell's legs and then past Tina.

Mr Creswell patted Sarah to calm her and then added, "I think the snake got a bigger fright than us."

"He did not!" Tina replied with conviction, her heart still hammering strongly.

They continued on but much more cautiously where there was any long grass. Luckily this was not very often, and Tina's nerves were able to settle down. She was helped in this by the birds. A dozen times she saw scrub turkeys scuttling off into the undergrowth and once she heard a rifle bird. That brought to mind that magical moment on Mt Tiptree when she had seen the Victoria's Riflebird raise its wings into the signature crescent shape before flitting away.

And there were white cockatoos, hundreds of them, in big, noisy flocks. They began to cackle and screech long before the group reached the trees they were roosting in and kept up the hideous din until long after they had passed underneath. Tina got frequent glimpses of them, but they did not really interest her, until the thought crossed her mind that there were lots of birds.

This would be a good place for those bird poachers to hang up their mist nets, she thought.

With the idea came fear and she anxiously scanned the jungle on either side then the road ahead. She even began to get creepy feelings up her back and she several times looked fearfully back to check they weren't being followed. She tried to tell herself she was being stupid and paranoid, but it took quite a while before the fear subsided back to an almost subconscious gnawing sensation.

She was helped in this by having to puff her way up several steep sections of road. The group passed a road junction going off to the right and at last came to the top of Python Hill. This was a relief but also a disappointment as the jungle was so dense that there was no view at all beyond the wall of vegetation.

From there the road went downhill for a kilometre to another road junction, this time on the left. They continued on and started up another slope, the road littered with twigs and dead leaves. As she went up the slope, Tina heard a bird somewhere ahead and looked up, only to walk into Mr Creswell who had suddenly stopped.

"Wha... what?" she gasped.

"Another snake," Mr Creswell replied.

Tina's heart again began to hammer and the adrenaline gushed, but Mr Creswell spoke calmly and had Michael by the arm. With his other arm he pointed, and Tina saw movement.

"Only a little one," Michael said in a disappointed tone.

Then Tina was able to calm down and focus her eyes. As she did, she was not sure if she should believe what she was seeing. It was another black snake and only about half a metre long and finger thin, but it had a blue underbelly.

"It's blue!" she said in surprise. She had seen both red-bellied and yellow-bellied black snakes but had never even heard of blue-bellied ones. But now there was one right in front of her and it was raised up in a warning posture and hissing at them.

"It's got a blue tongue too," Sarah added.

The snake was so small and far enough away not to be a direct threat, so Tina got control of herself and thought to use her camera. She took several photos, moving around to get the light at the best angle to do so. The snake shifted position to face her as she did, and then suddenly turned and slid away into the jungle.

The group resumed walking, discussing the blue-bellied snake as they went. The conversation then shifted to another flock of white cockatoos that squawked at them from the tall trees beside the road. It was only after she had passed beside a half a dozen that the trees finally caught Tina's attention.

"What huge trees!" she said, pointing to a giant that was more than three metres in diameter.

It was so tall she had to lean right back to look up. She marvelled at how tall and straight the trunk was and noted that there were no branches at all for about thirty metres. The tree was so tall it stuck up out of the main canopy of the rain forest.

"Emergents," Mr Creswell said. He then explained that trees that were able to do that got on best. "It is a struggle for sunlight as much as water and nutrient," he said. "So the thrust for rain forest trees is straight up." He then wondered how these very big trees had not been cut down back in the days when the timber cutters worked the North Queensland forests. "This is an old timber road we are walking along," he explained.

The road ran fairly level for the next 2 kilometres, with numerous very tall trees along each side. Then the group came to a gate and there was Mr Creswell's vehicle parked there on a cleared space at a road junction. Tina saw that the road junction was the one where the Danbulla Forest Drive did a sharp curve back to the right and then went winding down the side of the ridge.

They climbed into the vehicle, Tina with a thankful sigh of relief. It was just after 5pm by then and she felt quite worn out. Mr Creswell started the engine and drove them back to the campsite. They drove down the ridge past where Mr Creswell said there used to be a forestry barracks, past 'The Chimneys', Lake Euramo and the old schoolhouse to the Fongon Bay turn-off. There they turned left and went along the gravel side road through the pine plantations. Tina was again surprised by how far it was and how long it seemed to take.

It was 1730hrs by the time they reached the camp and already the sun was well down in the west and a strong, chilly wind was blowing off the mountains to the north. Mrs Creswell and Aiden had dinner ready but insisted the girls have a wash first. This was done in a washbasin in a screened off area at the back of the tent.

By then petrol and diesel generators were spoiling the evening quiet all around. Tina discovered she needed to go to the toilet, but as twilight was setting in she was scared to go on her own. This time she plucked up courage and asked Sarah to come with her. Mrs Creswell told them to hurry and added she would have the meal ready by the time they came back.

The two girls hurried to the toilet block. As they did several strong gusts of wind buffeted the camp and Tina shivered and commented that it might be a cold night. Afterwards, as they came out of the toilet, she found a cold wind blowing which set her shivering again. They hurried down the slope and through the edge of the camp. As they did Tina looked across the rippling waves on the lake to where lights were flickering in the campgrounds along the north shore. Movement against the last of the daylight caught her eye and she watched a flock of ducks fly across, heading south.

"Going to be a change in the weather by the look of it," she commented. Then she puzzled over another dark object that had appeared against the faint glow of the western sky.

Sarah saw it too and said, "What's that?"

Tina stared and saw a football shaped object with something hanging underneath. The object appeared to be drifting with the wind and was so low over the waves that she thought it would get caught in the pines further along the peninsula. But it just scraped across the top of them. As it did Tina heard a person yelling but she could not make out what they were saying over the noise of the wind and the generators.

As the 'thing' vanished from view across the southern arm of the lake, hidden against the darkening sky Sarah said, "Is it a balloon?"

Balloon? Tina thought. Then a conversation came back to her. "I wonder if it is Willy Williams' airship?"

"Airship?"

"You know, like his model zeppelin, but big enough to carry a person," Tina replied.

"There was a person under that thing. I could hear him calling out," Sarah said.

"I wonder...?" Tina mused. She felt quite uneasy about what they had just seen. "It didn't appear to be under control did it?"

Sarah shrugged. "I suppose not. It's a funny time to be trying to fly something like that."

Tina wracked her brain to try to remember what she had heard at school. *Willy was going to his aunty's farm this weekend with Stephen and Stick and that little tease Marjorie and they were going to fly his new airship,* she thought. *I wonder if something has gone wrong?*

She had a vague notion that the farm was nowhere near Lake Tinaroo. "I am just going to ask those people down there what the person in the airship said," she said to Sarah. "You go and tell your mum I will be there in a few minutes."

Sarah wanted to come with her but did as she was told. Tina hurried on along the vehicle track through the camp, past tents, barbeques, and boats on trailers until she reached the last few tents. Here she found a large group, several families by the look of it, all seated around pressure lanterns and tables of food. They were just starting to eat.

Hoping she wasn't being foolish Tina self-consciously moved forward into the light until she was noticed. A big, burly man in shorts and pullover saw her and said, "Hello. What do want Sweetie?"

Tina had to clear her throat to speak. "Did you see a thing fly past a few minutes ago?" she asked.

"We were just talking about that," the man replied. "Yes we did, a big balloon thing with some bloke hanging underneath it."

"He was calling out, wasn't he?" Tina asked.

"Yes he was, but we couldn't make out what he was saying, too much wind."

A woman sitting across the table spoke up. "I thought he was calling help. I told you that Jack."

"Yeah. Mighta been," Jack agreed.

"Have you reported it?" Tina asked.

The man shook his head. "Nah. We were just talking about what to do."

They discussed the sighting for a few more minutes and as they talked Tina's doubts became certainties. "We must report this," she said.

"You do it then," the man said. He looked a bit annoyed and lifted a beer to his lips.

Tina turned and made her way back the Creswell's tent. When she arrived, they were all seated at the table ready to eat but were also curious about the sighting. As Tina sat down, she apologised for being late, and then said, "I think it was Willy's airship and I think there is something wrong. Can we phone the police please?"

Mr Creswell at once looked serious and quizzed her about what they had seen and why she thought what she did. He then nodded and took out his mobile phone and called the police. As he talked Tina saw his eyebrows go up and her heart skipped a beat. He then confirmed that she had been right when he said, "So it was an airship?"

That comment got Tina really interested and also relieved her fears over possibly having made a fuss about nothing. After more talk, Mr Creswell held the phone aside and said to her, "This airship, which way was it headed?"

"South, towards Python Point," Tina replied instantly.

There was some discussion over whether it might have run into the ridge leading up to Python Hill. Tina could see that clearly outlined against the night sky but was sure the airship had been heading more to the west of it.

"Towards the Yunguburra end of the lake," she said.

This information was relayed to the police and Mr Creswell then ended the phone call. As he slid the mobile phone into his pocket, he looked at them all and then said, "You were right. It was Willy William's airship. It has been blown over the mountains from near Davies Creek and his parents have just phoned in to call for help to find it. The police were afraid it would be crashed up on the side of the Lamb Range and that they would not be able to look before tomorrow morning. Now they are going to start searching south of the lake. Well done you two."

As he said this Tina was simultaneously glad and anxious as an appalling thought came to her, along with images of the clutching hand sticking out of the water. "I hope he doesn't crash in the lake and drown," she whispered.

They had to calm and reassure her after that and then they settled to eating. Tina was so anxious she felt ill and said she was not hungry, but Mrs Creswell said that she had to eat and if she wouldn't they would call her parents to come and get her. Faced with that possibility Tina managed to force some food down.

It was then early to bed. There were no reports on the radio news and no return phone calls from the police so all they could do was speculate and look at the Lamb Range in wonder.

Right over those mountains! Tina thought. *Willy must have been terrified!*

After that Tina did not think she would sleep but found she was tired out from the boating and hiking and she was sound asleep within minutes of placing her head on the pillow.

Once again it was the motors that woke her up at dawn when campers switched on generators or started powerboats. For a few minutes she lay half-awake while she cursed them for being selfish and inconsiderate, she snuggled down against the cold and tried to go back to sleep. Sarah lay beside her, still sound asleep. Both boys and the adults were already up moving about outside. Through bleary eyes and a gap in the tent flaps Tina saw that there was a thick fog and that made her even more determined to sleep in. She burrowed into her pillow and drew her sleeping bag close around her neck to keep warm.

At that moment, the content of a conversation in the next tent penetrated her consciousness. She heard a man call, "Come and look at the TV John."

Another man, presumably John, replied, "Why? What is it?"

"Some kid on a homemade airship adrift over Atherton," the first voice replied.

Tina sat up, wide awake. *Airship!* she thought.

In a moment she was on her feet and struggling into slippers and dressing gown. Then she hurried out, barely noting the good mornings from the Creswells. Without considering the rudeness of her actions she went to the next tent and looked in. Two men and two women were there, and they glanced at her.

"Yes?" one of the women queried, surprised rather than hostile.

Tina pointed to the portable TV on a table. "May I watch please? The boy on the airship goes to my school and I was the one who reported it to the police."

That satisfied them and she was given room to see. As she did, Mr and Mrs Creswell came to the entrance and apologised and were in turn invited in. Tina stared in astonishment at the images on the TV. There was no doubt it was Willy's homemade airship. It was flying along just above the buildings in Atherton. It appeared to be floating in the top of a layer of fog and a person could be seen clinging to what looked like a bicycle frame hanging below the gas bag.

There was a large and growing crowd following it along the street, as well as a variety of vehicles. From time to time the TV camera was directed on the crowd and during one of these scenes Tina recognised some of the people.

"That is Graham Kirk," she gasped, pointing to him. "And there is Stephen Bell, and Peter Bronsky."

Sarah pointed at the screen "And that little minx, Marjorie," she added.

Tina also noted two air cadets: Marjorie's big brother Stick and Noddy Parker. "How did the boys get there?" she asked no-one in particular. She thought that Graham and his friends had been going to climb Lambs Head that weekend.

The group watched the drama for the next 20 minutes and Tina found she was biting her knuckles with anxiety as the airship drifted across the grounds of the Atherton State High School. As it scraped over the roof of one of the buildings Graham and Stephen scaled the outside of the building and tried to grab a rope dangling under the airship. Tina found she was holding her breath as they risked a terrible fall in their efforts. Finally it was Stephen who took a fearful risk and jumped off the roof as the airship began drifting clear. He grabbed the rope and hung on. His weight brought the airship down. Tina found she was disappointed that it had not been Graham who had made the heroic leap.

There were more surprises as the TV crew pushed through the crowd to where the airship was now grounded. The camera zoomed in on the boy on the frame underneath and she saw it was not Willy. "That is Roger Dunning in 9B," she cried.

"It is," agreed Sarah. "How did he get on the airship?"

"And where is Willy?" Tina added.

Chapter 30

WHERE IS WILLY?

That apparently was the question being asked in Atherton, but the answer was not forthcoming as the TV station switched back to its scheduled program. Tina could have cried with frustration. Amid the babble of talk and speculation she sat there trying to sort out in her own mind what on earth had gone on. But she couldn't. So all she could do was thank the owners of the TV and ask them to let her know if there was any more news.

She joined the Creswells at breakfast and again the main topic of conversation was the airship and what had happened. Tina was now consumed by curiosity and wanted to drive to Atherton to find out what had happened but when she hinted at this the Creswells would not hear of it.

"Your parents will be here to pick you up at lunch time. We aren't driving anywhere. We have to pack up the camp and that will take an hour or so."

At that both Aiden and Michael began to grumble. Michael said, "Aw Dad! Can't we go sailing again?"

"Only after the camp is packed and only for a short sail," Mr Creswell replied.

So they finished eating, washed up and began packing. As they did a red and white helicopter buzzed low overhead. Tina looked up and saw that it was heading towards Atherton. "That's the Rescue Chopper isn't it?" she asked.

"Yes, it is," Mr Creswell answered.

"Looking for Willy maybe?" Sarah suggested.

When Tina again saw the helicopter half an hour later, she was sure. It flew across the lake over near the town but high up and then began circling around the very top of the Lamb Range.

Searching for Willy alright, she decided.

They watched it for a few minutes, but it vanished out of sight over the other side of the mountain. Just looking up at the Lamb Range gave

Tina some uncomfortable memories and she hoped Willy hadn't fallen foul of the bird poachers. But there was nothing more to see so they went back to the chore of breaking camp. Each person packed their own gear and moved it out of the tent. This was then taken down and folded up.

While they were doing that Mr Creswell's mobile phone rang and he answered it. After a short conversation he closed the phone, and said, "That was the police. They want to question us about the airship."

That information got Tina all interested again and she became quite restless. But they did not just sit and wait. The remainder of the camp, except for a few chairs and a table, were packed and loaded into the vehicle. While they worked similar scenes were being enacted around them. Tina saw that some families were busy packing while others seemed determined to stay till the last moment. She noted the first vehicles towing boats already leaving the campground.

As she watched one vehicle drive off into the pines, she saw a police car coming into view from the other direction. That got her heart beating faster with a mixture of anxiety and anticipation. She drew Mr Creswell's attention to it and they stood and waved until the police saw them and drove over to their camp. A tubby sergeant and a skinny female constable got out.

The sergeant introduced himself to the adults and began questioning them but Mr Creswell indicated Tina and Sarah, so the sergeant questioned them. He asked which direction they thought the airship had been travelling in.

Tina had no hesitation in pointing to the Lamb Range. "From up there," she said. "It was being blown along by the wind and went across the pines down at the end of the peninsula and then went on out of sight to the south."

The sergeant looked doubtful but noted this and then went to his car to radio the information. Having done that he thanked them for helping. "Your information made it much easier last night," he said.

"How is Roger?" Tina asked.

"Roger?"

"The boy who was on the airship when it was brought down at Atherton," Tina answered.

The sergeant looked surprised. "How do you know about that?"

"Saw it on TV this morning," Tina answered.

"How do you know his name?" the sergeant asked.

"He goes to our school. So do the boys who grabbed the airship," Tina explained.

That satisfied the sergeant and he and the constable climbed into their car and drove away. Soon after that Tina again saw the rescue helicopter buzzing around the crest of the Lamb Range.

Poor Willy, if he is lost in all that jungle, she thought. Memories of pushing through where there was no track made her shudder and she feared for his life. *If he is down in that jungle they will never find him. If he is injured he will lie there until he dies,* she mused.

They returned to packing up and by 9am had this done. Mr Creswell looked at his watch and said, "We have two hours before your parents are due Tina. Do you kids want to do one last sail?"

Tina didn't but Sarah at once said yes and looked appealingly at her so she nodded.

"Canoe or sailboat?" Mr Creswell asked.

"Canoe," Sarah answered before Tina could say 'sailboat'.

Once again, vague and nameless anxieties related to her nightmare of two nights before surfaced to bother her. But she said nothing and helped prepare. It was decided that, as they had gone southwards on the previous trips that this time they go northwards. That suited Tina as it meant she could watch the helicopter as it buzzed around the top of Mt Edith.

The boat trailer was pushed across the narrow neck of the peninsula and the sailboat rigged and launched. Michael sailed with his parents while Sarah and Tina carried the canoe across and launched it. Aiden was checked to ensure he had his PFD on correctly, then the girls buckled theirs. Tina stepped in and went to the bows and got settled. Then she used her paddle to help push the canoe into deeper water. Sarah lifted Aiden in, and when he was seated she pushed off and settled in the stern.

They set off northwards across the lake but almost immediately Aiden began to ask them, in a very anxious voice, not to go too far from land. That suited Tina, so she suggested they coast along eastwards. Sarah was happy to do this as this was the direction the sailboat was also taking.

Aiden did very little paddling but that did not bother Tina or Sarah. They settled to a good rhythm and soon had the canoe skimming nicely along in the calm water close to the pine tree clad southern shore of that part of the lake. As the canoe coasted along Tina kept glancing up at the jungle-covered slopes of the Lamb Range. She was watching the helicopter when it was visible, and brooding over Willy's possible fate when it was not.

If he dies in the jungle the wild pigs will get at his body and chew it up and scatter the bones, she told herself.

The thought disgusted her, and she shuddered and found she was terrified of even thinking about dying. That got her worrying about the bird smugglers again and she knew she was very scared. Memories of her nightmare returned, and she kept scanning the lake, even while she tried to tell herself not to be silly. Knowing it would really frighten little Aiden she said nothing about her fears and managed to keep up a bright chatter.

Ducks and other waterbirds provided a safe topic and they paddled on in apparent happiness. The sailboat vanished through a narrow strait and then came back to skim around them. That cheered Aiden up and he waved and called out and had to be told to sit still in case he tipped the canoe over.

They soon covered a couple of kilometres and rounded a point into the most easterly extremity of the lake. There were half a dozen small inlets and bays and two large ones. In particular there was a large arm of the lake extending northwards. On the next point between this and a large southern inlet was a picnic area which Tina recognised as School Point. The sight of the deforested land behind it quite stunned her as it had been clear felled. She had to remind herself it was not a natural forest that had been cut down but a pine plantation.

The sailboat went northwards so the canoe followed. This had them heading almost directly for Mt Edith and once again worry about Willy dominated Tina's thoughts for much of the time. However questions about what type of bird was in sight brought her back to the present.

They paddled on for about another kilometre. The sailboat returned and then went off again, but always in sight, tacking back and forth across the steadily narrowing inlet. Sarah suggested turning back, but just as she did they saw the sailboat go briefly out of sight behind some jungle, only to reappear almost immediately on the other side of it.

"How did they do that?" Aiden asked.

"It is a little island," Tina replied, remembering it from a previous holiday trip.

"Can we go around it please?" Aiden asked.

So they paddled another half a kilometre until they came to the small island. Tina had forgotten just how pretty the small jungle covered island was and enjoyed the sheer beauty of the setting. She was even more pleased at Aiden's evident pleasure. The island was only a knoll 50 metres across sticking up out of the water but it had an enchanting appeal to it. *A kid sized island,* she thought, smiling at pleasant memories of reading Arthur Ransome's 'Swallows and Amazons' with their adventures on Wildcat Island.

Then she noted that a bitumen road came out of the water and went up over one side of the island and then plunged back into the lake. "Look. That must be the same bitumen road that goes up over our secret island," she said.

That made the island even more attractive and they nosed right in. Aiden wanted to land but at that moment the sailboat came sliding back past them and Mr Creswell called that it was time to start back.

Sarah waved her paddle and called back, "We will just go around the island."

Aiden got all upset at not being allowed ashore but there was no help for it so they back paddled away from the shore and then set off close around the tiny island. "We will come back another day and explore it properly," Sarah told Aiden.

"Can we camp on it?" he asked eagerly.

"If we are allowed," Sarah answered diplomatically.

Tina had to smile and agreed that it looked just the most perfect island for a secret camping trip. *Maybe we can camp on it when we do our D of E expedition?* she thought.

Then she concentrated on paddling. As they went around the northern end of the island, she noted that the jungle now loomed so close and so high that she could no longer see the mountain tops. Further around there were pine trees on the eastern shore and she noted a vehicle track come down through them to end at a thick wall of reeds on the edge of the lake.

That must be the continuation of the road that goes over this little island, she decided.

Further around again they crossed the mouth of a large creek that emptied into the bay from the east. But the place looked quiet unpleasant to Tina, being full of some sort of brown sludge and tall, brown reeds that looked dead.

Is that oil? she wondered. Still puzzling over whether the brown colouring was natural or not they went on southwards and retraced their route.

The sailboat kept them company, passing both ahead and astern, or sometimes sailing close alongside so that it was a cheerful trip back with the wind behind them. It took only half an hour to paddle back, the only thing that caught Tina's attention being the view down the long arm of the lake to Tinaroo after they passed the headland near School Point. As always, it surprised her at how large the lake looked.

When they arrived back at the campground it was to find that more than half the campers were gone and in their place was a lot of litter and worn grass. The canoe was beached and Tina jumped out and lifted Aiden ashore. As she did, she felt a curious sense of relief but also regret. In spite of her fears, she knew she had been enjoying the canoeing.

Her parents and Garth arrived 10 minutes later and Tina was very glad to see them. Her mother hugged her and anxiously asked how she was. Tina assured her she was fine, even though she felt very brittle inside. The conversation shifted to the search for Willy. Her father commented that they had just driven past the Search HQ, at which Tinna experienced a feeling of helplessness and then a strong desire to join the search.

"Can we drive home past it please?" she asked.

"We were planning to go back the other way," her father answered.

"Please dad! It's very important to me," Tina said.

Her father studied her face and then nodded. "OK Ti, if that is what you want."

"Thanks dad."

They loaded her gear into the Jackaroo and then thanked the Creswells.

Sarah said, "No, I need to thank you. It has been great having you here Tina."

"See you at school tomorrow then," Tina replied, warmed by her friend's evident sincerity.

The family climbed into their vehicle and set off homewards. As they travelled Tina described the sailing and canoe trips and tried to sound happy and relaxed. She also described how she and Sarah had seen the airship and then the police visit. By the time she had done this they had reached the Danbulla Forest Drive. Here, instead of turning right they went left.

Tina became quite pensive, fretting about Willy's fate. The road went northwards, winding through pine forests and then down across a concrete bridge over a fair-sized creek. *That is the creek that had all the dead reeds at its mouth,* she decided.

The road went uphill with pine trees on the left and jungle on the right, then came to a road junction. Tina noted a road that went off to the left. *That is the one that goes over the small island and then up that ridge through the pine trees.*

At that point the main road did a sharp turn to the right and entered jungle. A kilometre or so further along, after several sharp bends, it crossed another small concrete bridge and then went up around another bend with more pine trees on the left. Then it turned left and passed through a patch of rain forest.

At the end of this straight was a clearing and road junction. It was crowded with parked vehicles and tents and two large caravans, the Search HQ. As they neared, Tina saw police and State Emergency Services logos on the caravans. One of the caravans was a mobile canteen and a group of people stood at the counter getting food and drinks. Among the people Tina glimpsed two wearing army camouflage uniforms. She recognised Graham and Peter and was seized by the urgent need to speak to them.

She had intended asking her father to stop anyway but an SES worker was directing them to drive on. Despite this she cried, "Please Dad, stop!"

The SES worker came over as they came to a standstill and asked them to drive on. Tina leaned out and said, "I was the girl who reported the airship last night and those boys are in my class at school. May I speak to them for a few minutes please?"

"Oh, alright! Park over there," the SES worker directed.

Tina's father parked the Jackaroo, but Tina had her seat belt off and the door open even before the vehicle had stopped moving. Then she ran across the grass towards the group. As she did, she saw Graham turn to look and then recognition on his face. He stepped out of the group and Tina experienced an intense desire to throw her arms around him. Just in time she stopped herself, shocked at her behaviour.

He isn't my boyfriend, Andrew is, she chided herself. But she had to concede that Graham looked very rugged and handsome all the same.

Graham grinned and said, "Fancy meeting you here. Are you just passing through?"

"No. We've been camping here all weekend. I just wanted to know how the search for Willy Williams is going," Tina replied as the others crowded around.

Graham looked puzzled. "Did you hear about it on the radio?"

Tina shook her head. "No. It was on a portable TV, but it was me who first reported seeing the airship here," she said.

"You! You saw it?" Graham asked.

"Yes," Tina replied, a bit puzzled by his answer.

Peter now moved forward. "Where were you camped Tina?"

"At the Fongon Bay Campground. We had been sailing and canoeing all day," she replied.

"You must have been lucky to spot it last night. It was pretty dark."

Tina frowned and shook her head. "No. It was quite visible. There was still enough light to see it clearly," she answered.

"Still enough light," Peter echoed. He frowned and glanced at Graham, then turned back to her. "What time did you see the airship?"

"Just before sunset," Tina answered. "It came drifting across the lake from this area and went south after passing across the pine trees on the end of the peninsula at Fongon."

Stephen now pushed forward. "You are sure? You really saw the airship in daylight down over the lake?"

"Yes," Tina replied. She was a bit nettled at not being believed. She was also mystified.

So, apparently, were the boys. Peter turned to Graham and said, "What time was it when we saw the airship up on top of the mountain do you reckon?"

Graham bit his lip and said, "About 8:30 I think. We hadn't even got down from Lambs Head to the Davies Creek Road before it got dark."

Peter nodded. "That's right. And then we drove for hours."

A man who now introduced himself as Willy's father, said, "That is right. My mobile phone will tell me what time I made the call from up on top near Mt Edith." He took out the phone and began checking the call times.

Stephen turned to his friends. "You know what this must mean, if Tina really saw Willy's airship at Fongon at sunset?"

"Yes," Peter said. His mouth formed a grim line. "The airship we saw wasn't Willy's. So your theory might be correct Steve."

Willy's father now bit his lip and showed the phone screen to Peter and Stephen. "You were right. It was 8:49." He then turned to Tina again and said, "Thank you. Your report made the search much easier. My wife was able to get to Lake Eacham area in time to see the airship drift overhead."

"But where is Willy? Why wasn't he on the airship?" Tina asked.

It was explained to her that the airship had become snagged in a big tree, an emergent that stuck up out of the jungle canopy up near Mt Edith but while he was trying to tie the airship to the tree a gust of wind had blown it away and he had been left behind.

"So he is still in the tree?" Tina said.

"We hope so, but we can't find the tree," Graham replied. "We have flown around by helicopter and even walked through the jungle. They are searching that bit of jungle now in case he has fallen off and is lying on the ground. We did too." He explained in detail how he and Peter had taken compass bearings to pinpoint the exact position of the tree.

Tina was puzzled. "So where are you going now?"

Graham suddenly looked anxious and glanced at his friends. "We... er... we are going to look somewhere else. We... er... have a theory that the police don't agree with."

Peter interrupted, "We found the stump of a huge tree that had just been cut down, but no sign of Willy, or of how the tree was removed. We have an idea we want to check. And what you have just told us seems to confirm it. Sorry Tina but time is important. Come on Graham. We have to get moving."

That was all very mysterious to Tina and the vagueness of their statements puzzled her. She frowned but the boys exchanged glances and would not say any more. That nettled her a bit and she said, "Can I help?"

Peter shook his head. "Thanks for offering but we will check our idea first. Come on Graham," he said.

Graham looked embarrassed and then said, "We have to go. See you tomorrow at school."

They walked away and Tina was left standing there feeling quite puzzled and distressed. All she could do was say goodbye and then join her family who had just arrived.

"Well?" her father asked. "Where is Willy?"

Chapter 31

I WISH THAT WAS ME!

During the drive back to Cairns Tina hardly noticed the scenery. Her mind was occupied with worry about Willy and with trying to puzzle out what Graham had meant. The route they followed was west along the Danbulla Forest Drive to Tinaroo and the only places that really caught her attention were the concrete bridge over Kauri Creek and the dam wall. When they reached the northern end of the huge concrete dam Tina glanced at it briefly and noted just how high it was. There looked to be at least a hundred metre drop down the steep face of the wall. That gave her momentary flashbacks to her fears in the sailboat and to her nightmare.

You wouldn't survive going over that, she thought.

The road wound down the hillside to a concrete bridge a few hundred metres below the dam wall, giving her another good view of the huge concrete structure. Such massive engineering products both amazed and awed her.

From there they drove back uphill to the town of Tinaroo and then through kilometres of bush and open farmland to the small township of Kairi and then to Tolga. At Tolga they turned right and went back to Cairns via Mareeba and the Kuranda Range. Once home, Tina checked on her birds and fed them and then washed her camping clothes. Then she tried to relax and even began some homework. There followed a whole night of uncertainty. The search for Willy was a major item on the TV news but he had still not been found by the time darkness set in.

Tina was so upset she had trouble eating her tea and lay awake for hours worrying. Not normally religious she even did some quiet praying. Gloomy thoughts of death depressed her and added to her own fears.

On Tuesday morning there was still no news. Tina went to school feeling wretched. From time to time she stared back up at the jungle covered mountains to the west.

Poor old Willy, she thought. *He is lost up there somewhere.*

The very idea of being lost in jungle-covered mountains made her shudder and feel miserable. At school she was very glad of the company of her friends. Most were full of stories about how good their weekends had been. Only Sarah was really concerned about Willy and the lack of interest further depressed Tina.

While she sat talking to her friends before first bell, a stir among the students attracted Tina's attention. "What is it?" Sarah called.

Samantha called back. "A giant airship. It's circling over the inlet."

"An airship!" Tina cried in surprise. *I wonder if it is Willy's?*

Having seen it brought down the previous morning she could not imagine how it would be allowed up again. Puzzled and hopeful, she joined the throng of students lining the school fence and stared. She saw the thing at once, a gigantic object in the sky. It was an airship, but a glance told her it was not the home-made construction she had seen on the TV. This one was huge. It was painted black underneath and a dappled green and grey on top. Underneath was a cabin with motors on either side.

That is a real airship, she thought. She had seen them before advertising cars and football teams, 'blimps' she'd also heard them called. The airship was turning away and was just visible over the roofs of the houses.

Some girls pushed in beside Tina and Sarah. Tina glanced and noted that it was Barbara and her friends.

"What's it doing?" Fiona asked.

"Going round in circles from the look of it," Gillian said.

"What's that little plane doing?" Samantha asked.

Tina now noticed a tiny, single engine plane circling around the airship. The plane swooped and dived, then zoomed away, to circle round again.

Barbara gasped and cried, "It nearly crashed into it then!"

It was certainly unusual. Hundreds more students and several teachers joined them as the word spread. Tina watched fascinated as the airship circled round again, coming much closer and lower this time.

"It looks like it is trying to avoid the plane," she observed.

The plane swooped again. A sound, which could only have been a machine gun, came clearly to them.

"That plane is trying to shoot the balloon down!" Fiona cried.

Tina was horrified. She watched with her heart in her mouth as the plane circled and came racing in from behind the airship again. If it was trying to shoot the airship down it looked like it would succeed. The thought that she might be watching someone get killed made Tina sick in her stomach.

"Oh no!"

There was a united gasp of horror as a man jumped from the airship with a parachute, its lines tangling around the nose of the attacking plane. Both plane and parachute went spinning down, the man at the end of the parachute just visible as a tiny black dot like a spider at the end of its thread. Tina put her hand to her mouth and stared in horror.

Both plane and parachute vanished below the roof tops. Seconds later, the crunch of a crash reached their ears. "It's crashed!" a hundred people cried. Dozens of students, mostly boys, began running along the footpath towards the Esplanade. Teachers shouted at them to stop. Some did. Others kept going.

Tina felt like she wanted to vomit. She stared apprehensively at the airship, which she saw had now turned and was now heading straight towards them.

"It's getting lower," Fiona said.

"It might be going to crash too," Samantha suggested.

That was a horrible thought. Tina watched anxiously as the airship headed directly for her. The thought crossed her mind that she might be in danger. *If it crashes, I could be killed,* she told herself.

Through her mind flashed the ghastly images from TV programs of the famous *Hindenburg* crash with the explosions and roaring flames. But even as she began to wonder if she should run the airship began to turn. It then headed off to the north. The students all moved out onto the footpath to watch. Barbara saw that the airship was definitely getting lower by the minute.

When the airship was a block or so away it swung round and headed back towards the school.

"It's going to land on the oval!" a boy cried.

That precipitated a stampede by a thousand students. Teachers ran with them, shouting for them to stop. Most students just ignored them. Tina allowed herself to be carried along with the rush. She arrived breathless at the oval in time to see that the rumour was true. The airship was going to land there.

Now the teachers became almost frantic with worry, shouting and pushing to keep children back. Tina found her path blocked by Barbara who was trying to get past Mr Conkey.

"Stay back!" he shouted. "It may crash and burn. It is full of gas."

Again the newsreel images of the *Hindenburg* crash flitted through Tina's mind, and seemingly through the minds of many others as she saw many of the students begin to back away. She heard the rumour sweep around, whereby the students became more manageable. More teachers arrived, including the principal and deputy principal, and herded the huge crowd back to the edge of the oval.

Tina stood beside Barbara and her friends and stared up in amazement. Close up the airship was truly gigantic. It was longer than the football field on which it was slowly settling. She saw that it had propellers in swivelling nacelles on either side of the cabin. She was also struck by how quiet it was.

"It must have electric motors," Mr Conkey said to Mr MacLaren.

Someone pointed and called out. "That's Willy Williams!"

Tina felt her heart leap with hope. She saw a row of faces peering out through the windows at the front of the airship's cabin, and one of them was Willy. Now she was both puzzled and amazed.

Barbara gasped and said, "Surely this can't be the airship he was making at his aunt's farm? Wasn't he lost in a tree?"

"He was," Tina replied. "And it is not his homemade airship. I saw that, and it was much smaller."

"So how did he get this one?" Sarah asked.

Tina shook her head. It was a real mystery.

The huge airship settled gently on the oval, its nose resting on the football goal posts. As soon as it touched down a door flew open and out jumped Graham Kirk in his cadet uniform.

Mr Conkey let out an oath then said, "Bloody Graham Kirk! I might have known."

Stephen followed Graham out, then Marjorie. After a moment Peter climbed out holding a black briefcase. The motors then whirred to silence. Tina could clearly see Willy working at the controls. He was methodically doing things to the control panel. Then he stood up and walked to the door. Very slowly, as though he was reluctant to leave, he stepped down. As cool as could be he began walking towards them, his eyes scanning the crowd.

Willy stopped 30 metres away and turned to look up at the airship. After a few seconds he smiled and nodded. Once more he started walking towards where the others were standing with the teachers. A great buzz of conversation had broken out but the crowd now fell silent. Tina saw Willy's eyes searching the crowd and she suddenly realised why.

He is looking for Barbara! she thought, glancing sideways to see how Barbara was reacting.

Then Willy saw her and he stopped. Tina saw Barbara was staring back, mouth half open and her face all tense. Tina expected him to come forward and kiss Barbara or something. Instead Willy sighed and shook his head and turned away. He walked over to Marjorie and embraced her. Before the eyes of the whole school they kissed. A great roar of approval went up. Willy was the hero of the hour.

Tina felt an up-welling of emotion that brought tears to her eyes. She was thrilled by the sheer drama and romance of it. And she was jealous. *I wish* (she had to pause to move Graham's face and name out of her mind) *Andrew would do that to me!*

Then she remembered Barbara and looked at her. She saw that Barbara was also on the edge of tears and that she looked thoroughly miserable. *Willy has chosen Marjorie! He has rejected her!* Tina thought.

But Barbara's problems were forgotten as Graham and his friends walked in their direction. Once again, Tina had to suppress an urge to rush over and embrace him. But he saw her and detoured over to stand in front of her.

For a few moments Tina stared into his eyes and she felt such a mix of emotions she became very confused. "Hello. What happened?" was all she could croak.

Graham grinned, "What a thrill! I thought our goose was cooked when that bloody plane began trying to shoot us down," he said.

"So did I, but how did you get aboard this airship?" Tina asked.

At that moment, Mr Conkey appeared next to Graham. "Office!" he ordered.

"Yes sir. Tell you later Tina," Graham said.

He gave her another winning smile and began making his way through the crowd towards the office. Peter and Stephen followed him, then Willy, Marjorie and Principal. The Deputy Principal began ordering the students to move to class.

Andrew pushed his way through the milling throng and took Tina by the arm. "I've been looking for you," he said. But as he did, he turned and his eyes followed Graham.

Tina felt a surge of guilt which was almost immediately replaced by anger. *Why should I feel guilty?* she thought. *I haven't been cheating on him.* But she could tell that Andrew was both worried and jealous. *Good! Now he might lift his game,* she told herself.

They turned and began walking back towards the school buildings. Tina felt another niggle of annoyance, but she tried to control this. "How was your weekend?" she asked.

"Oh, alright," Andrew replied in an offhand voice.

His tone stirred up her own doubts and jealousies and that caused her to ask, "Did you see that blonde in Townsville?"

"Er... er yes," Andrew admitted.

Now Tina felt really threatened and she snapped, "Did you and her do anything?"

"No!" Andrew retorted in an angry voice. "I just met her when we went canoeing on the Burdekin."

Tina had heard of the Burdekin and vaguely knew it was a big river. Feeling quite hurt she said, "And did she take her clothes off?"

This time Andrew went bright red and Tina guessed that something had happened. Andrew shook his head and said, "It was... a family outing. That's all."

They walked in silence for a few paces and then Andrew spoke again. "How was your holiday? Did you go anywhere?"

Tina felt quite shocked. *I told him I was going camping with Sarah,* she thought. "You don't listen to what I say," she said, her anger still taking control of her tongue.

"I do!" Andrew cried, looking both hurt and baffled.

Tina relented a little and began to relate the events of the weekend. This kept them talking all the way to the classroom and once there the tension eased a little.

Classes began but the whole school was in a disturbed mood because of the airship incident. The unrest was maintained because of the physical presence of the giant airship. It was so large it was visible from much of the school Tina could actually see the top half of the airship looming above the buildings across the quadrangle and rumours kept sweeping the class. These were added to by the passing of various teachers, students and official looking people.

The period before morning break was English with Mrs Standish and after it Tina joined her friends down near the oval to gape at the airship. The oval had all been roped off by the police and safety people and the rumour went around that all the people in the light aircraft, and the man who had parachuted into its propeller, were dead.

Noddy Parker gave them his version. "They went splat into the mudflats off the Esplanade," he recounted with sound effects and hand gestures.

That made Tina feel awful and she tried to imagine such a horrible death. Andrew joined her and they moved back to the school buildings to eat and talk. Tina related how she had seen the homemade airship with Roger on it and then how she had met Graham, Peter and Stephen at the Search HQ. When she mentioned Graham's name, she noticed a distinct tightening around Andrew's mouth and eyes.

He is jealous, she decided. *It has got him worried.*

She considered that to be a good thing and deliberately mentioned Graham's name a few more times, just to check Andrew's reaction.

To her own surprise, she found herself thinking about Graham and she looked around, hoping to see him. But he was no longer at school. He and his friend had been taken away by police and parents while the extraordinary events surrounding the huge airship were investigated. The wildest rumours went around the school: that Willy had stolen the airship to escape a gang of crooks; that the crooks had tried to murder him and his friends; that Graham had saved Willy from being murdered.

"Graham is a real hero," Tina commented, deliberately saying it to test Andrew's reaction.

His response was to grunt and look unhappy. That caused the conversation to flag, and Tina found it a relief that the bell went and they had to return to class. It was a thoughtful and slightly unhappy girl who sat down to Maths A.

Andrew hasn't asked me for another date, she mused. In her dejection she could only surmise that he had regretted taking her out or now found her unattractive.

At lunch time they met again and then listened to the latest rumours. But Andrew was in a bad mood and Tina felt quite distracted and also intensely interested in the airship story. After school there was a suggestion by Blake that they go down to the Esplanade to watch the police trying to retrieve the crashed plane and the bodies from the mudflat. Tina was both appalled and fascinated but did not want to do that. Instead she went home. After a snack she went to feed the birds. Then she sat in her room, her unfinished homework open in front of her as she pondered who she loved and who loved her.

In her mind the image of Willy kissing Marjorie kept forming and she sighed every time, wishing she was the centre of a great drama and romance. *Oh! I wish something romantic like that would happen to me!* she thought.

For the first time she began to consciously consider a relationship with Graham. *He is certainly a hero. And he seems more interested in me than Andrew is,* she told herself.

But she felt guilty for having what she considered such disloyal thoughts, until she thought of the blonde in Townsville. Then the worm of doubt squirmed in her gut and all her fears and jealousies swam to the surface again.

It was a thoroughly miserable girl who tried to pretend she was happy and normal when her parents came home. The topic after dinner was the airship and Tina was able to add all the little details from the incident at school.[1] Tina tried to hide her unhappiness but she suspected that her mother had noticed, just by the looks and little comments she gave.

That night sleep would not come, and Tina relived the dramas of the last few weeks and found herself thinking seriously about Graham. Those thoughts made her feel guilty and disloyal but also aroused her anger.

Andrew hasn't said he loves me or that he is my boyfriend, she told herself. *So why shouldn't I?*

The following day Tina found her emotions under stress once more. Graham was back at school and during morning break, while they made their way from the classroom to downstairs, she asked him what had happened on the weekend. Graham walked with her right across to where Tina usually sat with her friends and then he sat beside her and continued with his story. Tina found that both embarrassing and enjoyable. She noted the glances other girls cast at them and it made her feel good.

---

[1] For the full story, read *Airship over Atherton* by C. R. Cummings.

Then the situation took an unexpected turn when Graham suddenly said, "You are beaut Tina. I would like to take you out. How about it?"

For a few seconds Tina was too flustered to answer. She was both delighted and flattered but was also assailed by guilt. But even so she gave an ambiguous answer. "Er... thanks. I er... when did you have in mind?" she stammered, aware that she was blushing and that her emotions were possibly clouding her judgement.

"How about Saturday night?" Graham suggested.

"Oh, I don't know," Tina replied. She was very tempted, but images of Andrew came to niggle at her conscience.

Graham looked her in the eyes and even as she marvelled at how blue they were he said, "Are you worrying about Andrew?"

"Yes," she replied. The thought that he must have read her mind while he gazed into her eyes came to her, but she tried to shrug it off as ridiculous.

Graham looked serious and said, "Is he taking you out?"

Tina shook her head and muttered no. Graham seized on this and asked, "Are you going steady?"

I wish we were, Tina thought. But she was too unsure, so she shook her head and said, "Not really."

"Good! Then you can go out with other people. You aren't married to him and you won't be cheating or two-timing or anything," Graham said.

The word married caused Tina a few mental twinges as she had thought about it but she had to concede Graham was right. Graham persisted by adding, "If he still likes you it might make him pull his socks up. You are too attractive to be left unguarded. So, if he is fair dinkum about you, he will lift his game."

"I'll think about it," Tina replied.

"Thanks," Graham replied. He stood up and walked away.

As he did, Tina noticed Andrew. He had been standing near the army cadet Q Store watching. Now he walked towards her. Not wanting the other girls to overhear any more of her private life Tina stood up and went to meet him.

As they met, Andrew gestured in the direction Graham had gone. "That looked very matey. What was he saying?"

The tone and the implication annoyed Tina. Her mind raced and she thought, *We need to settle this. I am not going to waste my time on a boy who doesn't like me.* So she said, "Graham was telling me about their airship adventure but then he asked me for a date."

"Oh did he!" Andrew growled. "And you said no I hope."

"As a matter of fact I didn't," Tina replied angrily.

"So you are going to go out with him then?" Andrew said in a challenging tone.

"Why shouldn't I? You don't own me," Tina snapped back.

Andrew looked upset but then replied, "You'll be sorry. He is a real fast operator with the ladies; besides, he already has a girlfriend."

Both comments worried Tina, the second more than the first. "Who?" she demanded to know.

"That little tubby girl in Year 8, Margaret Lake," Andrew answered.

Tina felt a surge of relief, tinged by sadness. "She likes him, but he doesn't take her out or anything."

"So you are going to go out with him?"

"Yes."

At that Andrew spun on his heel and stalked away. Tina watched him go with very mixed emotions. She knew she had been hasty and still believed that she really loved Andrew; but there was also the excitement and thrill of the new situation.

I will go out with Graham. Oh. I hope I haven't been a very silly girl, she thought.

Chapter 32

GRAHAM

Later that morning, Tina met Graham between classes. He smiled and said, "Have you made your mind up?"

"Yes. I will go out with you, if my parents agree," Tina answered

A grin lit up Graham's face and he said, "What would you like to do? Do you have a favourite place to go?"

That touched Tina. *He is allowing me to choose. That's nice.* But she said, "You decide. Will your parents let you go out?"

Graham nodded. "No problem. They trust me. Besides, my dad is away at the moment."

Tina knew that his father was a ship's captain and that he was often absent. They discussed possible venues and then went to their next class. During the lesson she spent most of her time daydreaming, feeling the thrill and anticipation of her daring new romance. One result was that she did very little work and was several times scolded by the teacher.

After school Tina wanted to speak to Graham, but as it was the 'Home Training' parade for the army cadets she only glimpsed him from a distance. Even so she found the look of him sent a little pulse of excitement and admiration through her. She had often seen him in his uniform before but now she found him particularly handsome.

Once she got home, she had to nerve herself for the bigger challenge of asking her parents for permission to go on the date. As both worked and did not get home for another two hours, she had plenty of time to work herself into a state of nervous anxiety. Then, when they were home, she found herself so afraid of them saying no that she had trouble bringing up the subject.

Finally, after the evening meal and washing up she broached the subject with them, having waited until Garth was in the bath and therefore out of earshot.

"A date?" her father queried. "Who with?"

That really put Tina on a spot. She went red and bit her lip and shook her head. "Er...With Graham Kirk."

Both parents turned to look at her. Her father raised his eyebrows and said, "So what happened to Andrew?"

Tina struggled for a satisfactory answer and finally could only shrug and mutter, "He didn't ask me. I don't know if he likes me. He..." Then tears came and she fled the room in shame.

Her mother followed her to her room and patted her back. "It's alright Tina. I understand, even if your father doesn't. Never mind Andrew. It is probably a good thing that you don't get stuck on one boy too soon. You need to meet a few to learn what they are like."

And Tina did on the next Saturday night. Graham accepted her suggestion of a very traditional movie date and she was also given the choice of movie. That warmed her towards Graham as she had expected him to be bossier and to want to see an action or war movie.

To begin with, Graham acted like the perfect gentleman. He was considerate and did not interrupt and did not spend all of his time talking about himself. As they sat side by side in the theatre, Tina began to relax and enjoy herself and was quite happy when he reached across and took her hand. She thought that was a bit fast, but his hand felt nice and she allowed him to hold it. The feel of his arm sent little tingles of excitement through her and she decided she was enjoying the experience.

Sometime later, Graham let go of her hand and placed his arm around her shoulders. That also seemed a bit quick to her and she became a bit anxious lest he try to do something she wasn't ready for (his right hand was over her right shoulder and close to her breast!). But he didn't and she slowly relaxed and then snuggled against him, enjoying the pleasure of being held and, she thought, of being valued.

Later they stood outside the theatre while waiting for her mother to pick them up. As they did, Graham kept hold of her hand and this made her feel both self-conscious and pleased. So far she had enjoyed the evening, and when he suggested another date she nodded and gave him a bright smile.

"When?" she queried.

"One night during the week?"

Tina shook her head. "Sorry. Mum and Dad won't let me go out during the week. It must be a weekend," she said. She was aware that she was disappointed at not being able to go out again soon.

Graham looked thoughtful. "It can't be next weekend. We have a cadet exercise that starts on Friday night."

"That is the Tri-service bivouac isn't it?" Tina asked.

"Yes, it is," Graham replied.

"So after that," Tina answered.

At that moment, her mother drove in and parked next to them. "We can talk about it at school," she suggested.

"That will be good," Graham agreed.

Tina wasn't quite so sure. The idea conjured up images of Andrew and of other girls whispering behind their hands. For a moment she wondered if she was doing the right thing, but then she felt a spasm of annoyance at Andrew and that decided her.

"Yes please. That will be nice," she said.

They climbed into the back seat and even as she clipped on her seat belt Graham took her hand again. That gave her a little thrill as her mother was just in front of her and could see them in the rear vision mirror. But it also increased her admiration for Graham.

I hope he isn't going to try to kiss me on the first date, she thought, then realised she would like it if he did.

But her worries were not needed. Graham chatted to her mother as they drove, answering questions about the movie and what class he was in and what his parents did. By the time they pulled up outside Graham's house, Tina was wishing he would try to kiss her, and she even felt an urge to give him a kiss, at least on the cheek. However her natural shyness kept her in check, and she could only say goodnight as he climbed out and then settle back in her seat with a sort of vague empty ache in her heart.

Is he the one? she wondered as she waved goodbye.

Feeling quite mixed up but sort of happy she chatted to her mother as they drove home. Later in bed she relived the evening and then found, to her own surprise that she was fantasising about the next date, imagining a much more torrid event where Graham would kiss her and during which his hands would do exciting things while exploring her body. These thoughts got her all hot but also made her feel ashamed. She knew what men did to women but was quite ambivalent about what she wanted. All she was sure of was that when she met the right man, they would do these things naturally.

Sunday was a flat event after that, and all Tina could do was fantasize and look forward to school. But when Monday came around she became every anxious. All her anxieties about being embarrassed or being an object of gossip rose to bother her and she became quite tense as she walked into the school.

But she had a wonderful day. Graham met her and chatted away with jokes and light banter which kept her entertained until class began. During lessons she felt both impatient for the breaks so she could see Graham again and uncomfortable when Andrew gave her several hurt and accusing stares.

During morning break Tina was embarrassed, but she loved it. She was sitting with Sarah in her usual place when Graham appeared. He gestured to Sarah and then turned and sat down, gently pushing both Tina and Sarah aside. He wriggled to get comfortable, his body touching both hers and Sarah's. He then took Tina's hand and began to chatter away about nothing much. Tina was surprised, then anxious lest a teacher see them (Holding hands being against the rules). Then she noted Sarah's interested and jealous expression. That caused her to feel good. It also raised her admiration for Graham.

He is brave enough to sit with me, she thought, glancing around to check whether other girls were looking. They were and there were a lot of smiles, grins and behind-the-hand whispering going on. That made her blush, but she was glad. *That has showed them I am not just a tubby frump!* she thought.

The only fly in the ointment of her happiness was seeing Andrew's hurt looks when she went back to class. But Tina then shrugged. *He had his chance,* she told herself. But somehow she felt she had made a mistake and felt upset.

Lunch time was similar, and Tina began to really enjoy herself. That set the pattern for the remainder of the week. Later it all melded into one happy blur and she had trouble separating one day from another in her memories. The only one she was sure of was the Wednesday when Graham had gone to army cadets and they had talked about the weekend tri-service exercise.

The outline of the exercise was that the Air Cadets were doing a basic fieldcraft weekend and would provide camps and HQs for the Army Cadets to try to find and sneak up on. The Navy Cadets were the safety signals network and were also practising their communication skills. The Army Cadets were really doing a hike to get them ready for their weeklong 'Senior Exercise'.

Before the training began Graham spoke to Tina. "What are you doing during this exercise?" he asked.

Tina grinned and shook her head. "I can't tell you. It is secret," she replied mischievously.

"I can keep secrets," Graham replied in a suggestive tone.

The implied double meaning made Tina blush. "If I told you we would have to shoot you," she said.

Graham laughed and said, "Are you going to be at one of the signal stations?"

"Yes," Tina admitted.

"Then I will find you," Graham said.

"Only if you can get past the guards," Tina replied doubtfully.

Graham laughed again. "They are only air cadets!" he cried. Then he said, "If I do, will you give me a kiss?"

Tina was thrilled but managed to say, "We are not allowed to fraternize at cadets."

"Then I will take you prisoner and will kiss you anyway," he boasted.

Tina blushed. "We will see," she said, secretly hoping he would be able to sneak in and kiss her but doubting he would even be where she was.

The cadets were called on parade at that moment, so the conversation ended but it stayed in her mind as fuel for a whole series of fantasies that night.

On Thursday and Friday Graham sat with Tina and repeated his boast and she took it up and made it a challenge. "I dare you," she said, then added, "And if no-one can see us, you can kiss me."

"You're on!" Graham replied happily, his face split by a grin. The twinkle in his eye sent a thrill through Tina and she went back to class to more fantasies and was even able to ignore Andrew's sulky looks.

At last school was over and she hurried home to get ready for cadets. They were moving that night and had to be packed and ready. Tina found she was quite excited, both at the idea of the exercise and at the thought of Graham trying to creep past the guards to get to her. It gave her a few happy fantasies while she packed at home.

Her mother drove her to TS *Endeavour* at 1845hrs and the evening provided a whole new set of experiences and entertainment. Not all of the unit were going on the exercise, so they had a normal training night. The 31 that were going were divided into 9 groups. While the names were being read out Tina found herself quite tense. She was both dreading and hoping that Andrew would be in her group. When she heard he was not she experienced mixed emotions.

Maybe I still like him? she wondered, glancing quickly at him. As she did, she saw his head start to move and quickly turned hers back.

The groups then prepared their camping and signalling equipment. This was both amusing and testing to Tina. All the cadets who had been training for the Duke of Edinburgh expeditions were organised and had all their gear neatly packed and ready to carry. But the others, about twenty in number, had the most amazing variety of bags and bundles. Tina spent the next hour helping others pack, including Arthur Blake who was their team leader. Blake seemed to have gear everywhere and so did Sarah, who was also in the team.

How could Blake be so disorganised? she wondered. *He has been on camps before!*

So had Sarah but it was obvious her parent's style of camping set the norm for her. She had loose items and three big bags full to overflowing.

Tina picked one up and was amazed at the weight. "Holy Moses Sarah! What have you got in this, the kitchen sink?" she cried.

Sarah looked quite hurt and got all huffy, but Tina apologised and helped her to re-stow it all and reduce the bulk. But it was still a lot.

Sub Lt Sheldon, the Training Officer, thought so too. "You lot are lucky you aren't in the army cadets. They only get a pack and basic webbing," he commented.

It was done at last and they settled down on their bunk beds for the night, the girls on one side of the hall in their own accommodation. This was so they could get away to an early start in the morning. Tina had trouble sleeping because she was now confused. During the night Andrew had ignored her and that had hurt. It left her wondering who she wanted, and she found her fantasies were not quite as enjoyable.

They were roused at 0530hrs and after a check parade they changed into their grey, blue and black camouflage pattern work dress. Then they set to work packing up and carrying out their morning routine. Tina was rostered for washing up in the galley after breakfast and that kept her busy almost right up until they paraded for 'colours' at 0745hrs. As soon as the parade was over those going on the exercise loaded their gear into a waiting Navy bus and were checked on board.

Tina sat next to Sarah and Andrew sat behind her. That made her feel quite uncomfortable, but she tried to ignore him and began chatting and joking. The bus set off, along with two support vehicles, at 0815. For the next two hours it was a familiar journey for Tina, south to Gordonvale, turn right and up the Mulgrave Valley and then up the Gillies Highway and across the Tablelands to Atherton. Tina tried to relax and enjoy the scenery but the knowledge that Andrew was there and the sight of the Lamb Range with its memories of mist nets and poachers both got her anxious and unsettled.

They stopped at Atherton for a toilet break and then continued on southwards up the main road to Herberton. As the bus ground up the steep, winding road to the pass Tina remembered what her father had said about the old railway and pointed it out to Sarah. They went over the crest of the pass and then crossed the old railway twice. Soon after that they pulled up behind two large coaches which were parked on the left of the road. What looked like hundreds of cadets in army camouflage uniforms were milling around and Tina's first thought was that they were army cadets but then she saw they were air force cadets, so she stopped looking for Graham.

The army cadets are doing a pack march to toughen up and are supposed to sneak in, she told herself. The army cadets had arrived in the area the night before but, by agreement, were not yet in the area to be guarded.

The navy cadets de-bussed and unloaded their gear. By then most of the air cadets had begun walking off along a dirt road into the bush. They were followed by three 4WDs and a truck loaded with packs and camping gear. The navy cadets were then separated into two groups. One group was starting the exercise in Herberton and the others at this point, which Tina now learned was called Moomin. Tina was in the Moomin Group. Because she was training for the D of E badge, she and the other candidates had to carry their packs. The other navy cadets loaded theirs in one of the support vehicles. The second group reboarded the bus, along with about twenty of the air cadets and they continued on to Herberton.

The vehicles headed off along a gravel road and the cadets followed them, first splashing through a shallow crossing of the Wild River and then walking under an old timber railway trestle. Then it was a 2 kilometres route march along the dirt road to the main campsite. This involved them in wading the Wild River again and this caused some dismay and unhappiness to those who did not have waterproof boots. To Tina it was no worry at all and she began to enjoy herself, thinking it was lovely forest country. The trees were tall and straight with a thick growth of waist high grass underneath.

Should be lots of interesting birds, she thought.

After a kilometre and a half, the navy cadets arrived at a boom gate where a group of air cadets were standing around on guard. Just beyond that the road became bitumen and went steeply uphill to the right. With her pack weighing her down Tina found it quite a puff and many of the others were unable to walk up it without stopping a few times. It made Tina glad she had done the walk over the mountains and that she had kept reasonably fit.

The road levelled out and became gravel again, curving to the left. A hundred metres along an old side road came in from the right and she saw two vehicles parked there and a group of air cadets setting up camp. She knew that the air cadets had one group of new recruits doing a weekend bivouac to learn how to live in the field and wondered if that was them.

The others are second years doing fieldcraft training and they will be the guards and patrols, she remembered. The third group, mostly third and fourth years, were the air cadet radio teams.

She puffed her way up another couple of hundred metres of road and around a slight curve to the right. The country was still mostly a pleasant forest with waist high grass, but she noted a few patches of ferns and thicker undergrowth off to the left. The navy cadets were halted and told to sit beside the road on the right-hand side. As they did Tina saw that three vehicles were parked in a clearing on the left and that people were setting up tents among the trees behind them.

The CO, Lt Cdr Hazard, walked across from the tents. "Those tents are the tri-service HQ," he explained. "We will have a safety control Command Post here with staff from all three services. Team One will be the staff for it. Team Two is to set up a signal station across the road where they can communicate with Team Five on Stewarts Head."

He pointed behind them and Tina swivelled her head to look and was able to get a glimpse of a rocky knoll on the next mountain range over. She knew that Team 5 comprised the biggest, fittest boys in the unit and that they had Sub Lt Sheldon with them, plus an air cadet team.

Andrew was in Team 1 with Cadet Midshipman George and Petty Officer O'Leary. Tina found she had mixed feelings about that. She thought she would have preferred him to be somewhere else but was glad he was close.

About twenty air cadets joined the navy cadets and sat down. Among them Tina recognised Willy Williams and his mates Stick and Noddy. Willy smiled and gave Tina a nod as he sat down. Then Capt Conkey appeared in his army cadet uniform and he also gave her an approving nod. The cadets were issued with photocopied maps and then given a ground orientation and safety brief by an air cadet squadron leader. It was then that Tina learned that the air cadets came from three squadrons: Cairns, Mareeba and Innisfail. It peeved her that the Air Cadets had three units in the region whereas the Navy Cadets only had one. They were then told to have lunch.

After that they were split into groups for signals training. Most of the afternoon was taken up with lessons by instructors from all three services on how to set up radios (army 77 Sets), on radio net diagrams, revision of the phonetic alphabet and radio appointment titles, then on basic RATEL procedures including writing and speaking letters and numerals, sending long messages and on relaying.

During the lessons Tina kept thinking about where the army cadets might be at that moment. She frequently looked around at the surrounding bush, half expecting to see Graham's face among the leaves. Each time she shook her head and told herself he would be better than that.

He won't be seen that easily, she thought.

Once the lessons were done the radios were netted in and radio checks carried out. Team 3 was then taken by vehicle back to the Moomin rail bridge where they were to set up a signal station and Observation Post with a team of three air cadets. They were to watch for any army cadet patrols trying to sneak into the area.

The remaining navy cadets were told to set up their tents among the trees across the road from the HQ tents. The ridge was fairly flat and open and from the crest of it they had a good view of Stewarts Head. Tina and

Sarah set up their tent on a nice open piece of ground and Tina decided that she was enjoying herself. She noted Andrew set up his tent about 20 paces away and closer to the road. Once that was done, they were told to set up their signalling torch aimed at Stewarts Head.

This was done as they had been trained, aimed carefully and then taped to a tree to stop it moving. Packs and folding seats were placed next to it so they could sit and work the light and keep watch for signals. The radio was placed beside them and they began watching and listening. Andrew and his team took themselves off to the HQ tent and soon afterwards Tina heard his voice on the radio as he called Teams 4, 5 and 6 for radio checks.

After that the exercise became a bit boring as nothing happened and apart from a few routine radio checks every half hour the time just dragged. It was only at about 1600hrs that the first report of army cadets came in. It was from Team 6 who reported that six army cadets had just walked past their position and were heading for Stewarts Head. Tina had to study the map to find the Grid Reference. She saw that Team 6 were on a high point on a long ridge that ran all the way from Stewarts Head to the hills overlooking Herberton.

Soon after that there was a report from Team 7 which was on Saint Patricks Hill, which overlooked Herberton. They reported another six army cadets walking past them near the very top of the hill. They were also heading east.

Team 3 reported next. "Five army cadets have just walked past along the road heading towards HQ," they reported.

That sent the excitement up and radio messages went out from the HQ to ensure that the guard team at the gate at the bottom of the hill had heard this report and were on the alert. A small patrol of four 2nd Year air cadets was sent off down the road to reinforce them. Another team, including Willy and Stick, went past along the road towards the Old Dam, which Tina's map told her was about a kilometre away along a side road.

It was from the Old Dam that the next report came in at 1710hrs. These were only air cadets and they reported that they had captured a team of five army cadets who had tried to cross the gorge there by walking across the dam wall. An air cadet patrol was instructed to bring them to HQ.

These reports all got Tina thinking about Graham, wondering if he was in one of the groups who had been spotted. Once again, she looked around and carefully studied the surrounding scrub.

A message from Stewarts Head then told them that a group of five or six army cadets was moving in the valley between them and HQ. On hearing that both Tina and Sarah walked across through the grass to see if they could see anything. But they couldn't. The ground curved away in such a fashion as to make it hard to see and in the floor of the valley the treetops hid much of the ground.

The two girls strolled back to join Blake. As they did Tina saw a group coming walking down the road. It included air cadets with blue shoulder slides and army cadets with light green ones. For a second Tina's heart thumped harder as she thought she saw Graham among the prisoners. To check she hurried to the side of the road to get a better look.

But Graham wasn't one of the army cadets. She felt quite guilty when she realised she was being disloyal by hoping he wouldn't get caught. She saw that Willy and Stick were among the grinning guards and then realised she even knew most of the army cadets. They went to her school. She recognised CUO Ian MacAistair and his pretty female sergeant from Year 11, Sheila Sherry.

A group of officers including Capt Conkey came out to meet them. Capt Conkey was in a bad mood and Tina at first thought it was because his cadets had been caught. Then she realised it was over a safety issue.

"Why were you crossing the top of the dam wall?" Capt Conkey growled at CUO MacAlistair.

"Because the lake has jungle all around it sir and downstream of the dam the gorge is too steep to safely climb down into," CUO MacAlistair replied.

"But that wall is only half a metre wide and 20 metres high! It has water flowing over it. If you had slipped you would have been killed," Capt Conkey cried.

"Not if we fell into the water sir," CUO MacAlistair replied.

"No! Then you would only have been drowned!" Capt Conkey retorted.

CUO MacAlistair looked embarrassed but shook his head. "We took our packs and webbing off and carried them in each hand sir,"

"Well, that's something," Capt Conkley replied. "Anyway, full marks to the air cadets. Now hand over a green slide to them and get going to your night location."

Tina watched as the army cadets undid one of their two green shoulder slides and handed it to an air cadet. The army cadets then refilled their water bottles from the nearby jerry cans. They then pulled on their packs and webbing again and set off back up the road. The air cadets had to be restrained from following them.

"But we won't to see where they camp sir," Stick said.

"Be fair Cadet Morton. Give them 10 minutes start," said an air cadet officer.

Tina watched the army cadets until they were out of sight before Blake called her and Sarah back. There was another report and he needed them to copy it down and mark it on the map. As she did, this Tina wondered where the army cadets were going to spend the night. She also studied the dams for the first time. She had heard them mentioned during the safety briefing but now she saw there were two, an Old Dam, and half a kilometre upstream, a New Dam. Both had lakes marked above them.

For a few seconds she wondered if the bird smugglers might use the lakes for their floatplane but then she shook her head. Both lakes were in among tall trees and surrounded by mountains, and low cloud.

I'm getting phobic, she told herself.

She looked around to see if any army cadets were creeping up, and got a shock. Visibility had dropped to only a few metres. She saw that dense wafts of drifting mist were swirling past through the trees. The low cloud even obscured Stewarts Head for minutes at a time.

Blake laughed and pointed at it. "It won't do our Morse code exercise any good if the cloud hides it tonight," he commented.

A report came in that an army cadet group had been contacted down near the gate and that they had run away to the east. That put them somewhere down the ridge from where Tina and her team were, and again she and Sarah walked 25 metres across to try to spot them. But they saw no-one. As they made their way back to the radio, Blake called to them excitedly.

"Army cadets are attacking the signal station on Stewarts Head!"

Tina and Sarah joined Blake and sat listening to the radio reports and looking towards the distant mountain top. The low cloud had gone and the rocky knoll was clear to see. It was only 2 kilometres away but without binoculars Tina could not see anyone. The reports said that six army cadets were being held off down on the ridge to the west of the signal station. Then more radio reports came in of army cadet groups attacking the signal stations on Saint Patricks Hill and Mt Ida and on the ridge west of Stewarts Head. For the next 10 minutes there were confusing reports and several call signs cutting into each other's messages.

Then Team 5 on Stewarts Head came on the air to report that a second army cadet group had snuck up behind them and captured them. They were staying on the air for safety. The air cadet group who were guarding the signal station had been drawn off by the first attackers and did not want to surrender but Tina heard the officers negotiating. Sub Lt Sheldon was there, and he arranged for all the cadets on Stewarts Head to move in to get a water resupply and for safety during the night. Tina knew they had a safety vehicle just near Stewarts Head and now learned that the army cadets had another one up on Saint Patricks Hill and that the three signal stations there were to claim they had beaten off their attackers.

Blake looked excitedly around. "I hope we get attacked. I would like a bit of a battle," he said.

Sarah scoffed. "How can we have a battle? We haven't got any guns."

"Nor have the army cadets but we can still pretend and go bang, bang!" Blake answered.

Tina also looked around, hoping to see Graham. Instead she noted that the air cadets had put several groups of guards out around the camp. The low cloud and mist still drifted through in patches but mostly it was clear.

Nothing further happened and Blake told them to have their tea while it was still light. "You first Tina, then Sarah. We need two here on duty at all times."

Tina took her food and cooking gear and made her way across to the clearing near the jerry cans as they were ordered not to cook in the long grass. As she settled herself and began preparing her food Andrew came out of the HQ tent and carried his gear over to join her. She nodded a greeting and felt both excited and embarrassed.

He shouldn't affect me like that, she told herself, but it did leave her wondering if she still loved him. *Or do I love Graham?* she thought.

Instinctively she knew the answer. Graham was fun and exciting, but she wasn't in love with him. That got her casting surreptitious glances at

Andrew and regretting her earlier actions. But she could not bring herself to make any overt peace moves so she ate quickly without speaking and then packed up and hurried back to relieve Sarah.

The sun was going by then and the evening shadows began to quickly spread. Sarah moved over to sit near Andrew and Cadet Midshipman George. Blake looked around as more drifting cloud billowed in. "I had better eat while it is still daylight," he said. "Will you be alright on your own for a few minutes Tina?"

Tina said yes and Blake hurried over to start cooking his food. More low cloud drifted in, the cold air making Tina shiver and think about a pullover. She settled lower and looked at the map and signals log and then around her. She saw that the air cadet guard groups were moving back in and settling to have their evening meal.

Then she looked around again. *I wonder where Graham is at the moment?* she thought.

And there he was!

Grinning at her from behind a tree, his face a camouflaged mask.

Chapter 33

MORSE AND MISCHIEF

Tina's mouth fell open in surprise. Graham! And only 10 paces away! A surge of excitement swept through her and she went to speak. As she did, Graham shook his head and placed a finger to his lips. He then glanced sideways toward where the other navy and air cadets were sitting having their meal.

Tina's eyes followed his gaze, and when she saw Andrew sitting there happily eating she felt a stab of guilt. *I should warn my team,* she thought. But she didn't, and that made her feel even more guilty. As a compromise, she whispered, "Don't you dare say you have blown us up or something or I will call out."

"What if I kiss you?" Graham whispered back. That made Tina squirm with delighted anticipation and at the same time blush.

She shook her head and cast another guilty glance across the road. "Not now! We might be seen," she hissed.

"Later then. The exercise goes until 2100," Graham replied, his eyes twinkling and his face alight with a mischievous grin.

That idea excited Tina but she again shook her head. "You won't get a chance. There are usually two of us on duty here."

"I know," Graham replied. "But I'll bet you two kisses that I do."

His answer gave Tina an uncomfortable hint that he had been watching her from under cover for some time, but she accepted the dare. "If you can sneak in without the others knowing, I will give you a kiss," she agreed.

At that moment, a rustle in the grass nearby made her glance and she saw another camouflaged figure raise its head behind a tree. She had known in her mind that Graham would be part of a patrol, but she had not thought the others were so close.

Oh dear! I hope he didn't hear, she thought, now recognising the black and green camouflaged face as belonging to a Year 11 boy from her school.

That person softly clicked his fingers to attract Graham's attention and then made a signal to withdraw. Then he also gave Tina a grin before lowering himself back into the long grass. Tina saw the tops of the grass moving as he crawled away.

Graham smiled and hissed, "See you later." Then he was also gone, slipping away on his belly in the grass.

Tina shook her head at that. *I wouldn't like to crawl around in the long grass,* she told herself, anxious worries about snakes and spiders flitting through her mind. But it only confirmed in her mind how brave Graham was and how determined he might be. It made her glad she was a navy cadet. *I wouldn't like having to get dirty like that,* she thought.

The encounter made her feel very guilty. *I should have cried out and yelled bang!* she told herself. She resolved to do so next time, even if it meant going without a kiss. *I shouldn't be disloyal to the Navy Cadets,* she told herself.

Her guilt returned when Blake and Sarah came back. *I have let the side down,* she thought. *Now the enemy know how our camp is guarded.*

The others seated themselves beside her and they started talking. As they did, Tina began to worry that one of them might walk around and notice the crushed grass where Graham and the other army cadet had crept forward. But they didn't and it was something else that caught Sarah's attention.

"You seem happy," she commented.

"Er... I am," Tina replied.

She groped for a suitable answer and could only lamely add that she was enjoying the exercise. To escape from the conversation she said she needed to go to the toilet. There was a portable toilet parked over at the vehicles, so she stood up and made her way over to it.

As she came out of the toilet, the group of air cadets, which included Willy and Stick, came back from their search for the army cadet's night location. Andrew called to them as they arrived, "Did you find them?"

An air cadet sergeant shook his head. "No," he replied. "But we found where they left the road. They are hiding in the bush somewhere around near the Old Dam."

At that moment, an army vehicle arrived from down the road. Tina saw that Lt Hamilton was driving it. He called to Capt Conkey, "I'll just take them some water and come back."

The army Land Rover was driven on up the road and Willy said, "If we follow that we will find their camp and we might even catch them while they are refilling their water bottles."

Images of Graham being caught came to Tina and she wanted to say no but Lt Cdr Hazard saved her. He said, "Fair go! We need to keep the water up to everyone for safety. Give them half an hour and then you can go looking."

"Oh sir! But it will be dark by then!" Willy answered.

"You can use a torch," another officer added.

The grumbling air cadets moved to start cooking their tea and Tina made her way back to the signal station. By then twilight was almost over and she wished she had her torch. She dug this out of her pack and then re-joined the others.

Wondering if Graham could still see her, she settled and looked around. As it got darker, she found herself listening and staring into the dark bush. The exercise orders allowed the army cadets to creep in during the night and she knew from overheard conversations that the army cadets practiced this on their weekend bivouacs. But the thought of walking or crawling through the scrub in the dark made her shudder with fear.

Air cadets went off in groups to set up guard posts at road junctions and to patrol the roads. Sentries were posted around the camp and Cadet Midshipman George came and cautioned them to be on their guard. That made Tina blush with shame and she was glad it was dark.

At 1900hrs another signals exercise began. They were joined by all the navy cadets and both Lt Cdr Hazard and Sub Lt Mullion. That caused Tina very mixed emotions.

Graham won't be able to sneak up on me now, she thought, then felt ashamed at being both disappointed and relieved. What really niggled was the suspicion that the relief was only because it meant she would not have to be disloyal to her own team again.

The signals exercise was the sending of messages by Morse code using flashing lights. To do this the big torch was turned on but with a piece of thick cardboard held over the front. One cadet would then raise and lower it to make the longs and shorts for the dots and dashes.

"You don't try to turn the torch on and off," Lt Cdr Hazard reminded them. "All that does is blow the bulb or break the switch mechanism."

The messages were to be sent to the signal station on Stewarts Head who would relay it on to Saint Patricks Hill and then to Herberton. Blake pointed at Stewarts Head and said, "But sir, weren't they captured by the army cadets this afternoon?"

Lt Cdr Hazard nodded. "They were, but the signals exercise is still going ahead," he replied. "There are about twenty army, navy and air cadets grouped up there for safety tonight," he added.

But not Graham, Tina thought. *He is somewhere near here.*

At that moment they were engulfed in swirling mist and Andrew chuckled and added, "We won't see much if this cloud keeps up!"

Having Andrew near her made Tina feel uncomfortable and doubly guilty but perversely she was glad he was there. She peered into the fog, looking for lights on the distant knoll and around for any sign of Graham.

Then the mist cleared and they began flashing the torch. An answering flicker of light told them that the people on Stewarts Head were ready to receive their message. The exercise began, interrupted from time to time by more drifting low cloud. First Lt Cdr Hazard gave each message a number and then he had two cadets convert it from letters into Morse dots and dashes and then one of them read it to the torch operator who made the 'shorts' and 'longs' by lifting the cardboard over the front of the torch.

It all went much slower than Tina had expected, and she began to appreciate just how skilled the navy signallers on ships were. She had been on navy ships and watched the rapidly flashed signal lamps sending messages from one ship to the other, the signallers spelling the letters as fast as they were sent and doing it with almost no apparent effort.

When it was their turn to receive a message it was even worse. They were all told to write it down on their notebooks and then to turn the dots and dashes into letters. Almost none of them knew the Morse code well enough to just watch and write the correct letter but to Tina's satisfaction both Andrew and Cadet Midshipman George had this skill. She didn't and she kept making little mistakes.

The messages were all short and apparently easy, such as: 'Weigh anchor', 'Set sail', '20 knots' or 'Enemy battleships' but it took them about 15 minute just to get one of them right. This was made harder by more cloud drifting across Stewarts Head or by an occasional drifting of fine drizzle.

Tina found it quite challenging and entertaining but only half her mind was on the job. The other half was wondering about Graham and half hoping he would try to creep up to her. But she did not think any opportunity would present itself as she was with such a big group. However at 2030hrs Lt Cdr Hazard organised supper and they were told to leave two people at the signal station while the others had hot Milo and biscuits over at the tents.

"I'll stay," Tina volunteered.

The other person was Blake. He was told to stay, and the others all trooped off across the road. Tina took it on herself to do the writing as Blake called to her the dots and dashes. As she did, Tina wondered if Graham was close enough to be able to see her face in the glow of her torch.

I hope so, she thought.

But the grass was now wet and it was getting cold, and she doubted if the army cadets would be crawling through the bush in those conditions. She knew from the radio that there had been a few 'contacts' along the roads and at various other signal stations during the previous hour but nothing had happened near the HQ.

Then a thick bank of cloud obscured Stewarts Head. Some even drifted in among the trees where Tina was, making the lights of the HQ camp go misty. Blake grunted and said, "Can't see a blasted thing now! I will just do a pee while I get the chance."

"We are supposed to always have two people here, just in case," Tina reminded him, her heart lifting with both hope and anxiety.

Blake stood up. "It'll be alright. I won't be long." With that he hurried off across the road.

Tina suddenly felt very isolated and anxious and she turned to look towards the camp. As she did, there was the sound of rustling grass near her and she jumped with fright and turned to look.

It was Graham. He came forward at a crouch, all covered in some sort of woolly, shaggy camouflage cover and with his face smeared with camouflage cream. He was grinning from ear to ear and obviously really enjoying himself. "Good! I thought he would never go," he said.

Tina was thrilled, but also torn. *I should cry out,* she told herself.

But she didn't. Indeed all she seemed able to do was sit and let him kneel and put his arms around her. It was only when he tried to kiss her that she stopped him. "Not with all that horrible muck on your face!" she cried softly.

Graham nodded and used his sleeves and handkerchief to hastily wipe most of the cam cream away. Then he moved closer, his eyes continually flicking from her to the HQ camp. Tina felt a surge of delight.

He's going to kiss me! she thought. She knew that was what he had said he would do but she had expected a bit more of preliminary cuddling and talking.

Instead he just took her in his arms and covered her lips with his. For a few moments she was so surprised that she did not react. Then she felt the warmth of desire pulse through her and she responded. The sheer thrill of the risk excited her, but she also felt it was very romantic. They drew apart for a few seconds and Graham again studied the camp.

"That was nice," he murmured. "You feel great."

With that he pulled her to him and kissed her again. This time Tina returned the kisses with interest and she began to heat up as she felt his strong male body pressing against hers. *He is aroused,* she noted, both pleased and anxious at the same time. She thought it was terribly romantic that he had crept through the bush in the night to be with her.

They drew apart and looked at each other. Tina found she was breathless and she licked dry lips. "Have you been watching us all the time?" she whispered.

Graham shook his head. "No. We went back to our hide to have a meal."

"Hide?"

"A secret camp," Graham explained.

"Where is it?" Tina asked.

Graham pointed up the road. "Just off an old side track up near the New Dam," he answered. Then he smiled and said, "Stop talking. They might hear us and I didn't crawl through all that wet grass just to talk."

Tina was thrilled at that and despite his wet clothes and the smell of his sweat she happily allowed him to hold her tight. They kissed again. As they did Tina saw that Graham was glancing past her even as he kissed but she understood that he did want to get caught and forgave him the lack of attention. And she was in no doubt that he was physically aroused. As he kissed, he stroked her body with his hands, sending waves of heat through her.

Then she realised that his right hand was actually gently caressing her left breast. For a few moments she was so surprised that she did not react. It was what she knew lovers did, but she was still shocked, even as his touch set her on fire with desire. And it felt very nice.

But this is too fast, she told herself, afraid she might lose control and do things she would really regret.

Firmly she reached up and moved his hand away. His response was to stop kissing and whisper, "Sorry." Then he kissed her again and she forgave him and let him.

Suddenly Graham stiffened and he stopped kissing. He drew back into a crouch and stared towards the camp. Tina heard the sound of voices and footsteps heading their way.

"Got to go!" Graham whispered. He knelt forward and gave her a last quick kiss, then turned and slipped away into the long grass.

No sooner had he gone than three people arrived: Lt Cdr Hazard, Petty Officer O'Leary and Andrew. Lt Cdr Hazard said, "What is that message saying?"

Message? Tina wondered. Then she experienced a sensation of ghastly shock when she saw that the signal lamp on Stewarts Head was flashing. *Oh no!* she thought, wondering how long it had been going.

"I don't know sir. I didn't see it," she said, hot with shame and anxiety.

Lt Cdr Hazard grunted with annoyance and came closer, "I thought there were supposed to be two of you here. Where is the other person?"

"Blake was here sir, just a moment ago. He just went to the toilet," Tina answered. She knew her answer wasn't the whole truth and she blushed with shame at the lie.

Lt Cdr Hazard shone his torch down on the open notebook beside Tina and said, "Did you copy any of the message?"

"No sir," Tina replied, shame and guilt making her burn.

"What's that on your face?" Petty Officer O'Leary asked, his torch moving to shine full on her.

Tina felt another burning stab of guilt and anxiety. She knew instantly it was camouflage cream but did not know what to say. Not wanting to openly lie she said nothing. The others bent to look.

It was Andrew who answered. "It looks like camouflage cream to me," he said, his voice both hurt and accusing at the same time.

Tina rubbed at her face and some cream came off on her fingertips. She saw it was green cream and she could only swallow and feel even worse. A swirl of sickness began to form in her stomach.

"Camouflage cream?" Lt Cdr Hazard said in puzzlement.

"Army cadets!" Andrew growled. Then he bent closer. "Tina, has Graham Kirk been here?"

Tina could only sit and nod. Tears were forming and she was beginning to feel nauseous.

Lt Cdr Hazard asked, "What army cadets?"

Andrew answered him a very hurt, hard voice. "Tina is going out with an army cadet from our school sir."

"Are you? Has he been here?" Lt Cdr Hazard asked, anger sounding in his tone.

"Yes sir!" Tina sobbed. Now the tears did come, along with shame and burning memories.

Worse still all the others were now arriving back and there was a babble of conversation and whispering to add to her hurt. Then it got worse. Petty Officer O'Leary moved his torch to look around and then said, "What's this?"

He held up a sheet of paper which had been taped to the signal torch. Tina looked at it in horror, suspecting what it was. She had to blink to clear her tears to see better. Then she experienced an even deeper wave of shock and embarrassment. Clearly printed on the paper was:

2 Platoon Army Cadets
CUO MacAlsistair
CDTSGT Grenfell
CDTCPL Kirk
CDTCPL Bell

The awful realisation burst on Tina that while Graham had been kissing her at least one other army cadet had been there, taping the paper to the torch. The name Stephen Bell flitted through her mind. A fierce wave of embarrassment coursed through her as she remembered those passionate kisses and then Graham's roaming hand. Then the shame of being watched was replaced by a much darker and more hurtful idea.

Did Graham just do that so the others could sneak in? she wondered.

The thought that she might have been used in that way really stung and even though she had doubts she could not push the idea out.

It got rapidly worse as the paper was thrust under her nose by an angry Petty Officer O'Leary. "How come they could sneak up and stick this on the torch if you were guarding it?" he asked in a very accusing tone.

Tina could only shake her head and sob. She looked up and saw a row of hostile faces all looking down at her in the torchlight. She noted a reproachful look on Sarah's face and felt so awful she just wanted to earth to swallow her up.

At that moment Blake returned and Tina had the irrational urge to shout at him to say none of this would have happened if he had stayed there. But in her shame and misery she said nothing.

Blake looked around and said, "What's going on?"

Six voices all spoke at once and Tina heard comments like: 'Let us down,' and 'Let the enemy in'. To her shame Petty Officer O'Leary made the aside, "Sleeping with the enemy eh?"

The connotation of disloyalty and of promiscuous sex both stung Tina but she had no answer. Into her mind swirled heated images of Graham's aroused state and of his hand on her breast.

Lt Cdr Hazard snapped, "That is enough talk like that thank you Petty Officer!" Then he turned on Blake. "Well, where have you been?" he snapped.

Blake explained and after hearing the lame excuse Lt Cdr Hazard then blasted him for leaving his post. Blake obviously did not realise what had gone wrong until the paper was shown to him. He then became very defensive and kept muttering he had to go to the dunny. Others now used their torches to look around and trails of flattened grass were quickly found that showed at least three or four army cadets had crawled right up to the signal station. Some cadets started following the tracks but Lt Cdr Hazard called them back.

"You are not going to run around the bush in the dark trying to catch army cadets. You don't have the training or the right equipment. Now get back to running this signal station," he snapped.

Petty Officer O'Leary then said, "Sir, Tina probably told the army cadets where to find us. She might be in communication with them."

"I did not!" Tina cried, horrified at the accusation.

"You could have been sending them signals," Petty Officer O'Leary retorted.

"That's enough!" Lt Cdr Hazard said. "Seaman Babcock, go over to the HQ tent. Sub Lieutenant Mullion, you go with her please."

Tina stood and walked towards the camp, stumbling frequently as her tears made it hard to see. Sub Lt Mullion walked with her and took her elbow to steady her. Once there Lt Cdr Hazard joined them, and they stood in the darkness near the vehicles. It was obvious to Tina that Lt Cdr Hazard was very angry.

He hissed at her, "Did you know the army cadets were going to sneak up?"

"No sir," Tina replied, her voice almost cracking with anxiety. She then explained Graham's dare, a task made harder and more humiliating because she could not stop sniffling and tears kept trickling out.

"So he said he would kiss you if he could?" Lt Cdr Hazard said.

"Yes sir."

"And did he?"

Tina hesitated and was tempted to lie but then sobbed and said, "Yes."

For a few seconds Lt Cdr Hazard said nothing but Sub Lt Mullion added, "That's obviously how she got the camouflage cream on her face."

"Fraternising , and with the enemy!" Lt Cdr Hazard added.

At the word 'fraternising' Tina felt a spasm of fear grip her stomach. She knew it was against all the rules and she suddenly realised that she was in real trouble. *I could be chucked out of cadets!* she thought.

Pulses of hot shame swept through her as she pictured the humiliations, the behind-the hand whispering, the sneers of her enemies, the hurt it would cause her family. Then another even worse idea struck her: *Graham could be in trouble too!*

Her mind raced as she tried to find a way to save him. In desperation she cried, "Oh sir, it was only a little kiss! We didn't... didn't do anything!'

But even as she said it the image of his hand burned in her mind and she mentally squirmed and loathed herself. But then she stiffened her resolve. To save Graham she would lie!

Lt Cdr Hazard shook his head. "What are we going to do with you?" he said.

Chapter 34

DAWN AT THE DAM

For several seconds Tina stood, so appalled at what might happen that she was unable to speak. Then she sobbed, "Oh Sir, please don't chuck me out! And please don't get Graham into trouble!"

She felt so upset that she shook, and nausea swirled in her stomach.

Lt Cdr Hazard gave her a sour look and scowled. "Why not? You have broken the rules and you have been disloyal to us and let us down."

"Sorry, sir," Tina whispered, her voice breaking with sobs.

"I suppose you thought it was just a bit of harmless fun?"

Tina could only nod as her throat was choked with emotion.

At that Sub Lt Mullion spoke. "It is only an exercise Sir," she said.

"Yes, I know, but I will still have to show this paper to the army cadet OOCs and they will crow about how good they are and we have nothing to reply with. Our reputation will take a dive, and when they learn about how it was achieved we will be the butt of their jokes. I don't like being the laughingstock."

That idea scorched Tina's pride too and she felt even sicker when she realised that her name was going to become common gossip. *Serves me right!* she told herself bitterly.

She didn't blame Graham or really regret letting him kiss her. But she could see no way of stopping the stories and she did feel bad about having harmed the unit's reputation.

Sub Lt Mullion looked thoughtful. "Perhaps if we could sneak into their camp or catch them out somehow?" she suggested.

"How could we do that?" Lt Cdr Hazard queried.

Sub Lt Mullion gestured to Tina. "Seaman Babcock might be able to tell us where they are camped."

"Can you, Seaman Babcock?" Lt Cdr Hazard asked.

That really put Tina on the spot. *First, I have betrayed my own unit and now they want me to betray Graham,* she thought.

In her misery she felt she just wanted to collapse. Then she resolved to be truthful. "I don't know exactly sir but Graham, that is Corporal Kirk, said they are camped beside an old side road up that way. Somewhere near a dam. He called their camp a hide." She pointed up the road, feeling more upset than ever.

Lt Cdr Hazard was thoughtful. "Hmmm. You don't know exactly where?"

"No sir."

He took out a map and moved to where the light from the nearest tent provided sufficient illumination. He pointed to it and said, "This is the road that goes around this hill to the New Dam and there is a vehicle track shown as cutting across from the next bend to re-join the road just upstream of the New Dam. I suppose that is the track."

Sub Lt Mullion studied the map and agreed but Tina could only shrug. "I suppose so sir. But he did say they were in a hide, a secret camp, and I don't think we will find it in the dark."

Lt Cdr Hazard looked thoughtful. "No, I agree. The army cadet patrols won't have any lights and are probably all in bed by now. But we might catch them at daylight."

Sub Lt Mullion nodded and said, "Possibly sir."

Lt Cdr Hazard looked hard at Tina. "So that is what we will do. We will get up early and send a couple of groups to search for them. And you will go with them Seaman Babcock."

"Yes sir."

"Now, is your boyfriend likely to come back tonight?"

Tina guessed that a trap would be set if Graham had planned to but she was able to shake her head. "I don't think so sir. He didn't say anything about that." But the idea of Graham sneaking up in the night to be with her sent another little thrill through her.

This was instantly quashed when Lt Cdr Hazard said, "Were you planning to go and see him?"

Tina was both shocked and hurt. "No sir!" she cried. The knowledge that she had lost their trust really stung. She had to calm herself to answer. "I won't do the wrong thing again, sir."

"I hope so. But just in case you will sleep next to Sub Lt Mullion and we will maintain a guard all night," Lt Cdr Hazard said.

That hurt even more. Tina began to bitterly regret those minutes of romantic passion, until she thought about them and wondered if she would choose love over Cadets if that was the option. *It was nice, and*

Graham really knows how to kiss, even if he is a bit fast, she thought. But then the niggling doubt about whether he actually liked her or was just doing it to distract her while his friends snuck in caused her to wonder.

The memory of Andrew's hurt look when he had discovered that she had been kissing Graham also bothered her, as did the look he gave her as they re-joined the group. When Lt Cdr Hazard told the other navy cadets the plan for the morning Tina burned again with shame and with the knowledge that she had hurt both herself and Andrew. During the briefing she caught him looking at her intently.

He must still like me, she decided.

Later, in the privacy of her sleeping bag she wept with misery at the mess she had made of things. *And does Graham really love me, or am I just a bit of fun? Was he using me?* she wondered. It was all unpleasant and on top of that was the knowledge that she had damaged her reputation in the unit. She did not think she would be thrown out of cadets but she did think that she had damaged her chances of being promoted. *The officers won't trust me,* she thought unhappily.

The group were sent to bed at 2200hrs, except for two who were on guard nearby. These were to be changed every hour on a roster and Tina was thankful she did not have to share the duty with Andrew. When her turn came, she spent the first hour with Blake and the second with Petty Officer O'Leary. Neither said much to her and she felt even more miserable than before.

It was a cold night with low cloud and occasional light showers of drizzle and Tina felt so wretched she considered saying she was sick. But then pride kicked in.

I got myself into this mess. I will now get myself out. And if Graham did use me then I don't owe him anything. Anyway, I am a navy cadet and he is an army cadet and they are our opponents, she reasoned.

So when they were roused by Cadet Midshipman George at 0500hrs she dragged herself out of her sleeping bag and set about preparing without complaint. Lt Cdr Hazard briefed them at 0530hrs, handing each one a map photocopy and two small radios. They were grouped into their two teams so Tina was with Petty Officer O'Leary and Sarah and Andrew was with Cadet Midshipman George and Blake.

Lt Cdr Hazard pointed at the map in the torchlight. "One group will go clockwise around the road and the other anticlockwise. You need to be up near the New Dam by First Light which is in about half an hour's time. But don't leave the road except to attack the army cadet's camp if you find it. If you do find it radio at once and wait for the other team to join you. Be back by 0730 for breakfast. Now, off you go."

It was still dark except for a lantern in the HQ tent and none of the air cadets or army cadet officers was awake as the group made its way out onto the road. Mist drifted thickly through the trees and the road was just a grey blur. Blake turned on his torch but Cadet Midshipman George at once told him to turn it off.

"We don't want the army cadets to see us coming," he explained.

"They won't sir. They will still be asleep," Blake replied, but he switched the torch off.

Tina walked at the back of the group as they trudged up the gravel road in the dark. She felt ill and miserable and was shivering with cold even though she had her pullover and a beanie on. All she carried was a torch and a water bottle. The map she shoved into her pocket. She really did not feel like any silly games in the cold, wet bush at that hour.

It was only a 5-minute walk to the junction of the side road, just enough to make her puff a little. The side road was blocked by a fallen tree, but the turn-off was obvious even in the darkness. Cadet Midshipman George pointed to it and said, "OK PO, take your group along that and when you get to the dam turn left and you should end up back here. We should meet you along the way."

With that he led Andrew and Blake off to the left along the good road. Petty Officer O'Leary led Sarah and Tina around the end of the fallen tree and on along the old road. It was deeply rutted and several more logs and fallen trees blocked it further along. This meant frequent detours but there was no danger of getting lost as a clear foot track wound its way along the old road. The cadets had to go slowly to avoid tripping or slipping and Tina found it both unpleasant and spooky. The dark bush was dripping from the fog and drizzle and to her it all looked hostile.

Petty Officer O'Leary stopped after a hundred metres and said, "Six O'clock. That is when the army cadets have reveille, I think. We might hear them getting up if we are quiet. You go first Tina, and if Kirk asks who we are you tell him it is you. Then you go ahead on your own and keep him busy while we radio the others."

"What do you mean by keep him busy?" Tina asked, feeling very hurt at the implication.

She was right. Petty Officer O'Leary snickered and said, "Same way he kept your attention last night."

Tina wanted to cry, or scream at him. But all she did was bite her lip and hold back the tears. Sarah's face was just a pale blob in the darkness so she could not tell what she was thinking, and she said nothing. But Tina saw no option if she wanted to redeem herself except try her hardest to find the army cadets.

"You keep your crude thoughts to yourself!" she hissed. Then she pushed past him and walked on along the track. The others followed.

Another 100 paces along the track Tina came to a track junction. Another old road led off to the right and she halted and stood listening. But all she could hear was the splatting of drips from the leaves overhead. Otherwise it was very still. There was no breeze and the bush was silent.

Not even a bird, she thought.

Through the trees Tina could just see a flat patch of lighter grey ahead so she kept going. "That must be the lake," she said. The others agreed and followed her.

It was. Another hundred and 50 paces brought them to yet another track junction, this one only a few metres from the shore of a small lake. Tina halted and looked around. The lake was about half a kilometre long and slightly less than that wide. Because there was no breeze the surface was completely still. Wisps of mist were rising from it to form a thin layer of fog above it. The fog half obscured the dark jungle on the hills surrounding the lake.

Down to the left the straight black line of the concrete dam wall was visible through the mist. Petty Officer O'Leary pointed to it and said, "There's the actual dam. That is the way we have to go. We should meet the others there."

"What about this other track?" Tina queried, pointing to the rough vehicle track which led off to the right around the shore of the lake.

Petty Officer O'Leary just shrugged and started walking. Sarah followed him and, after a moment's hesitation, Tina did likewise, now falling to the rear. But they had only gone about 20 paces when a faint metallic noise came from the far end of the lake to their right rear.

"What was that?" Sarah asked.

Tina pointed back up the other vehicle track. "Someone over there I think," she replied. She stopped and stared across the misty water but could only see fog and dark leaves.

Petty Officer O'Leary stopped and said, "Come on. We are supposed to go this way."

"We are supposed to find the army cadets," Tina replied.

"Then you go and look. I don't feel like walking further than I have to," Petty Officer O'Leary replied.

Tina turned and started walking back towards the track junction. "Come with me Sarah."

But Sarah shook her head. "No. I will wait with Petty Officer O'Leary. Hurry up. It is nearly six thirty and we have to get back."

Tina did not want to go looking on her own but she was now determined to find the army cadets, so she kept on walking. Twice she glanced back. She glimpsed Petty Officer O'Leary and Sarah, both just standing there watching. Then they were lost in the gloom and behind the bushes and tall reeds that lined the shore of the lake.

When she reached the track junction Tina stopped and looked at the muddy ground. It was just past 'First Light' and the sky was lightening so she was able to see fairly clearly. She noted vehicle tracks and then an unmistakeable boot imprint which pointed along the side-track.

Boot tracks! They might be along here, she thought hopefully.

She set off at a cautious walk. By now she was feeling both excited and anxious. The gloomy silence pressed down on her and she felt quite alone. *That is silly,* she told herself. *The others are only a hundred metres back and it is just a cadet exercise.*

But after another 100 paces she felt even more tense. All was quiet and barely a ripple disturbed the surface of the dam. *Not even a duck,* Tina thought as she glanced through a gap in the reeds to study the lake. It was now shimmering with a faint silver tone as the light improved.

Then she heard another metallic clink and the murmur of voices. These definitely came from further along the track. Tina felt a surge of excitement and hope and moved quickly in that direction, only halting at the bends to peek around them. A few times she considered going back to get the others, but she decided she would take them definite information first.

I will at least count how many army cadets there are, she thought.

By this time she was approaching the head of that arm of the lake and the trees loomed darkly overhead. She could quite distinctly hear voices, even above the excited beating of her heart. A tremor or anxiety made her admit she was scared but then she told herself not to be silly.

It is only a cadet exercise, she reminded herself.

She moved forward at a stealthy crouch, heading for the next bend. But before she reached it she passed a gap in the bushes and reeds on her left and that allowed her a good view out to the water. What she saw caused her to freeze in shock. Floating close under the trees only 50 metres away was a grey painted floatplane.

The smugglers! she thought as a wave of fear swept through her.

She stepped back a pace to get a better look and then had no doubts. The floatplane looked ghostly in the half light and mist and was partly hidden by a camouflage net. *Single engine, high wing,* she noted. By now her heart was hammering rapidly and her throat had gone dry.

Then a squelching sound further along the track made her flinch and she looked that way. To her horror a person stepped around a muddy puddle at the bend. It was man and he saw her at once. He stopped and his mouth fell open.

So did Tina's. *Neville!* she thought, recognising her back neighbour.

He obviously recognised her as well. For a moment he just stared and then he shook his head and called, "You! You little interfering bitch! Come here!"

With that he ran towards her. For a heartbeat Tina was frozen with fear, but then she turned and fled.

Chapter 35

TERROR

For a few heartbeats Tina stood and stared in frightened disbelief. Then her mind registered that Neville was running towards her and a spasm of sheer terror flooded through her. She turned and ran.

As she did, she heard Neville call loudly: "Danny! We've been spotted. That girl's here. Help me! Kostis, get that plane out of here, fast!"

The mention of Danny sent new waves of terror coursing through Tina. She ran as fast as she could, aware that Neville had started in pursuit. Almost at once she knew she was in trouble. The track was muddy, and she was unfit. A glance over her shoulder revealed that Neville had already halved the distance. It was obvious he would catch her very quickly.

The thought flashed through Tina's mind that only her friends could save her. She did not know what Neville might do to her when he caught her, but she had seen the ranger shot and Danny's horrible threats flooded into her mind adding to her fear. *And he is here!* A glance over her shoulder showed Danny's angry face as he came running around the corner behind her.

"Help!" Tina shrieked. "Help!"

But the cry came out as a strangled screech and its immediate result was to send a startled white cockatoo flapping up from its perch. As it rose the bird began to squark and screech. This caused a whole flock of cockatoos to rise in alarm, their cacophony drowning out Tina's cries. All she could do was sob in fear and keep running.

As she ran, she kept looking ahead, hoping to see her friends but all she could see was mist and bushes. Twice she nearly slipped and fell on the muddy track. Each time she regained her balance and kept running but at the cost of some hot pains in her left leg and groin.

But it was no good. Neville was fitter and faster and she could hear his thudding and squelching footsteps getting closer every few seconds. Panic surged in Tina's heart and she tried to push herself to run faster.

She also tried to call for help but the sound came out as a shrieking gasp which set the cockatoos screeching again.

Then he had her. She felt his hand grab at her shirt, and she sobbed with terror and kept running. Just ahead of her was the track junction where she had left the others but to her dismay there was no sign of them. *They must be close!* she thought. In desperation she sucked in air to scream for help. But As she did, she was spun off her feet by Neville's grasping hand.

Tina found herself rolling in mud and grass, then in shallow water. But in the process Neville had lost his grip. Hope surged and Tina scrambled to her hands and knees and tried to get up to run. She was now to the right of the vehicle track and she found herself on the edge of the lake, in among the reeds and shallow water. But that was away from Neville, so she scuttled in that direction, then tried to dodge to the left to get back to dry land.

As she did, she realised she would not make it. Neville came splashing across and grabbed at her again. She screamed as loud as she could. Neville swore and pushed, and Tina fell heavily face first into the shallow water. Fear lent her strength and she raised her head and gasped more air and screamed again. As she did, she heard what sounded like a whole flock of cockatoos begin screeching and she even glimpsed some of the birds flapping up from the nearby trees.

Tina mentally cursed the birds and opened her mouth to suck in more air. As she did, she heard Danny's voice.

"Drown the little bitch! Shut her up!" he called.

Neville acted on that. He jumped on Tina's back, knocking the wind out of her and driving her face under water with his hand. Now absolute terror coursed through Tina and she squirmed in desperation.

They are going to kill me! I am going to die! her terrified mind thought.

Tina knew that death was very close. With her face shoved into the mud and slime she had only a minute or so of life unless she could break free. A desperate desire to live gave her strength. She heaved and wriggled with all her might in a frantic attempt to break free.

And it worked. Neville lost his balance and rolled off her. As soon as Tina felt the weight lift off her back, she rolled the other way, ignoring the pain of her water bottle pushing into her side. In desperation she got her head above water and gasped air, then rolled again and scrambled to her hands and knees. Her mind kept screaming to run as she knew that Danny was also after her. But mud and slime had got into her eyes and she could not see clearly and had no idea how close he was. But she did know that when he arrived she had no chance at all.

So she sprang to her feet, wiping her face to clear her vision as she did. Through one mud caked eye she glimpsed Neville rising to his feet. He was only a metre or so away, just out of reach. But already his hands were clawing to grab her, and he looked very angry. Tina turned, then slipped and almost stumbled. By desperately jerking away she managed to avoid his rush and fled.

Splashing through the shallow water and reeds she ran away from him, only to see that she was now running back towards Danny. His angry face came briefly into focus before her eyes watered and closed. But it was enough to send a new spasm of terror through her and to change the direction of her flight. She fled gasping up out of the water.

Half blinded and choking with fear and water which had gotten into her mouth, she fled along the only clear path she could see. As she did, she wiped at her eyes and blinked repeatedly in an attempt to clear her vision. In this she was partly successful, and she saw that she was on the vehicle track. That cheered her up until she realised that she was running back into the forest instead of along beside the dam.

My friends are the other way, she thought, her hopes plunging. Then she shook her head and told herself to keep going. *This is the way we came. I can go this way back to camp,* she reasoned.

The image of the adult officers gave her hope and she pushed herself to keep running. A glance over her shoulder showed Neville splashing ashore 20 metres behind and Danny arriving at the track junction. She did not know if she could outrun the men again, but she was not going to give up.

Neville pointed and yelled at Danny: "Go back and help Kostis to get the plane away, then bring the vehicle, and your gun. I will catch her."

The pause gave Tina another 10 paces head start and she pushed herself to keep going. By now she was feeling winded and was gasping for air but dread kept her moving. She did not even waste any more breath in trying to call for help.

As she ran, she continued to try to clear her vision and slowly she succeeded. She was able to get her right eye to water and partially clear, but the left was full of grit and she could only keep blinking and hoping. Then both eyes came open and she was able to see clearly enough to avoid the worst of the ruts that threatened to make her tumble.

It was only after she had run another 20 or so paces that her mind became puzzled. The track did not look familiar and was sloping slightly downhill. She looked around and noted that the ground sloped up to a hill on her right. *That hill should be on my left,* she reasoned.

Then the horrible truth dawned on her: while clearing her eyes, she had run past the track junction and had taken the wrong track.

I am running away from the camp! she thought with dismay.

But Neville was again hot on her heels and she had no option but to keep running. Tina briefly considered leaving the track, but the surrounding area was all forest with an undergrowth of waist high ferns and long grass.

I won't be able to run through that faster than him, she reasoned. So she kept on.

The track went downhill for a hundred metres to a muddy creek crossing. On the upstream side was a large muddy pond, and the sight of it caused Tina another bout of terror. Images of Neville trying to drown her kept her moving.

But then it was a long uphill slope and she quickly began to weaken. Her breath was now coming in hot gasps and the beginnings of a stitch began to stab in her lower belly. Tina had never been a good runner and she could only curse as her large breasts were now causing her pain and balance problems as they bounced wildly. To stop that she held them with her arms. But that gave her a cruel dilemma. She needed to pump her arms to run properly so she released her breasts and accepted the painful bouncing as the lesser problem.

The effort of breathing and the pain in her side melded into one great burning pain that caused her to consider giving up. But then fear of death overrode the pain and she pushed herself on. And Neville was catching up! The sound of his thudding boots kept getting closer and each frantic glance over Tina's shoulder showed him catching up fast. His rasping breath began to sound close behind. Tina felt her hopes sliding down as she knew she was weakening and was near the end of her ability to run.

But she gamely kept on pushing herself. Again her eyes watered, and she blinked to clear them. Just in time she noted a muddy rut and was able to sidestep to avoid it. As she did, she felt Neville's fingers grasp at her shirt. Then she heard a strangled obscenity and a loud thud. A glance back revealed Neville tumbling in the muddy wheel rut.

He's fallen! Tina thought, experiencing a surge of hope. For a few more moment's she kept on running before her mind took control. *You can't keep running,* she told herself.

She knew she needed to get her breath back, if only to be able to fight. Now she resolved to make Neville pay dearly for her life. Knowing that it might be a potentially fatal mistake she slowed to a walk.

As Tina strode up the long slope, she found her heart hammering so hard that her vision was blurring and black dots danced before her eyes. She was gasping in great shuddering gulps of air and the pain in her side was so intense she had to double up several times in an attempt to ease it. Every few steps she glanced back.

Neville got to his feet and started after her, cursing and swearing as he did. He called on her to stop but she ignored him and kept going. To her surprise he did not resume running but only followed at a fast walk. It occurred to her that he was winded too and that cheered her enormously. A faint hope of actually escaping began to grow.

But he was able to walk faster than her and he began to slowly but steadily catch up. Tina's hopes began slipping again. But she grimly kept trying. The slope levelled out and the track turned left to wind along a ridge top. Out to her right Tina got glimpses of the rocky face of Stewarts Head but it was so far away that it was no more than a familiar landmark rather than a place of hope. Through her mind ran vague hopes of meeting other cadets or of the others following and saving her.

They must be wondering where I am, she thought. She even hoped that they had heard her or even seen her being chased. But whether they would be in time was another matter.

For at least 200 paces Tina kept walking. All the while Neville slowly caught up. Tina kept hoping as her breathing slowed and the pain of the stitch eased. But she was also very wary. It was just as well she was because, when Neville was about 20 metres behind, he suddenly broke into a run. Tina was expecting this and at once fled as fast as she could go. Both broke into a desperate sprint.

Tina knew within seconds that she was in real trouble. Her body felt like lead and the pain in her side at once returned with almost crippling force. After 100 paces her heart was thudding so hard she was feeling dizzy. Her breath was again rasping hot gasps.

Oh! I can't go on! she thought. But fear of dying kept her trying.

She came to another track junction. Without hesitation she took what looked to be the better track and went to the left. This led down to a small creek. Before she reached it she cast another frantic glance over her shoulder. Neville was now almost within arm's reach, his arms working as they pumped furiously. His face was red and contorted and he was also gasping for air. But there was a pool of water beside the shallow ford that brought back all of Tina's terror of drowning and it gave her the energy for a frantic effort. She splashed across the ford and started up the slope beyond, driven by absolute desperation.

At every step she expected to feel Neville to grab her and she tensed to fight. But she managed to hold her lead and suddenly she was aware that he was not breathing down her neck. Another glance showed her what she had not expected at all, Neville had slowed to a gasping walk. He met her eye and uttered a disgusting expletive, then shook his fist.

"Bitch! Come here!" he croaked.

Tina felt a surge of hope. *He is out of breath,* she thought.

Even so she forced herself to keep running until she had increased her lead to about 50 paces. Then she also slowed to a gasping walk. She was so exhausted by this time that she just wanted to flop down and give up but fear kept her leaden arms and legs moving.

Neville kept following at a fast walk and Tina decided that his tactic now was to exhaust her and then catch up. She gritted her teeth and kept walking. With an effort that she knew was rapidly weakening her she managed to maintain the gap between them.

As she regained her breath and cleared her eyes, Tina took stock of the country. It was still forest, but the trees were larger and taller and the undergrowth was still waist high or even chest high ferns and long grass. Off to her left the ground sloped slightly downwards to a dense wall of jungle about a hundred metres away. That gave her a vague hope.

If I could get into the jungle I might be able to hide and sneak away, she thought. But her rational mind told her that any attempt to force a track through the weeds and ferns would be her undoing. *He will be able to follow the track I make faster than I can make it,* she reasoned. So she kept on along the vehicle track.

This wound through the forest with a low ridge on her right. This seemed to block escape in that direction, so she began pinning her hopes on the jungle to her left. The chase continued with both walking fast but with Neville still trailing 50 metres or more behind. Tina had no idea where she was and kept hoping she would come to a house or a road. An awful feeling of loneliness now added to her apprehension. Several times she sobbed at the apparent hopelessness of her case.

Nearly 5 minutes of fast walking brought only a change of direction in the track. Tina was only vaguely aware of this from a change in the angle of the sun. Its rays were now slanting in through the trees to produce a dappled of light and shade. She felt quite disoriented and could think of no other plan than to keep on along the track.

Another 5 minutes of gasped walking brought no obvious change to the situation. To Tina it just seemed to take her further away from her friends and her hopes of rescue went down even lower. Then suddenly she got a flash of hope. She glanced back and saw that Neville had stopped and was crouching down to retie a shoelace. He was wearing some sort of trainers or joggers she noted.

It increased her lead to about 70 or 80 paces and as she went round a bend she again considered trying to hide or to try to reach the jungle. But then Neville's head reappeared over the ferns and she abandoned the idea.

And then Neville was running again, sprinting to catch her. Tina gasped and fled, the terror welling up again as she doubted if she could keep running much longer. The track wound around the trees now and the grass and ground were wet from dripping mist. Low cloud swirled around her and the chill seemed to grip her heart. Pushing herself with grim determination she ran as fast as she could manage.

But once again Neville's lighter build gave him the advantage and he gradually overhauled her. Tina could only gasp and run, tears clouding her vision. That was nearly her undoing as she several times slipped in muddy wheel ruts where the last vehicle along the track had bogged down to its axles in soft patches of ground. But she regained her balance and ran on.

Once again Neville closed up until he was almost within reach. Tina started to sob and knew what real terror was. But then her heavier cadet boots with their cleated tread were the saving of her. She sped across another set of muddy wheel ruts in a sloshy dip. Behind her she heard a cry of alarm and a thud. Glancing back she saw that Neville's joggers had not given him the grip he needed on the slippery ground and he had fallen.

Encouraged to keep trying Tina continued running. This time she did not immediately slow to a walk. *I need to increase the lead so I can hide,* she reasoned. Through eyes clouded with watering from the grit still in them she noted that the jungle appeared closer. *I might make it this time,* she thought hopefully.

She glanced back and saw Neville roll over and scramble to his feet. Then, to her joy, she saw him wince and crouch to rub at his ankle. By then he was almost lost to sight in the low cloud. Tina rounded another bend and ran on, her breath again coming in sobbing gasps and pain spreading through her chest and body.

Ahead of her through the mist she saw that the track forked again. The left fork went into the dark wall of jungle, which was now much closer, and the right fork went up over a low ridge in a clearing. The sight of that slope immediately made her mind up. She turned towards the jungle, hope growing with every step as Neville still hadn't appeared behind her.

Beside the track she noted a scatter of white feathers. *From a white cockatoo,* she thought without making any mental connection.

Another glance behind showed no sign of Neville and for the first time she really did think she might get away. She turned her head to look at the jungle ahead and noted that the cloud between her and it seemed to be thicker than ever. Only at the last moment, much too late to stop, did she recognize her danger.

A mist net! she thought.

She tried to stop but was running too fast. To her complete horror she ran into the net. Its soft nylon mesh enfolded her in a clinging chill and she came to a struggling standstill. Terror surged.

Caught! she told herself.

The sickening knowledge that Neville was just back along the track swamped her with a sense of hopelessness.

Chapter 36

COCKATOO

Tina struggled frantically, sobbing with fear and exhaustion as she did. But her struggles seemed to snare her even tighter. Only by a conscious effort of willpower did she make herself stand still to study the problem. But she was so frightened she had trouble focusing her eyes and she kept flicking her gaze to try to locate Neville. Because she had been spun around she had trouble even working out which way to look, and only the dark mass of the jungle and the brightness of the rising sun gave her some orientation.

Back up! she told herself.

Gripping the net with both hands to try to untangle it from her water bottle and belt she worked out which way to move. Shaking with fear she took several cautious steps backwards. As she did, she noted a small bird snared high up in the net which was suspended across the clearing by ropes tied up over high branches.

By turning her head from side to side Tina was able to detect the pattern of the net and saw that her plan was working. So she kept easing back, pausing only to glance back along the track for signs of Neville.

And there he was!

He came limping around the bend in the track about 50 paces away. When he saw her predicament his face split into a cruel grin and he began to hobble faster. Panic gripped Tina and she struggled frantically to get free, pulling back hard. This stretched the net, but its strength dismayed her.

How can a mesh so fine be so strong! she thought.

It looked as though she would be caught and she started to sob and scream. Then she realised that her water bottle was snagged and she fumbled at her belt. Neville hurried towards her and began to gloat and make obscene promises of what he was going to do to her.

Total disgust mingled with terror to give Tina strength and calm. She felt the belt snap open and then she was tumbling backwards on the grass. By then Neville was only 20 paces away. Driven by a desperate desire to survive Tina rolled away and scrambled to her feet. Then she bolted, even as Neville broke into a lurching run and reached out to grab her.

Tina had the jungle in mind as the best place to hide so she ran towards it, running along beside the net which stretched most of the way to the wall of vegetation. The place where the track vanished into a tunnel of vegetation was her objective and she dodged around the end of the net and headed for it, only to swerve and gasp. Movement in the jungle shadows caught her eye and this resolved into the shape of a man.

And not just any man but Marco!

Marco was hurrying along the jungle track towards her, his face showing puzzlement. In his right hand he carried a bag and in the left a cage containing a white cockatoo. Tina blanched with terror and felt despair well up.

Caught! she thought. *Trapped between two of them.*

Still she didn't give up. She immediately changed direction and ran away from Marco, brushing the net and almost being snagged by it as she did. Just in time she swerved to keep clear. By then Neville was just on the other side and he pushed at the net in an attempt to snag her. His attempt failed but sent her heart rate shooting up so that the blood pounded in her ears. But it did not look as though she had any chance as she was now running up the vehicle track over the low grassy ridge.

A glance behind showed Marco's bulky form running up the slope behind her, urged on by Neville who was now limping around the far end of the net. Tina pushed herself to the limit, pounding up the slope. It was only 50 metres, but the last bit was steep and she was soon gasping for breath. The only shred of hope came from a backward glance that showed that Marco was no runner. He was too bulky and was not catching up.

Tina turned her head to look ahead to pick the best route and got another shock. What she had taken to be more low cloud she now saw was another mist net. This was stretched right across the crest of the ridge including the vehicle track. In a flash she noted that she was closer to the right-hand end.

If I go left, I will have to angle back towards Marco, she decided.

So she ran to the right, straight into the rays of the rising sun. These dazzled her and added to her already gritty sore eyes made it very hard to see. She could see well enough to avoid the big trees but realised she had no choice but to run into the long grass and ferns.

With a sob of despair Tina ploughed into the tangle. Within a few steps she knew she was in trouble. The grass and ferns dragged at her legs and there were even thin vines that snatched at her boots and threatened to trip her up. A glance behind showed she was over the crest by then and that the two men were still out of sight. The thought that she might be able to hide flashed through her mind, but she as quickly discarded it.

They will just follow my tracks and find me, she reasoned.

Again she glanced back. Now she was 20 metres into the tangle and still no sign of the men. She turned her eyes to the front, just in time to spot a fallen log across her path. A frantic jump got her safety across, but she only managed another 5 paces before a vine snagged her left boot. Down she went, her hopes crashing with her.

Whimpering with shock and fear she tried to scramble to her feet, but the vine still held her and she fell again. Frantically she lay on her side and clawed at the ensnaring plant. To her dismay, it was too strong to break and she had to try pulling it clear. But her haste made it worse as the creeper seemed to snag on every eyelet of her boot.

Then, just as she was free and had rolled onto her hands and knees preparatory to rising, she heard the sound of thudding boots and of men crashing into the undergrowth.

"Where'd the bitch go?" Marco called.

Tina froze and decided to make a virtue of necessity. *I will try to hide,* she thought.

So she crouched, panting for breath and trembling in every muscle. Her heart was beating so hard she had trouble hearing but from the sounds deduced that both men were off to her left, Marco closer than Neville. She did not dare raise her head to look but tensed ready for flight.

The two men crashed on into the weeds until they were almost off to Tina's left front. Then they stopped. Both swore and Marco muttered, "Where did the bitch go? She can't be far."

"Hiding in the weeds," Neville suggested. He began to walk around, obviously searching the ferns.

Tina felt ill as both men began to thrash around the long grass only 20 paces to her left. She managed to get control of her gasping breath and tried to get the wind for another run. But she felt so exhausted and dizzy that she doubted if she could run much more. Then the men began searching in her direction and she half rose and tensed to start running.

Neville's voice stopped her from breaking cover. "We are nongs. Let's find her tracks and follow them," he said.

From the noises Tina decided that he had started walking back towards the vehicle track. Then Marco followed him.

At the mention of tracking her Tina again felt her hopes slide down. *They will find me easily,* she decided. But still she didn't give up. *I will try to crawl further away,* she told herself.

So she began pushing through the grass and ferns on her hands and knees. It was very unpleasant as the grass and ferns were dripping with dewdrops and she was soon soaked again. She also found it hard to move without making a noise and could only hope that the sounds of the men's own progress drowned hers.

And I hope they don't see the tops of the grass moving, she thought.

Only after she had crawled for about 10 metres did the thought that there might be snakes in the tangle occur to her. The idea made her pause and shudder but then she kept on. *I am dead anyway if I don't get away,* she told herself.

So she kept pushing through the thick mass of long grass, ferns, and vines. The grass scratched her hands and face, but she ignored that. Pieces of wet grass also stuck to her sweaty skin and she scraped them away irritably. Then she gave a wry smile at the thought that Graham had crawled through the same sort of tangle to be with her the night before.

I'm glad I'm not an army cadet, she thought.

Then the sounds began behind her and the fear flooded back, almost paralysing her. She heard Neville call: "Here we are! Here are her tracks. Come on!"

There was no doubt in Tina's mind that they would soon catch her. Now she wrestled with the cruel decision, when to start running? *How close do I let them get before I run?* she wondered.

A moment's pause allowed her to gulp more air (She was amazed at how puffed she had become while crawling) and she decided to go early rather than late. *Neville has a hurt ankle and I think I can outrun Marco,* she reasoned.

So she took a couple of deep breaths and then stood up. They saw her at once and both men yelled out and started running. Tina bolted. Her whole focus was on not tripping again. Her estimate was that the men were 25 metres behind, and she focused on keeping that lead. But it was hard. The long grass and ferns dragged at her legs and the vines still snagged at her boots. And to run directly away from the men drove her directly into the rising sun, making it hard to see.

Then Marco went down with a swearing crash and she realised it was just as hard for the men. Hearing his curses lifted Tina's spirits and she managed a grin. A glance back showed her that Neville was still leaping and jumping in her wake, but he was not looking happy. Nor was he catching up. Marco scrambled to his feet and set off after her again.

The frantic pursuit went on for another hundred metres. Tina floundered and pushed her way down a long slope to an overgrown creek line. This baulked her for a few seconds, but she then gritted her teeth and leapt into the long grass and water of the small creek and then clawed her way up the other side.

Marco was close behind by then and almost grabbed her by the ankle as she scrambled up the steep slope out of the creek. Neville came slithering down into the creek as she pushed through a tangle of vines and scrub on the other bank. Marco began climbing after her, uttering a stream of revolting threats and obscenities as he did.

Fear had Tina in its grip and desperation drove her on. She crashed through a belt of scrub, tripped on a vine, rolled over and sprang to her feet and continued running even before Marco was up out the creek bed.

Tina ran on, her breathing laboured and her legs and arms feeling heavier every second. She knew she was close to the end and there seemed to be no end to the forest. It changed slightly to include thickets of smaller trees and more ferns than grass, but she was still able to force a path. For lack of a better option she kept running towards the rising sun, angling slightly to the left to keep the direct rays out of her eyes.

The men began closing the gap. After another 100 paces Marco was only 10 paces behind and Neville only twice that. By then Tina was almost reeling with exhaustion. She was gasping in great gulps and the agonizing stitch was gripping her lower abdomen. She began to despair.

Then Marco slowed. Tina heard Neville snarl at him to keep running and she risked a glance behind. She saw Neville limp over to Marco and grab his sleeve.

"Keep running! We've almost got her," he shouted.

"Can't! I'm buggered," Marco gasped in reply. Tina saw that his whole huge frame was heaving as he sucked in air.

"But she will get away," Neville cried, turning to glare at Tina.

Marco shook his head, "So what? Let's get out of here while we still can."

Neville swore and then lifted a small radio or mobile phone to his head. "Danny, bring the vehicle to the old timber cutter's camp," he said. Then he turned to face Tina and shouted, "I will get you, you bitch!"

When Tina heard the threat she shuddered and a chill seemed to grip her heart. Despite the fear her mind told her to get her breath back, so she slowed to a walk. All she felt like doing was collapsing but she made herself keep on moving as fast as she could. The men followed but only at a walk. Tina suddenly felt a ray of hope.

I am getting away, she thought, noting that she was now nearly 50 paces ahead of the men.

For the next 10 minutes she pushed on eastwards through the forest, ignoring the bruises and scratches and the leaves sticking to her skin. She recovered her breath but felt very tired. But the knowledge that the men were still following kept her moving. Gritting her teeth she pushed herself. Slowly the distance between them and her increased until they were at least 100 paces behind.

She increased this lead until they were out of sight for seconds at a time and then for a minute at a time. Now she really began to hope. *I might get away,* she thought.

Suddenly she came out of the ferns onto a well-used vehicle track. It was so unexpected that for a moment she could only stop and stare. *A track! Should I follow it? And which way?* she wondered. Her mind told her that she should go right as that was the way back to her friends and the dams.

But even as she turned that way and began walking, she heard the sound of a vehicle engine. She stopped to listen. No doubt about it, a motor, and getting closer. *But is it one of ours or is it the vehicle with Danny in it?* she worried.

So frightened of Danny was she that she did not dare risk being caught by him. *He will be fresh and will be able to outrun me for sure,* she thought. Then another thought chilled her even more. *And he will probably have his gun!*

Tina did an about turn and began hurrying the other way. As the vehicle got closer, she began to panic and tried to run. But a stumbling trot was the best she could manage. She began casting glances into the bush looking for hiding places.

I must take to the scrub, she thought.

But she kept on along the track as the easier route to put distance between her and the men. A hundred panting paces further along Tina came to a sort of clearing. There were a few giant trees and a couple of side-tracks and it looked man-made to her.

The old timber cutter's camp? she thought.

At that point the vehicle track swung sharply off to the left and wound off through a stand of thicker timber. As Tina plodded along it she glanced back to listen for sounds of pursuit and then had a thought which made her stomach turn over. *I am leaving clear boot prints!* she observed.

As she looked in horror at the clear imprint of her boot in the muddy black soil, she heard loud yells in the forest. At first she thought the men had seen her again, but then she heard the vehicle come to a stop.

"Time I took cover," she muttered.

Reluctantly she stepped off the track into the waist high grass and head high ferns on the right of the track. For a few steps she experienced fearful thoughts about poisonous snakes, but the men were more deadly, so she ignored the possibility of snake bite and pushed her way rapidly into the tangle. Within a couple of minutes she had covered more than a hundred metres and could no longer hear the vehicle or the men's voices. Just as reassuring was the observation that her tracks were not obvious enough to follow except by patient tracking.

Then the problem of which way to walk bothered her. She stopped and looked around and noted that she was on a wide ridge top which was gently climbing. Noting the sun she thought, *Right is east but that is downhill. And left is back the way I came from through all that scrub. So my friends must be back past the men. Oh, which way should I go?*

Tina bit her lip and then remembered her photocopied map. With trembling hands she dug it out and studied it. But she had trouble working out where she was.

Which tracks did I run along? she thought. All the while she was still gasping in air and shivering with over-exertion and fear. Every instinct was to keep on running, to get as far as possible away from the men.

She decided to go on east, reasoning that going down the slope would take her to the Wild River and then to Moomin. *It's only a few kilometres,* she reasoned. Unsure how steep the slope ahead might be she started pushing through the tangle eastwards to where she could see the ground starting to drop away.

Suddenly she heard the sound of movement nearby and she experienced a spasm of terror so strong it all but paralysed her. She froze and looked frantically around. Her eyes seemed to blur and sweat trickled into them, making her blink. Part of her mind told her that the men could not have gotten that close without her hearing them, but her ears told her it was the sound of people pushing their way through the undergrowth, and very close.

And there they were!

Through eyes made blurry by terror and perspiration Tina saw people moving only about 20 metres away. Then, even as she began lowering herself to hide, her mind registered what her eyes were seeing. They were not the men. Instead, she noted army camouflage uniforms. Blinking sweat from her eyes she peered through a bush.

Yes, army camouflage uniforms. Army cadets! she thought.

A wave of intense relief swamped her and she felt dizzy.

Safe! she told herself.

Chapter 37

GRAHAM?

Tina let out a sob and tried to call out. She now saw that the army cadets had not seen her and were walking across her front from right to left. There were four of them, faces and hands camouflaged and all carrying packs. All were boys and one had glasses. Then recognition came.

"Graham!" she croaked.

The army cadets halted and went into a crouch, their heads all swivelling in her direction. Tina began pushing towards them. Graham's camouflaged face was all she was now focused on. He looked puzzled, and then grinned and said to the others, "I told you I heard someone moving."

Tina got tangled in some vines among chest high ferns and she came to a sobbing, struggling halt. Graham saw this and at once moved to help. A few seconds later she was in his arms.

"Tina! What are you doing here? Are you alright?" he asked.

Tina found herself quite unable to answer for a few minutes. All she could do was sob and cling to him. Waves of trembling shook her so much she could hardly stand. Dimly she was aware of Graham's sweaty clothes and smell and the thought crossed her mind that she must smell as well. But she was safe!

The other army cadets crowded around and a clearing was quickly trampled and packs dropped. By then her trembling legs could no longer support her and she flopped down onto one of the packs. One of the army cadets, obviously the leader, said, "Steve, keep watch."

Tina now recognised him. He was a Year 12 from her school: Cadet Under-Officer Mike Masters. With him were a Year 11 boy she had also seen and Graham and Stephen Bell. Shame at her weakness and fear mingled with her sobs of relief and she kept panting and could not bring herself to speak to answer their questions until it occurred to her that the men might not care that she was with them.

Danny shot at us when we were in a group. He might shoot at them too, she thought.

"Shhh!" she hissed, placing her fingers to her lips as CUO Masters again asked if she was alright. They looked puzzled but she shook her head and croaked. "Keep quiet. There are men after me. They have guns and might shoot."

At that Graham's eyes widened and he held her shoulders and crouched close. "What men Ti? Why are they chasing you?"

"Bird Poachers," Tina whispered. "The same men who shot the ranger at Koombooloomba Dam," she replied.

Graham nodded and instantly understood. He went into a half crouch and peeked over the top of the scrub. CUO Masters said, "You are a navy cadet, aren't you?"

"Yes," Tina nodded. Her throat felt so dry and constricted she could hardly speak.

"And you go to our school," CUO Masters added.

Tina nodded. "Yes, I'm in Ten 'A'," she said, barely able to speak her throat was so dry.

Graham crouched again and pulled out a water bottle. "Here have a drink," he said.

Tina gulped at the water then found she was gasping and shivering so much she could not drink without spilling some. She stopped drinking and tried to get control of her trembling muscles.

Graham looked her up and down. "Geez Tina, you look a wreck. I didn't recognize you to begin with," he commented.

"They... they tried to drown me!" Tina croaked. Another fit of trembling shook her and there were more tears.

CUO Masters whispered, "Are you alone?"

Tina nodded. "There were three of us, but I got separated," she explained.

"What happened?"

Tina steadied herself and said, "We were sent to find your camp at First Light. We were to try and surprise you," she explained. "So we walked along that old road to the New Dam."

On hearing that all four army cadets looked at each other and chuckled. Graham grinned and said, "You wouldn't have caught us. We packed up in the dark and moved. We were just back there in the scrub by First Light," he said.

That annoyed Tina as it made her feel foolish. But she had to concede it was the sort of thing she had expected. However the spurt of emotion gave her voice some strength and, after another gulp of water, she quickly explained how she had seen the floatplane and then been chased. "They are just back there a few hundred metres, near that clearing," she said.

CUO Masters looked serious and said, "I thought we heard a vehicle. We'd better put a bit more distance between us and them. Sgt Grenfell, try to get HQ on the radio to warn them. Cpl Kirk, you help Tina and Cpl Bell, you bring up the rear. Let's go."

Tina did not think she had the strength left to stand but she tried. Graham offered his hands and she took them. With apparent ease he hauled her to her feet. For a few moments she could only stand with both legs trembling so much she doubted if they would function. But CUO Masters was already moving and she forced herself to take a step.

"Ow! Oooh!" she muttered.

Every muscle in that leg seemed to complain and she just wanted to stop but she made herself move the other leg. It hurt as well and forced a low groan from her. But she gritted her teeth and made herself walk.

I won't place the boys in danger just because it hurts a bit, she told herself.

As she limped along Tina kept glancing back but there was no sign of the men and the sound of their own thrusting progress through a thickening tangle of head-high ferns and shrubs made it difficult to see very far anyway. She noted all the army cadets continually looking in all directions and particularly behind them and it reassured her.

They are used to sneaking around the bush, she thought. That was a very comforting idea.

For 10 minutes the group pushed its way through the fern scrub. Tina noted they were going slowly uphill, but the ground was so rough and the undergrowth so thick it made little difference. Soon she was sweating heavily and gasping for breath. Every step was an effort and she kept getting snagged by spikey little vines which either held her back or tripped her up. Graham went just ahead of her and made an effort to clear a path for her, using secateurs to cut the worst of the vines.

Frequent detours were made to avoid particularly thick patches of scrub and fallen trees but there were so many of these they had to climb over dozens of them. Tina found it exhausting and she came to a sobbing standstill.

Graham stood and held her arm. "All the logs are from that cyclone last January," he said. "See how they are all lying at the same angle? That shows the wind direction."

Tina could see that and vividly remembered the cyclone which had briefly battered Cairns on its way down the coast. *That was the cyclone that Andrew and his sister got caught in on some lighthouse near Townsville,* she remembered.

Then she also remembered that she had heard that the blonde had also been part of that adventure and she experienced a spurt of jealous annoyance. She then remembered that Graham and his friends had made a dramatic march over the mountains near Mt Bartle Frere during the same cyclone to save a gold miner who had been trapped by a fallen tree.

It's easy for him. He's done things like this before, she thought. Panting with exhaustion she croaked, "Sorry," then sobbed and added, "I need a rest."

CUO Masters stopped and gave the signal to halt. "This will do. We are half a kilometre from where we found you. We will rest for a while. If they follow us we will hear them and will hide you and tell them a story," he said.

Tina was again given Graham's pack to sit down on and then almost went into hysterics when he reached down and flicked a leech off her trousers. She hated leeches and in her current state it was almost too much.

"Oh! Get them off me!" she wailed softly, shuddering and then groaning as cramps seized her calf muscles.

To her annoyance Graham just chuckled and treated the leeches as a joke. He picked up all the leeches he could see on both her and him, rolled each into a ball and flicked it away. Even one that was fastened to his neck he just scraped off and flicked away. When she told him that he was bleeding he just wiped the blood onto his hand to look at it and shrugged. "Nothing much. It will stop soon," he said. Then he went on looking for more. It was so obvious that he was really enjoying the situation that Tina got annoyed with him.

Silly boy! she thought. *It's all right for him. The men aren't chasing him.*

But it was a new insight into Graham's character, and she found his obvious toughness a bit off-putting. She was also surprised at how well

Stephen Bell was coping. He kept making little jokes and smiling but never relaxed his careful scrutiny of the surrounding bush.

During much of this time Sgt Grenfell had been talking quietly on his radio. It was obvious to Tina that reception was poor, and because he had a small earpiece and microphone she could not hear any of the answers but it was enough to know that they were in radio communication with HQ.

I like Grenfell, she thought.

He was a solid, chunky lad with short fair hair and a calm disposition. She had often seen him around the school but now she saw he was very cool and efficient.

He crouched and said to CUO Masters, "I've told HQ that we have Tina with us. They already knew she was missing but did not know why or where."

"Did you tell them about the men and the floatplane?" Tina asked.

Sgt Grenfell nodded. "Yes. They said that they got a report from the navy cadets of a floatplane taking off just after sunup."

An idea suddenly seized Tina. "Tell them to call the police and get them to stop the crooks escaping," she said.

Sgt Grenfell radioed HQ and passed on the message. Then he listened to the reply, nodding his head as he did. In her impatience to know Tina felt the urge to reach for the headphones but he then looked at her. "Too late I think. Capt Conkey says that a civilian Four-Wheel Drive has just driven past going down the mountain."

"Oh bother blast!" Tina cried. It was actually genuine swear words that were going through her mind, but she was able to restrain herself from swearing in front of the boys.

CUO Masters took the radio and called Capt Conkey. "What do you want us to do now sir? Over."

He listened to Capt Conkey's reply then said, "We are closer to Stewarts Head now sir. Is the safety vehicle still there? Over."

The answer obviously was yes. CUO Masters looked at her and said, "Are you up to a bit of a climb? Whichever way we go we have to walk a kilometre or so."

Tina thought hard. *There might still be some of those men back along the track,* she thought. That sent a shiver of fear through her and she decided a bit of pain was the better option.

"I would rather go over Stewarts Head," she said.

So they did. It took over an hour and left Tina feeling utterly exhausted but at least she felt safe. To begin with there were more ferns and leeches. After a few hundred metres of that they came out into open forest and waist high blady grass. A rough foot pad wound its way along an undulating ridge. There were frequent detours to avoid fallen trees and large rocks but because there were three people in front of her flattening the grass and because they were following a trail that had been recently used it was not too bad.

"Did you come this way?" she asked Graham during a short halt to have a drink.

Graham shook his head. "No. We came across the mountains from the highway. We had to cross the gorge of the Wild River and boy, wasn't it rough going!"

"Were you some of the group that crossed the wall of the Old Dam?" Tina queried.

The boys all laughed. "No," Graham replied. "That was One Platoon."

Tina frowned. "But they said that the gorge was too steep to cross. That was why they walked across the top of the dam wall."

"It is," Graham agreed. "So we made the effort and detoured down around it and then crossed near the gate at the bottom of the hill."

"Were you the group the guards at the gate chased?" Tina asked.

Again Graham shook his head. "Not us. We just photographed the guards and then followed the water pipe up the side of the gorge to near the Old Dam. Then we came cross country to where you and Andrew were at your signal station."

At the mention of Andrew Tina experienced a vivid feeling of hurt and guilt. She nodded and then looked at Graham. *Do I love him? Or do I still love Andrew?* she wondered.

Heated images of Graham touching her breast came to disturb and confuse. She hadn't really minded and had to admit she was aroused by it, but somehow she felt he had been taking liberties.

It was a bit fast, she told herself.

They continued on, climbing up a few hundred metres of steep rocky slope which brought Tina to a panting standstill with cramps a dozen times. It began to look as though they had made the wrong decision about which way to go but then another radio call came in to report a second civilian 4WD with two men in it passing HQ on the way down the mountain.

"Oh! Why didn't they stop them and arrest them?" Tina cried.

"Fair go!" Graham answered. "The cadet officers aren't the police and if these men are armed it would have placed them in danger. Don't worry. I'm sure they have taken their registration numbers. Let the cops catch them."

Tina had to admit that was sensible, but it still rankled that the crooks had apparently escaped. *Maybe the police have caught them further down the road,* she hoped.

They continued on and reached the rocky summit of Stewarts Head 10 minutes later. There they found quite a large group of cadets waiting, including Graham's friend Peter and also Sub Lt Sheldon. Tina flopped down and broke into fits of shivering for a while. Then she was given a hot drink and a meal. Graham cooked this for her on his hexamine stove and she was grateful for it. She had not realised how hungry she was until she was asked.

It was after 0900hrs by then so the whole group moved on down the other side of the knoll along quite a well trampled walking track. The first few hundred metres were steep and rocky but as they came out of a stand of dense timber onto a small knoll Tina saw a parked vehicle. The sight caused her to begin sobbing with relief and it took all her efforts to hobble the last 100 paces.

The driver was Lt Hamilton from the Army Cadets. He had two female cadets with him and they took Tina's gear and then helped her into the passenger's seat. They then climbed in the back. As she settled herself more comfortably Tina saw Graham standing nearby and grinning. She had expected him to come with her but now she saw it had not even occurred to him. When she asked him, he shook his head.

"No room. Anyway, we have to finish our patrol," he said.

Tina felt quite disappointed even though she knew his reply was perfectly reasonable. *It is me being unreasonable,* she told herself. But it did give her niggling doubts. Then a spasm of cramp seized her left calf in an agonising grip and she could only cry out and pummel it while the vehicle was started up.

She did not enjoy the drive down. The track was very steep and bumpy and wound through the trees along the crest of a steep ridge.

But it only took 10 minutes to reach a track junction where more cadets from all three services waited. Another vehicle joined them, and both vehicles continued on down a steep slope and across a steep little saddle and then up onto another ridge. The vehicle track ran along the crest of this and Tina had to hold on tight against the bumps. It was all a bit much and she felt even more exhausted when they went down off it and up along another ridge line and onto the side of what she learned was Saint Patricks Hill. There were more cadets there but after that the road was easy and good and they were soon down among the houses of Herberton.

As they reached the bitumen Tina sighed with relief and just wanted to collapse. But she kept herself awake and alert until they reached the main HQ at Woodleigh College. She had never been there but liked the place. It was not large, only half a dozen buildings and had a very relaxed air about it. The vehicle was driven in the back way onto a lawn and she was then helped out amid a crowd that included police and paramedics. Lt Cdr Hazard and Sub Lt Mullion were both there and they helped shield her from the curious eyes and questions while she was whisked into a room at the end of one of the dormitories.

There was a lot of fuss including tactful questions about whether she had suffered any sexual assault. Her kit bag was produced and she was allowed a chance to have a shower and change of uniform. Feeling much better but still limping and shivering she was then led to an office where she was questioned by police and other government officials. Lt Cdr Hazard and Sub Lt Mullion sat in with her and that made her feel less stressed.

When the questioning reached the stage of discussing the bird poacher's vehicles Tina turned to Lt Cdr Hazard. "Did you get a good description of them sir?" she asked.

"We did. We not only noted their make and registration numbers but also took photos. They were both a dirty brown colour and had covered trays on the back," Lt Cdr Hazard explained.

"Did you see the men?" Tina queried.

Lt Cdr Hazard nodded. "Yes. One in the first vehicle and two in the second. We got photos of both and they did not look happy but kept on driving."

"One of them is my back neighbour, Neville," Tina said. It was only then that the awful realisation came to her that now she might really be in danger.

Neville recognised me and he knows where I live and he will have a real grudge. He might come back for revenge, she thought. It was a chilling idea and set her shivering again.

When they had calmed her there were more questions until Tina just wanted it to end. To her own dismay she found that it was not Graham's face she was picturing to comfort her but Andrew's.

Do I love Graham at all? she wondered.

To test this she badly wanted to see him, but she got no chance. By the time the questioning was done the army cadets had departed the area in their coaches. Nor did Tina get to see Andrew as the other navy cadets had also departed.

Nagging at the back of her mind was worry about what consequences she might face over her 'fraternization with the enemy' incident. When Lt Cdr Hazard made no mention of it she was left in a state of some anxiety. As the issue still had not been raised by the time, she was led out to a car she plucked up the courage to ask.

"Sir, what... what about my misbehaviour?"

Lt Cdr Hazard glanced at Sub Lt Mullion and then looked her in the eyes. "I think perhaps you have been punished enough. It was sufficient for you to promise not to misbehave again and for you to try to catch the army cadets," he answered.

"I am not going to be chucked out of cadets?"

Lt Cdr Hazard shook his head vigorously. "No, definitely not! You are good cadet with great potential. Discharging you might be a warning to others, but it won't make you a better person. If you stay you will be. I think you have learned your lesson," he said.

"Are you going to tell my parents?" Tina asked, voicing a deep worry.

Lt Cdr Hazard shook his head. "No. It wasn't a serious incident. I think it can be kept within the unit as a disciplinary incident, so I will leave that to you. Besides, all the others know and are sure to gossip," he said.

At the thought of having lost the good opinion of her peers (and Andrew) Tina bit her lip. Knowing there would be malicious gossip both at cadets and at school made her burn with shame. She nodded and said, "Thank you, sir."

"But we will ask you to promise to behave in future," Lt Cdr Hazard added.

Tina swallowed and had to struggle to hold back tears of relief. "Yes sir. I promise," she said. She wanted to ask if she would still be eligible to attend the promotion course, but the tears were now so close she could not bring herself to do so. So she took her seat in the back of the car and driven back to her home in Cairns by Lt Cdr Hazard and Sub Lt Mullion. With her in the car was Sarah, who was full of sympathy and questions.

As they drove down the Gillies Highway Tina was a bit annoyed with Sarah and the others and she peevishly asked, "Didn't you hear me call for help?"

Sarah shook her head. "No. Sorry. We heard lots of cockatoos, but the first unusual sound was that plane starting its engine," she explained.

"Did you see it?" Tina asked.

"Yes. It took off right past us. We thought it was going to crash. At first it couldn't take off because the lake was so calm, or so Petty Officer O'Leary said. So it roared backwards and forwards across the lake a couple of times to make waves and then did a take-off run. We didn't think it would get off in time but it just cleared the wall of the dam and then sank down into the valley until it nearly hit the treetops and then it flew off around the bend," Sarah explained.

Tina pictured this and shuddered. A whole series of flashbacks set her trembling and gripping the seat and hand grips. Then the terrifying thought of Neville and the other bird poachers coming to get her flooded in to fill her with dread.

I wonder if Neville went home? Or have the police arrested him? she worried. Anxiety about what she might find at home got her biting her nails.

Chapter 38

WORRY

Neville and the fear of revenge attacks were on the top of Tina's mind when she arrived home. Her parents had been informed of the incident and both the police and Lt Cdr Hazard also explained the situation. As soon as Tina was released from her parent's sobbing hugs her mother cried, "Oh Ti-bub! Every time you go away you seem to get into some scrape. We will have to ban you going on camps."

"Mum! Fair go! It was just a coincidence. Anyway, nothing happened on my trip to the Mitchell River lakes or to Lake Tinaroo," she said.

"Yes, well, but we have been wondering if you shouldn't take up some other interest rather than Navy Cadets."

Other interest! Tina thought, shocked and instantly worried that she might not be allowed to stay in the Navy Cadets.

"Mum! That's not fair! I love being in the cadets. It is the main interest in my life."

As she said this, she had a vivid mental image of Andrew and knew that it was the social aspect of Cadets that appealed the most.

As though she could read her mind, her mother said, "I thought it was now the Army Cadets you were interested in?"

Graham's image flashed onto the screen of Tina's mind and she experienced a surge of very mixed emotions. A surge of shame about allowing Graham to sneak in and kiss her made her burn and she wondered if she should now confess to her parents. But she was too scared of making things worse and could not bring herself to tell. Instead she shook her head vigorously and denied it, but in her heart she knew she had strong doubts.

Graham is certainly very nice; and very... brave. But I don't think he is right for me, she told herself. To change the subject she said, "Never mind that. What about the back neighbours, Neville and his family? Did the police catch him?"

Her mother shook her head. "We don't think so. We did see the police there a while ago and the police who called on us asked about them. But

I did notice that Mrs Tallboy went into the cage and took all those black cockatoos away earlier this morning.

"Clearing out the evidence," Tina suggested. Then the awful thoughts crept back in. "Mum, did the police say anything about us being safe?"

"From Neville because you identified him? They didn't but we will ask," her mother replied.

Tina's father patted her and said, "We will keep you safe Ti-bub."

"You can't dad. You can't be with me twenty four hours a day." Tina replied.

Her father looked uncomfortable but continued to reassure her. He then made a point of asking the police, when they returned a few hours later, more questions. They did not seem to think that Tina was in any real danger but she was not really reassured.

They didn't hear Danny or Neville making threats, she thought unhappily.

She was so afraid of the back neighbours that she did not want to go out to see her birds. That caused her to feel ashamed of her cowardice and she forced herself to make the move. But it was a bit of an ordeal. Her birds were glad to see her but she could not relax and kept glancing at the empty cages and the blank back windows of Neville's house.

They know where I live. They can easily come and get me, she thought.

Then a sharp pain in her forefinger made her cry out. "Ow! Beaky!" Beaky had bitten her as she rested her hand on the wire mesh. She rubbed the finger and then felt guilty. "I haven't fed you, have I, poor bird?" she said.

But as she fed the cockatoo she had sharp flashbacks to the screeching cockatoos up at the New Dam. Images of the cockatoo feathers lying beside the track caused such a wave of fear that she found herself looking anxiously around and breathing rapidly.

As she went back inside the house the niggling thought that perhaps it was cruel to keep birds in cages came to bother her. *Would Beaky be happier if he was free?* she wondered.

That night she had trouble sleeping. She kept imagining the poachers sneaking up to her window and breaking in to get at her. The fears became so real she found she was shivering and sobbing. It took her an effort to calm down. But then she had several bad nightmares. One was a variation of the grasping hand coming up out of the lake. In this dream she then fell out of her canoe and was unable to right it or drain it. It was dark and a strong current pulled her away from the shore. Then ghostly shapes were chasing her and she knew she was being dragged towards a high waterfall but could not swim fast enough to break the grip of the current!

In the morning she felt exhausted and frightened. Despite this she did not want to stay home. *I will be here on my own unless mum or dad stay home with me,* she thought. Not wanting to be the cause of any concern to her parents, or the reason why they lost a day's income, she said nothing.

At breakfast her mother noticed and asked if she wanted to stay at home. Tina shook her head. "No mum. I will be alright. Anyway, exams start today," she replied, glad of an excuse that avoided the truth.

But that truth nagged at her with a gut-gripping tension. She made a point of listening to the morning news on the radio but there was no mention of either her adventures or the bird poachers.

The police haven't caught them, she thought.

But there were other reasons than exams and fear of being home alone to make her want to go to school. Was it Graham or Andrew that she loved? She had a deep concern that she had made an awful mistake going out with Graham but wasn't sure if she could make it up with Andrew.

Her initial reaction at school was that she couldn't. She made a point of walking around to find him, without making it obvious. When she saw him her heart did a little flip and began to beat much harder and that got her worried.

Do I still love him? she asked herself. But she knew that she did. So she deliberately did not approach him, wanting to see what he would do when he saw her.

To her relief, Andrew came over at once. "How are you Tina? Are you alright?" he asked.

Tina was so overcome with emotion that it took all her will power not to throw her arms around him. Instead she just nodded and said, "Yes."

For the next few minutes they discussed the incident. Tina described what had happened to her and Andrew told her about what had happened back at the camp. "There was a rare old flap when the others came back and said they did not know where you were. We were all organised into search parties by Mr Conkey and went up to where you were last seen."

"What did you find?" Tina asked.

"We found a place where all the reeds had been flattened by someone and for a while we wondered if you had drowned in the dam," Andrew explained. At that point his voice trembled and he looked as though his eyes were moist.

Maybe he still likes me? she wondered.

Andrew then described how they had searched around the dam and decided that she hadn't drowned as the crushed reeds did not extend out into the lake. "Then it was suggested that you might have been in that floatplane that took off," he said.

"Did you see the floatplane?" Tina asked.

Andrew shook his head. "No. But Blake and Sarah did, and Cadet Midshipman George and Petty Officer O'Leary."

"What about the smuggler's camp? Did you find that?"

"Yes, but there was just rubbish and muddy boot tracks and wheel tracks. Their vehicles drove past while we were there but would not stop," Andrew said. He shook his head, "Anyway, by then the army cadets had radioed that you were with them and safe so we weren't worried."

They talked a bit longer, but Tina had the impression that Andrew appeared so cold and distant that she feared that he now resented her. Then she had another test of her emotions a few minutes after Andrew had left when Graham appeared.

Graham smiled when he saw her and at once came over to ask how she was. But he made no move to hug or kiss her and Tina noted that she was glad of that.

Maybe I don't really like him at all? she thought. Then she blushed hot at the memory of his hand on her breast and she felt confused.

For the next few minutes Graham talked about what had happened but he had plainly enjoyed the experience and gave the impression he did not really understand how terrified Tina had been.

Or how scared I am that the men will come back for revenge, she told herself. But at least he was contrite when she told him how much trouble she had been in when their kissing had been discovered.

"Are you going to be chucked out of cadets?" he asked, looking worried.

Tina shook her head. "No. But I might not get promoted this year." she replied.

"Sorry. I didn't mean for you to get into any trouble," he answered.

It was on the tip of Tina's tongue to ask if he had only kissed her to distract her from the cadets leaving the note but she couldn't bring herself to ask. So the ugly suspicions remained. However nothing in his manner suggested he did not like her so she became even more confused.

When the bell went for classes Graham walked with her, still chatting happily. Tina noted other students eyes on them and that made her feel uncomfortable. Partly it was certainty that the story of her letting Graham sneak in to kiss her was now common gossip and partly it was just doubts about her own attractiveness and worth. That bothered her as well because she sensed that she should be glad to be seen with a boy.

Maybe Graham isn't the one? she decided. But was Andrew?

Then there was another worrying incident when they met Andrew outside her classroom. When Andrew saw them together, he all but scowled and then he gave Graham quite a hostile look. Tina felt even more upset when she noted that the two boys were not even on speaking terms. Graham glanced at Andrew and merely nodded, then went on his way.

Oh, what have I done? Tina thought unhappily.

She realised that because Graham had been in the patrol that rescued her it gave the appearance of strengthening his position as her boyfriend. But if Andrew was the one how could she counter these rumours and win his affections back? For a moment she met his eyes, but he just gave her a hurt and slightly puzzled look in return.

Tina found it a relief to be absorbed by the need to concentrate on exams. She had two that day, both lasting for two hours. First was English, supervised by Mrs Ramsey. That was easy and Tina was sure that she did well. The second, after lunch, was Commerce, supervised by Mrs Massey.

During the lunch break Tina sat with Sarah and she had to describe the whole chase again. Then Carmen Collins joined them and the tale had to be related again. By then Tina was feeling drained out and upset. Having Carmen being nice to her did not help as she did, not know how to act. Once again, she found it a relief to go to class.

After school Tina hoped to see Andrew (or Graham!) but to her disappointment neither was around. So she went home feeling unhappy and unsure. Her dejection increased when she got home as she had to feed the birds and that meant going into the back yard. Once again, her anxiety level shot up and a wave of fear almost made her not go. It took her an effort of willpower to go out through the back gate. The whole time she was in the back yard she felt anxious and she scuttled back inside as quickly as she could, thoroughly ashamed of her weakness.

That night was no better. The news contained nothing about the smugglers being caught and after she had gone to bed Tina lay awake, trembling with nervous exhaustion and fear.

This set the pattern for the remainder of the week. Tina became so ill and drained that she wondered if she would collapse. But she also made a big effort to hide her state from her family and friends so that they would not worry. Not once did she suggest staying home as she felt safer at school.

The only person who seemed to notice was Capt Conkey. He supervised her exam on Maths A on Wednesday morning and asked her if she was alright. "You look pretty down," he commented.

"I'm alright sir," Tina lied.

"You don't look it. We can arrange to have your exam postponed if you don't feel up to it," he added.

That made Tina feel better, but she insisted she was well enough to do the exam. So she did. It was only during the break after it that she finally broke down in tears. The main cause of this was Graham asking her if she would go out with him again.

The request was so unexpected that Tina could only shake her head. But it also caused her feelings to crystallize. *No,* she thought. *I don't love Graham. I love Andrew.*

So she shook her head and said, "No, Graham. Sorry."

"You are sure?" Graham asked.

"Yes," Tina replied.

As she did, she felt tears well up and not wanting him to see them she stood up and hurried away. She took herself into the girls' toilet as the only place close where he could not follow. As she did, several other girls gave her curious or sympathetic looks, but she made no explanations and locked herself in a cubicle until the weeping dried up.

After about 10 minutes she wiped her eyes and nerved herself to come out again, only to find herself witness to a confrontation between Andrew and Graham. The two boys were standing glaring at each other, clenched fists on hips.

Oh no! Tina thought. *This is all my fault.*

As she hurried towards the two boys, she heard Andrew snarl, "What did you do to upset Tina?"

"None of your business," Graham retorted belligerently.

"Leave her alone or I will smash you!" Andrew threatened.

"You and what army?" Graham snapped. He sneered and raised his fists.

By then Tina was close. *Andrew must still care about me,* she thought. But she was also anxious to prevent a fight that might get both boys into trouble. So she pushed between them.

"Stop it!" she cried. "It's my fault. Don't fight please."

Andrew glanced at her but then faced Graham again. He growled, "Don't you hurt Tina."

"I'll do whatever she wants!" Graham retorted.

"Stop it!" Tina cried. "No fighting!"

Andrew gave her a cold look and then glared once more at Graham before walking away. Tina stood and flapped her arms in distress. More tears misted her eyes and she felt utterly defeated and miserable. Graham grunted and looked resentfully at her then also turned and walked away.

That look made Tina feel even worse. *I've lost with both of them!* she thought. Once again the tears came, but this time she was so upset she didn't care who saw. All she could do was slump down on the seat and weep.

Sarah came and put her arms around her shoulders and then a couple of the other girls joined in. That helped calm Tina but not as much as her pride when she heard the other girls asking each other what had happened and speculating on what the boys might have done to upset her so.

With an effort Tina steadied her breathing and then sat up straight and dried her eyes. "I'm alright," she said.

"What did they do?" Sarah asked.

"Nothing!" Tina cried.

A Year 9 girl named Melissa snickered and said, "Nothing? Well, that isn't any fun. It is a real disappointment when a boy doesn't try his luck. You don't want a cold fish for a boyfriend."

Another girl let out a chortle. "I thought you said your boyfriend was like a fish," she said.

"He is, a groper!" Melissa replied with a chuckle.

Heated images of Graham's hand on her breast caused Tina to blush, and she said, "It's not like that!"

Sarah asked, "What did Graham do?"

"Nothing," Tina denied, sniffling again but blushing.

"Nothing!" cried another girl. "I can't imagine Graham Kirk not trying something, not from what I've heard."

A Year 10 girl named Caroline let out a theatrical sigh and added, "He can try his luck with me any time he likes!"

Tina was both annoyed and amused. Angrily she snapped, "Well you can have him then!"

That caused a wave of speculation and tittering, much of it salacious or malicious. Tina burned with embarrassment and could only end it by standing up and walking away to be on her own. For the rest of the break she wandered the far end of the oval and tried to calm her thoughts and feelings.

But she could think of no plan to win Andrew back, other than telling him straight that she had made a mistake and she was too shy and proud to do that. So she went miserably back to the next exam with only half her thoughts on Chemistry.

After school she went home and locked herself in her room and sobbed until her parents came home. Then she pretended she was normal and happy. But the effort hurt and she went out to feed the birds as a way of getting out of the house.

Once again, she was almost overwhelmed by fear but she also found the nagging worry that keeping caged birds might be cruel was becoming a torment. Of a sudden she came to a decision.

I will sell the budgies and I will let Beaky go free, she told herself.

This was discussed at length with her parents. But the worry that freeing a bird used to captivity was tantamount to being a death sentence was also considered. They decided on a compromise.

"After your cadet camps we will start leaving Beaky's cage door open and allow his wings to grow," her father said. "Then he can come and go and if he decides to fly away that is his choice."

That seemed to be the best plan and Tina felt better. And the conversation got her thinking about the cadet exercises due to begin in two days' time. *I will be with Andrew a lot of the time,* she mused. *Maybe I can win his affection back somehow?* The fact that the first week also involved being with the army cadets who would include Graham was a worry but she shrugged that off. *I've told Graham no,* she thought, hoping that was the end of the affair. But she did briefly consider not going to the camps. But stubborn pride made her decide she would not run away like that. *I will go and just make the best of it,* she told herself.

Thursday was more exams: Maths B and Information Technology and Tina thought she did well at both. She stayed away from where the boys might be and hid herself in the library to study. The whole time her mind was in a ferment of worry: worry about the bird poachers, worry about Andrew; and worry about there being more unpleasantness between him and Graham on the cadet exercise. The anxiety drained her and left her feeling exhausted.

Despite this she did not get much relief during the night. Fear of the men nagged at her while she was awake and bad dreams spoiled her sleep. Only her optimistic nature and a slight sense of growing interest and excitement in the exercise gave a counterweight to her dejection. She had never been on one of the 'Senior' exercises run by the Heatley army cadet unit, but she had heard a number of stories. What she was sure of was that nobody except the officers running it knew where they were going or what was going to happen next. That sense of mystery began to intrigue her.

I hope I enjoy it, she thought.

So Friday was a more interesting day and Tina found herself looking forward to the next week, event though she was also still gripped by nagging anxieties. During the day she discussed the exercise with Sarah but made a point of avoiding the boys. After school she hurried home and set to work packing and preparing.

That evening she went out to feed Beaky and nerved herself to ignore her fears. She told herself that her real worry was how to win back Andrew.

I will come up with a plan, she told herself.

So she went off to cadets full of a mixture of anxiety, hope and determination.

Chapter 39

SENIOR EXERCISE

Tina had heard several stories about 130ACU's 'Senior' field exercises, and these were enough to give her some concern about whether she was good enough. She was also worried that she might not enjoy the experience. But she resolutely put these thoughts aside by telling herself that others were depending on her.

It will be good training for our D-of-E expedition, and we can get that out of the way after the promotion course, she told herself.

But then another worry surfaced: would she be allowed to do the promotion course after her 'fraternization' incident? So far the OC had not spoken to her again about her misbehaviour. Nor had she told her parents about it and that omission made her blush with shame at her cowardice.

But she did not want to be a problem to others, so she hid her concerns and chatted happily to her parents and little brother until she was dropped off at TS *Endeavour* at 1845hrs that evening. By then the more personal worry about her relationship with Andrew had grown to dominate her emotions and much of her conscious mind. Even the worry about not being promoted was a long way second to that.

Andrew was there but he was just distantly friendly and so fragile were Tina's emotions that she was willing to accept that. Instead she tried hard to focus her thoughts on the preparation and training for the exercise. Also gnawing at her was the worry about whether she was going to be allowed to go on the promotion course the following week. She felt deeply ashamed of herself for not being brave enough to ask. There was also the nagging fear that her parents would find out.

If I am not allowed to go mum and dad will want to know why, she thought unhappily.

Seeing Lt Cdr Hazard standing on his own watching the training Tina suddenly resolved to settle the issue. *I have to know,* she told herself. So, sick with apprehension, she marched smartly across the hall, halted facing him and gave him a snappy salute.

Lt Cdr Hazard returned the salute. "Yes, Able Seaman Babcock?" he asked.

Tina opened her mouth to speak but was anxious that she had to swallow and moisten her lips. "Er sir. Excuse me but am I still allowed to go on the promotion course?" she asked.

Lt Cdr Hazard nodded and pointed to the nearby notice board. "Yes. Your name is on the list there."

Tina glanced at the notice board and felt very foolish for not having first checked. She blushed and saluted again. "Thank you, sir," she said, then about turned and marched away, her heart pounding with relief.

After that it was a normal Friday night parade except those attending the Senior Exercise were given separate training. This included sessions on knots and lashings, blocks and tackles and on flag and light signals. To Tina's relief none of the other cadets seemed to be treating her any differently because of her letting down the unit the previous weekend. There were only some questions about her escape from the bird smugglers from cadets who did not go to her school.

Curiosity about the exercise also led to many questions but the officers either would not, or could not, answer them. Lt Ryan, who was the senior rank attending, just kept shrugging and saying, "You will find out tomorrow. Even we don't know where you are going or what the exercise story is about. All we know is that there will be some boat work to give us some special naval type opportunities."

AB Davidson, Andrew's most serious rival, said, "I've heard that each of these exercises is in a different place each year. Is that right, sir?"

Lt Ryan nodded. "That is what I have heard; that each exercise is in a different area and has a different story."

"Story?" Dimity Bates queried.

Lt Ryan nodded. "That's right. Each exercise has a story, a fictional scenario to set the scene and then to provide reasons for what happens," he explained.

Petty Officer O'Leary spoke next. "I heard they did a weeklong exercise in the Charters Towers area last year."

Cadet Midshipman George agreed. "They did, and the year before they did one in this area. They went up Smiths Track to Speewah and then back along Douglas's Track to Kuranda and on north through the jungle. I helped but only for two days."

It sounded interesting to Tina and she hoped she would be fit enough. But her real worry was about how she and Andrew would relate when they had to spend a week in close company. That was tested that night when they finished training. At supper she found Andrew standing beside her and she was quite unable to think of anything to say to him.

The cadets and staff who were attending the army cadet exercise stayed that night at the depot. That was something they quite often did and was no problem as there were separate male and female accommodation and Tina did not have to see Andrew until they did a 'Check Parade' for roll call the following morning.

Breakfast was cooked for them in the galley and then the cadets packed up ready to travel. Cleaning duties and inspections took up the next hour and then Lt Ryan called the group together. There were four teams of four: two 'Bronze', one 'Silver' and one 'Gold'. As well three of the adult staff were attending the camp: Lt Ryan, Sub Lt Mullion and Instructor Petty Officer Evans, the 'Boats' officer.

When the depot was cleaned and 'ship-shape' to Lt Ryan's satisfaction he sat the group in the classroom. "Ok troops, now I can tell you things I was not at liberty to tell you last night. Firstly, it has been confirmed that the Bronze D of E teams may get a chance to qualify for your Duke of Edinburgh Award on this exercise; so you may not have to do your own later."

That raised a cheer and Tina found herself grinning at Andrew. Andrew smiled back. "That's good. Now we can just concentrate on the promotion course," he said.

Tina nodded and noted his smile, but also that it did not seem to reach his eyes and that he looked anxious. She felt her emotions start to churn. *No good thinking about relationships now,* she told herself. *Remember the rules: no fraternisation at cadets!* So she refocused on what Lt Ryan was saying.

"We are not moving right away," he explained. "We have to take boats with us as part of this exercise. So we need to check them and get them loaded onto a truck or trailers."

"Boats on an army cadet exercise sir?" Andrew queried.

"Search me," Lt Ryan replied. "I don't know the scenario for this exercise. We will find that out after lunch."

Intrigued and happy to be doing 'nautical' things instead of possibly crawling through wet grass or jungle Tina happily helped check and load 8 Canadian canoes onto a canoe trailer, along with all the necessary PFDs (Personal Flotation Devices). Then they were told to check four of the unit's small 'Laser' sailboats. While the cadets did this the adults did a thorough check of two power boats to be used as safety boats. Radios and other items were then checked and loaded.

Lunch was only sandwiches and was served early at 1130. As soon as it was over the cadets cleaned up, loaded their gear into a navy coach and were checked on board. As she settled into her seat next to Stella Tina found she was gripped by a delicious sense of mystery as they had no idea where they were going or what the story might be about.

In fact they only went for a 20-minute trip to Gordonvale. Gordonvale is administratively part of the City of Cairns but is in fact a separate town which is dominated by a huge sugar mill. The coach turned off the Bruce Highway and made its way to the park which constituted the town square. As the coach pulled up Tina saw a large group of army cadets sitting in groups on the lawn opposite the police station.

The sight of those army uniforms sent Tina into a bit of a tiz.

Is Graham there? she wondered. She knew he was taking part in the exercise, but she also understood that there were different groups. Anxiously she scanned the group. *There he is!* she thought, noting that her heart rate had shot up with anxiety rather than love. *No, it is Andrew I love. I just hope there isn't any friction or unpleasantness between them.*

To her relief Graham did no more than give her a friendly smile and a wave as he went about packing his gear. But Tina did note him and Andrew exchange unfriendly glances. That was good news for her she decided.

It must mean that Andrew still has some feelings for me, she thought.

There were then more pleasant surprises. Seated to one side were a dozen navy cadets. "From Townsville and Mackay," Petty Officer O'Leary commented. Tina recognised a few but did not know any very well. However Andrew and his sister Carmen did and they at once went over to say hello. Seeing several blonde females among the Townsville navy cadets sent Tina's anxiety level shooting up.

I wonder if any of them is the blonde nudist he keeps seeing? she worried.

But she wasn't introduced and stayed with her own group until they were told to be seated next to the other navy cadets. The Navy Cadets were then organised into two 'watches': Port and Starboard. The TS *Coral Sea* group were added to the Port Watch which included Tina's Bronze Team and CDTMID George's Gold Team. The cadets from Mackay were put in the Starboard Watch.

The exercise then began. A tubby, middle-aged major of army cadets moved to the front of the group and introduced himself. "I am Major Wickham, OC of 130 Army Cadet Unit, Heatley," he said. "And I am the Exercise Director."

Major Wickham then gave a very detailed safety briefing and explanation of how the exercise was organised and who the staff were and the rules and expectations for behaviour. Tina now learned that she was about to take part in a 'One-sided, controlled exercise'. This meant that all the incidents were carefully planned and were to be staged by a separate team called the 'Control Group'.

"The Control Group," Major Wickham explained, "is primarily there to provide safety check points and radio relay stations but they also provide the people who give you the action or the story. Sometimes they will be acting as innocent civilians such as woodcutters and, if you treat them correctly, they will give you the correct information. At other times they will act as the opposing force. You need to observe carefully how the people you meet are dressed."

That was a novel idea to Tina, but she liked it. Major Wickham explained that the exercise was designed to be as real as possible, to 'feel' real, but not at the expense of safety. "Also we will stop to teach any necessary lessons and also, after every action, you will move in and sit like this so we can count heads. The exercise moves continually, and we must keep careful track of where everyone is," he explained.

For that reason the group leaders were then required to make their own roll books, and this allowed an opportunity for people to flex muscles and go to the toilet. The briefing then resumed with a lot of information on road safety and safety with vehicles and water.

"You will not take any chances with safety," Major Wickham emphasised. "If you have any concerns or doubts then stop the exercise and check everyone is safe. We will not risk hurting anyone just for a cadet training activity."

As she sat listening Tina decided that she liked Major Wickham. *He seems very thorough,* she thought. She knew from what Capt Conkey had told her that no other army cadet unit in Australia did anything comparable.

"It is only because Major Wickham makes the effort to plan and write the exercises," he had explained.

After nearly two hours of briefings, the cadets were told to stand and put their kit bags beside a truck and then pull on their packs and webbing. Tina had no trouble with hers and thanked their earlier expeditions in preparation. But it was obvious many of the other cadets, both army and navy, were not as ready. There were many groans and looks of dismay as the strain came on.

The whole group, now about 80 strong, marched off along the side of the park past the main shopping centre. They crossed two streets, practicing how to do it safely as a single group side by side. Then they walked two more blocks, past a caravan park to the Gordonvale State High School. Tina was surprised to learn that the cadets had hired the school hall and they were seated in long lines inside.

For the next hour, all packs and webbing were re-packed. Each cadet was then weighed twice, once with their pack and webbing on and once without. If the load exceeded 40% of their body mass the cadet was sent back to take things out. Officers and NCOs continually inspected and checked to ensure that the equipment was fitting correctly and the load well balanced.

The army cadets then spent an hour walking around the oval to test the load and to toughen them up. They stopped every 15 minute to check and adjust. During this time the navy cadets unloaded all their canoes and boats and laid out all the paddles, sails, PFDs and other items of equipment. While they did Tina several times noticed Graham. He was smiling and joking and his fitness was very obvious.

That's because of all those hikes he and his friends do, she thought.

The evening meal was then prepared outside in section and platoon groups. For the navy cadets this meant in their teams which meant that Tina was in close proximity to Andrew much of the time. The cooking she enjoyed and she managed to relax a bit. It was a very social event and Tina got to know a couple of the Townsville navy cadets, including one of the blondes. She learned that her name was Anne and that she was not The Blonde who she now learned was not a navy cadet.

But her brother was and Tina was introduced to Martin Schipholl and thought him a very nice person. Apparently Andrew had saved him from drowning and later Martin had joined the Navy Cadets. Now he was an Able Seaman and nominated for the same Leading Seaman course she was to attend in the second week of the holidays.

At 1900hrs the whole group was seated in the hall in their section groups and the 'Story' was begun. Major Wickham explained that the exercise was usually set in a historical time that precluded aircraft or motor vehicles. "Definitely no helicopters so you have to walk," he said. "So this one is not set in North Queensland but in North America two hundred and fifty years ago. That is back in 1758, during a war called by the British 'The Great War for the Empire', by the Europeans the 'Seven Years War' and by the Americans the 'French and Indian War'. We are playing the role of the British."

This was all a bit hard to follow for Tina and she puzzled over the map and handout that was then issued to everyone. From it, and the briefing that followed, she learned that in the 1750s the French, who owned Canada and much of the Mississippi valley, and their Indian allies, had set out to block British expansion inland in North America by establishing a chain of forts along the rives and lakes.

Major Wickham pointed to a large wall map that had been hung up. "Most of North America was trackless forest or mountains. The easiest way to move both people and goods was by water. So the rivers and lakes were vital transport arteries. At key points, such as where two rivers joined, or at the 'portages', the tracks which led around rapids or waterfalls, both sides built forts. They even built huge stone forts armed with dozens of cannons at narrow choke points on the big lakes. The most famous was Fort Ticonderoga."

A picture of Fort Ticonderoga was displayed and Tina was amazed. *I had no idea any of this went on,* she thought, uncomfortably aware that she was very ignorant of world history.

Major Wickham had another map displayed. "Now, the Special Idea for our exercise. We are pretending that the Atherton Tablelands are being fought over by the British and French. We are advancing from the sea and the French are coming from the big rivers of the interior. For our exercise we are using the Mulgrave River, Barron River and Lake Tinaroo. The town of Tinaroo is the key and the French have just set up some new forts there and near it to control the lake and the portage where the dam is. We will pretend there is no dam."

Tina had a vivid image of the black wall of the dam coming closer and closer as she and Sarah had sailed across the lake a few weeks before and she found she was now very interested.

Major Wickham then explained the importance of artillery. "Most of the forts were just timber stockades but the more important ones like Fort Ticonderoga were built in peace time of stone and earthworks. The forts in our story are all new and have just been constructed so are earthworks and logs. As far as we know none of them yet has cannons in them but the only effective way they can be attacked is by battering down their walls with artillery. That is the crux of our problem, to get cannons close enough to fire at the forts."

He paused and looked directly at the navy cadets. "That is to be the special role of the navy cadets. The sailors of that era were all trained in the use of cannons on ships so for the story you are crew members of the British Line-of-Battle Ship HMS *Renown* and you have been put ashore with a cannon and boats and the mission of supporting our expedition to provide our artillery. You must get a cannon to where it can fire on the town of Tinaroo. And to add a bit of rivalry and provide teamwork opportunities we have two cannons and the Port Watch and Starboard Watch get one each."

As she heard that Tina felt a surge of excitement and anxiety. *This is good. It will be a real challenge,* she thought. And she wondered where the cannons were coming from.

As though in answer a group of cadets wheeled a small 18th Century ship's cannon out of a side room. It had a black painted barrel about 1.5 metres long which was as thick as a person's leg. The gun carriage had four black wheels about 30centimetres in diameter and was made of timber and painted a deep yellow. It was then explained that it was not a real cannon, just a timber replica.

That was a bit of a disappointment, especially to the boys who wanted to fire it. Tina could only smile at their hopeful comments. She now learned that part of the challenge was the requirement to move all the necessary items needed to make a cannon work. These included one 'cannonball' (a tennis ball) and one 'gunpowder' cartridge (a packet of plain flower that had to be kept dry!) per cadet, plus felt wads, two rammers, two sponges, two wormers (for extracting misfires and cleaning), fuzes (plastic coil), cleaning cloths, plus tools to construct a gun position (an axe, two picks, two shovels and a couple of handspikes (long poles). It all added up to a quite formidable pile as five cadets brought it all out of the side room and laid it out.

Major Wickham pointed to the extra items. "Most of this will be the navy's responsibility to shift. The army cadets will carry some but will be there to do the infantry job." He then explained that the exercise was not to teach warlike tactics. "But nor will we use all the drills of the time. The Seven Years War was when the modern tactics began to evolve. The British Army formed several units who specialised in forest fighting with rifles. The main one was the Royal American Regiment. They have evolved over time into the Rifle Brigade and still exist. The other unit was Roger's Rangers, from which the American Ranger units claim descent."

He did some more explanations of organization and tactics then went into details of the exercise. There was a 10-minute break and then the leaders were seated for what the army cadets called an 'Orders Group'. Tina sat at the back and took notes and was impressed. The orders were highly detailed and in a very definite sequence and at the end she was quite sure of what they were going to do the next day.

The navy cadets then moved to one side and began a discussion on how to best move all the equipment and the cannons. This led to some quite animated arguments and some very good suggestions. Each team then was then allocated a task. To her dismay Tina found that her team had to move the gun carriage and the rammers and sponges.

Andrew made the best suggestion. "We make catamarans out of the canoes to give them stability," he said.

"And how do we load the cannon? We have to pretend it is the real weight," Petty Officer O'Leary asked.

"Block and tackle," Tina suggested.

"Suspended from what?" Lt Ryan queried.

"A tree branch?" Tina replied.

Andrew nodded. "Or we make a sheer legs from two poles."

"Good thinking. So we need more ropes and some blocks," Lt Ryan said.

"Yes sir. Can we go back to the depot and get them?" Cadet Midshipman George asked.

Lt Ryan grinned. "No need. Major Wickham thought of that and they are here."

Again Tina was impressed. She was also now very interested, alive with the challenge of getting the cannon to Tinaroo. *This is going to be good!* she thought.

That night they all slept on mats on the floor of the hall. The army cadets were up at 0400hrs and started moving in the dark at 0500hrs. The navy cadets were roused at this time and through eyes made bleary from sleep Tina picked out Graham among the army cadets swinging on their packs. He was smiling and looked very happy but to her annoyance he did not even glance in her direction. As he tramped out the door, she felt a twinge of regret and then of relief.

He isn't the one, she told herself.

As she thought this, she looked around and found herself looking at Andrew. He met her eyes for a second and smiled, then bent to roll up his sleeping bag.

Well, that is something, she told herself.

But how to rebuild the relationship?

Chapter 40

UPSTREAM AND UPHILL

Morning routine kept the navy cadets busy until 0630hrs. By then all of the army cadets had gone except one lieutenant who was there to lock up the building. The navy cadets cleaned up and swept the hall and then carried their gear out to the vehicles. At 0700hrs they began moving. The first activity was a simple navigation exercise with each group taking a different route through the town to the bank of the Mulgrave River. This involved marching with their packs. As there were only four different routes but 6 groups they were sent off 10 minutes apart in time.

Tina's group marched back to the main square and then along a road beside the railway. This led them past the Catholic church and on along a light railway which crossed under the Bruce Highway bridge. On the other side, the group turned left off the railway and followed a vehicle track down to a park beside the highway bridge over the Mulgrave. The walk was about 2 kilometres and took about half an hour but was far enough to have them perspiring and to make Tina glad it was no further.

She had often been to the picnic area at the highway bridge so there was no mystery yet. The only thrill had been the odd one of marching through the sleepy town, noticed only by the dogs and the occasional early riser. At the picnic area they found a truck and three 4WDs towing boat trailers. Two carried the unit's power boats and another had four 'Laser' sailboats and the last trailer had 8 canoes on it. These were all unloaded and then work began on preparing them to carry the cannon and its accessories. Because it promised to be wet work, they all stripped down to their bathers, Tina a little self-consciously.

Then they set to work tying knots, lashing poles and boats together and loading stores aboard. This was all good teamwork activity. During the next hour they lashed two canoes together using the rammers and poles to make a catamaran. Then two long poles were placed side by side at right angles to the riverbank. They were lashed loosely together with a diagonal lashing near their top ends and a block and tackle set up and lashed on above that. Then another block and tackle arrangement was secured to a tree well back from the river bank and also secured to the top of the two poles. The two poles were slid forward until much of their length was out over the water and then the shoreward ends of the poles were spread apart and the butts dug into the river bank. The whole arrangement was then hauled up using the rear block and tackle until they were nearly vertical to form a sheer legs.

Lt Ryan pointed out that if they were really going to lift a one tonne cannon, they would have need much longer and stronger poles than the ones provided but they were to pretend for the sake of the exercise.

One of the wooden gun carriage was then rolled in underneath the block and tackle dangling from the cross lashing. This was then used to haul the carriage up a few centimetres off the ground. The Starboard Watch canoe catamaran was pulled in close to the bank and then the rear block and tackle eased off so that the dangling gun carriage was swung out over the catamaran. Very carefully the gun carriage was lowered down onto the cross beams and then moved until the trim of the raft was even. It was then unhooked and lashed in place.

Tina enjoyed all of this and so did the others. She found it very satisfying work even if they got very wet doing it. In fact she deliberately made the most of being in her bathers to try to attract Andrew's attention. Knowing by now that he liked to see breasts, she used every opportunity to lean forward in front of him to give him an eyeful, or she squeezed her arms together to push up an eye-popping amount of cleavage. All the while she pretended that she was not aware of what was happening. That she succeeded she was sure of by the way he kept glancing at her and when she noted him lick his lips a few times she secretly smiled with satisfaction.

Good! He knows I exist, she thought.

Then she blushed with shame, being well aware that everyone else there could also see. She noted, to her embarrassment, that even some of the adult males were giving her surreptitious glances. After that she eased up on her flaunting but still enjoyed the naughty thrill.

There was a short break for breakfast, cooked on a portable BBQ, and then the work continued. By 0930hrs the other gun carriage, both cannon barrels and all the heavy stores had been loaded into three other catamaran rafts. The sheer legs was then dismantled and the parts also loaded aboard. Eight more canoes arrived on another trailer and were launched. Then the open tinnie-type power boat was launched, along with the four sail boats. Two cadets were tasked as crew for each sailboat. No attempt was made to rig the sail boats as their masts had been used as beams on the catamarans and because it wasn't possible to sail on such a narrow river anyway, the Mulgrave generally only being less than 50 metres across. So the four sailboats were tied on behind canoes. Personal gear was then packed aboard.

Lt Ryan then insisted they all put on long sleeve shirts and sandshoes. "If you try walking on the rocks in rapids in bare feet you might break a toe," he cautioned.

PFDs and hats were added and then they were ready. Radios were tested and placed in plastic bags. Then a few shouted commands got the cadets to scramble aboard their respective craft and the expedition got under way.

Tina sat in the front of the starboard side canoe with Andrew behind her. Stella and Blake went in the port canoe. For the first few minutes it felt like sheer joy to Tina. It was a lovely day, sunny but cool, a gentle breeze, crystal clear water, lovely scenery.

It is great to be alive! she thought.

And it was also exhilarating to be part of such a group. Tina had never seen so many canoes or boats on a river at once. She did a count and noted 16 canoes, 4 sailboats and one powerboat.

It certainly looks impressive, she thought.

Their flotilla 'commodore' was Cadet Midshipman George, and he did a fair amount of shouting before the flotilla spread out in the order he wanted them in. Leading the group were four canoes with cadets from Townsville and Mackay. These were sent ahead to scout for the best route and to watch for enemy.

"We are heading into Indian country remember," Cadet Midshipman George said. "We don't want you getting scalped by a Mohawk."

Tina smiled at that and remembered the exercise story line. For a few seconds she looked at the walls of trees lining both banks and wondered if any 'Indians' were watching them. *I wonder if they will ambush us or anything like that?* she thought.

Anxious to do the right thing, she asked what they would do if that happened and Andrew said they would pretend to shoot back and head for the bank to fight the ambushers.

"But we shouldn't need to. The army cadets are ahead of us and are supposed to be making sure it is safe for us," he added.

At the words 'army cadets' Tina thought she noted a sour puckering of his lips and she wondered if he was thinking about Graham. *I hope so. A bit of rivalry will keep him on his toes,* she told herself.

After 10 minutes of paddling, the mood subtly changed. Muscles began to tire, and people began to perspire. It became very obvious that they were going upstream. By then they were at the end of a long, smooth straight and had arrived at the bottom of a long set of rapids. The rapids were not fast, or deep, but they were strong enough to stop any canoe being paddled. There was nothing for it but to get out and then drag the rafts and canoes up against the current.

This turned out to be harder than expected as well and it quickly became apparent that tow ropes were needed. These were taken out of the rope bags and secured to the bows, the other ends being made up with bowlines. Andrew looped one over his shoulder and began dragging the raft upstream. Tina and the others helped by poling or pushing. But being close in to the trees was a problem too. Many branches overhung the water and blocked progress. Worse still many of the branches grew pointing downstream, forced that way permanently by the fast current and floods of the wet season.

It was quite a laborious task to haul the raft up to the next reach of still water. Rivalry began to develop between the Port and Starboard Watches and Tina could only laugh and enjoy it. By the time they got there Tina was puffing and feeling bruised and tired. She also realised that her legs were getting sun burnt despite getting out frequently to wade. The best she could do was apply more sunscreen and hope it wasn't all getting washed off. And wading up against the current on the rocky stream bed was hard work. Thankfully they re-boarded and resumed paddling.

This went on for the next two hours, by which time they were about another 4 kilometres upstream. *We are barely moving at walking pace* Tina decided.

They came to another long, smooth section of the river and were able to re-board and proceed by paddling. The scout canoes were sent hurrying on ahead in response to a radio call and the other craft all waited for the tail end to catch up. Then, grouped as a flotilla, they proceeded.

Two hours later they reached a long set of rapids which needed another wet haul to get above. A 'portage' was suggested but voted against as too much effort. At the top was another long stretch of deep water and the cadets were able to re-board the canoes or rafts and continue paddling. This stretch of the river curved in against the hills on the right-hand side of the valley and Tina thought it just the prettiest place she had ever been.

At the top end of the stretch of calm water was another set of rapids. Right at the bottom of them, on the right was a deep backwater crossed by a railway bridge. Here they met up with the army cadets. They had 'captured' the bridge by sending a group up through the jungle to by-pass it. Now they were walking the main body across and the safety boat was positioned close by in case any fell in. Tina briefly glimpsed Graham as he strode confidently across and the sight caused her some very mixed emotions.

Am I glad we broke up, or sad? she wondered. But the sight of his almost arrogant self-confidence made her feel sure that he wasn't the right man for her. A glance at Andrew reinforced this feeling. *He is the one,* she told herself.

But how to win him back?

An opportunity to get Andrew's attention almost immediately presented itself. As they struggled up the next rapids, Andrew lost his footing. Tina was close and grabbed his sleeve, holding him tightly until he had regained his footing.

Andrew looked her in the eyes and said, "Thanks," but Tina was left wondering if he hadn't resented being rescued by her.

These rapids were in a section of the river valley designated as national park and the place was unusually beautiful. The rapids were small and shallow and studded by dozens of small islands and trees, giving it a picturesque appearance. A halt was called to have lunch and the navy cadets beached their craft and made their way to a line of small sandy beaches to sit and eat. The beaches were among green ferns and reeds and all shaded by overhanging trees. Nearby sat some army cadets who were also eating, but Graham was not one of them so Tina was able to relax and try to use her conversation to interest Andrew.

After lunch the upriver haul was resumed. The army cadets walked along the sugar train light railway but most of the time they were out of sight from the river. Only briefly at Pete's Bridge did Tina see them in the distance, and then again an hour later at the Ross and Locke Picnic Area.

Here the light railway crossed the top of the rapids on a low timber bridge and as the navy cadets hauled their craft up and under it the army cadets walked across. This time Graham saw Tina and he waved and called a cheerful greeting. Tina replied in a friendly way, hoping that Andrew would not read the wrong message into it.

The canoes then traversed a wide deep curve around to another rail bridge. Here the army cadets, rather than cross the long bridge, turned off and walked along a foot track in the jungle on the edge of the river and the navy cadet group paddled beside them on the deep water. They passed the mouth of the Little Mulgrave River and again Tina was struck by the sheer beauty of the place.

Another set of rapids was encountered, and everyone climbed out and began dragging the rafts and canoes up to the next level. By this time Tina was feeling very sore and tired and her hands had gone all wrinkled. Worse still she was feeling badly chafed in her arm pits and around her bra and on her buttocks. Her watch told her it was 1630hrs and she could only wonder where the day had gone.

"I hope we stop soon," she said, then immediately regretted it, fearing that Andrew would despise her for being a weakling.

To her relief he smiled and said, "Me too. I am worn out. I needed more training for this."

At the top of the rapids the navy cadets were called on to do a real 'seamanship' activity to support the army cadets. Two long ropes (taken from a navy cadet vehicle that was now parked on the far bank) were secured on the bank near the army cadets. Snatch bocks were attached and other ropes secured to them to make a running pulley arrangement on each rope. A raft was tied to each block and then used to ferry army cadets and their gear across. By having a work party on the far bank who moved the end of the rope upstream or downstream of the anchor point on the other bank they were able to use the force of the current to push the rafts across with minimum effort.

Tina enjoyed this exercise immensely and even forgot how wet and cold she was. It took 6 trips for each raft to ferry all the army cadets across, 8 at a time. To Tina's relief, Graham was not on her raft and she was able to watch from afar as he was taken across on the other raft.

The reason for the ferrying was that the bank the army cadets had been walking along had turned into a cliff whereas the other bank was flat for about two hundred metres and had a lovely park-like appearance from the stand of tall trees that shaded it. That the activity was planned was obvious to Tina because all the vehicles now arrived and parked. Once all the army cadets were across the ropes were untied and rolled up and then the cadets were grouped for a roll check and briefing.

Tina was amused to see a male cadet dressed as a Mohawk Indian brought forward. The cadet wore only shorts and cloths hanging down in front and back of his crutch. He was bare-chested and covered in war paint and had two feathers in a headband. He had information about another 'war party' of Iroquois led by French officers that was nearby.

As the Mohawk talked, Stella nudged Tina and giggled, "If we have to act as Indians, I hope we don't have to dress like that!"

Tina had a brief mental image of herself standing bare breasted and covered with war paint and feathers and felt a peculiar sense of thrill. She was ashamed to admit that it was a fantasy she liked.

It would get Andrew's attention for sure, she thought.

With that in mind she glanced at him. He turned his head and their eyes met and then he smiled. Tina blushed and looked away, experiencing the peculiar feeling that he had been able to read her mind.

But I would like him to see me like that, she told herself.

The 'expedition' resumed its journey, the army cadets marching out along a side-track and the navy cadets re-boarding their canoes and continuing by water. The two groups met again 10 minutes later when the canoes went under another bridge over which the army cadets were trudging. The two groups then separated for 20 minutes, the river curving in a wide loop with cane fields on the left and steep, tree covered slope on the right.

Both groups came back together at another set of rapids right at the base of a steep spur of the main range that seemed to block off the valley. Another bridge crossed at the top of the rapids, but the army cadets merely secured the bridge with a patrol while the main group moved in among the trees in the river bed. The navy cadets beached their canoes at the bottom of the rapids and were joined by their officers and vehicles.

Lt Ryan pointed to the nearby strip of clean sand. "We eat, then, when it is dark, we unload everything," he explained.

A cadet petty officer from Townsville put his hand up. "Excuse me sir, why not unload now in daylight?" he asked.

"Part of the exercise story and part of the challenge," Lt Ryan answered. "The story is that enemy patrols may be watching so we have to deceive them as to out destination and intentions. We want them to think we are proceeding further upriver but in fact we are going up that ridge to the top of the range." He pointed up to the west.

Tina looked up and her mouth fell open in surprise. Towering up for 700 metres beside them was the escarpment of the Atherton Tablelands and while she had known they were going up there it had not occurred to her that it might be on foot and in the dark!

Now this will be a challenge! she told herself.

And it was. The sun went down and then the hard work began. Patrols of army cadets went on ahead and the others stayed to help with the hauling and carrying. Now the rivalry between the Port and Starboard Watches became more overt. For two hours the navy cadets worked setting up sheer legs and unloading the cannon parts onto sleds made of timber lashed together. All the small pieces were then distributed so that every army cadet had a piece to carry. Then the canoes and boats were dragged ashore. The safety boat was placed on its trailer, but the canoes were carried a hundred metres over the stony river bed to the bridge. Then the group had to go back and carry their gear to that point. Then they had to return and drag the cannon parts up. By the time this was done they were all sweating and Tina was feeling very tired.

But that was only the beginning. Now the teamwork and character-building part of the exercise really came into play. They had to organize work parties and set up blocks and tackles tied to trees on the hillside opposite and then the cannon parts had to be hauled up, metre by metre. Then the canoes, personal gear and other pieces all had to be carried up, taking two more trips.

It was exhausting and hard work in the dark and there were tears and swearing and many frayed tempers, but Tina enjoyed it immensely. *This is a real challenge!* she thought. It certainly tested the leaders and the teamwork. *And us navy cadets couldn't have done this on our own,* she decided, looking at a group of thirty army cadets hauling on ropes attached to the cannon barrel and the block and tackle easing it up. *And all in the dark with no lights or torches!* she marvelled. The army cadets had insisted on that 'so the enemy don't see us'.

Throughout all this the officers stood watching, careful to make sure what was being done was safe, but they deliberately left most of the organising and control to the Cadet Midshipmen and Cadet Under-Officers. The senior ratings and NCOs all had a part in the leadership.

In all it took five hours to haul the cannon parts and canoes 500 metres up a hill covered with savannah woodland. On the crest they came to a gravel road that led up the spine of the ridgeline. By then it was past midnight.

"We have to be at the Gillies Highway by First Light," Major Wickham said after congratulating them during the rest stop and roll call on the road.

Maps were taken out and Tina noted that the highway was 2 kilometres away and 300 metres higher. In the moonlight she could just make out the scar of the highway as it snaked its way diagonally up the side of the steep escarpment. The point where the gravel road joined the highway was at a prominent knoll on the spur called The Knob on the map. This was pointed out to her and looked a dismayingly long way away and above them.

Work parties were again organised and patrols sent ahead to scout for enemy. By now they had the procedure well organised. First carry the gear and canoes up the next hundred metres or so. Then carry up and secure blocks and tackles to trees and then sort out the ropes and place work parties on them. Then haul the heavy items up to that point and secure them. The process was then repeated.

By having three parties setting up the blocks and tackles they were able to keep up an almost continuous flow. As soon as a cannon or carriage reached the top of a haul it was secured and the next tackle attached to it. It was then cast off and hauled up the next slope while the first tackle was run back down to the other heavy item. During this the third tackle set was untied from below and carried up above the first one to be ready by the time the first heavy item reached the top of Number 2 set. It was all really hard work and very good teamwork stuff.

Tina and Andrew were part of the team responsible for setting up tackle set Number 2. She found the hardest part was slogging up to the next place while carrying both the tackle set and her personal luggage. A team of army cadets carried their canoe and paddles for them and then helped to haul the ropes.

The temperature dropped, the moon crept across the sky and the hill seemed never ending. Tina sweated and swore and had to put on gloves to stop her hands from being chafed red raw. She became so exhausted she was disoriented. It was certainly the hardest thing she had ever done in her life. And she loved it. After a rest for drinks and a snack she was able to continue.

Several times she found herself working close to Graham, but he just said hello or grinned and focused on the work. That he was very fit and a real asset to the team was obvious, but Tina felt no spark of romance about him and found herself feeling easier. Instead, she found being in close proximity to Andrew comforting and helpful.

It seemed for a couple of hours that they weren't making any progress and that the swapping over of tackle sets was becoming never ending but suddenly Tina realised they were at the base of a very steep slope which rose into the stars and she realised they were on the lower slopes of The Knob. By then they had moved the tackle set over twenty times, at least four or five times an hour and she was losing track of time.

She now saw that it was almost 0500hrs. *Daylight won't be far away,* she thought, glancing back along the valley behind her and being thrilled and awed by the view.

The valley was a play of shadow and moonlight and the moonlight was reflecting off the river as it wound its way down past the distant cluster of lights that marked the location of Gordonvale.

We have come a long way! she thought with satisfaction and surprise.

A report came back that one of the patrols up ahead had clashed with an enemy patrol and that brought the story back into Tina's mind. But also in her mind was the thought that they were only halfway up the side of the mountain.

Can I do it? she wondered, looking up the steep, rugged and forested slopes ahead of them.

Chapter 41

CONTROL GROUP

Tina gritted her teeth and kept on trying. The tackle and gear were carried up to the top of the steep 'pinch' and secured to yet another tree and the hauling process resumed. Slowly the light improved and Tina noted the mountains to the east standing out in clear silhouette. Then, to her intense relief, the road levelled out and the next few hundred metres were almost flat. The road curved left around The Knoll on a bench cut and went into a cutting.

By the time the expedition arrived at the bitumen Gillies Highway it was daybreak and the sun was just peeking over the ranges. Parked at the junction were seven vehicles including the truck and all the navy vehicles with trailers. The army cadets were instructed to keep marching. They did this by keeping to the side of the highway which, even at this time of the morning, was busy.

The navy cadets were told to stop and have breakfast. That was an even bigger relief to Tina and during the meal she kept hoping that the vehicles meant that they would not have to drag the cannons and canoes up the other half of the mountain. This hope was reinforced when the three army cadet vehicles drove on up the highway.

She was right. Lt Ryan explained that it was not safe to try to move the cannon and canoes up such a busy mountain highway so the navy cadets were to load them onto the vehicles and then change roles to become part of the 'Control Group'.

It took nearly two hours to construct sheer legs to hoist the cannon and parts onto the truck and to load and lash on the canoes, spars and other items. Their own gear was then loaded aboard except for basic webbing. They were checked to ensure all had their lunch and water bottles full.

"And your raincoats," Lt Ryan added as it had come over all overcast and was starting to drizzle.

Once the loading was completed the navy cadets were instructed to walk up the highway for the next kilometre, taking care to keep off the bitumen. Tina did not enjoy this experience. There was lots of traffic, all roaring and rushing by only metres away with a steep slope on the left. As well as that a strong, cold wind began blowing down the valley and with it came showers of rain. It showed her very clearly why it would have been unsafe to have tried to pull the cannons and canoes along that section of road.

At 0915hrs they reached the gravel car park at the bottom of Robsons Track, a foot trail that follows an old wagon road up the continuation of the same spur. Most of the navy cadet vehicles drove on up the range with one team of cadets from Mackay on board. The other vehicles joined the walkers in the car park. Lt Hamilton of the army cadets was waiting there with three army cadets dressed in old civilian clothes. He then briefed them to become part of the enemy group.

"You are a raiding party of Iroquois led by two French officers and you are following up the tracks left by the British. When you catch them up you are to attack and battle with them but not actually close on them. There is to be no physical contact and no throwing things. They will do a withdrawal in contact exercise with platoons leapfrogging to cover each other. You will always stay at least 50 metres from them and try to be a bit realistic," he explained.

Costumes were then organised. Raincoats came off and the navy cadets were all issued with blue headbands. Feathers were stuck in these, the number going up with each rank. Two of the army cadets put on tricorn hats with white plumes on them and a gold *fleur d lis* badge on the right front. They were the French officers and now took command, grouping the navy cadets into their two watches.

After a safety brief and check on the map of where they were and where they were going, the groups set off up the walking track. To begin with this was relatively easy, but the slope quickly became steeper and the pace slowed to a puffing slog. Once again Tina had to grit her teeth and push herself to keep going. She was starting to feel lightheaded with exhaustion and lack of sleep but knew it was all part of the challenge to test them, so she clenched her jaw and struggled on upwards.

But others didn't. A boy from Mackay soon sat down gasping and complaining. The group came to a halt while a sub lieutenant from Townsville and some of his friends attended to him. Tina stayed out of the way so only overheard a bit of what was said but did learn that the boy had given up, saying he was getting cramps and had blisters. There were a couple of radio calls and then two of the older boys from Townsville were sent with the boy to help him back down to the safety vehicles. As she watched them go, Tina vowed she would not give up like them. When the order was given to continue, she hoisted herself to her feet and after a few groans at sore and stiffening muscles began plodding uphill.

Despite the showers of cold rain she found she was sweating and very quickly she drank one of the water bottles on her belt. To compensate, she found the view dramatic and beautiful and the open forest they were moving up through interesting and pretty. The foot track wound back and forth in short 50 metre zigzags. The mountainside was steep but most of the time the walking was just a panting slog up the rough trail.

At 1115hrs they caught up with the army cadet company. From the rocks up at the next bend came loud shots of 'Bang! Bang!' and the leading navy cadets replied. Tina hurried up the track and followed Andrew out onto the grassy slope to the right. She then joined in the 'Cowboys and Indians' 'battle' with both relief and pleasure. For a few minutes she was happy to pretend to be shooting at the heads she could just see further up the slope.

Then the army cadet rear-guard began to withdraw up the slope. Tina heard the shouted orders and glimpsed the backs of running figures and joined in the rush to chase, only to be shouted at by Cadet Midshipman George to stay under cover and let them go.

"Let them get a bit of a break, then we follow," he instructed.

They did. As soon as the last army cadet had vanished from view, the Control Group were ordered to follow up. They did this in a scrambling rush, which soon had Tina gasping for breath but cheerfully excited. Because the Control Group were not carrying packs, they quickly caught the army cadets up but by then another group of army cadets further up the slope and to one side were 'shooting' to cover the withdrawal of their fellows. The navy cadets were told to take cover and shoot back. They did so until the next group of army cadets began pulling back. Tina was glad to crouch behind a tree in the wet grass as it gave her a chance to get her breath back.

The process repeated itself several times until they were told to stop and have lunch at 1200hrs. By then they were at least halfway up the mountainside and all feeling quite worn out. "But not as buggered as those army cadets with their packs, I'll bet," Andrew commented.

The group sat along the track and Tina took out some biscuits and a small tin of tuna. She had several drinks and emptied one of her water bottles. Cloud and drizzle closed in and there were a few heavy showers which soaked her despite her raincoat. Despite the cold and discomfort Tina found she was still enjoying herself.

But not so some of the others. Grace Rushbrook sat and complained and told everyone she was feeling sick and that she had blisters on her hands as well as her feet. A couple of the boys from other units were also grumbling and not looking as though they were enjoying the experience.

"This is bloody stupid!" muttered a Leading Seaman from Townsville.

"No it's not," Tina retorted. "It was designed to test our fitness and character and it is obviously doing that."

The Leading Seaman glared back at her, making her fear she had made an enemy. But he then stopped complaining so openly.

Andrew chuckled and nudged her arm. "Good for you kiddo!" he whispered.

For a moment their eyes met and he smiled. Tina smiled back and wanted to throw her arms around him. But she just sat and glowed inside. *He has noticed me and I think he still likes me,* she told herself. *There is hope!*

Buoyed up by that Tina joined in the renewed battle with even greater enthusiasm after lunch. Despite feeling very tired, chafed, wet and cold she found she was really enjoying the challenge. The battle went on for hours, the army cadets pulling back section by section and platoon by platoon, holding just long enough to allow the last group to plod on past the new rear-guard before pulling back. Heavy rain began to drench them.

Tina emptied her second water bottle but then refilled it when they crossed a clear running mountain stream at the point where the walking track changed direction from running up the spine of the ridge to heading up a small valley. The vegetation changed from short grass and she-oaks to long grass, ferns and eucalypts. There were even a few old steel telegraph poles standing beside the track and Tina learned they were put up in the late 19th Century when this was the main road to the Tablelands.

"I'm glad we aren't travelling up and down this in a horse drawn stagecoach," Tina gasped as she set herself to tackle another steep and now slippery section of track.

The next battle took them up to a clump of large boulders on a ridge line. When she at last reached it, soaked and sweating, Tina saw that the ridge levelled out ahead and that a wall of dense jungle lined the crest ahead.

Uh oh! Rainforest, she thought.

There was a very confused 'battle' at that point and only when the navy cadets moved up did Tina discover that a second group from the Control Group, including army cadets she had never seen before, had been holding the company up from its front while her group had been pushing them from the back. As she plodded on along the track, she passed several drenched 'Indians' and 'Frenchmen'.

The foot track came to a vehicle track on the crest of the range. This was just two wheel ruts and went to the left and wound along just on the edge of the jungle. It also went up and down over some steep little rises that got Tina panting again. The battles continued but so did the rain which got heavier and heavier. Soon she was soaked and shivering, despite her raincoat.

At 1530hrs they reached Gillies Lookout: a park and lookout with vehicles parked on a gravel ring road. The place was also a launch point for hang gliders and from the lookout Tina got a few brief but dramatic glimpses of the whole Mulgrave Valley. Through the clouds and rain it looked very rugged and beautiful. She was even able to see all the way back to Gordonvale, now just a distant blur.

Andrew stood beside her and pointed down. "You can see our whole route so far," he said.

He was right. Tina was able to identify the Mulgrave River, Little Mulgrave, the bridge where they had unloaded the cannon and the ridge they had come up in the dark. The sight impressed her and also made her feel very proud of what she had achieved.

But she was now so exhausted, cold, and chafed that she doubted if she could go much further. To her intense relief she heard that they could rest until it got dark. The adult staff had set up several tarpaulins in a sheltered corner out of the wind and the cadet's packs were there. Thankfully, Tina limped over, found her pack and slumped down on it.

Carmen Collins and Petty Officer Page set up two plastic sheets to make a change room and the girls were told to get into dry clothes. Tina dug out a change of clothes and when it was her turn thankfully stripped and dried herself, then dressed in the dry clothes. She felt so cold she was trembling, and it took her quite a while to warm up. Like the others she pulled out her sleeping bag and snuggled into it to warm up.

The heavy rain eased just before dark and they were able to move out and heat some food on their stoves. A hot drink of Milo helped and by then Tina's feet had dried out a bit and she felt much better but still needed a real rest. So she groaned with all the others when her patrol and Carmen's were told to change back into their wet clothes and get ready to continue the exercise.

Pulling on the wet clothes and socks was a bit of a challenge but she managed it and then packed all the dry things carefully, all wrapped in plastic. She then refilled her water bottles. The work of packing was interrupted by several heavy showers of rain. After a briefing on what to do next she pulled on her pack and set off into the damp darkness with the others. It was so dark they needed to use their torches to keep on the road which plunged into a tunnel of rainforest.

The next hour was a bit of an ordeal as they sloshed, slithered, and trudged for 2 kilometres up and down some quite steep hills through the rainforest. It was so dark and unpleasant that Tina found it quite scary and daunting, but the presence of her friends helped to keep her calm and moving. Twice she lost her footing when going down steep slopes and fell heavily on her bum. Mud and water coated her and she became so filthy and wet that she could only shrug and stop caring. Each time Andrew helped to heave her to her feet and that helped a lot.

As expected from the orders, they met an army cadet patrol but the actual challenge from the darkness still came as a surprise. There was a loud call to surrender and torches shone on them. As ordered, the navy cadets did not at first surrender so there was a short battle. During it Tina just stood in the rain and made no attempt to take cover in the jungle beside the roads. Several others did and quickly regretted it when they were snagged by wait-a-while or thorns.

"Surrender!" shouted a voice from the jungle beside them.

Tina recognised Graham's voice and gave a wry smile. *It had to be him,* she thought. "He sounds like he is having as much fun as a pig in mud!" she commented.

He was. When Carmen's group withdrew according to plan Tina's team did as instructed and surrendered. A grinning Graham came out and recognised them. "Gotcha!" he chortled.

Andrew snorted and muttered, "Pig in mud alright."

He did not sound very friendly and Tina felt a stab of concern that her actions had driven a wedge between the friends. But Graham appeared not to notice and became busy radioing his HQ and then organising the 'prisoners'. He then kept them waiting until another patrol arrived to relieve his and then led them back to where the army cadets were 'harboured' in the jungle.

They did this without torches and in a slow, slithering line. It was so dark they had to hang onto the webbing of the person ahead of them and Tina marvelled that Graham could find his camp in the dark. They passed two parked vehicles near a bend and then were led in along a rope tied from tree to tree at waist height to where a shelter was strung between six trees.

Major Wickham and several CUOs and others were waiting there and now torches were allowed. After a check that everyone was present and unhurt, they were questioned according to a printed script. Blake had a copy of this in a plastic bag and he did the answering. Tina just stood and listened, shivering but still interested in spite of herself. Blake's answers gave the army cadets the information as to which Indian war party they were from and a clue that there were other war bands which could be moving to cut off the 'British' advance.

As they talked, Tina watched Graham's face and was again struck by how ruggedly handsome he was. He was obviously enjoying the exercise even though he was just as soaked as she was and had carried his pack up the mountain during the day.

He is very fit, but he isn't the man for me, she decided again.

While speculating on how she might get Andrew to pay her attention, she followed the others back out to the road. The navy cadet team was then led further on along the muddy gravel road past some sentries and then on for a hundred metres to a sharp bend in the road where a patrol challenged them. At that point, their guides left them with instructions to keep following the road until they came to the Control Group camp. By then heavy rain was pouring down again.

The navy cadets took out their torches and trudged on. Tina felt ready to just flop down and now found it a real effort just to put one foot in front of the other and Stella was moaning and complaining all the time.

I don't think I can go on much longer either, Tina thought.

Luckily, she didn't have to. Just a hundred metres further along the road they came to a line of parked vehicles and a camp on the right of the road between the vehicles and an open field. Sentries challenged them and then Lt Hamilton met them and showed them to where several shelters were strung up to trees and the fence. Packs were dumped in out of the rain and bedding unrolled.

"Sleep dry. Don't get your sleeping bags wet," Carmen reminded them.

Feeling very daring, even though it was almost so dark she could barely make out her neighbours, Tina stripped and slipped naked into the sleeping bag. The knowledge that Andrew was only in the next shelter along added to the thrill.

Oooh! I wish he was in here with me! she thought.

She slept well, except for a few cramps and aches. They were woken while it was still dark and ordered to get dressed. That was a challenge, especially in the dark but by 0545hrs they all stood out in the light drizzle being briefed.

The first activity was a dawn attack on the army cadets. This included having to push through the edge of the rainforest in the dark, the wet leaves feeling clammy and horrible in the darkness. Tina expected to be snagged by wait-a-while but was lucky and met none. There was a lot of shouting and banging and then the dim forms of the defenders became visible. As instructed Tina pretended to die, an unpleasant experience as it meant falling down on the soggy leaf mould.

I hope I don't pick up a tick or a leech, she thought.

The battle was ended and she joined everyone out on the edge of the road where they sat in their section lines for a roll check and then a briefing. One of the army cadets had lines to read to move the story along, the attackers were from two of the 'French' war parties who had marched all night to block the advance.

As soon as that was over the Control Group hurried back along the muddy road to their camp and carried out their morning routine. This had to be done under shelters as the heavy rain began again. The radio news informed them that it had rained heavily all night long right across the Atherton Tablelands. That caused some speculation that the exercise might be cancelled.

"Oh, I hope not," Tina commented. "I am starting to enjoy this."

It was obvious to her that others weren't, but she was pleased with how well she had performed and after a good night's sleep felt ready for more.

The rain eased during breakfast and then the cloud began to shred and open out so that by 0800hrs they were experiencing watery sunlight. During this time there were several small 'actions' as army cadet patrols tried to sneak up on the camp. Tina enjoyed the action but was then taken away with Stella by Lt Hamilton. Both girls were given long dresses and old-fashioned bonnets and the story line that they were two 'English' girls who had fled wounded into the forest when 'Indians' had attacked their farm. Carmen and Hayley Page, both also dressed as girls, came with them. Lt Hamilton and two army cadet sergeants made up the remainder of the party. With radios and packs they made their way west along the road for 300 metres to where there was jungle on the left and open fields on the right. Here they turned left and walked 200 metres into the jungle on a compass course.

Lt Hamilton led the way and the going was not as bad as Tina had feared. There was very little wait-a-while in this patch of rain forest and the ground was a gentle down slope. On reaching 400 paces, Lt Hamilton showed the girls where to wait.

"You are to put the costumes on when we call on the radio and then pretend you are badly hurt. One is to have an arrow stuck through them and the other has been hacked up by a tomahawk. Here are some bandages and fake blood. Don't get it on the clothes please. And here is the arrow."

He handed over these items and then said to Carmen and Hayley, "You two are to come back with me and I will put you in hiding beside the road. When the company arrives you are to run out and ask for help to find your friends. The company will then do search patrols to find you and then we will do a First Aid and casualty evacuation exercise. During that you will be carried out to the road on stretchers."

Stella looked very anxious. "But what if they don't find us sir?"

Lt Hamilton smiled. "Don't worry. There will be a patrol every 50 paces. Even if they don't see you, you will hear them and are to call out to attract their attention. And you have that radio if there are any problems and I will come immediately," he explained.

That satisfied Tina who was confident she could find her way out if she needed to. The others made their way back to the road and the two girls sat on their packs and waited. "We may as well make ourselves comfortable," Tina said. "We have a couple of hours to wait."

The timings included an attack on the 'French' camp at 0930hrs and then there had to be briefings, roll checks and orders so it would be 1030hrs before the search patrols began. At Tina's urging, they put up a shelter and then unrolled their groundsheets and sleeping bags under it. Then they sat or lay and talked. It was damp and gloomy in the jungle and Tina found it unpleasant and scary, but she was glad of the training expeditions they had done.

But that reminded her of the men with the mist nets and she began to imagine that they might be somewhere in this jungle so she started to look anxiously around whenever she heard an unusual noise, and to her most of the jungle noises were unusual. When she became aware of this, she told herself to stop scaring herself by imagining things. Seeing a leech wriggling up Stella's leg helped. Watching for them then took up much of their mental effort until the search exercise began. At the appointed time they put on their costumes. Then they waited.

A patrol led by Stephen Bell found them and then they packed up and waited until the whole company had grouped there. The First Aid exercise and stretcher carry followed, and Tina did not enjoy that she as she was scared of being dropped. But Major Wickham supervised this activity personally and there were always eight cadets carrying the stretcher, so she made it safely out to the road.

It was bright sunshine by then and Tina found the glare hard to take until her eyes adjusted. After the roll check she had lines to read to describe how she and her sister had fled the attack by the Indian war party. She also told them that their brother, a fur trapper, had seen French sailing boats on the big lake.

After her act Tina and Stella were sent back along the road to change back into uniform. They then joined a group of Control Group cadets including all of the navy cadets at the rear of the company. At 1330hrs, after lunch, the company hoisted on their packs and began a route march. This hurt. Tina's sore shoulder muscles and chafing at once began to bother her but she gritted her teeth and ignored it. It was now a lovely clear day, even though she could see dark rain clouds in the distance, and she was determined to enjoy the exercise.

I wonder what will happen next? she thought.

Chapter 42

NAVAL SUPREMACY

Tina walked along the muddy road, happy despite her aches and pains. She was now really enjoying the exercise and one of the aspects she liked most was not knowing what was going to happen next.

We have to get the cannons and the canoes to the lake and then set up the guns to bombard the French forts, she thought. But how was that going to be organised? A study of her map photocopy showed her that the nearest arm of Lake Tinaroo was about 5 kilometres away. *But we aren't dragging the cannon or canoes,* she thought.

She had so entered into the spirit of the story that she thought they should be. *It isn't right. We should be doing it as realistically as we can,* she told herself. But she had to admit that they were all very tired and dirty and she knew she must stink from sweat. But 5 kilometres wasn't that far. *We could march that in a couple of hours,* she decided.

But could she? After passing a gate where several safety vehicles and staff were waiting, they came out into open farmland on a fairly gentle ridge. The road went westwards through a small clump of trees and then down across a wide, grassy valley. About a kilometre away the road reached a wall of dense rainforest and that got her a bit concerned. In the distance Tina saw that there was still a mass of dark rain clouds, but apart from a few light showers none fell on the company.

After half an hour, the company reached another gate at the edge of the jungle. By then Tina was really feeling the strain and wishing they could stop. She noted that the side road they were on now joined a bitumen road and her map informed her it was the Danbulla Forest Drive.

I know where I am now, she thought. *Only 3 kilometres to the lake.*

But they didn't go to the lake. The march was directed to the left around a bend past a farmhouse and there they found a coach and the truck parked beside the road. It took a few minutes for the truth to sink in: They were not marching all the way but were to travel by vehicle! But where to?

Their gear was loaded on the truck or in the bins under the coach and the cadets then checked aboard. Once the coach was full it set off and Tina was able to sit back and relax her trembling muscles. The coach went south along the winding Danbulla Drive through rolling farmland to the Gillies Highway where it turned right. It drove past Lake Barrine and then Lake Eacham and on across the rolling hills. As they went Tina got a good view of the country and of the distant mountains. She also got several glimpses of Lake Tinaroo off to her right. There was also more rain and she noted that the mountains on the far side of the Tablelands were being deluged by heavy rain.

That is the Herberton Range, she mused. Vivid flashbacks to being chased by Danny at the New Dam caused her to shiver and she shook her head. *I hope those men have left the country,* she told herself.

Just 5 minutes later, the coach stopped in the main street of the lovely small town of Yungaburra. To many of the cadets the place was a novelty, but Tina had been there many times. The cadets were told to unload everything and to place it in the park across the road. Here she noted the cannon parts and the canoes.

Looks like we start hauling from here, she thought.

And they did. After an hour, during which the remainder of the company were ferried to join them and during which they were allowed to go to the shops, they were organised into work parties and began hauling or carrying. Tina and her team had the job of carrying their own gear and the canoe. The other navy cadets did likewise. The army cadets hauled the cannons and all of its parts.

The route they followed led them north to Tinaburra. This was 3 kilometres and was along a bitumen road with houses on both sides for the first kilometre. After that it was along the crest of a wide, gentle ridge with short grass on both sides. The grassy slopes led down to two arms of the lake. Seeing the water cheered Tina and she began to look forward to being 'naval' again instead of military.

When they were halfway along the road clouds came over and it began to drizzle in intermittent showers. But there was nothing for it but to trudge on. The main problem, apart from the chafing effect of wet clothes, was that the canoe began to fill with rainwater, and they had to stop from time to time to empty it out. They could only carry it for about 100 paces at a time anyway.

It took over an hour and a half to reach their destination and it was 1630hrs by the time they reached the Tinaburra Waters motel and caravan park. Here they were directed to the line of pine trees on the eastern side of the motel area. By the time they arrived heavy rain was falling.

Part of the Control Group were already there, and Tina saw that they had driven in several lines of star pickets on the gentle open slope leading down to the lake. The canoes were placed upside down and the cannon parts stacked and covered with a tarpaulin. The cadets were then organised into males and females and then into pairs and they were set to work to erect their shelters between the pine trees or star pickets. Tina shared with Stella and had Carmen and Hayley in the next shelter.

Tina was then part of a navy cadet work party that rigged three tarpaulins between the motel rooms and the swimming pool fence. These were secured to posts and trees and quickly provided a large area of concrete which was free of rain. The cadets were then organised to have showers. These were in the caravan park facilities, but Tina found it wonderful to stand under the hot shower. Her aches and pain seemed to melt away and despite the sharp itching and pains from her chafing and scratches she felt revived.

In dry clothes and wearing a pullover and raincoat she took her wet clothes to where the officers were collecting them to be laundered and tumble dried. Luckily, the cadets did not have to try to cook in the rain. A barbeque had been organised and was held under the tarpaulins outside the rooms. Two of the rooms had been hired to allow the adult staff to use the showers and toilets and for the female staff to sleep in.

Tina's happiness increased when she went with the other girls to sit under the tarpaulins. The cadets were seated in section lines for roll check at 1800hrs. They were then allowed to relax and mix socially. To Tina's delight Andrew moved to sit beside her and nudged her with his elbow.

"Do you mind if I sit here?" he asked.

Tina was so pleased that all she could do was smile and nod. Her whole being seemed to tingle and heat up and she became so excited that she had to restrain herself from acting too soon. But she found that she had to know how he felt about her so to test the situation she slowly moved so that she was leaning gently but firmly against him. To her relief and delight he made no move to end this and several times pressed against her. Taking heart from this she pressed herself firmly against him.

In return he gave her another smile and a gentle hug, and sitting under the tarpaulin with the other cadets as it got dark became a very pleasant experience for Tina. Despite the wind and rain she felt warm and safe and loved as she snuggled against him. Her main concern was that the adult staff might suspect them of fraternising.

But with seventy people crowded in under the tarpaulins nobody seemed to notice and after a while they had to get up and join the queue to get their food. The hamburger and grilled sausage was very welcome and when they both had theirs they stood on the side of the group and ate. From time to time their eyes met and Tina was sure that Andrew was sending her signals of affection. She chewed and in between mouthfuls chatted about the exercise. She was pleased to find that Andrew was really enjoying it as well and hoped that the second half would be as interesting.

After an hour of socialising and eating, the cadets and staff were all moved to sit in a tight group outside one of the rooms. Major Wickham then briefed them on the next part of the story, using a data projector to illustrate his talk. He then gave everyone a two-page summary of the history of naval warfare on the lakes and rivers of North America in the 18th Century.

Tina read this with amazement. She had vaguely known that there were big lakes in North America but now learned that some were like inland seas, being hundreds of kilometres across. They were so big that large ships had been constructed on their shores for both trade and warfare.

She now learned that two lakes in particular had been of vital strategic importance: Lakes George and Champlain. The French had built a huge stone fort, which they named Fort Carillon but which the British and Americans called Fort Ticonderoga at the narrowest point of Lake Champlain. The pictures quite amazed her. She had always assumed it was all log huts and timber stockades, not stone barracks and huge stone walls topped by dozens of heavy cannons and with a regular army garrison.

She read how in 1758 the French, led by the Marquis Montcalm had moved south along Lake George in hundreds of bateaux (flat-bottomed lake boats) and canoes with 1500 regular French soldiers plus hundreds of *couriers du bois* (messengers of the woods, French hunters, and trappers who acted as scouts and messengers) and Indians.

Major Wickham put up another picture showing Mohawk Indians using tomahawks to kill white people, including women and children. "Some of you will have read a book called *The Last of the Mohicans* or perhaps seen the movie of that name," he said. "This was when the British garrison of Fort William Henry surrendered to Montcalm and were allowed to leave but most were then murdered by the Indians."

He then showed a picture painted at the time of thousands of boats and canoes on a lake. "The British did a counter-offensive with 6,300 British regular troops, thousands of American colonial militiamen and hundreds of Indians. This is them moving north and the canoes stretched from one side of the lake to the other and 15 kilometres long. Unfortunately, through bad tactics they lost the battle and were driven back."

Next he put up a map of the area and showed how a British force of 3,600 regulars and colonials had travelled 430 miles up the Mohawk River and across to Lake Ontario, then along the lake to capture Fort Frontenac at the eastern end of that lake, thereby cutting French North America in half.

"They did 84 portages and fought dozens of skirmishes with the Indians. It is this expedition which gave me the idea for this exercise," he explained.

And a good idea too! Tina thought.

Major Wickham then quickly summarised how Fort Ticonderoga had been captured and recaptured by both sides during the American War of Independence. "This time both sides built fleets of small ships: schooners, gunboats and even brigs to gain control of the waterway. The British even built a three-masted ship, a sloop-of-war named HMS *Inflexible* with 18 cannons. There was a naval battle which the British won, mainly because they had bigger and better ships and had drafted crews from their Royal Navy warships to man them."

Tina studied the pictures of the ships and the battle and was again amazed. *Building big ships so far from the sea,* she thought. *They must have been very determined.* She now learned that there were even bigger naval battles with bigger ships on the large lakes of the Great Lakes system during an event called the War of 1812. *I didn't even know that Britain and America fought such a war,* she thought.

Major Wickham now faced the navy cadets. "Your mission over the next two days is to gain naval supremacy of the lake. For reasons of safety and expedience we are going to ignore reality a bit and will be starting from this end of the lake instead of from the north end. You will be divided into two teams, each with four sailboats. You are to pretend that the sailboats are actually small warships with cannons, and you are to seek each other out and then we will decide who wins by how well the two fleets manoeuvre."

That idea really appealed to Tina and she listened with interest as the rules of the 'naval battle' were explained. "This will be really good!" she commented, to which Andrew agreed. The Port Watch was designated the 'British' fleet and would start from where they were. The other half of the navy cadet group were the 'French' and their start point was not revealed. The army cadets were to be moved by coach back to where they had been picked up and were to march to the lake.

The first major objective was to get the cannons to the lake at its narrowest point. When Tina studied the map photocopy, they were all give she gave a little cry of delight. "That is Python Point, our secret island," she said. Images of the recent holiday added to her pleasure.

The cadets were then sent to bed. As she made her way out into the wind and drizzle, Tina experienced a strong urge to cuddle up to Andrew but she resisted this and just walked with the other girls and said a casual 'good night' to him. But as she lay in her sleeping bag, she found herself wishing that she was snuggling up to him, even if it meant they ended up doing some very naughty things.

He can do it if he likes, she told herself.

Despite frequent heavy rain Tina slept well that night. She woke feeling refreshed and happy to a grey world of dense fog. The cadets did a check parade at 0600hrs for roll call and then they settled to their morning routine. The rain had stopped but during breakfast Tina heard the weather report on the radio news which informed her that there was still very heavy rain on the Herberton Range.

The effect of the rain was obvious when they went to launch the canoes and sailboats. The level of the lake was up by about half a metre and brown plumes of silty flood water were coming down the creeks to mingle with the darker waters of the lake. While the navy cadets worked at preparing their boats dark clouds began building and showers and drizzle swept over them.

By the time the army cadets boarded their coach it was raining steadily. The army cadets, including a grinning Graham, hurried aboard and soon afterwards were driven away. So were half the navy cadets, the 'Blue Team' representing the French. With them went the canoe trailers. Tina and her friends donned raincoats and hats and continued their preparations. Their bags were placed in the truck and then four 'Laser' sailboats were unloaded off their trailers. Only a bag with a water bottle and lunch plus radios and other safety gear were taken on the sailboats.

Small British red ensigns of the 18th Century design were issued to each sailboat and this was hauled up on a halyard rigged for the purpose. They then rigged the single mast and sail and launched their boats. Only when they were afloat did they raise their ensigns. Andrew thought this should have been done with more ceremony, but it was raining heavily and blustery gusts were whipping the lake into small whitecaps.

As soon as the Safety Boat was afloat and the radios had been tested, the flotilla set off. The wind was blowing from the southwest, so the boats had a good run. All the way north along the lake the conditions were challenging but none of the boats capsized. Tina enjoyed it immensely despite the showers of rain and cold spray and the wind that cut in around her collar. She was also cheered by seeing how much Andrew was enjoying it. He laughed frequently and his eyes seemed to sparkle.

Around 2 kilometres and 20 minutes sailing had them at the point where they changed course to NNE. In that area the Barron River emptied into the lake and the change in water colour was very obvious. The boats then ran with a stern wind for another two kilometres to where another long, indented arm of the lake came in from the Northeast. Ahead of the boast was the rain shrouded mass of jungle covered hills around Python Hill and Tina looked at it and wondered how the army cadets were getting on.

They are hiking down the Python Road through the jungle, she thought, picturing the muddy road and the blue bellied snake as she did. *It must be miserable in this rain. It will be all mud and slush.*

She was very glad she wasn't with them, even though the story was that they were dragging the cannon along that road to Python Point.

The rain eased as they changed course again to run north up through the narrowest section of the lake. On the starboard side were the jungle covered hills and peninsulas and to port open farmland and the dominating height of Tobacco Hill. According to the original story line the French had a fort with cannons on Tobacco Hill and they controlled the narrows but for safety reasons that reality had been glossed over. So the flotilla sailed past the bare grassy hill in watery sunlight and Tina appreciated just how such a place must have dominated in the old days.

She pointed this out to Andrew, and he nodded. "A couple of cannons dug in up there would certainly control all this part of the lake," he agreed.

Blake looked around and then said, "What about at night. It should be easy enough then."

Andrew shook his head. "If they were efficient, they would have guard boats down here and some form of illumination ready to light." Suddenly he sat up and pointed off to port. "Sail ho! Enemy in sight on the port beam!" he cried.

Tina looked and felt a pulse of pleasurable excitement. Coming out of the bay behind Tobacco Hill were four sailboats flying white flags with gold *fleur de lis* on them.

"The French fleet," she commented.

Blake looked and frowned. "They aren't flying French flags. That is red, white and blue isn't it?"

Sarah answered that. "Blue, white and red, but no, that was only the French flag after the French Revolution. The flag before that was that one."

Cadet Midshipman George began shouting orders and the four sailboats swung around into line abreast and sailed directly towards their opponents. For the next half hour it was all rapid sail handling and dexterous sailing. Spray and rain soaked the cadets and Tina found herself laughing with enjoyment and excitement. Twice they came within a whisker of capsizing and only frantic shifts of balance and easing of sheets (her job) saved them.

Three times the little flotillas manoeuvred into line astern, the two 'battle lines' sailing parallel and only metres apart. Tina knew that the officers in the two motor launches were marking them on how well they kept the distance between boats and how well they steered in line so she concentrated on doing her very best.

The boys kept yelling out 'Bang!' and 'Boom!' to pretend they were firing cannons. This elicited similar shouts from the 'enemy' who also jeered and made derogatory comments about their seamanship. Then the enemy flagship suddenly veered out of line and cut across between the lead boat and Tina's. A glance showed Tina that the cause was an attempt to avoid capsizing and a momentary loss of control by the enemy.

"Lookout!" Blake shouted.

"Hard a starboard! Jibe!" shouted Andrew.

He put the helm over and the boat's bow swung round. Just in time Tina pulled in the sheet to hold the boom steady until it had swung through the eye of the wind. Then she gripped it with her free hand and passed it over her head, calling a warning to the others as she did. Then she eased the sheet out.

They narrowly avoided both a collision and capsizing but then found themselves right alongside the enemy flagship. The enemy were all in a fluster and still trying to get under control and before they knew it the hulls of the two boats bumped and then ground together. Tina had an impression of anxious and scared looking faces turning in their direction.

Suddenly, Andrew called, "Sarah, take the helm. Tina, hold this course. Quick!"

Sarah scrambled aft past Tina and took the tiller from him. As she did, Andrew stood up and only then, as he shouted to Blake to join him, did Tina understand what he intended. She opened her mouth to say don't but was too late. Andrew sprang across the gap between the two boats and pushed hard at the enemy captain. Blake followed, also crashing into one of the crew.

The enemy captain went tumbling over the side, still pulling on the tiller as he did. The enemy flagship swung into a vicious turn that nearly capsized it. The bow jerked round and for a moment Tina thought it would ram into her boat and crush her. But it missed, merely bumping into the stern and then sheering off. It ended up facing into the wind, its sail flapping wildly.

Tina saw that the enemy flagship was now cut off from its fellows by the British battle line. She yelled to Sarah to come about and in two smart manoeuvres they wore round and came head to wind close alongside the enemy captain. He was bobbing in the water shouting angrily and at first did not want their help and tried to swim away. By then the safety boat was heading towards them so Tina let him go and got Sarah to ease them up alongside the enemy flagship.

By the time they reached it Andrew had untied their halyard and he quickly pulled down their flag. "Captured her!" he shouted.

It led to quite an argument of course and the other side claimed they couldn't do that. Andrew's retort was that it was how they did it in the old days and, anyway, they were only responding to the ramming attempt. This was disputed as a simple mishap which Blake loudly labelled poor seamanship. This earned him scowls and a rebuke, but the point was gained. The sailboat was counted as captured.

To Tina's surprise it was only 1030hrs and she wondered what they would do for the remainder of the day. Both teams, plus the safety boats, then sailed across the lake into the lee of Tobacco Hill. Here, in a sheltered little bay, they beached the sailboats and made their way to a houseboat tied to a jetty. The houseboat had been hired by the adult staff as the HQ Afloat and the cadets were given morning tea on board. They were then briefed for an orienteering exercise which was afloat.

Tina was glad of the chance to get out of the wind and rain, particularly while they got out their maps and calculated what to do. It was a typical orienteering exercise with more check points than they could possibly reach in the allotted time. Each check point was allocated a number of points and those with the most marks were upwind.

After some argument about which check points to try for the magnetic bearings were worked out for the desired course. At 1200hrs the signal to start was given and the teams raced out to their sailboats and set off. For the next three hours they zigzagged across the lake, mostly in drizzling rain. At least the wind had died down so the waves were much smaller. Even so it was all wet and fun. The check points turned out to be notes in plastic bags that were taped to poles driven into the bank of the lake. Each note had a letter and a secret message to prove that the boat had actually been to it. These were noted and then they immediately set out on the next leg.

By 1515hrs all eight boats were back at the start. Tina's team did not win. They came third but she did not mind. It had all been a lot of fun. They were then told to unrig the sailboats and load them on trailers. That took half an hour and then they unloaded their canoes and gear and launched the canoes. The rafts were lashed together and the gyn erected to reload the cannon and its parts aboard. Lt Ryan told them to pretend they were actually doing this on the other side of the lake. By the time they stepped aboard the wind had died almost completely and the rain had eased to a misty drizzle.

The rafts, canoes, motorboats and houseboat then set off due north down the lake. It was easy going with the gentle wind behind them and Tina told herself she was still enjoying it, despite goose bumps, wrinkled skin, chafing and blisters on her hands. To add to her pleasure she even knew where they were going, to Secret Island at Python Point. It was visible to her all the way.

The flotilla arrived at 1630hrs, the motorboats beaching on the bitumen road where it vanished into the lake and the canoes along the inland shore of the small island. The HQ boat moored itself just off the north shore of the island in its lee. Tina felt very proud to show off 'her' island but was surprised at how much the water level had risen.

At least half a metre, she calculated.

Where the road dipped down into the water and it had been only ankle deep and 25 metres wide it was now waist deep and 50 metres of water. The whole island appeared to have shrunk and instead of 150 metres from end to end was less than a hundred.

The cannons were unloaded and the rafts prepared for ferrying the troops. When the army cadets arrived, tired and muddy from their 14 kilometres march at 1715hrs they were ferried across to the island on the rafts and canoes. This provided the navy cadets with another opportunity to show off their special skills as ropes were secured from trees on the mainland to trees on the island and single blocks with pulling ropes looped onto these. The navy cadets were then able to haul the rafts back and forth with the minimum of fuss.

Tina had the pleasure of helping Graham aboard her raft. He was soaked and splattered with mud but was still smiling. "Did you have a good day?" Tina asked.

"Great! We have had some really good battles in the jungle," Graham answered.

At the mention of the jungle Tina shuddered. "You can have all the jungle to yourself," she said.

The raft was pulled across by Andrew and Blake and Tina saw Andrew give Graham a wary greeting. She was tempted to make a comment to set Andrew's mind at rest but was interrupted by shouts and yelling back along the road. It was the rear-guard battling some French and Indians and the navy cadets had to quickly move the canoes and rafts back across to pick them up. During this part of the exercise Tina saw several of the 'enemy' flitting from tree to tree and pretending to fire so she pretended to shoot back.

"Bang! Bang!" she shouted.

"Boom!" added Andrew. "Cannon," he explained.

Then Blake went: "Tat-atat-atat-atat-a-tat!"

At that Major Wickham laughed and yelled at him, "No machine guns! They hadn't been invented then."

The good-natured little battle ended with the whole British force on the island, the canoes and rafts hauled up on the bitumen roadway. For a time they 'stood to', but then Major Wickham detailed a section for outpost guard duty and they were ferried back across to the mainland. They deployed a hundred metres forward and the others were all told to eat while it was light.

The navy cadets were grouped near the western end of the island and Tina and her team found cleared places among the small trees where they could sit on their packs and cook their food. She was in a good mood, made better by Andrew sitting beside her. Several times she was tempted to hint to Andrew that she wouldn't mind a bit of loving but then guilt at even thinking of breaking the cadet fraternization rules held her tongue.

Tents and shelters were erected and the cadets prepared for the night. The navy cadets were rostered to keep guard on the boats and the 'seaward' sides of the lake, leaving the army cadets to guard the landward approach. Dusk set in. As the last of the sun set below the band of dark clouds off to the west, the wind had died completely and the rain had stopped.

Just on last light the 'enemy' attacked again. The outpost was driven back and rescued by ferry. Then a group of 'painted' Indians, boys wearing only shorts, boots, feathers and paint, made an 'attack', splashing through the shallows. They were all 'shot' or retreated. They obviously had a good time getting wet and falling over but Tina was glad it wasn't her.

Not in water that cold, she thought.

As soon as the enemy retreated another section was ferried across to set up the outpost again. Then girls who wanted to use the portable toilet were also ferried across. Two navy cadets were rostered to operate the ferry. They were kept busy by people going to the toilet or by patrols being ferried across as the army cadets kept up the action far into the night. The other navy and army cadets were sent to bed. This gave Tina a chance to change into dry clothes and to take her wet boots off.

The action settled down by midnight, which was when Tina was rostered to start duty. She found it cold, dark and very still when she went to the raft. Pulling on a pullover she sat next to the male navy cadet from Mackay who was the other 'ferryman'.

For the next hour she sat there listening. From time to time one or the other made a comment or they heard the army cadet sentries nearby being changed but otherwise the only sound was the soft sighing of the light breeze in the leaves and the lap of tiny waves.

At 0100hrs Andrew was woken and came on duty so that Tina found herself alone in the dark with him. *This should be my chance,* she told herself. *It should be romantic.* But she would not put him in a position that might compromise his sense of duty or his conscience. *It would not be fair to tempt him.*

So they sat quietly side by side. As the next 10 minutes ticked by, Tina's attention was divided between the nearness of Andrew and doing her duty as a guard. Then he surprised her by nudging her and whispering. "Tina. er... You were great today. I... I have really come to admire you over the last few days. You are tough, and brave and strong, and you are really intelligent."

Say I am beautiful, Tina thought hopefully.

But Andrew said, "And you are really good looking and desirable."

"Thank you," she managed to croak, her heart hammering with hope.

There was a pause and Tina thought he had finished but then he said, "I would like to ask you out again, if you want."

"I do," Tina replied, leaning against him and giving his forearm a squeeze.

She half expected him to put his arm around her and to do things like kissing and she wasn't sure if she would break the rules or not. To her relief he muttered, "Good. Thanks for that. But sorry, no frat at cadets."

That increased her respect for him even more and she again squeezed his arm and whispered, "After camp." She nearly added that he could enjoy as much as he liked but was then shocked at her own thoughts and stopped talking. She took her hand away and sat in happy silence.

And it was into that silence that she thought she heard a sinister sound that sent a shiver of goose bumps up her spine. *Was that an aero engine?*

she wondered. She cocked her head and looked in all directions but could not be sure.

"What's the matter?" Andrew whispered, sensing her tenseness and movement.

"I thought I heard a plane coming in to land," Tina replied.

"A plane! Fair go. I didn't hear anything," Andrew replied.

But now Tina was certain. "But I did. It came down over there." She pointed to her left front.

"But why would a plane land here at night?" Andrew queried.

A shiver of apprehension went through Tina. Into her mind flashed the image of the grey painted floatplane. She whispered back, "The bird smuggler's floatplane."

Andrew listened. "I can't hear anything," he said.

Tina stood up and stared into the night. "I am going to have a look," she said.

Chapter 43

WRONG TURN

A ndrew stood up beside her. "You can't. We are on duty," he reminded her.

"I know. I will go as soon as I have been relieved," Tina replied.

"You will not! You are not going on your own," Andrew said fiercely.

But Tina got stubborn, "I will, but I will be very careful. Anyway, you are just here and I can yell if I need help."

Andrew argued some more but Tina was adamant. At last he relented and agreed. "If you aren't back in 15 minute, I will tell the officers."

"Twenty, and don't wake them until we have some definite information," Tina agreed.

So they sat and waited until 0150hrs came around. Tina went off to wake Stella and then returned with her to the sentry post. When they got back there Tina asked Andrew to ferry her across. Stella wanted to know where they were going. Tina blushed, thinking that Stella suspected them of sneaking off for a pash, but she said, "Andrew is just taking me across so I can go to the toilet."

It was the work of a minute or so to climb onto the ferry and haul it across the water gap. On the other side Tina stepped off and waded ashore. Andrew wished her luck and then sat there waiting. Tina first told the army cadet sentries she was going to the toilet and not to shoot her when she came back. Then she set off along the bitumen road into the night.

She did go to the toilet too. Fear made it an urgent necessity as soon as she was on her own. Memories of being chased by Danny and Neville got her feeling really anxious and she had to talk herself into continuing on past the portable toilet.

The night was dark and still and there were even hints of mist as Tina walked slowly forward along the old bitumen road. She was very glad that she had been there before as her objective was clear in her mind.

That place where the bitumen road goes back into the water would be an ideal place for the smugglers. They could easily drive to there with a boat and the floatplane could land in one of those sheltered bays where nobody lives, she reasoned.

There was some concern that she might encounter cadets from the Control Group but that was a minor worry compared to her very real fear of meeting the smugglers. It took her an effort of willpower to keep walking. In a few minutes she was at the place where the dirt vehicle track that led up to the Danbulla Road joined the bitumen. After stopping there to listen for a minute she continued on around the curving bitumen road.

Another 3 minutes of silent but steady walking had her at a point where she could again see the lake, or would have been able to if there hadn't been thick fog. Tina stopped and gaped in surprise at the dense woolly mass that had rolled in across the water. It was cold and felt clammy and visibility dropped to 50 paces within seconds.

But the fog will hide me too, she reasoned.

Knowing that her 20 minutes were rapidly running down she continued on, eyes and ears alert for any hint of danger. But there was no vehicle and no men. She reached the place where the road went down into the water and stopped. Straining her eyes to try to penetrate the fog and darkness she looked for the floatplane.

There was no sign of it. Several times gaps opened in the drifting mist and she was able to take in the whole of the starlit bay and still she could see nothing that resembled an aircraft. *But I am sure I heard it,* she thought. Biting her lip with anxiety and frustration she stayed a couple more minutes to be sure.

Then a sound off to her left attracted Tina's attention and she moved right down to ankle deep in the water to see better in that direction. A light came into view and her heart at once leapt and began hammering. Then she realised she was looking at the anchored HQ houseboat.

I must have been wrong, she told herself, reasoning that no floatplane would land if it saw the riding lights of the houseboat. *Maybe it landed in the next bay over?* she wondered. That got her trying to remember if there was another similar bay or just the big one with Fongon Campground on its north shore.

But she could not remember well enough. What she could remember was paddling across in the canoe and then images from her nightmare coming to her: of the dark shapes under the water and of the grasping hand reaching up out of the lake. That got her trembling with self-induced fright and she hastily backed out of the water and away from the lake, her eyes scanning frantically for signs of the horrible things.

Thoroughly scared now, and also very ashamed of being so, Tina turned and walked quickly back along the old bitumen road. As she walked, she kept glancing back at the fog and dark water. Even As she did, this she berated herself for being silly. But part of her mind still conjured up fears of things in the water. It took her an effort not to break into a run.

Then she did break into a run but only because she heard Andrew's voice from the darkness ahead. He had no sooner spoken than other voices started calling out: "Bang! Bang! Gotcha!"

Tina had opened her mouth to call back but now shut it and ran. *Andrew has run into the enemy,* she thought. Now she had new worries: that Andrew might be captured; and that they might be in trouble for leaving the bivouac area.

There was more shouting ahead and Tina clearly heard Andrew yelling 'Bang! Bang!' in reply. Then she was rounding the bend and saw several dark shapes ahead of her. They were between her and Andrew and she decided that the best tactic was to run past them in the darkness before they realised who she was. To add to the confusion she also shouted loudly, "Bang! Bang!" as she came up behind the figures.

The enemy were surprised by this attack from behind them and they ran back up the dirt vehicle track, almost tripping over themselves in their haste. Tina took the opportunity and dashed past, still pretending to shoot. A few seconds later she was with Andrew.

"Are you alright Ti?" he asked.

"Fine. Let's get out of here before they realise there are only two of us," she said.

So they retreated back along the road at a quick walk. The enemy made a half-hearted attempt to follow up but when the army cadet sentries joined in the firing they withdrew. Tina and Andrew identified themselves and then boarded the ferry and crossed back to the island.

As they waded ashore Andrew asked, "Well, did you see anything?"

Tina shook her head. "No. Just fog and the HQ houseboat."

"So there wasn't a plane."

"No. But I thought I heard one," Tina replied.

"Just the wind in the trees or something. You are starting to get obsessive about those people Tina. Now, let's get to bed, I'm cold," Andrew answered.

Tina did not reply but went with him back to their bivouac. *I am sure I heard something,* she told herself. But she did not discuss it. Instead she went reluctantly to her own shelter (she really wanted to join Andrew in his), took off her wet socks and boots and slid into her sleeping bag.

But then she could not sleep, wondering if she really was becoming obsessed with the smugglers and if she had only imagined hearing an aircraft.

She was shaken awake by Carmen while it was still dark. "Get dressed, get packed and get up quietly," Carmen whispered.

"Why? What's happening?" Tina queried.

"The army cadets are doing their 'stand-to'," Carmen answered. She then explained how the army cadets, when doing a tactical field exercise, always got up in the dark and packed everything so they were ready to 'march or fight' before dawn.

Stella really grumbled. "More fool them! I'm glad I'm not an army cadet."

It was not well done. Many of the navy cadets began using torches and this drew hisses and rebukes from the army cadets and from the adults and senior ranks. With some difficulty Tina pulled on her socks and boots and then rolled up her bedding in the dark.

She was just finishing this when an eruption of shouting back along the road announced an enemy attack. The only navy cadets involved were two gun crews for the cannon and as Tina was not among their number she could only listen and watch. As a result she only got fleeting glimpses of figures flitting from tree to tree and then splashing into the water towards the island. The gun crews did a lot of shouting and all yelled 'Boom!' in unison to indicate they were firing. That amused Tina and she wished she was with them.

The cannon helped split the attack, but two groups of enemy made it across to the island. Major Wickham had a section of army cadets sitting on their packs nearby as his company reserve and he called them to reinforce the platoon defending the ferry area.

The attack was beaten off and the enemy withdrew except for one who remained as a prisoner. The battle was then ended and everyone on the island was called in for a roll call and briefing. They were seated on their packs in section lines and once Major Wickham was satisfied that nobody was hurt or missing her had the Intelligence Section question the prisoner. He informed the cadets that the French were calling in more tribes of Indians and some *couriers du bois,* plus regular French troops to contest their advance.

"The French have started building a new timber fort at the northeast end of the lake," the prisoner replied. But no, he could not show them where it was on a map as he had not paid attention in school. What he was sure of was that it blocked the roads which went around the north shore of the lake.

Major Wickham then took over. "We must destroy this new fort before it can be completed or it could delay our advance badly. Then the enemy could concentrate a superior force against us and wipe us out." He showed on a map how other British forces (notional only) were advancing on other routes into the area.

Then he indicated the local area on the map. "First we will move as a company to the Danbulla Road. Then we are going to advance on two axes. 4 Platoon will advance north along the Danbulla Road while 5 Platoon advances along the old Boar Pocket Road and connecting timber tracks to come in on the enemy's flank. The cannons are to move by water to RV with us at this creek just north of School Point Campground."

That was the bit that interested Tina and she studied the map with interest. Then she recognised the place. It was just near the small island she had mentally nicknamed 'Swallows and Amazons'.

"Oh, I know that area. We went canoeing there during the holidays," she commented to Andrew.

Breakfast followed and then an Orders Group. By then the first army cadet recon patrols were moving. Graham was in one of these and he gave Tina a cheerful grin and wave as he went. Then the shelters were pulled down and packed, despite showers of gentle drizzle that were starting. The main body of the army cadets was then ferried across to the mainland. Once they had moved off the navy cadets set to work to rig the sheer legs and then to load the cannon and their parts back on the rafts and into the canoes.

Navigation was then worked out and communications checked. The wind was only a stiff breeze, but it was enough to push up a lively chop which made the canoes difficult to handle. The rafts were in no danger of capsizing but the small waves threw up a lot of spray so Tina and her friends were soon very wet. Having a raincoat and Souwester helped keep her warm but not dry.

It was 0930hrs when they set off and nearly 1000hrs when they rounded the next point and headed for Fongon Peninsula. As they did, Tina studied the town of Tinaroo which was only 2 kilometres to the west. It looked closer across the choppy water.

As part of the exercise, the navy cadets landed on the south shore of Fongon Peninsula about 500 metres east of the tip and recon patrols were sent ashore to check whether the French had built a fort or had any cannons on the tip.

"If they have we couldn't sail past," Lt Ryan explained.

This is where Willy's airship drifted overhead, Tina thought.

She was then sent in one of the recon patrols along with Carmen, Stella and a girl from Mackay. Her patrol had to scout the north shore so they pushed their way through a pine plantation along an overgrown fire trail. That was quite unpleasant as the grass was long and wet and there were lots of waist high ferns. The result was soaked trousers and boots.

There was a small group of enemy, but Tina only got a fleeting glimpse of them as they pulled back from the tip when Cadet Midshipman George's patrol attacked them. The patrols were then recalled to the boats. The enemy withdrew inland along the road through the campground and were picked up by a vehicle.

The whole activity took nearly 2 hours, so they stopped for lunch as soon as they had moved the boats to the lee of the peninsula. The HQ houseboat joined them and they were able to get hot cocoa or Milo.

During the lunch break orders for more patrols were issued and four canoes moved out ahead. They were to check the headlands on both sides of the eastern arm of the lake, plus the campground at School Point and a headland near the Kauri Creek Campground which was visible only a kilometre away on the north shore of the lake. Tina and her team stayed on their raft to move the cannon.

The rafts and HQ houseboat waited for half an hour and then followed the canoes. In the lee of the peninsula the waves were minimal and as the afternoon went on the wind died down, even as the rain increased. By the time they passed the narrows into the eastern arm of the lake the waves had died away to almost nothing and the rain had stopped. It was still overcast and quite cold but the hard work of paddling the raft kept Tina warm.

They were re-joined by the canoes which then hurried on ahead again. This time they were to check the small island (Swallows and Amazons Island as Tina had nicknamed it) and their landing site at the end of a headland near it. Tina enjoyed paddling up that stretch of the lake as she had good memories of it from the holidays and she thought it was very pretty.

The HQ houseboat moored itself to a tree on Swallows Island and the rafts came alongside and they waited until all the canoes had reached the shore. That was on the point at the northeast corner of the lake where a road ran up from the lake into an extensive pine forest. As the canoes neared the shore they were fired on by a small group of enemy. The canoes spread out and fired back and then pushed in to beach themselves. As soon as the canoe crews were ashore and skirmishing the HQ houseboat and rafts set off to join them.

Half an hour later Tina was also ashore, but by then the enemy had withdrawn back up into the forest. The navy cadets set to work erecting the sheer legs to unload the cannon. While they were doing this a sentry post of three was placed 100 metres up the vehicle track at a track junction in the pine forest. Half an hour into the task one of the sentries came walking back with Lt Hamilton of the army cadets.

"We need four girls to play a female role for the Control Group for a couple of hours," he explained.

Tina did not really want to be a girl. She wanted to be part of a gun crew. But she was detailed for the task along with Carmen, Stella and Dimity. They left their gear in the canoes and followed Lt Hamilton back up the track. It was easy walking and from the track junction onwards the road was almost straight and clear of grass. As they walked Tina noted two more track junctions where other roads went off through the pine trees. 'Fire breaks?' she wondered.

At the second one of these they found a group of four 'enemy' waiting under cover to contest the advance of the cannon. Lt Hamilton spoke to them and they grinned and promised to make a good battle of it. The girls were led on past them along the vehicle track.

They came to a large clearing. In the middle were several stacks of logs placed there by timber cutters. Lt Hamilton said the logs were the new French fort under construction. Several members of the Control Group were there wearing black tricorne hats with fluffy white trimmings. They were supposed to be French regular troops and a French flag flew from a pole inside the 'stockade'. Inside the fort were parked four vehicles and a portable toilet and there was a 'west wall' just inside the tree line. It was made of hutchies draped over ropes tied at chest height from tree to tree and from a distance looked quite realistic.

"This is good," Tina commented to Carmen.

Carmen nodded and said, "I am really enjoying this exercise story. It gives us navy cadets lots to do."

Lt Hamilton led them on past the fort to a road junction 50 metres further along. As they crossed a good gravel road at a bend Tina recognised it as the Danbulla Road. To her surprise they plunged into the jungle on the other side of the road. For a few moments Tina worried that she might be in for another jungle experience and was not happy. But then she saw that they were now following an old, partly overgrown road.

"An old timber track," Lt Hamilton explained.

A hundred metres along this, in a grassy clearing surrounded by jungle, the group came to an 'Indian village' consisting of three tepees made of sticks and hutchies and some more of the Control Group. There were seven 'Indians'. All were boys and four of them had no shirts on. Two wore only breech clouts, cloths hanging down from front and back. All wore war paint and had feathers attached to their headbands and to sticks they were carrying.

Stella giggled, then turned and whispered behind her hand, "I hope we don't have to dress like those boys!"

Tina imagined herself wearing only two tiny pieces of cloth and a few feathers and went hot with embarrassment. But then she began to fantasize. *That would get Andrew's attention,* she mused.

But that was not the costume they were required to wear. Lt Hamilton held up a long, old fashioned dress. "You girls are to wear these clothes. You are to play act that you are white women who have been captured by the Indians so the British can rescue you."

"Where do we change?" Stella asked, looking first at the flimsy 'tepees' and then at the surrounding rainforest.

"Just pull the dresses on over your uniforms or go back along the track a bit if the shelters aren't good enough," Lt Hamilton replied. He then handed them each an old-fashioned bonnet with ribbons.

The girls pulled on their costumes and as Tina placed the bonnet on her head she had to smile. Watching Dimity tie the ribbon under her chin looked so charming she had to compliment her. "You look really pretty Dimmy," she said.

Dimity blushed but was obviously very pleased. Not so Stella who scowled and said, "Have you become a lemon then?"

"No, why?" Tina replied, hurt by the catty comment but also aware she had probably hurt Stella's feelings by not complimenting her.

It was Carmen who kept the peace and the girls were then positioned at trees on the side of the clearing. The 'Indians' pretended to tie them to the trees and then began a war dance around a pretend fire. One of them began to beat a drum and the others did a lot of whooping and shrill yelping. From time to time they came over and made threatening gestures with plywood tomahawks and knives. Tina did not enjoy that and wondered how she would cope if she was ever tied up by men who really meant to harm her.

As she thought about this, images of Danny, Neville, and Marco formed in her mind. Fear made her look into the jungle in case they were there. But instead of seeing bird smugglers she saw army cadets. They had crept forward and now called on the Indians to surrender. The Indians refused and began a battle. For the next 5 minutes there was a lot of shouting and banging and the Indians either pretended to die or ran away. Tina found a grinning Graham crouching behind a tree facing the way they had gone.

"How are you Ti?" he asked.

"Good. Are you enjoying yourself?" Tina answered.

"Too right! This is a great exercise," Graham answered.

Tina expected to be set free, but Lt Hamilton again appeared and the girls were 'recycled'. "You can be hostages in the fort as well," he explained.

So while the army cadets re-organised and checked the Indians the girls were led back along the old road to the 'fort'. Here they were again tied to trees at the back of the clearing. A few metres away was the west 'wall' of the fort. By then the action had begun. To start with the navy cadet team fought their way up from the lake and as they got closer Tina was able to recognize some of the voices.

I wish I was with them, she thought.

That desire increased when she heard the firing reach the other side of the west 'wall'. The defenders on that side fell back inside the fort and began firing over the top of the wall, their faces flushed with excitement. By that time the army cadets had driven back the outposts from the direction of the Indian village and were in action with the defenders of the fort. Tina was able to spot some of the attackers flitting through the edge of the pine plantation as they encircled the fort.

There followed a series of probes and attacks that revealed that the fort was surrounded. There was a lot shouting and pretend shooting and then a 20-minute lull. During that the girls were allowed to have a drink and sit in the shade.

Then came what Tina had expected. From the west sounded the loud shouted 'boom!' of the cannon pretend firing. She had to smile at that and when one of the army cadet OOCs walked over and untied one of the ropes holding a hutchie, allowing it to drop she grinned at the other girls and teased the French.

Carmen grinned back. "Our cannon are blowing down their wall," she said.

The army cadet OOC nodded and said, "Making a breach to assault through."

As that was the whole point of dragging the cannon all that way Tina felt really pleased. "I wish I was one of the gun crew," she commented.

Carmen gave a nod and answered, "We will make sure we have a go next time."

The cannon 'fired' four more times and each time a section of the north or west wall was 'blown' down. Then the British infantry attacked from the north. As they did the cannon fired from their flank and the OOC told half the defenders to die. "They have just fired grape shot," he explained.

The battle then raged fast and furious for a few minutes and Tina saw a yelling and wildly excited Graham clamber up over a pile of logs to shoot down at the defenders. *He is really having a good time,* she told herself. Then she blushed at her memories but that made her sure that she did not love him. *It is Andrew,* she told herself.

This idea was reinforced a few minutes later when the navy cadet team came running in to join the attack and she saw Andrew run across. When he saw her, he immediately detoured and set to work untying her. While he puzzled over the knots, Tina grinned and just unwrapped the ropes.

"It's alright Andrew. They are only pretend knots," she said.

For several seconds the pair stood looking at each other and Tina experienced a strong desire to fling her arms around his neck. He must have been feeling the same way as he suddenly leaned forward and kissed her on the cheek.

"I love you," he murmured.

Then Tina did put her arms around his neck and return the kiss but this time on his lips. "My hero!" she whispered.

She was then interrupted by Stella calling loudly, "Hoy! None of that you two!"

Carmen turned and added, "Save that for later. Come on, we are being called in for roll call and briefing." Then she met Tina's eyes and smiled.

Tina saw that the battle was over and that the army cadets were moving to sit in their section lines. She smiled and blushed but felt extremely happy. *I have succeeded,* she thought. *He has noticed me!* Feeling almost euphoric she joined navy cadet team and sat to have her name checked off.

There was then a 20-minute briefing by Major Wickham who explained the action. A prisoner was then questioned and he explained that the Indians had captured a group of missionaries and nuns and that they planned to kill them at sun rise in a ritual sacrifice at a place called Platypus Lookout. This was located on the map and Major Wickham told them it was 16 kilometres away.

"We will march there during the night and try to rescue the prisoners. The navy cadets will transport the cannon there in case they are needed as the Lookout may have been fortified. We will now have orders for these moves," he said.

Lt Ryan then called the navy cadets aside. Once they were away from the army cadets he said: "Navy, listen in. We will drag the cannon back to the lake and have our orders there. We will be moving in daylight to camp near Platypus Lookout. We have 7 kilometres to go and that will take about two hours, so we need to move. It is 1600hrs now, and if we move we can be afloat by 1630hrs and at the Platypus Campground by 1800hrs. So work parties to the gun and you girls get out of those costumes and come and join us. Let's move!"

They moved. Tina and the other three girls walked back across the clearing to where Lt Hamilton was collecting items of costume from a group of army cadets. While standing in line Tina learned that these cadets had only been in the Control Group that day. The exercise was planned so that every section was rostered to provide the Control Group with extra numbers at key times.

By the time the girls handed back their clothing the navy cadets and the cannon had vanished back along the road through the pine forest. Tina was last in line and as she turned to follow them her eye noted the nearby portable toilet. Thinking it might be more pleasant to use than squatting in the long grass and weeds she turned to Stella. "I will just go to the toilet. I won't be a minute."

Stella made a face and kept on walking while Tina hurried over to the toilet. But she was a few seconds too late and a female army cadet beat her to it. So she stood and waited. When the other girl came out Tina went in, and wondered if the bush might not have been better as the tiny cubicle had a horrible chemical and waste smell. But she did what she had to and then hurriedly dressed.

To her annoyance when she stepped out there was no sign of Stella. *She could have waited,* Tina mentally grumbled.

But she was not worried as she knew the canoes and rafts were only a few hundred metres along the road. So she hurried across the clearing and on along the dirt vehicle track through the pine forest. Her only concern was keeping the others waiting. With that in mind she walked as fast as she could. At almost every step she expected to see the other girls or the teams dragging the two cannon.

The pine forest was very peaceful in the late afternoon and she sniffed the odour of resin and felt very happy. *I am really enjoying this exercise,* she thought as she hurried past a road junction.

A minute later she came to the second one. Here she hesitated but only for a second or so as she could clearly see that the left hand one had been recently used, the grass having been crushed by wheels. So she went left.

The vehicle track curved slightly and went downhill through more pine forest. As Tina hurried along a niggling worry came to her that things didn't quite look right.

Have I taken the correct track? she wondered.

Now feeling somewhat worried she hurried on around the bend. Ahead of her she caught a glimpse of water glinting in the sunlight. *The lake. Not far now,* she thought.

Then the back of a vehicle came into view and that bothered her more. She came to a stop and looked around. As she did, she heard the undergrowth crackle beside her and she glanced that way. Into her horrified gaze stepped Danny the smuggler!

He said, "Go back! No cadets allowed down this... Holy Moley! You, you bitch!"

Oh no! I have taken the wrong turn, Tina thought.

Even As she did, she spun round and started to run, fear pulsing into her veins.

Chapter 44

KNOTS AND LASHINGS

But this time there was no escape. Within 10 paces Danny had caught up with her and grabbed her shirt from behind. Tina was so terrified she almost lost control of her body. Frantically, she struggled to break free but then his arm went around her neck.

"Help! Hel..." she cried.

Whack!

A smashing blow to the side of her head half stunned Tina and she staggered and gasped. Danny held her up and then clamped a hand over her mouth and gripped her throat. Tina began to choke and as the panic stabbed through her she was sure he was going to strangle her to death.

But he didn't. Instead he changed his grip and then shoved a dirty, oil-soaked rag into her mouth. The fumes at once caught at the back of Tina's throat and she began to cough and feel nauseous. She tried to pull the rag out, but Danny smacked her again and snarled, "Leave it in! Stop struggling or I will really hurt you."

Tina did. Danny was much too strong for her and she was almost paralysed by terror. She was so afraid she was sure she was going to lose control of her bowels or bladder. Only a residual shred of pride helped her keep control.

Wait your chance, she told herself, hoping there would be an opportunity. At the front of her mind was the certainty that the cadets would come looking for her in a few minutes and she would be saved. *These men won't dare do anything to me with all the cadets in the area,* she told herself.

Danny then disconcerted her more by dragging her down the vehicle track to where two vehicles were parked. As she was hauled around the bend Tina was dismayed to see both Marco and Kostis sitting in folding chairs under a tarpaulin strung between the trees. Further down she saw a tent and then got a glimpse of the floatplane floating under a camouflage net.

I was right. I did hear the plane land, she told herself.

But it was small compensation for the fear that was gripping her. Danny held her tight and said gloatingly. "Look who I caught!"

"Her!" Marco cried angrily. "What is she doing here? Hey girl, how come you always finding us? Who tell you, eh?"

Tina could only shake her head. Marco went to pull the rag out and snarled, "Answer me!"

But Danny held her away. "No Marco. Leave the gag in. There are hundreds of those bloody cadets just up the track and if she screams they will hear her."

"So they come looking for her anyway when they find she is missing, eh?" Kostis suggested.

"Yeah, but we will say we ain't seen her and then we will help them look for her," Danny replied.

"What we do with her?" Marco asked.

"Put her in the lake," Kostis answered.

Tina was so shocked and terrified when the meaning of that sank in that she whimpered. Ghastly images from her nightmares of the clutching hand sticking up out of the lake swirled across the screen of her mind. She would have begged but was only able to shake her head vigorously and use her eyes to plead.

To her relief Danny said no. "We can get rid of her later, out over the sea," he said, chilling Tina even more so that she was almost reduced to a quivering wreck.

"What we do with her until then?" Marco asked.

Danny answered, "We tie her up and hide her in the tent or in the plane. Then we keep the cadets from looking in the tent," he answered.

"But I want to know how she find us each time," Kostis said.

"We can question her later, after these cadets have left the area," Danny replied.

"What if they stay?" Marco countered.

Danny shook Tina and turned her to look into her eyes at very close range so that she could smell his foul breath and sweat. "Are the cadets staying here? Answer me girlie."

Tina shook her head and got a smack for her pains. Danny snarled, "You better be tellin' the truth kid."

Marco looked worried. "We better tell the boss, eh?"

"Yeah. I will call the boss on my mobile phone. We will keep her out of sight until he tells us what to do. You two tie her up and I will go back up the track and keep any nosy cadets from coming down to the camp. We don't want them to see the plane," Danny answered.

On hearing that Tina's hopes plummeted. To her dismay, Marco took hold of her, clasping his huge hairy arms around her body, squashing her breasts as he did. But Tina was so frightened she barely noticed. He picked her up and carried her down to the tent pitched near the edge of the lake. Tina got a chance to look around but was disappointed to see that a screen of reeds and bushes largely hid the tent from the creek that the plane was moored in. She realised it was the creek that had all the dead reeds near its mouth.

Oil from the plane has killed the vegetation, she surmised.

What really galled her was knowing that Swallows Island was just out of sight around the bend and that meant the HQ houseboat. To add to her distress was the knowledge that Andrew and the others were only a few hundred metres away.

Just around at the end of the peninsula, she thought. Then she heard faint shouts which could only come from her friends. *Oh they must notice I am missing soon,* she thought.

Marco stood her in the tent and gruffly ordered her to turn around and to put her hands behind her back. Tina reluctantly did as she was told. But As she did, she remembered something she had read about a person escaping by holding their hands as far apart as they could. So she placed the sides of her hands together and hoped that Kostis would not notice. He didn't. He picked up some rough sisal rope which lay in a tangle on the ground amid the litter of camping gear and personal possessions. Using it he quickly and roughly bound her wrists together. As he did, Tina tensed to stop her wrists slipping together. In this she was only partly successful as it felt like the whole of her forearms had been wrapped up by some sort of lashing.

While this was being done to her Tina looked hopefully out through the open back of the tent. As she did, she again heard distant shouts and that sent her hopes up. But then a canoe appeared out on the lake. It was being paddled rapidly away.

They aren't leaving surely? she wondered in dismay. Her hopes received another blow when she clearly heard the command 'heave'.

That told her that the navy cadets were loading the cannon onto the rafts. *They must have noticed I am not with them,* she thought anxiously.

But more canoes appeared out on the water. By then the first was well across the lake and as she watched it vanished from view behind a headland. Tina felt such a sense of desperation she began to hyperventilate. Coupled with the fumes from the oily rag it made her dizzy and nauseous. She reeled and staggered and was then roughly pushed down.

"Lie down bitch so we can tie your legs," Marco ordered.

Tina had no choice but obey. She was so shocked she did not even kick or struggle. But she did have the presence of mind to place her ankle bones touching each other. Marco took another piece of rope and quickly bound her ankles together. That was painful as the ankle bones pressed on each other, but Tina could only whimper and shake her head. Tears came and trickled down her face. She was rolled into the corner of the tent behind a row of stretchers and the two men set to work to close the flaps.

As the tent was laced up Tina felt crushed by despair. She rolled on her side to watch but felt too ill and frightened to do anything. Then she heard Kostis say he would check the plane was ready. "Just in case we need to make a da quick getaway."

Silence settled, broken by an occasional sound that indicated that Marco was still outside. 20 minutes went by during which Tina was tormented by fear of dying and images of death.

Then she heard voices. Marco said, "What the kids do Danny?"

"I think they are gone," Danny replied.

"Both lots? The ones at the clearing too?" Marco answered.

"Don't know," Danny replied. Then he asked, "Where's the girl?"

"In the tent."

Tina heard footsteps and the flap over a small window was lifted. Danny looked in and their eyes met. Danny nodded and let the flap drop again. "Good," he said.

Marco asked, "What the boss say to do?"

"Keep her prisoner and Kostis is to take her with him in the plane. The boss wants to question her to find out how it is she always seems to be bumping into us."

"What we do with her after that?" Marco asked.

Danny grunted and said, "Get rid of her somehow. Chuck her out

425

over the sea would be a good idea. Now, let's check that these bloody kids are gone. Get Kostis. He can wait at the track junction while I go one way and you go the other."

On hearing that Tina felt a surge of hope. *If all three leave I might have a chance of getting away,* she reasoned. But she waited until she heard the three men walking away before she began feeling the knots and lashings which bound her.

Almost at once her hopes went up. The knots did not feel right to her. Frequent competitions at Navy Cadets where she had raced others in tying knots blindfolded made her familiar with them. *These noddies don't know their knots,* she thought. Carefully she explored the knots with her fingers and having found an end tried to push it back through the knot.

When that didn't work she wriggled her wrists and was gratified to feel a slight easing of the pressure as her hands slipped off each other so that the narrower wrists were together. She then moved her legs so that the ankle bones slid off each other. The relief from the burning pain made the effort worthwhile, she decided. But more squirming and wriggling did not seem to loosen the ropes.

Despite that she did not give up hope and began to patiently feel around each rope and then to work out which way it had to be pulled to loosen it. Using fingers that were rapidly going numb she twisted, tugged and pulled. Her training on knots and lashings at Navy Cadets told her that the way to get a rope to move was to twist it in the direction of the 'lay'. This tightened it and made its diameter smaller. But 20 minutes of struggling and twisting did not seem to have any effect.

Then she heard the men coming back and bitter despair welled up in her. *Oh blast!* she thought miserably. Feelings of absolute failure and terror swamped her for a few minutes.

The tent was then unlaced and Danny came in and he roughly rolled Tina over and examined the knots. With a grunt of satisfaction he left the tent and laced it up again.

"She's still trussed up like the proverbial turkey. You did a good job Marco," he said with a cruel laugh.

When the tent had been opened Tina had noticed that the light outside was considerably dimmer. Dusk was setting in and the sunlight had already gone off the treetops. *Surely my friends have realised I am not with them?* she thought.

The men thought so too, as Marco said, "I'm surprised nobody come looking for her, eh?"

"You'd think they would have noticed," agreed Danny.

"They must be slack lot," Marco opined.

Tina thought the same. *Surely, they have noticed? Surely Andrew knows I am not in his canoe?* she puzzled. But it seemed that they had not and she was plunged into even deeper despair.

A lantern was lit and then a gas stove. The two men began cooking tea. As they did, they talked and Tina gathered from what she overheard of the conversation that the navy cadets had indeed gone but that the army cadets were still at the clearing.

They won't be leaving until midnight, she remembered. *So I must escape before then.*

The smugglers were particularly annoyed as they could not drive their vehicles out and did not want to risk the sound of the plane taking off being heard. "As soon as we have had a feed I will go and check if those bloody cadets are still there and you can take over from Kostis as guard at the track junction," Danny said.

The smugglers settled to their eating and Tina lay in the tent, her moods alternating between terrified despair and frantic hope. Once again, she set to work on the knots but after another half hour nothing seemed to have loosened. By then it was quite dark, the sun having gone and no moon being up. Inside the tent it was pitch black.

When Danny again checked her bonds 10 minutes later, he had to use a torch. Seeing that she was still tied up he called out, "OK Marco, you come with me and take over as guard at the track junction just in case there are more of these bloody kids around."

Tina then heard the sound of the men's voices fading away as they walked off up the track. *Now is my chance,* she told herself. *There is no-one here.*

But how to get the knots undone? Her mind turned to knives and other sharp tools, but she had seen none in the tent. In the hope that there might be one outside where the men had been cooking, she rolled and squirmed across to the front of the tent. But to her dismay she found she could not push her way under the laced-up flap. She tried the side of the tent, but it was pegged firmly down. Black despair engulfed her and she began to sob and shake. Then she prayed as she had never prayed before.

Images of being thrown out of the floatplane, presumably still tied up, to fall into the ocean caused her to sweat with terror.

After a few minutes, she lay back exhausted and quietly cried. But she was now dehydrated and her eyes became hot and scratchy. In the grip of chest-tightening apprehension she slumped down and shook her head.

Oh what am I to do? Why haven't the others noticed I am missing? she thought miserably.

Then her hopes crashed once more when she heard voices. The men came back: Marco and Kostis. *Danny must be guarding the track,* she decided. A torch shone on her through the tent window and she heard Marco say she was still there and well and truly tied up.

I am too, Tina thought.

Despair welled up and she wept a few more scratchy tears. For a while she lay there all but overcome by black despair. The men sat outside and talked, a lantern providing some light.

Then Tina became desperate. *Time is slipping away. I must get free,* she told herself.

Having failed to undo the knots she set herself to try to cut a rope. She wriggled around feeling for something sharp but was unable to find anything. That disheartened her but she stubbornly persisted. For several more minutes she tried to get her wrists free. Then she stopped and lay back panting from the effort. *Silly!* she told herself.

Get your feet free. You can walk away then and worry about the hands later.

So she concentrated on the ropes binding her lower legs. Arching her back she reached behind her to get at the ropes more easily. For lack of any other plan she set to work with her fingernails, sawing at a single strand of the sisal fibre.

It took her perhaps 10 minutes to sever just one strand, but she was able to peel it back and felt better. The exercise also helped to take some of the numbness out of her fingers and wrists. She then picked and sawed at another fibre. This one was cut through in only a couple of minutes. With each one Tina improved her technique until she was able to slice a fibre a minute. With each one she cut she was able to feel the rope getting thinner.

Finally she was able to sever the entire rope. It took her more than two hours, during which the men outside twice looked in. They saw nothing unusual and then she heard Marco say it was time to relieve Danny. He walked off and Kostis sat down again. Tina resumed her work on trying to unravel the severed rope.

Danny returned and shone a torch on her. Tina pretended to be asleep and Danny just grunted and moved away. He began talking to Kostis but she was unable to hear most of what was said. What she did understand was that the smugglers were going to fly out over the Coral Sea to rendezvous with a motor launch at some atoll or reef. That was obviously how they had been operating.

But it was sour satisfaction to learn this if she was about to die and could do nothing about it. That, added to her terror of imminent death, sent her to work again, twisting and pushing the loose strands of fibre through the tangle of ropes. Cramps and aching muscles caused her to sob and stop from time to time and dehydration and dizziness added to her woes. But she kept on trying.

Suddenly Tina went still. Very cautiously she moved her fingers. *Is it?* she wondered.

Yes it was! The rope around her ankles was definitely loose. Hope surged and she flexed the fingertips on her left hand. For several more minutes she tried to get her wrists free. Then she stopped and lay back panting from the effort. Almost at once she found the ropes were looser. She was just able to grip with her fingers enough to twist and push at the coils. To her joy the rope began to move. Wanting to rush but knowing she must be careful she kept on pulling strand after strand of the hairy sisal rope back through the tangle.

Suddenly the ringing of a mobile phone broke the silence. Then Danny's voice spoke. "Yes boss. No, I don't know if they are still there. Yes boss. Call you in half an hour." Tina heard him ring off and then he said, "Kostis, you guard the camp and the girl. Marco, come with me. The boss wants to know if he can drive here."

"What time is it?" Marco asked.

"Nearly ten O'clock. If they are still there, they are probably staying all night so we might have to risk them hearing us and take off. Come on Marco."

Tina heard the sound of receding voices. Then Kostis shone his torch in on Tina. Satisfied she was still there he resumed his seat, muttering grumpily in some foreign language. Tina set to work on the ropes in feverish desperation.

This might be my only chance, she thought.

Then suddenly the bindings came undone. Tina found one end loose in her hand and she sobbed with happiness. *Oh yes!* she told herself. In a fever of impatience she began unwinding the rope from around her ankles.

Nearly ten, she told herself. She wracked her brain to try to remember what time the army cadets were going to move but could not. *They had 16 kilometres to march. How long will that take in the dark?* she wondered. She fervently hoped they were still there. *I must try to get to them,* she thought.

Suddenly she went tense. Footsteps were approaching the tent. *Oh no! They are coming back!* Tina thought, the terror clutching at her heart again.

Trembling with anxiety she quickly wound the rope back around her ankle, then lay on her side, arching her back to keep hold of the rope behind her so that it looked tight.

It was Danny. He unlaced the tent and said, "Bloody cadets are still there. I am going to have a lie down. Marco is on guard. You have a sleep and take over from him at midnight Kostis."

That dashed Tina's hopes. She lay still and pretended to be asleep while almost quivering with fear as Danny came in. *Oh I hope he doesn't discover I have cut a rope,* she thought.

Danny's first act was to walk over and shine his torch on her. Tina lay still and tried to not tense up. To her intense relief Danny apparently saw no problem as he walked to the stretcher nearest the front and lay down on it. Kostis also came in, carrying the lantern. He rearranged the bedding on the stretcher right next to Tina. He also glanced at her before turning off the lantern. Tina was left lying in the dark only a metre from the man.

At first she was gripped by a sense of bitter defeat, but after a while, when it became obvious that the two men had gone to sleep, she determined to try to escape. *They have left the front unlaced. If I can get my legs free I can walk away,* she told herself.

Quietly she set to work on the ropes again, tensing and stopping every time Marco moved. But when he began to snore loudly, she moved with more confidence. Even so it took her more than an hour to completely unwind the ropes from her ankles. The hardest bit was untying the knot that secured one end of the rope to her right ankle.

But it was done at last and Tina lay and gently eased her legs and tried to warm the cramped muscles by moving them. By then she was in a lather of anxiety despite the cold. *If I don't hurry then Kostis will wake up and find I am free,* she thought. She presumed Kostis had an alarm in his wristwatch.

As soon as she felt sure that her legs would work, she rolled onto her front and tried to stand up. But that proved to be much harder than she had expected. With her hands still tied behind her all that seemed to happen was to push her face into the mud and grass. But fear of death gave her the desperate strength to ignore such petty discomfort and she quickly found she could recline. Even then it took some struggling to get over onto her knees. Twice she fell and each time she lay still for fear the noise might have woken the men.

Then she was on her feet! Very carefully she stood upright. For a few seconds she stood listening while her legs trembled almost uncontrollably. Then she began tip-toeing towards the front of the tent. A sudden noise and movement by Kostis caused her to freeze and she stared hard at him in the darkness. Then he grunted and let out a huge fart.

Men! Tina thought. *Disgusting creatures!*

But she had to smile and continued moving cautiously past the sleeping men. Passing Danny she found more of an ordeal but a few seconds later she was at the front flaps and very slowly pushed them apart and slid through.

I'm out. Now I must free my hands, she thought, as a sense of exultation surged in her chest.

It was dark with no moon, but it was light enough to see and Tina noted the folding table and barbeque. And there was the instrument she wanted. A knife lay on the table, its blade gleaming in the starlight. Then she discovered that having the knife and being able to use it were too quite different things. For a few seconds she was tempted to start walking up the track without waiting but now she paused.

Marco is on guard somewhere along the track, she reasoned. *How do I sneak past him?* But the only other choice was down to the lake. *Do they have a boat?* she wondered.

With that in mind she turned and walked slowly down past the side of the tent, still with her hands tied. There was a boat, a large tinnie with an outboard engine. But it was on a boat trailer and was 10 metres away from the water.

I will never be able to get that in the water without making too much noise, she thought.

Once again, a feeling of defeat gripped her. There seemed to be no option but to try to locate Marco and sneak past him. So she turned and started walking back past the tent.

But As she did, she heard a twig snap up the track and then the crunch and thud of footsteps. A dark bulky figure came into view among the trees.

Marco! He is coming back! Tina thought in panic.

Chapter 45

TRAPPED!

Tina froze in shock. Panic welled up but she managed to keep control. *Hide!* she told herself.

The nearest place was behind the boat. In two steps she was behind it and then she crouched. But even as she did, her whirling thoughts told her she was in real trouble. *They will discover I have escaped. I must get away,* she told herself.

But Marco reached the tent and went inside. Through her mind fitted the concept that the devil was in front and the deep blue lake behind. Trembling with apprehension, she tried to think out what to do. There seemed to be only three options: run up the track as soon as Marco went into the tent; try to escape through the forest, or the water behind her.

Suddenly her thoughts crystallised. *The lake!* she thought.

She felt sure that the men would hear her and catch her if she tried to run or if she attempted to push through the forest in the dark. Knowing she had only seconds to act she turned and walked quickly down to the edge of the water. Here she hesitated, but only for a second as an angry yell erupted from the tent behind her.

They know I have gone, she thought.

Impelled by fear she waded slowly into the water, trying not to splash or make ripples. To her surprise the water did not feel cold and she was soon knee deep. By the time Danny's angry voice sounded as he woke Kostis she was up to her waist. The bottom was sludgy mire, but she did not hesitate.

Moving sideways out of the cleared lane leading up from where the boat had been launched, she waded in among the reeds. To her dismay she found that water weeds were entangling her feet, making it hard for her to move or keep her balance. *If I slip over, I could drown,* she thought.

So she slowed and edged further along the outside edge of the reeds. There she stopped and turned her attention to trying to cut the ropes without dropping the knife.

"If I drop the knife I am done for," she muttered.

By then the camp was in uproar with Danny roundly abusing both Kostis and Marco. Tina saw torch beams flashing in various directions and lowered herself until only her head was out of the water. Someone ran off up the track and another person went hunting around the tent. Then a torch beam was directed out onto the creek. This lit up the floatplane which was floating at the end of a rope just near Tina. Tina could see numerous ripples caused by her movements but apparently the man noticed nothing and most of the time the beam was swept over the aircraft.

Then she heard Danny call and say, "Check the edge of the forest Kostis. Look for tracks, look for vegetation that has been crushed or flattened."

As soon as the torch beam moved away Tina resumed moving to put more distance between her and the camp. It was only after she had moved another 10 metres that she realised she had instinctively moved in the direction where the navy cadets had beached their canoes. That direction led her towards the open lake and away from the army cadets.

I should have gone up the creek. she thought.

The thought that she could not swim with her hands tied stopped her and she resumed her sawing at the ropes. It was difficult as she had to turn the knife around and shove the blade upwards through the bindings. Then she could only push it up and down without much pressure on the actual rope. But desperation lent her strength and she kept cutting until she realised she was stirring up quite large ripples.

She paused and found she was panting for breath. *Slow down! Get control!* she told herself.

For a minute or so she stood shivering in the water and recovered her breath. The search was still going on and she could hear angry mutterings, but it seemed the men were focused on the forest up the track from the camp.

Tina resumed her efforts to cut the rope and she was rewarded by feeling a rope come loose. By then she had cut herself several times, but she ignored that and began flexing her hands while continuing to saw. Suddenly the bindings all came loose, and several coils fell down over her hands. She wanted to cheer and felt such a surge of hope she gasped and trembled. Then she carefully wriggled, plucked and cut at the ropes until they fell away and her wrists came free. With a sob of relief she moved her hands around to her front.

For another couple of minutes she could do nothing but stand and shiver as waves of pain swept through her wrists and hands. Then she gingerly cut or untied the remaining bonds. As she recovered, she began to plan her next move.

She was helped by hearing Danny say, "Kostis, you guard the camp. I am going to check if those army cadets are still there."

"What if the girl is there?" Kostis queried.

"Then I will shoot the bitch and then we get out of here. Now keep watch," Danny snarled.

That comment chilled Tina and also told her that Danny was armed. Memories of him shooting at her at Koombooloomba made her very conscious that it was no idle threat. *I must be very careful,* she thought.

At that moment, a torch beam swept out across the creek and lit up the floatplane again. It then moved away and Tina saw it moving around the tent. Suddenly an idea came to her. She was still clutching the knife and now determined to use it.

Placing the knife between her teeth in the best pirate fashion, Tina lowered herself into the water and began a slow breaststroke towards the plane. It took her a real effort of willpower to swim out into the dark, deep water as all the horrible images from her nightmares welled up to frighten her. But now she was determined. Being very conscious of the danger of either drowning or being shot, she swam out across the creek to put more distance between her and the men. Then she angled in until the floatplane was between her and the camp. A minute later she was clinging to the port float and peeking over it.

It was the smell that gave her the next idea. *I need to disable this plane if the crooks are to be caught,* she told herself. But how? She knew very little about the mechanics of aeroplanes and she saw that to do anything she would have to haul herself up out of the water. *That will be hard to do without making a lot of splashing noises,* she thought.

Reluctantly, she opted for the lesser nuisance of casting the floatplane adrift. *That will at least hold them up for a while,* she thought. She knew it was only petty revenge and that it could backfire on her by telegraphing which way she had left the camp, but she went ahead with the plan. *They won't know which way I swam after I set the plane adrift,* she decided.

The knife came into use and a few seconds later the mooring rope was cut. Tina slid the knife into her waistband and then gripped the end of the rope in her teeth and began to breaststroke towards the lake. It took an effort to get the aircraft moving, but once it was she was able to tow it fairly easily. At each stroke she glanced back at the camp to check that she hadn't been seen.

As soon as the mouth of the creek came into view, she changed her mind about what to do next. She had considered swimming across to Swallows Island, or even to the far side of the lake, but now she gave that idea up. *It is too far. I am weakening too fast. I will drown,* she thought.

So she cast the plane off and gave it a last shove then turned and swam back the way she had come. She knew that was a risk too but reasoned that hiding among the reeds and bushes on the shore of the lake was not a good plan. *The crooks can come searching for me in their power boat and a spotlight will quickly pick me up,* she thought.

She decided that trying to reach the army cadets remained her best option. So she angled across to the far side of the creek and very cautiously breast stoked past the camp. As she did, she saw only one brief flicker of a torch and that appeared to be up the track beyond the tent.

By this time she was feeling both exhausted and cold. Despite the danger she floated to get her breath back and then eased into a sidestroke to keep the camp under continuous observation. As she swam, she kept having to fight down panicky fears about what might be lurking in the black, slimy water. When she did touch weeds or reeds, she let out little gasps of fright and had to calm herself.

Then the camp was out of sight behind her and she was able to relax a bit. She saw that the creek was narrowing in and she began to encounter more and more floating weeds. A thick, dark tangle of bushes and reeds hemmed her in on both sides. After another 50 metres there was no longer a clear channel and she had to push through an ever-thickening tangle.

It became harder and harder for Tina to swim and she resorted to hauling herself forwards across the matt of floating lilies and grass. She began to consider pushing through the tangle of vegetation to reach dry land. *Maybe it will be easier to creep through the pine forest?* she wondered. But her memory told her it would be awful, all ferns long grass and prickly weeds.

Behind her she heard an angry shout. She turned and looked back but was around a bend in the creek and only glimpsed a few flickers of torch light. *They have discovered that the floatplane is gone,* she decided. Now the fat was in the fire! *They will really be after me now!* she thought. But it was with a mixture of fierce satisfaction and fear.

Behind her she heard angry voices muttering and some metallic noises followed by splashing. *Launching their boat?* she wondered.

Then she heard more voices and clearly the words 'lake' and 'that way'. She went all tense with anxiety in case the crooks followed her muddy trail. Next came the purring putter of a boat's outboard motor and, to her intense relief, it faded away.

They have gone out onto the lake! She thought. *Once they have retrieved their float plane, they will look for me.*

Spurred by fear, Tina continued on up the creek and again found a narrow channel but it was now so shallow she could touch bottom. But that was no use as the bottom was all slush and mud, so she had to keep half-swimming, half-crawling. She came to a stop, gasping and worn out. Ahead of her she could see a black wall of dense vegetation and a dark, horizontal line.

That is the bridge on the Danbulla Forest Drive, she thought, *and the trees are the jungle where the Indian village was.*

Cheered up she pushed forward and then came to a terrified stop. Something had slithered across the lilies near her and had slipped into the water. *Snake?* she wondered.

For a few seconds she floundered there on the edge of hysteria. She was gripped by an intense desire to pull her legs up and kept cringing at every touch from a weed or reed. Then she knew she had to get out of the water.

Driven by a phobia induced panic she clawed, stumbled, and floundered up out of the creek into the belt of weeds and bushes on her left. Almost at once she was brought up short by thorns and prickly bushes. She came to a panting, sobbing halt and crouched trembling and shaking in the dark undergrowth. For several minutes she was quite unable to move.

It was the sound of a motor that brought her back to her senses. *A vehicle, and it is just up there where the fort clearing is,* Tina thought.

She stood up and tried to look over the top of the bushes. She was just in time to see the beam from the headlights of a vehicle flicker across the treetops and then she heard it accelerate away from her along the main road.

Was that the army cadets, or the crooks? she wondered. Another spasm of panic seized her. *I must catch up with the army cadets.*

But were they gone? She began pushing through the undergrowth, almost heedless of the scratches of lantana and the pain of thorns ripping her arms and body. It was a log that stopped her mad rush. She banged her shins against it and went sprawling in the weeds. Tears welled up and the pain was so intense that for several seconds all Tina could do was grip her ankles and rock back and forth whimpering.

Then she heard another vehicle. The sound came from the forest off to her left and she knew at once it was the crooks. Fear helped her regain control and she crouched behind a tree and tried to recover her breath. She saw the light from the headlights flicker on the trees and then heard it slow. It then turned towards her and she saw the beam of the headlights shine out just over her head.

Have they seen me? she wondered.

But the vehicle did not stop. Instead it swung around the clearing and then turned and went out onto the Danbulla Road. But this time the vehicle turned right. Tina got a glimpse of it as it roared off down the road to the bridge. She expected it to stop there but instead it drove on up the next hill and vanished from sight. As the sound of its engine died away in the distance Tina puzzled over what it might mean.

Have the crooks run away? she wondered. And what did they do about the floatplane?

Having no answers she resumed forcing her way through the forest but this time much more cautiously, feeling where she put each foot and pushing the worst of the prickly plants away from her face. Gnawing at her was the fear of Danny waiting for her at the clearing. She pictured him crouching behind some logs or behind a tree on the edge of the clearing, the gun ready. So she crept forward, straining her ears to listen and cursing very sound she made herself.

Because the undergrowth was so thick her progress became a crawl. Soaked as she was, she began to shiver as the temperature dropped. Once she thought she heard something and stayed crouched and tense for several minutes. Eventually she decided she was mistaken and resumed her painful progress.

At last she reached the edge of the 'fort' clearing. Here she knelt behind a tree and carefully looked in all directions. Her worry that she was much too late to meet up with the army cadets was quickly confirmed, sending her hopes plummeting again. In the starlight the place had a deserted and sinister look about it, the piles of logs making pools of shadow that could hide anything. There were certainly no vehicles there and she did not dare call out. She knew that any army cadets there might be very quiet but not that silent.

They aren't that good, she told herself.

But was Danny still waiting for her? The thought almost paralysed her with fear. Again she waited and listened while straining her eyes to search the numerous blobs of shadow. After a while she shook her head.

He might be, but I can't afford to wait. I have to catch up with the army cadets.

Wondering how much of a head start they might have, she crouched behind a pile of logs and pushed the button to light up the display on her watch: 0145hrs!

Tina was shocked. She then did a quick calculation. *If the army cadets left at midnight they must be a long way away now,* she thought. *That was a demoralising idea but she had to accept it. The sooner I start the sooner I might catch them up,* she decided.

But it took a real effort of courage to start walking. Her mind had already worked out that one or more of the smugglers might be waiting along the road. *They could just sit beside the road in the darkness and I will have no warning at all,* she thought, picturing them jumping out to grab her, or worse.

But despite her fear she forced herself to get moving. *I will freeze to death if I just sit here,* she told herself, although all she really wanted to do was lie down and sleep. By this time she felt utterly exhausted and was both hungry and very thirsty.

Skirting carefully around the right-hand edge of the clearing she made her way along the dirt road to the Danbulla Road. At the junction she stopped and listened, her imagination conjuring up smugglers waiting in the darkness under the trees. But the only sound was the whisper of the wind in the leaves so she reluctantly resumed walking.

Within 100 paces her courage almost failed her. The road went into a tunnel of rainforest and in under the trees it was so dark she literally could not see her hand in front of her face. All she could discern in the blackness was a vaguer tone of dark grey that indicated the gravel surface of the road. But even that was a poor guide and she kept straying into the slushy verge or even into the edge of the jungle. Only by walking on the crown of the road, and that by feel, could she make good progress.

Tina was dismayed at how loud the crunch of her boots sounded on the gravel and sand but after a time she became resigned to that. *If I creep along it will take days to walk the distance,* she told herself. But 16 kilometres seemed to be a daunting distance. *Can I do it?* she wondered.

Then it began to rain. That really lowered her spirits and she was soon soaked again. This undid all the warming effect of walking. The dripping and gurgling at least helped cloak the sound of her boots but the road surface became muddy and several times she slipped. Only by muscle wrenching effort did she keep upright.

Then she encountered a real problem. The sound of running water warned her she was coming to a creek. Her boots suddenly thudded on concrete overlain by sand. Then her shins struck the concrete kerbing of a bridge and the next thing she knew she had fallen heavily. She landed across the concrete kerb, the blow slamming into her right knee and chest, winding her. Just in time she realised she was falling, and she gripped the kerbing and pushed away. It was so dark she could not see anything of the bridge or road, but she fell back onto the roadway with a painful bump which bruised her buttocks.

For several minutes Tina sat there, whimpering and rubbing her smarting knee, ankles and elbows. Her heart rate had shot up to a rapid hammering. As awareness sank in of how close she had come to a potentially disastrous fall she broke into a fit of trembling. She felt the urge to cry and call for help.

The creek sounds a long way down, she thought.

The knowledge that she could have been killed or seriously injured made her shiver. Images of lying in the flooded creek below the bridge until she died caused her more bouts of shaking.

Nobody would look for me there, she thought.

So she made herself get up and keep walking. Cautiously she inched across the bridge, one boot at a time. On the other side she paused to check the time. Her watch told her it was now 0245hrs.

And I have only walked a kilometre or so, she thought unhappily.

She was so exhausted she just wanted to sit down but driven by fear she plodded on in the darkness and rain. After a while sheer exhaustion numbed her mind and she just slogged grimly on. Each step became an effort and she seemed to be just one mass of weak muscles and aches. She tried drinking the falling rain but quickly gave that up and at last sucked a handful from a puddle beside the road. The road wound up and down and through more rainforest and then along stretches where there was pine forest beside it. There were two more bridges and she crept across them, inching one boot forward at a time.

At 0320hrs she came to a clearing and a road junction. Once she realised what it was she paused and crouched at the side of the road listening. *Are they waiting for me here?* she wondered.

But all she could hear was the wind in the trees and the trickles and drip of water. Cautiously she walked forward, and she recognised it as the junction where the Mt Edith Road went off to the right.

This is where the search HQ was when they were looking for Willy, she remembered.

The knowledge that she had made some progress cheered her and she pushed herself to keep walking. A few minutes later she came to Robsons Creek and this time there was enough light in the clearing for her to make out that the creek had only low banks. By now feeling dehydrated she carefully made her way to the edge of the water to have a drink. She drank greedily until she felt bloated and then staggered back up to the road and plodded on.

The road went up over a hill that seemed to go on for ever. Worse still, the rain began again and the road became slick and greasy. Several times she slipped and fell, getting bruised and coated in mud each time. After each fall she lay in shivering shock for a minute or two, just wishing the nightmare would end. But then she gathered her strength and struggled to her feet.

Going down the other side was nearly as bad and once she slipped and landed heavily. *Just as well I've got a big bum,* she thought ruefully as she regained her feet.

The drizzle stopped and she plodded on. The road crossed a causeway with swamp on both sides and there was just enough light for her to make out the marshes and water. *I remember seeing this,* she told herself.

But she could not picture where it was on the map. Now she regretted not paying more attention on all those drives around the lake she had done in the last few years.

The road went up a slope and then into more rainforest. The road then levelled out and wound around through pitch black darkness. Tina steeled her nerves and kept on moving.

I must come to somewhere soon, she told herself.

She pictured the army cadets marching with their packs somewhere ahead and kept hoping she might catch them up. But in her heart, she knew this was a faint hope.

Unless they have some battles to fight which delay them, she decided. Further thought brought her to the conclusion that such activity was unlikely. *Major Wickham won't risk injuring cadets by trying to move in the jungle in the dark.*

Depressed and sore she plodded slowly on. At each bend she experienced a surge of hope and then a dash of dejection when only more blackness and jungle was revealed. She was now so tired and hungry she felt both exhausted and disoriented. Several times she stumbled and her eyes began to play tricks on her. It made her fearful she was starting to hallucinate, and she sobbed with despair, just wishing it was all over.

Another low causeway was crossed and then the road went steeply up a large hill into pine forest. It was hard going, and she was forced to stop every 50 or 100 paces to get her breath, but it still cheered her.

I remember this hill. I am getting closer, she told herself. And then she was like the little engine that could and grimly told herself, *I think I can. I think I can.* until she reached the level ground on the crest.

For several minutes she stood gasping and trembling at a road junction. The dark wall of pine trees seemed to hem her in and oppress her but despite the cold wind that began to chill her she felt better.

I am winning, she encouraged herself. *Just keep walking.*

So Tina did. And then her heart leapt with hope when she saw a distant pinpoint of light. It was far away and she knew it was off across the other side of the lake, but it was human.

There are people there, she muttered.

Then the distant light had the opposite effect, making her feel very much alone. She shivered and sobbed and could not go on. Exhausted she slumped down on the wet grass at the side of the road and began to cry.

If only a car would come along! she thought. But then she realised she did not dare stop any vehicles. "It is just as likely to be the crooks looking for me," she muttered.

But why aren't the cadets looking for me? she wondered. It all seemed very unfair and disheartening but after weeping a bit more she realised she was shivering with cold. *I must keep moving or I will get hyperthermia,* she reasoned.

But it took a real effort of willpower to raise herself to her feet and to lurch into motion. Every muscle seemed to be stiff and sore and chafing burned with a sharp sting under armpits and between her thighs.

But at least it was downhill. The road went down quickly, and the distant light was lost among the tops of the pine trees. The road was slippery, and she had to go carefully and her feet and legs hurt so much she whimpered with pain. But she kept on. First the road curved down to the right and then back to the left before levelling out on a long straight.

Tina plodded along this, almost tottering with fatigue. The darkness was still almost complete, the road being just a grey ribbon that wavered before her exhausted eyes.

At least it has stopped raining, she thought.

And then she got a really great boost to her hopes. On the right she came to a clearing with some buildings in it. "I know where I am! This is the Kauri Creek Picnic Area," she muttered. She had done nature rambles and picnics there with the Girl Guides and Brownies when she was a little girl. Just being somewhere she knew made her feel very much better.

But the place was in darkness and she knew it was not a campsite. *But the Kauri Creek Camping Area isn't far and there are people there,* she thought, remembering a Guide camp there two years earlier.

Heartened but now needing a pee she stepped off the road and limped across to the toilet, intending to use it. But when she got there Tina could not go in. In the darkness it just seemed too creepy and she backed away and just peed on the lawn.

Hot with shame at doing such a bad thing she pulled up her pants and hobbled across to a picnic shelter shed. She sat on one of the bench seats and considered her next move. For a few minutes she contemplated staying there until it was daylight.

At least I will be out of the rain, she told herself. But not dry. Her clothes were still wet and she was shivering. *I am not taking my clothes off,* she told herself, remembering the camping advice about sleeping dry.

Then the loneliness and spookiness of the place began to get at her. All around was dark forest and she could not hear anyone creeping up on her because the nearby creek was flowing fast and making a lot of noise. Her imagination began to get the better of her tired mind and several times she felt a cool breeze up her back and the hairs on the back of her neck stood up. Terror began to clutch at her heart, and she jumped at every unusual sound.

Then the image of the campground as she had seen it that afternoon from her canoe came to her. *There are people camped there,* she thought. *If I can get there, I will be safe.* She knew it wasn't far as her memory told her it was only a pleasant stroll for little Brownies. *Maybe 10 minutes' walk for me?* she decided.

So she heaved herself to her feet then stood on trembling legs until the muscle spasms calmed. A check of her watch told her it was 0430hrs. Slowly and painfully she walked back across the lawn to the road. It seemed to her that the light had improved but it was still very dark. Once she was back on the muddy gravel she turned right and began limping along. Just 50 paces on there was a concrete bridge across the creek and she remembered standing on it with the Guides and looking down at a beautiful clear stream which wound off through the jungle.

Worried by the memory of her earlier fall on such a bridge Tina went slowly and kept to the middle of the roadway. Because she was in a large clearing the starlight was good enough to make out both road and bridge safely, but she was still very wary. The creek looked to be flowing five or six metres wide and was gushing and gurgling under the bridge, swollen by the recent rain.

It was only a little noise when heard above the sound of rushing water, but it was metallic and it sent Tina's heart rate shooting up. She stopped in the middle of the bridge and strained her eyes while scanning the jungle and parking area on the far side. Down to the right on the other bank was a small shed and beyond that a turnoff to a car park and walking track. She stared hard, wondering if she had really heard anything.

Then, just as she wondered what it was, she was looking at two car headlights blazed out directly onto her from a vehicle parked in the car park over to her right front. Even as her dazzled eyes registered the lights terror surged through her veins.

The men! she thought. *It is a trap!*

Chapter 46

DESPERATION

For a few seconds Tina stood in the middle of the bridge, rooted to the spot by paralysing fear. The dazzling beams of light blinded her and seemed to pin her to there. But then came another metallic noise and a flicker of light told her that someone had run across in front of the car.

They are coming to get me! her terrified mind screamed, or she did. She wasn't sure. But the stab of pure terror broke the spell. *I must run. I must get away,* she thought. But she knew she could not run far. *I am too exhausted,* she reasoned.

For a second or two she thought of trying to run back to hide in the jungle, but she rejected that too. Then the crunch of running boots on gravel decided her. Her memory of the creek was of it being about knee deep and with a clear sandy bottom. In desperation she turned and sprang off the bridge into the darkness.

She knew the drop wasn't too far, perhaps 4 metres, but instead of sand she landed on rocks. A sharp pain stabbed up her right ankle and she went under water and crashed onto more rocks, tumbling over and over in a welter of foaming current which swept her away. Bruised and knocked half senseless she struggled to get her head above water, but the turbulence was very much stronger than her and much stronger than she had expected.

For several seconds Tina feared she was going to be drowned or would have her skull cracked by the rocks but then her feet and hands felt sand and the swirling eased and she was able to get her head up. Spluttering and gasping she realised that the creek was half in spate from the rain and that it was sweeping her along at a rapid rate. Flickering lights showed her that the bridge was already 50 paces behind her, and it flashed through her mind that swimming was not only her fastest method of travel but possibly her only. Sharp pains in her right leg made her suspect that she had broken her ankle or lower leg bone.

Suddenly she suffered a savage blow on the back and back of her head and she came to a stop, pinned against something by the force of the current. The blow was so severe that she was almost knocked unconscious and only desperation kept her struggling. Bruised and battered and gasping for breath it took her quite a few seconds before her stunned mind worked out that she had been swept into the branches of a dead tree that had fallen into the creek.

I'm going to drown! her terrified mind cried as the force of the water began to push her under.

Desperate to live she grabbed at the wet timber and struggled to free herself. But both legs seemed to be stuck in a fork by the force of the current and it felt as though her left leg might snap at any moment. Frantic and gasping she squirmed and struggled. Somehow, she managed to get a better grip, enough to keep her head just above water.

By a desperate heave she managed to drag her legs free and let them trail in the current. As she did, her eyes made sense of the pattern of light and darkness upstream. She noted the straight dark line of the bridge and in the glow of the car headlights two men running about on the bridge. Then a point of light appeared, and just as Tina puzzled over what it was, she realised it was a powerful hand torch. The beam swept down to light up the swirling waters of the creek. And then it shone right into her eyes and stayed still.

"There she is!" shouted a man.

Danny! Tina thought in terror.

"Get after her! Go down the creek," shouted another man.

On hearing that Tina renewed her efforts to get free of the snag. As she did, she heard Danny arguing with the other man, the 'Boss' she gathered.

The Boss shouted angrily, "Get after her or else! I will go along this track here beside the creek.'

Tina knew at once which track. It was a pleasant little walking track maintained by the National Park service. Having walked along it several times she knew it ran close beside the creek much of the way and that a grown man with a torch would find it easy going even in the dark. Her fear and desperation grew and she struggled furiously to get free, even as she glimpsed Danny run down the bank on the left of the bridge.

Here he comes! He is in the water! her terrified mind cried.

Slithering and scrambling frantically Tina dragged herself through the branches and slid free into clear water. As she did, her feet touched the bottom and she manage to get to her feet. The water was only waist deep, but the current was strong and she found it hard to keep her balance as she floundered desperately along. The whole time she was illuminated by a powerful torch. This induced a sense of intense nakedness and the terror was so great she kept sobbing.

Then the terror was notched up when Tina heard a sharp cracking noise close to her left ear. Almost stunned by fear she glance back to confirm what her racing mind told her. She was just in time to see a tiny stab of red. There was another snapping sound beside her.

He is shooting at me! she thought.

And Danny, who was floundering and splashing along the creek towards her, was already closer!

Tina heard the Boss shout, "Catch the bitch! Move man, move!"

Terrified Tina turned and stumbled, just as the boss fired again. She did not know where the bullet went but her mind made several instant decisions.

Underwater, she told herself. *And don't try to run. Swim.*

So she ducked under and began to breaststroke, her eyes closed and fear of crashing into more snags or rocks warring with the fear of being shot or caught. Because she still had her joggers on it was hard to use her feet, so she had to depend more on her arms. She couldn't stay under long, more from fear than lack of breath but when she came up, she at once realised that the torch beam was no longer on her.

She gasped in air and allowed the swift current to push her along. Behind her she could hear Danny splashing and cursing. Glancing back she got glimpses of the torch again. It was now in the jungle and rapidly catching up.

The Boss is running along the walking track, she decided.

Desperate to escape Tina swam as fast as she could, managing to keep ahead of the flickering, bobbing light. Luckily for her the creek curved away to the left and she gasped with relief when she saw the torch shine down on Danny. The men shouted to each other and then Danny resumed floundering after her, his swearing audible.

The creek went left and then curved back to the right and Tina realised that creek and track were again converging. A vague memory of looking down on some rapids added to her anxiety.

Rapids mean rocks, she thought.

Worry about injuring herself by being tumbled over the rocks caused her to start to try to pick her course. It was hard to do in the darkness as the creek flowed in a tunnel of rainforest but there was just enough light to make out the pattern.

Tina dragged herself to the left bank and tried to stand. There were sharp pains in her right ankle, but she was able to do so. Shaking violently from overexertion and gasping from breath she staggered up onto a grassy bank and began to hobble quickly along it. Twice she tripped and that made her slow down. But within seconds she realised her cautious plan would not work. Danny came into view only 25 paces behind and she saw the flicker of the torch almost directly in front of her.

For perhaps a second she hesitated. Then, with a sob of dread, she dived back into the creek. *Nothing for it but to take the risk,* she decided.

She began swimming with an overarm stroke until she glimpsed white foam in the blackness. There were rapids. And they were rough and dangerous. Tina hesitated for another second or two over whether to try to go down them feet first or headfirst and then decided on headfirst.

If I go feet first and strike my spine on a rock I could be crippled, she thought.

So she faced the rapids and tensed herself. The white showed more clearly, and the noise increased and suddenly she was over the first rocks, scraping her tummy and banging her knees. She slid into a swirling pool, but her hands were already working, feeling and clawing to keep her moving. Up to her right she glimpsed the torch, but its beam swept over her and she ignored it. All she could do was cringe and hope.

Tina went over a bigger drop and was almost tumbled over in the back eddy and swirl but was able to keep going. Dimly, above the roar of the rapids, she heard shouting and a frantic glance back showed her that the torch beam was directed on Danny. He was waving his arms and yelling. Then he hurried after her.

Tina went down another set of small rapids and then over a small waterfall about a metre high. This jarred her and she struck several rocks with knees and elbows. Excruciating pains shot through her and the fear of injury increased. But by desperate paddling she managed to slide out of a swirling pool and over another low fall and into the next section of creek.

Suddenly she realised she could see fairly clearly. *The moon is coming up!* she thought.

Her satisfaction lasted only for the second it took for her to work out that it made it harder for her to hide. But at least she could see better. There were more rocks ahead and what looked like another big snag. Rather than risk being dragged into its branches she windmilled with her arms to struggle to the bank.

Gasping for breath she hauled herself out and began staggering along the uneven grassy bank, ignoring the shooting pains in the right ankle. From behind her came a shout and she saw Danny hurrying down her bank of the creek, clambering from rock to rock. He had obviously decided that the rapids were not the best option. Worse still he seemed to be catching up fast.

Then he went down with a loud cry as he tripped. Tina heard him swear and then call on her to stop but she kept on going. The rapids seemed to have ended but she kept on along the creek bank until she also tripped, again wrenching her ankle. But it was the sight of the torch bobbing along through the jungle up to her right rear that really galvanised her into frantic action.

She slid into the water again and began to swim. The bottom was again sand and the creek seemed to have opened out so that the trees did not meet overhead. The creek curved right and then left into a straight reach of at least a hundred metres. Tina struggled gamely to keep swimming but her muscles quickly tired and her arms and legs began to feel as though they were made of lead. Her breath came in hot gasps and several times she splashed or swallowed water that made her choke and cough. Her eyes watered and she had to blink them clear.

Sobbing with despair and fatigue she swept past the point where the creek straightened out and became wider. To her dismay it became so shallow she began to scrape along the bottom and had trouble swimming. To make any progress she had to drag herself forward with her arms. A glance behind showed her the torch at the bend only 25 paces back and then into view came the splashing, swearing shape of Danny, now another 50 paces behind.

Desperate to escape, Tina decided to try running. She staggered to her feet and started floundering towards the grassy bank on her left. As she did, there was a loud snapping noise, which she now knew was a bullet.

The Boss is shooting at me again, her terrified mind screamed. But a corner of her mind was still rational and that worked out that he was firing a handgun. *If it was a rifle or shotgun, I would be dead,* she reasoned.

Being shot at sent spasms of terror through Tina and she broke into a frantic, floundering run. She heard another shot and saw a spray of water 10 metres ahead. To try to make it harder for the man to aim she tried swerving. As she did, she felt a heavy blow in her right buttock. The blow was so hard and hurt so much she thought she had been kicked by a large boot. But a glance behind showed Danny still 50 metres back and only just past the bend in the creek.

Then it dawned on her. *I have been hit!*

At the same moment she realised that running along the bank was not a good option. The grass was much longer and much of what she had taken for long grass was actually mostly reeds growing in water. Rather than be shot again she fell flat, and only just in time. Another bullet cracked close over head as she went down. Once again, she tried swimming underwater but quickly gave it up as hopeless as she encountered reeds and water weed and was quickly snared.

Frantically she wrenched herself free and then slid on down the stream. As she did, she tried to stay as low as she could. To achieve this she floated on her side and used her arms underwater. A throbbing pain was now spreading outwards from her bum and she began to despair. In the first pale beams of moonlight she saw Danny climb onto the bank He began forcing his way along it through the long grass. That allowed Tina to draw another 10 metres ahead. But then Danny realised he was not winning and splashed his way back into the creek.

Then Tina saw the torch off to her right rear. It was further away, just a pinprick of light in the dark wall of jungle. That gave her hope. But that was instantly dashed when she heard the Boss yell out: "Hey Danny, you keep on after her. We will go to the campground to make sure she doesn't get to contact anyone."

Danny stopped and called back, "What do I do if I catch her?"

"Make sure she doesn't call out. Drown the bitch," the Boss yelled back.

Tina was almost paralysed by fear when she heard this. Her stomach heaved and she trembled and gasped. But she was still free and 50 paces ahead and now she decided to change tactics. She slowed and drifted as she went around the next bend. This was to the left and the creek became even wider. Better still it was lined with a thick belt of reeds and these gave her the idea.

As soon as she was out of sight of Danny and no longer able to see the torch she stopped and began sliding into the reeds, taking care to angle back so that any track she left would only be visible to a person looking behind themselves. The reeds were full of slime and sharp ends, but she ignored both and even pushed fear of snakes to the back of her mind to allow herself to keep going.

She didn't go far, had barely pulled her body in off the clear water so that her boots were still not in the reeds when Danny appeared. He was wading and was cursing and swearing as he splashed along. The water was waist deep and the bottom a muddy sludge and it slowed him right down. Several times he floundered and slipped over, getting a dunking each time. As he passed close to where Tina lay with hammering heart he began looking in all directions. He came to a stop in chest deep water only 10 metres away and stared hard.

"Now where has the little bitch got to?" he muttered.

Tina was so winded that she had the urge to gulp in deep breaths, but she did not dare. It took all of her self-control to stop wheezing and gasping. Instead she sucked in slow, quiet breaths. To make herself harder to see she sank down so that only her nose and eyes were out of the water and hoped that he wouldn't notice the disturbed reeds. All the while she trembled and shook from overexertion and terror.

Then Danny turned his head to stare straight at her and she tensed.

Chapter 47

SAILOR SKILLS

Tina crouched in the cold water, her heart hammering and apprehension gripping her. For what seemed like ages Danny stared at the reeds. As he did, Tina tried to decide what to do next. Her options seemed very limited as she felt she was near the end of her strength.

I won't be able to outrun or outswim him, she thought.

Indeed her whole body now seemed to be a pulsing, throbbing mass of aches and pains. To make matters worse she was suddenly assailed by a fierce cramp in her left calf muscle. The pain was so sudden and so intense that she had to bite down on her left hand to stop herself crying out aloud. Tremors of shivering swept through her and tears sprang to her eyes. All she could do was grit her teeth and try not to make a noise.

Part of the problem was that she could not reach the cramping muscle without standing on one leg and she did not dare risk losing her balance. The other option was to duck under water and crouch submerged. But that would cause ripples and also deny her the chance to watch what Danny was doing. So instead she stood and endured the agony.

At last the waves of pain began to ease but it warned her that swimming in deep water might be very dangerous. *I could get a cramp and go under and drown,* she thought.

Then she noted a flicker of light off to her left front on the far bank of the creek. A surge of hope went through her. *That might be the campground,* she reasoned. *Now, if only I can reach some people unseen.*

To her intense relief Danny turned and continued wading on down the creek. This now curved to the right and became even wider. As Danny made his way downstream Tina saw him go down several times so that only his head was visible. Then he began to swim and she relaxed. Standing on one leg she tenderly massaged the sore calf muscle. Then she gingerly felt her right buttock. It had now become one great throbbing mass of pain.

To her dismay she found a tear in her trousers and then the torn edge of a hole in her skin. There didn't seem to be much blood, but as she was in the water she assumed it was just seeping out and washing away. Satisfied that the bullet wound was not immediately crippling or life threatening she relaxed a bit.

Just as well I have a big bum! she thought. But an almost paralysing sense of apprehension remained to chill her. She had absolutely no doubt that the men would kill her if they could.

Then another idea came to her. *Danny has gone downstream. Should I go back up the creek and continue on along the road to try to get to the army cadets?* she puzzled.

For several minutes she thought about this before shaking her head. The problem was the car. She did not know if it was still at the bridge. *Or it might be at the turn-off to the campground and they will still catch me,* she thought. Not knowing where the other gang members were induced a deep sense of uncertainty. *Marco and Neville might be around as well,* she thought.

That meant that the campground remained the best option. And that meant crossing the creek and going close to the men. For several more minutes fear held her in the reeds but her shivering increased and she realised that it was not only overexertion and shock that was causing it but also the cold.

I can't stay in the water much longer, she told herself. So, with a gulp of dread, she began to ease her way out of the reeds.

Tina then began wading across the creek. Within 10 paces she gave this up. The bottom was soft mud and sludge and she kept slipping and sinking in so that her head even went under. Instead she began a slow breaststroke. As she did, she kept scanning the water for signs of Danny.

Where has he gone? she wondered.

He had vanished from view and she did not know which bank he was on or near. To make matters worse she realised that the current, while much weaker in the wider and deeper stream, was still carrying her downstream at quite a speed. To counter this she had to swim harder, risking making more noise. But she was so worn out and her muscles so overtaxed that it took a painful effort to make her limbs move fast enough. What particularly worried her was that she was making waves and big ripples as she swam.

I hope they don't notice them, she thought anxiously.

Several lights appeared ahead of her and the beam of a torch suddenly swept across the creek down at the next bend, which she was now rapidly approaching. Tina's heart leapt in fright and she gulped several deep breaths ready to dive under. Then she saw a black shape in the water near the edge of the campground and recognised it as Danny's head. She heard voices call and then clearly heard the Boss say, "Swim ashore."

Danny did, and so did Tina. It was only twenty 5 metres and she had to increase speed or be swept down close to where the Boss stood. To make matters worse at that moment the cramp returned and all she could do was gasp and then grit her teeth and use her arms and good leg to keep moving. Only by the dint of extreme effort, summoning up her last reserves of energy, did she make the other side.

By then she was close in under some trees and she could see a tent and a parked vehicle only 10 metres away up on the bank. But an equal distance to her left were Danny and the Boss. All Tina could do was haul herself in under the small clumps of grass and reeds at the tree roots while she tried to recover her breath and dealt with the cramp.

If they hear me now, I am done for! she told herself, knowing she could neither run nor swim.

Then the Boss's torch beam swept close over her and then across the creek and along it in both directions. "So where the hell is she?" the Boss growled.

"Dunno. She might be hiding, or she might be dead. She went down pretty hard when you shot at her. I reckon you hit her," Danny replied.

"Yeah, maybe. But we don't want a body drifting around the lake. So we will look for one later. Right now we have to make sure she doesn't reach any of these campers to tell them her sob story. Come with me and help me speak to the people."

"What will we say Boss?"

"That we are detectives trying to catch a gang of druggies and that one is on the run," the Boss replied. With that he turned, and Tina saw his torch beam light up the nearest tent and vehicle. As he and Danny walked up towards it, he said, "You go and get Neville and get him to bring that car down here. Get its headlights on the mouth of the creek where it joins the lake. Tell Marco to stay at the junction to catch her if she goes along the road."

On hearing that Tina breathed a sigh of relief. *I was right,* she thought.

But now she was in a terrible quandary. *What should I do?* she wondered. One option was to swim back up the creek and make her way up into the forest on the other bank. *They will never find me in there,* she reasoned.

But nor would it get her any help and she was suddenly gripped by a fear of bleeding to death from the bullet wound. Another option was to try to get past the campground before the car arrived.

That seemed the better choice and she knew she did not have long, only a few minutes. Her ears told her that Danny was even then walking away up the gravel road through the campground and the sound of voices suggested that the Boss was talking to the campers.

Now or never, Tina told herself.

So she began side stroking downstream, keeping right in close to the bank. It was just as well she did because the Boss came back from the tent and shone his torch out across the creek again. All Tina could do was huddle in against the fringe of longer grass at the end of a small 'beach'. Then the Boss turned and directed his torch up the slope. That was a real help to Tina as it showed her that there were about 50 metres of open, mowed grass between her and the next tent. Seeing that sent her hopes plummeting.

I will have real trouble getting across all that open ground unseen, she thought miserably.

Then the torch beam swept around again and her gaze followed it. This time what it revealed gave her hope. Only about 20 metres further along to her left were four canoes. They had been dragged up out of the water, but they were still right near the edge.

If I can get one of those, she thought.

But how? All she could do was lie flat against the bank and try to stop her teeth chattering and her cramping muscles from trembling. At every second she expected the Boss to walk down and discover her and she winced at the terrifying images that her overwrought imagination conjured up of him aiming his pistol at her head, of the bullet shattering bone and sending blood and brains spattering; and of her dead body slumping into the water.

Then her chances of being discovered seemed to dramatically increase as a vehicle came driving down through the campground, its headlights lighting up the whole creek and lower campground.

Too late! she thought, her despair deepening.

The vehicle came to a stop about 10 metres away to her right rear, the beam of its headlights shining straight across the creek to the forest beyond. Doors opened and slammed and two men appeared near the Boss. Tina crouched in the mud and grass and bit her lip to avoid whimpering with fear. The Boss pointed in her direction and a stab of pure terror froze her.

Then the Boss said, "Neville, you take one of those canoes and a torch and go back up the creek to see if you can find this girl. Danny, you help me watch the creek and the tents."

Tina bit back a tiny sob of relief and lowered herself until only her eyes and nose were out of the water as she lay on her side along the bank. Neville went striding past and she heaved a sigh of relief. She twisted her neck around to watch and saw him shine a torch over the canoes, then push one into the water. He moved to get in and it gave her a stab of malicious pleasure to note that he had trouble getting in, nearly capsizing the Canadian he had selected. Having lowered himself in he took up a double paddle and began to use it, propelling the canoe out into the creek with unsteady strokes.

As he turned and went up the creek only 5 metres from Tina she slipped right under, fear clutching at her bowels. But she could only keep that up for half a minute. The experience of being under water in the dark and of having trouble holding her breath was too ghastly. It made her think of Andrew and his 50-metre underwater swim.

Andrew, she thought. *I love him but will I ever see him again? I wonder where he is?*

But she knew she could only get out of this by her own efforts so she eased up to the surface and blinked her eyes clear when she could no longer hold her breath. Breathing as silently as she could she looked around. To her intense relief Neville was now 20 metres upstream and full in the beam of the vehicle's headlights. A few strokes later and he was beyond them and vanishing around the bend. *Safe!* she thought.

Then she heard Danny say, "Nearly five O'clock boss. Be daylight soon. We should find her then."

"I want to be gone by daylight," the Boss replied. Then he shone his torch up at the next group of tents and said, "I will keep watching this tent near the creek. You go and check the next tent past that one."

To Tina's intense relief they both walked away up the lawn. But the thought of daylight really bothered her. *It will be hard to hide then. I had better get out of here,* she told herself.

She decided to move on past the campground but to stay in the water and then to hide in the forest. So she used her hands to drag herself slowly along in the shallows next to the bank. Every few seconds she glanced to check where the Boss and Neville were. And every few seconds she felt safer as she moved further away from the beam of the vehicle's headlights.

Then she was at the beached canoes and an idea came to her, partly driven by the knowledge that she would have trouble walking. *Can I use one? Will they notice?* she thought. *And can I take one without being spotted?*

She resolved to try, feeling that she would be safer afloat. So she slithered past the canoes and then crawled up the bank beyond them. Secure in their shadows she raised her head to check where the Boss and Danny were before looking into each one. The first was a kayak but it had no paddle. The next one was a Canadian and to her relief it had a short single paddle in it.

It will have to do, she reasoned.

She then glanced around and saw that both the Boss and Danny were a good hundred metres up the slope near another cluster of vehicles and tents. The flicker of a torch up the creek showed that Neville was still searching the far bank.

Now or never, she told herself. Taking a big gulp of air she grasped the canoe and began hauling. It slid easily down into the water and she edged her way backwards with it, taking care not to splash or make ripples. Soon the whole canoe was in the water and afloat and after another careful glance towards her enemies Tina carefully stood up and slid aboard. With her heart beating wildly with both fear and hope she pushed herself upright and reached for the paddle. Now training and experience both told. She dipped the paddle in and eased the canoe away from the shore.

Done it! she thought as she took another careful stroke.

She looked around and began to plot her course, noting that the creek opened out into the left-hand side of quite a wide bay. The whole shore of the campground right across the bay was just mowed grass with open water beyond it. And the moonlight did not help. But she was committed so she began to paddle with all the stealth she could manage, forcing her aching arms and tired muscles to function.

Suddenly, a yell rent the silence. Tina's blood froze and her heart leapt into her mouth. She glanced over her shoulder and saw a torch shining in her direction. It was Danny and he came running down the grass towards her.

Oh no! Seen! Tina thought. She dug the paddle in and used all the strength she could muster to get the canoe moving faster. *Can I get out of range of that pistol in time?* she wondered.

Terror gave her strength and she paddled frantically, casting frequent glances over her shoulder as she did. She saw Danny reach the canoes and look in each one and then swear and go running back up the lawn.

No paddles? Tina surmised.

The Boss came running down the lawn as well, yelling angrily for Danny to find a paddle and for Neville to come back. *Oh no, Neville!* she thought. He was already in a canoe and had a paddle.

She was gasping by this time and her tired arms were having trouble keeping up the pace and her whole body seemed to ache and throb. But dread kept her at it and she cringed and her flesh crawled in anticipation of being hit by a bullet. But the Boss did not shoot, just yelled angrily.

Tina kept on paddling, but she was so tired she had to slow to get her breath back and to allow her racing mind to make a sensible plan. *Where should I go?* she wondered.

Straight ahead of her was the open lake and she was already approaching the entrance to the bay and was obviously out of range of the pistol. Directly opposite her was the Fongon Campsite and she could see the twinkle of a few lights there.

There are people there, but can I make it in time? she wondered.

She glanced back and again her heart seemed to stand still as she saw the dark shape of Neville in his canoe come sliding into the beam of the vehicle's headlights.

She shook her head. *No. I can't make it. It is a kilometre or more and he is stronger and will catch me up. And even there I will still be right on the far side of the lake from the police and the crooks can drive around there to get me,* she thought. But what to do?

Go to starboard and keep close to the shore, she decided. *That way I can take to the jungle if it looks like Neville is going to catch me.*

So Tina turned the canoe and shaved the point and paddled as hard as she could westwards. As she rounded the end of the point Neville and the other crooks slipped from view and she felt a real surge of hope. But within seconds this turned to dismay as she discovered that around the other side of the point was another deep bay. Tina at once realised she could not hug the shore or Neville could cut across and get ahead of her.

I have to take the risk of him catching me and go straight across, she reasoned.

It was a sickening thought, but she nerved herself and took it, aiming her canoe for the nearest land on the far side of the inlet. Almost at once she regretted her decision as once outside the bay she found there was quite a stiff breeze and a chop of waves about half a metre high. This made it quite difficult to both steer and balance the canoe. The wind and waves were coming in from her port quarter, almost from abeam, making the canoe roll alarmingly. Several times she almost capsized but by a dint of skill and effort she managed to keep it upright.

Pushing herself to the limit Tina battled on, sobbing with despair and exertion. Every few strokes she cast a fearful glance over her shoulder. But before she was even halfway across the two or 300-metre wide inlet Neville came into view. He was paddling furiously, his paddle and canoe both throwing up spray as he pursued her. Tina sobbed again and felt the despair tighten in the pit of her stomach and in her chest. She knew she was close to the end of her strength and could only grimly force her exhausted muscles to function. Tears began to trickle down her cheeks, cold in the wind.

Another glance back showed Neville appreciably closer. *I might just reach the other side,* she thought, summoning up her last reserves to keep arms apparently made of lead moving.

Another rogue wave almost had her over and she shivered with fear and cold as the spray drenched her. By then the jungle on the far shore looked to be less than a hundred metres away. But was Neville closer? She glanced over her shoulder again.

And sobbed with relief.

Neville had capsized. Tina stopped her desperate paddling and eased up to just keep moving and under control. She looked back and saw that Neville was struggling to get the canoe the right way up. As it was the same design as hers, she guessed that its inbuilt flotation would stop it from sinking but she could not see how Neville could drain it on his own out in the open water.

He will have to drag it to the bank to drain it. I have a chance, she thought.

So she resumed a slow but steady stroke that pushed her canoe onwards. And she was right. By the time she reached the other shore Neville was at least another hundred metres behind and was struggling to drag his canoe towards the shore. For the first time Tina began to really think she had a chance.

That got her looking around. It was still dark, with the moonlight becoming fitful as low clouds began to cover the eastern sky. There was just a hint of grey and she knew that 'First Light' was at about 0615hrs. A check of her watch told her it was 0525hrs. Less than an hour.

So where do I make for now? she wondered.

By this time she was paddling close along a scrubby bank backed by an extensive pine plantation. Off to her left across the lake was the Fongon Campground. For a few seconds she again considered it. But then she rejected it.

There are several more campgrounds somewhere along this shore, she remembered. *And the cadets have gone to the one near Platypus Lookout. I will make for it.* To help her with her decision she remembered that the army cadets were going to march 16 kilometres to the western end of the lake. *The road wiggles all over the place. I can go much more direct and I am already halfway there,* she reasoned.

So she continued on along the north shore, heading west. Her decision was reinforced by the sight of twinkling lights in the far distance. *That is the town of Tinaroo. I can even go there,* she thought.

But the desire to catch up with Andrew and the Navy Cadets was stronger and motivated her to keep on paddling despite her aches and cramps. A few minutes later several lights came into view ahead of her.

That is another campground, she thought with relief. *Downfall Creek Campground, I think.*

It was and she made steady progress towards it so that by 0540hrs it was only a hundred metres away across another deep inlet and the tents and vehicles of campers were just visible in the watery moonlight.

Soon, she told herself, thinking of mobile phones and the police.

But when she was halfway across the inlet and aiming for the tip of the grassy open cape on which the campground stood she saw the headlights of a vehicle swing out of the jungle and come hurrying down the slope. At once her heart began to hammer in anxiety.

Oh no! Is that the crooks? she wondered.

A wave of fear so powerful it was almost paralysing coursed through her and she stopped paddling for a few seconds. When the vehicle came to a stop on the edge of the lake with its headlights shining out towards her, she knew she did not dare go ashore.

If it is them, I will just walk into their arms, she reasoned.

So she turned the canoe and headed out into the middle of the lake, a procedure that took all of her skill to prevent the beam sea capsizing her canoe. That her decision was the right one she was almost at once sure as she heard angry voices and glimpsed figures moving on the shore near the car.

Disheartened but glad she forced her tired muscles into action once more. *Platypus or Barrabadeen Campgrounds then,* she told herself, knowing that were definitely going to be cadets at the latter.

Once she was several hundred metres from the shore and she felt confident that she was safe from rifle fire, Tina turned her canoe west once again and kept paddling slowly. By then the pine trees on the western end of the Fongon Peninsula were only a few hundred metres off to her port side and she was again tempted to go there. But more lights and tents were now appearing only a kilometre or so ahead at the Platypus Campground, so she held her course towards it.

All the while she kept glancing frequently back. To her dismay she saw the vehicle reverse and then drive off up the slope. It vanished among the trees and then she got the worrying shock of seeing the flicker of its headlights off to her right as it drove along the road. Several times the headlights stopped, and she got the uneasy feeling the people in the car could see her and were keeping level with her. That got Tina fretting about how to avoid them when she finally got ashore.

Then she got another shock. It was just starting to get light, 0600hrs, and she was in the narrowest part of the lake between Fongon and the north shore, when she spotted a splash of white spray about half a kilometre behind. *Neville!* she thought.

"Oh no!" she sobbed. It was all too much, and she felt her hopes plummet. Despair gripped her insides and she wept with pain and fear.

But despite that she kept grimly on. Every minute she calculated she covered another hundred metres. Platypus Campground grew closer with every exhausted paddle stroke. But so did Neville's canoe. It became a black dot amid splashes of white spray. Then her despair deepened when the headlights moved on out of sight and a few minutes later reappeared among the pine trees and tents at the Platypus Campground.

Or is it another vehicle, just innocent people? she wondered.

But she knew she did not dare go ashore to test her theory. When the vehicle came to a halt on the edge of the lake with its headlights shining out across the water her suspicions deepened into certainty and she wept from fear and frustration. To add to her dejection she could see no sign of any cadets at the campground.

Gasping and sobbing with fatigue she pushed herself to keep paddling, again angling out into the lake and away from the shore. By this time she had the forested peninsulas of Python Point away off to her left but one look at those dark, jungle-covered ridges made her shake her head. They offered neither comfort nor help, even if she could hide there.

The 0610hrs came, and then 0615hrs, and the first grey paleness among the low clouds off to the east. By 0620hrs she was off the end of the peninsula that the Platypus Campground was on and the tip of the peninsula occupied by Camp Barrabadeen slid into view.

Oh please God! Not far now! she thought.

It looked to be about a kilometre away. So did the town of Tinaroo off her port bow. Directly in front of her she made out the straight line that marked the spillway of the dam. It was a few hundred metres further than Barrabadeen.

But only about half a kilometre back was Neville in his canoe and he appeared to be still paddling strongly and to be overhauling her fast. The sight of him made Tina sob and bite her lip.

Oh, can I make it in time? she wondered.

She could only try. But her arms were now so tired she could hardly lift the paddle and she was starting to lose her technique, the paddle frequently striking the water and throwing up 'crabs' of spray.

Worse still she was getting fierce cramps in her legs and her lower back muscles were starting to stiffen and seize up. Her muscles were trembling and she was shivering with cold. Blisters were forming and starting to break on her wet hands. Then, as the daylight strengthened, she made the shocking discovery that the bottom of the canoe was slick with blood!

I am bleeding to death! she thought with dismay.

It was now 0630hrs. Half a kilometre to go, but Neville only a few hundred metres behind.

It is going to be close, Tina thought, whimpering with pain from her cramps, chafing and blistered hands which were now starting to sting and bleed.

Suddenly she heard a noise which made her heart seem to stop and she looked back and up in despair. She was right. It was the smuggler's floatplane!

Tina watched in horrified disbelief as the floatplane flew low overhead and then swung round when over the spillway to come back in her direction. To her dismay she watched it land. As its floats hit the water, they threw up showers of spray. Then the aircraft began taxiing straight towards her.

Caught! she thought in despair. *And so close!*

Chapter 48

WORST NIGHTMARE

Tina stared at the approaching floatplane in horror. Sick despair engulfed her, and she slumped in her seat. All she could do for several seconds was shake with exhaustion. But then the terror began to mount and along with it a pent-up fury of frustration. Desperately she looked around, hoping for some help, any help!

To her left front was the line of the spillway and to the left of that the buildings of Tinaroo, now showing some reds and blues as the light improved. But the houses were now an impossibly long way away, a kilometre or more. To port was the vast expanse of the southern arm of the lake and behind her the tumbling grey of waves and then the dark masses of hills back from Python Point. And there was Neville, now overtaking her fast.

Her focus shifted back to the hilly peninsula ahead of her. She saw that there were tiny figures on the lawn near the buildings at Camp Barrabadeen and she thought they were wearing the mottled grey camouflage DPNU of navy cadets, but she couldn't be sure. But though they were only four or five hundred metres off they also seemed hopelessly far away.

Can they help me? she wondered.

In desperation she put down her paddle and stood up in the canoe, risking a capsize to do so. On shaking legs she balanced precariously and then held her arms up high. Then she dropped her right arm to horizontal and her left arm to point downwards at 45 degrees, making the letter 'S' in the Semaphore Code. After a pause of a second or so she dropped both arms and then immediately put her right arm back to the horizontal and reached across her front to hold her left arm up at 45 degrees, forming the letter 'O'. Then she made another 'S'. Twice more she repeated the SOS but by then was almost weeping with frustration and despair as she could not tell if anyone was even looking in her direction.

And they will probably not know semaphore, she thought. It was, after all, an archaic set of knowledge and only by being a navy cadet and for this exercise had she learned it.

Then the floatplane surged alongside and she saw heads leaning out of the side windows. Close up the plane was larger than she remembered. It had two windows behind the windscreen and then a sliding door on the port side just abaft the struts supporting the high wing. Looking from the rear side window on the port side was Danny and he had a pistol in his hand. Peering through the windscreen were Kostis and a middle-aged man who Tina assumed was The Boss.

The plane surged to a stop, Tina flinching away from the whirling propeller. Danny leaned out and shouted above the sound of the engine, "Get aboard girl!"

"No!" Tina shouted back. She felt frozen with fear but was also desperately determined.

"I will shoot if you don't," Danny called back.

"You will shoot me anyway," Tina retorted, the terror of imminent death causing her to tremble and want to puke.

"No we won't! The Boss just wants to talk to you," Danny answered.

Tina again shook her head. "No," she replied.

She did not believe the man and was so overwrought she could not help being defiant. Instead she took up her paddle and moved to paddle away. As she did, she crouched and her flesh crawled in anticipation of being struck by a bullet. The canoe began to move and she heard angry shouts but no shot.

Out of the corner of her eye she saw Danny move and she realised he had taken up a boat hook from inside the cabin. Just in time she raised her paddle to protect herself as he swung it in a vicious scything sweep. The action partially saved her but she was not strong enough to ward off the blow. The boathook struck her paddle and smashed it back into her face. Then the boathook slammed into the side of her head, sending her senses reeling.

To her dismay Tina found she could not see properly as she wavered on the edge of being unconscious. Then it got worse and she felt the canoe roll as she lost her balance in the waves. The next thing she knew she was in the water. As she went under panic swamped her for a second as she struggled to get free of the canoe and to work out which way was up. The water was cold and dark and terror made it hard to think straight.

But there was still a spark of defiance in her and she decided to try to swim away underwater.

But even as she did, she felt a sharp blow on her shoulders and then a burning, scraping feeling down the middle of her back. The next moment she experienced the odd sensation of being hauled backwards. Even as a sharp, stinging pain swept across her back she knew she had been gaffed by the boat hook and that Danny was pulling her back. Then her head banged against something, a float she presumed, and she blacked out for a few seconds.

When she came to, her whole being squirming with terror and panic, she realised that strong hands had her and were hauling her up out of the water. She felt the cold wind on her wet skin and clothes and a spasm of coughing wracked her as she instinctively tried to clear water from her throat and nose. Then she blinked her eyes open and saw that Neville was there in his canoe, helping to heave her up while Danny now stood on the port float and lifted. In the process her shirt ripped and they grabbed at her arms, breasts and bra in an attempt to get a firm grip.

It was all humiliating, painful and upsetting to Tina. Even so she tried to squirm free, to get back into the water. The result was a stinging blow to the side of her head that sent her senses reeling again. Danny snarled in her ear, "Stop struggling you stupid bitch or I will really hurt you!"

Tina now retched and a wave of intense trembling shook her so much she felt helpless. The men hoisted her up and rolled her into the cabin of the floatplane. In the process she banged her knees and shins and was bumped and bruised some more so that her whole being seemed to be one throbbing mass of pain. Reeling on the edge of unconsciousness she felt herself being rolled over and then dragged away from the door.

As she was being dragged Tina heard Neville say, "Here comes a boat."

"Forget it," Danny answered. "Just get in."

"What about Marco?"

The Boss answered this, "I have phoned him and told him to take the vehicle and get out of the area. He will be alright if he moves fast, before any coppers arrive."

Tina lay on her back, her head and neck jammed up against the far side of the cabin behind the seats. Despite her nausea and weakness she had the wit to glance around. She saw that she had two seats side by side on her right and a stack of locked boxes strapped to shelves on her left at the rear of the cabin.

Neville clambered in and stepped over Tina, giving her a kick as he did. "Little bitch! You have given us a real run around. You will pay for that!" he snarled.

That terrified Tina but also made her unreasonably angry. *I am the innocent victim here!* she thought indignantly.

But wisely she kept her mouth shut and her eyes almost closed, pretending to be more stunned than she actually was. Not that it took much pretending she was so battered. Danny next climbed up, and as he did Tina heard the buzzing sound of an outboard motor.

Help, but too late, she thought. She was sure there was no way the crooks would allow her to escape now. *They will use me as a hostage if it is the police,* she decided.

The Boss called, "Get this thing in the air Kostis. Let's get out of here."

"Where dat boat?" Kostis called as he opened the throttle.

"Somewhere behind us. You won't hit it," Danny answered as he slid the side door shut. He then stepped over Tina and moved to seat himself.

Tina felt the aircraft start to surge forward and then its engine bellowed as it began its take-off run. *Done for!* she thought, black despair flooding through her.

The engine roared and the plane dug its tail in and began to surge across the lake. As it did its floats smacked into every wave, sending up showers of spray. Tina tensed for the lift off and wondered what she might do next.

I'll die with dignity I hope, she thought gloomily. She resolved to tell the crooks nothing and to try to be defiant to the end. *I just hope they don't rape me and do disgusting and humiliating things,* she thought.

Then the aircraft's engine eased up and she heard the Boss say, "What's wrong?"

"We not moving right. Something holding us back," Kostis called back.

"Danny, have a look," the Boss ordered.

Danny swore but got out of his seat and stepped back over Tina. As he did, he gave her a savage kick to move her legs out of his way. Tina cried out in pain and curled up into a trembling ball. Then Danny unlocked the door and slid it open. Leaning out he looked back. He swore then leaned back in and yelled, "We are dragging that boat. Some kid, a navy cadet. He's tied on to us and has the outboard reversed."

Tina's heart leapt in hope. *Some kid! A navy cadet!* she thought. Was it Andrew?

But then the Boss's next order chilled her. He shouted, "Shoot the little bastard and get us free."

Tina saw Danny pull out his automatic pistol. After cocking it he took a firm grip on the doorframe with his left hand and leaned out to use the gun. *Oh no! He will shoot Andrew!* Tina thought.

She was sure it had to be Andrew. In desperation she acted. There in front of her was Danny's backside. Curling her legs up she lashed out, kicking as hard as she could. The blow caught Danny completely by surprise and he went flying out of the doorway and was gone in an instant.

There were angry shouts and Tina saw Neville leaning over the back of his seat and glaring at her. A stab of terror reminded her that she was still in mortal peril.

And I have really made them angry now! she thought.

In a panicked reflex she jerked away from Neville's clawing hands. But the boxes blocked her attempt to get clear. In desperation she grabbed at them, clicking open locks and catches. As Neville stood up and turned to come at her she flung the first box left-handed hard at his face.

Neville saw it coming and was able to put his hands up to ward it off but what happened next so astonished Tina she was frozen for several seconds. The box burst open and out of it rained a shower of wriggling brown objects.

Snakes! she thought as the reptiles showered over Neville, the Boss, and Kostis.

Pandemonium resulted. All the men began to yell and scream in fear and Tina saw a snake slither over the Boss's shoulder as he struggled to release his seatbelt and get up. Kostis seemed to go completely berserk and began swatting around him with his arms, letting go of the controls in the process.

One of the snakes wrapped itself around Neville's arm. He began to shriek in terror and flailed his arm to try to flick it off. As he did, the snake bit at him, striking repeatedly at his upper arm and face.

Another brown snake slid off the back of the seat onto the floor near Tina and she jerked her legs away from it in terror. Then she clawed her way to her feet, her eyes bulging with fright as the reptile slid towards her. She did not hesitate. There was the open door and the lake and she dived. She went through the door headfirst and landed with a hard belly flop among the waves.

The bad dive winded her but she had the presence of mind to not struggle until her eyes could detect which way was up. Then she swam and floated to the surface. As she did, she saw a tinnie-type power boat go past with a person in DPNU sitting in it, his mouth agape in astonishment at the sight of her.

It was Andrew and, as the first shock of recognition wore off, she saw him start to turn the boat. Then a wave slapped her in the face and she went under. When she came up, coughing and gasping she had trouble seeing until she blinked her eyes clear. Then she saw that Andrew was struggling to untie or cast off the rope that he had secured to the struts which held the floats under the floatplane.

She saw the powerboat and the floatplane both arc around in a semicircle. Then Andrew whipped out his sailor's knife and slashed the line. The floatplane went on weaving away from her, obviously not under control. Andrew sent the boat sweeping around in a wide curve, shielding his eyes as he searched for her among the waves. Now terrified that she might drown Tina struggled to keep her head above water even as she waved an arm.

It seemed to take Andrew some time to spot her, but she realised it was actually only a few seconds. Just As he did, a large dull red buoy went bobbing across Tina's field of vision. It was so unexpected that she could only gape at it and wonder. Then its meaning struck her like a physical blow.

That is one of the warning buoys near the spillway to the dam, she remembered.

A stab of terror, mixed with dark images from her nightmares, caused her to look around. She was just in time to see the tail of the floatplane suddenly tilt sharply upwards. That also puzzled her but then she saw it tilt further even as a man leapt out. The wing swung crazily and then the whole thing just vanished from sight.

As it did Tina's eyes focused on the straight line of water, beyond which was the sky. Again the shock of comprehension almost paralysed her. *That is the lip of the spillway. There is water going over the top of the dam,* she thought.

Remembering how much rain there had been the previous week, she was not really surprised but terrifying images of just how high and steep that massive concrete wall were flooded her mind, sending her into a panic.

Then there was more horror. Right near the spillway was the man who had jumped from the doomed plane. She recognised the Boss. He was swimming frantically, his face towards Tina. But even as she watched she saw him glance back and a look of despair cross his face. He made several more desperate arm movements but then he was gone, plucked over the edge by the current.

Only then did it dawn on Tina that she was next. *The current is dragging me towards the edge,* she told herself. *Swim girl, swim!*

In desperation she did. But she was so exhausted and winded that it was a feeble effort and she knew she was going backwards despite her best efforts. Several times she cast despairing glances back at that horrifying line that marked both the lip of the spillway and the boundary between life and death and each time it was closer. Frantic to live she struggled to keep swimming. Almost blinded by panic she looked around for Andrew and his boat.

Oh where is he? she thought.

There he was. She saw the boat powering in towards her, angling across the current. Another glance backwards. The lip seemed very close. She could hear the roar of the fall now.

My worst nightmare come true! she thought.

Then Andrew was there. He brought the boat surging across the current so that she washed down against it. In an instant he had seized her wrist. Her other hand snatched at the gunwale and she clung on desperately. Andrew cast a worried glance over his shoulder towards the dam. Then he leaned down and grabbed her torn shirt and the waistband of her trousers and hauled with all his strength.

Tina tried to help but she was too weak. Worse still her breasts and bra got snagged on the side of the boat. Andrew heaved and grunted and then had to lift her, the boat rocking dangerously as he did.

Then he lifted and dumped her unceremoniously on the bottom. In a flash he turned, grasped the throttle of the outboard and twisted it open. The motor spluttered and coughed and then burst into a healthy roar. The stern of the boat dug in and it began to move across the current.

Tina lifted her head, noting Andrew's worried frown and anxious glances over to port. He swung the boat to starboard and, as she did, Tina looked over the side. To her horror, she saw that they were only metres from the lip of the dam spillway and she could see right down into the valley below. The water racing over the lip was smooth but streaked with white and looked to be running very fast. Fear made Tina gasp but all she could do was cling on.

By then Andrew had turned the boat to face into the current and he gingerly opened the throttle as far as it would go. For several seconds Tina was sure they were done for. The boat did not seem to be winning against the force of the current. But then she noted a tiny creeping motion and she began to hope. She was right. Ever so slowly the boat began to make headway. And the further it got from the edge the weaker the current became so the faster it went until it was surging away from the danger.

Tina just wanted to slump down but images of the Boss going over the lip swirled up to haunt her conscience. *What if Danny dies too? I will have killed him,* she thought. So she struggled to a sitting position and mastered her dizziness.

"Danny," she gasped. "I kicked him out. We must save him."

"Bugger Danny," Andrew snarled.

"Please! I don't want his death on my conscience," Tina said. Already she felt responsible for the deaths of the others and it made her feel ill and terribly guilty.

"OK," Andrew answered.

So he went searching, zig-zagging back across the lake until they found Danny swimming feebly for the shore. He was obviously near the end of his strength as a swimmer and made no resistance when helped aboard. Tina ordered him to sit in the bow and he just slumped there looking glassy eyed until Andrew drove the boat up onto the beach at Camp Barrabadeen.

Andrew switched off and stepped into the shallows to help Tina up. As they did others crowded round and Andrew pointed to Danny.

"He is a murderer. Tie him up and call the police," he said.

Then he held Tina upright and hugged her firmly to him. Ignoring all the others crowding around and asking questions he said, "I love you Tina."

Then he kissed her, and she felt a surge of warmth and emotion such as she had never experienced.

* * * * *

After that it was hospital for Tina. She collapsed from exhaustion, blood loss and hyperthermia and was carried up the slope in Andrew's arms until a stretcher was organised. Then it was a ride in the Emergency Services helicopter to Cairns Base Hospital. The following day she was awake but very weak and Andrew was sitting by her bed. Her parents seemed to thoroughly approve of this, once they learned of his role in her rescue.

It was only then that Tina was able to ask the question that had gnawed at her: why had nobody noticed she was missing? Andrew told her that when he had asked before they even launched the canoes Stella had said something about her being with the army cadets at the fort. As she had just done a Control Group job it was assumed by everyone that she was doing that again. It was only after the dawn roll call by Major Wickham that her absence was noticed.

"We were standing on the lawn at Camp Barrabadeen ready to be briefed for the last battle when I realised you were not with the army cadets either," Andrew explained. "Lieutenant Ryan got on the radio and checked who had been at the previous action at 0400 at Platypus Lookout and then we discovered you were not with them either."

Andrew had then explained that he was sick with worry and while he was standing looking out over the lake watching the floatplane land and wondering where you were he saw a person in DPNU stand up in a canoe and start sending semaphore.

"It could only be you," he said. "Nobody else would be trying to send an S.O.S. by semaphore. Then I saw the other canoe and the floatplane and realised it was the bird smugglers. I just ran down to the boats and took the safety boat without waiting."

He then explained how he had seen her caught and bundled aboard and had reached the floatplane just in time to hook his anchor to the struts of the floats. "It was just enough to slow them down and prevent a take-off," he explained.

"You could have been killed," Tina cried.

"But thanks to you I wasn't," Andrew answered, and he kissed her again.

From then on everyone treated them as boyfriend and girlfriend and true romance did blossom. And Tina needed the support as she had been so traumatised by the experience that she suffered severe nightmares for a long time afterwards. Bouts of deep depression resulted from her deep feelings of guilt and she wondered if she would ever recover and be normal again.

It was made worse by the strong sense of guilt she had over the deaths of the three men. When a friend showed her a picture of the crumpled wreck of the floatplane at the bottom of the dam wall she broke down in hysterical weeping.

The knowledge that the trial of Danny was an ordeal she would have to face in the future, and the nagging worry that one day he might be out of jail and come to get her did not help her state of mind. But the best cure was love and she received that in big doses from her family, Andrew and her friends.

And the D of E expedition? Major Wickham signed off on that, assessing that their three days on the lake in boats had fulfilled the requirements. But there was no promotion course for Tina. She insisted that Andrew go and he did, to be promoted to the rank of Leading Seaman, but it took her another year to catch up, because no matter what her parents said, she insisted in staying in the Navy Cadets.

Enjoy more C.R. Cummings stories

The Air Cadets

The Navy Cadets

The Army Cadets

 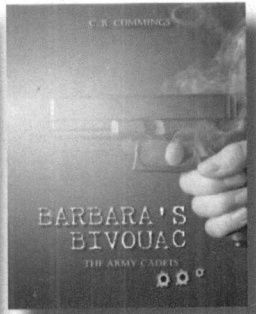 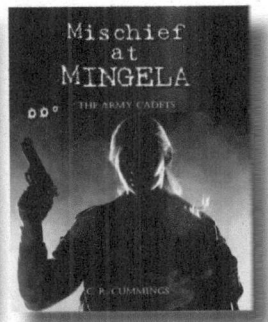

www.ingramcontent.com/pod-product-compliance
Lightning Source LLC
Chambersburg PA
CBHW011339010726
47493CB00009B/2876